W9-AMC-844

CHERRY BLOSSOMS

CHERRY BLOSSOMS

KIM HOOPER

TURNER PUBLISHING COMPANY

Cherry Blossoms
Copyright © 2018 Kim Hooper

Cover Design: Maddie Cothren
Book Design: Meg Reid

Library of Congress Cataloging-in-Publication Data

Names: Hooper, Kim, author.
Title: Cherry blossoms / Kim Hooper.
Description: Nashville, TN : Turner Publishing Company, [2018] |
Identifiers: LCCN 2018014788 (print) | LCCN 2018015278 (ebook)
ISBN 9781684421787 (ebook) | ISBN 9781684421763 (softcover)
ISBN 9781684421770 (hardcover)
Classification: LCC PS3608.O59495 (ebook)
LCC PS3608.O59495 C48 2018 (print) | DDC 813/.6--dc23
LC record available at https://lccn.loc.gov/2018014788

9781684421763 Paperback
9781684421770 Hardcover
9781684421787 eBook

Printed in the United States of America
17 18 19 20 10 9 8 7 6 5 4 3 2 1

Turner Publishing Company
Nashville, Tennessee
New York, New York
www.turnerpublishing.com

馬鹿は死ななきゃ治らない。

Baka wa shinanakya naoranai.
Unless an idiot dies, he won't be cured.

—Japanese Proverb

I am standing in drifts of dry sand, alone, coaxing the waves to crash harder, extend their reach far enough to touch my toes, maybe wet the cuffs of my jeans. I can hear Sara at an undefined distance—that high-pitched, breathless laugh of hers. She is happy, running, with an energy normally reserved for children in wide-open fields.

The sun is swallowed whole by the horizon, and the moon takes its place, assuming the night watch. It casts a path of light on the water, and I hear Sara in my ear, whispering "Let's swim out there. Let's go." I can feel strands of her blond hair grazing my cheek. But she's not here. I am alone. My mind deceives. Still I say, to this empty space beside me, "I'll swim anywhere for you."

I close my eyes—for how long, I don't know. The rhythm of the waves fades and the ocean starts to seem far away, as if I am being carried inland by a god I believed in when I went to Catholic school all those years ago. But when I open my eyes, I am sitting in the same spot. I haven't moved. God hasn't moved me. It's the water that's moving—receding, pulling back slowly.

"Jonathan! Come!" Sara says. She is out there, somewhere, seemingly unconcerned with being swept into the unknown. "It'll be okay."

I believe her because I always have. I've always seen having faith in her as better than the alternative—having faith in nothing.

I run toward the water, stepping on now-exposed shells and flopping fish, nearly slipping on mounds of seaweed and scraping my feet on coral.

I don't see her. "Sara?"

My voice has that artificial quality, like when you hear a recording of yourself. I keep running, wondering how it is that I am not out of breath. It must be that adrenaline they talk about, the kind that allows weak-armed women to lift cars off their unlucky offspring. I stop, blink hard, confirming the impossible. Yes, the water is returning. I know what this is; I've heard of this phenomenon before, seen footage of it on CNN. Tsunami: "standing wave" in Japanese. That's exactly what it looks like—a gigantic wave, paused at its greatest height and pushed forward by some hidden, malicious force. It's as tall as the high-rise where I work—fifteen, maybe twenty stories.

"Sara!"

"I'm here," she says, her voice coming from land now. How did she make it to land? I still can't see her. Her voice becomes frantic: "You have to run, Jonathan. Run!"

And I do. I run. But the wall of water is moving faster than my legs, catching up with me, about to overtake me. When it slams into me, it's like every bone in my body breaks. I am a miniature version of myself, tossed around in a washing machine of chaos. I flail and thrash, struggling to keep my head above water and, when this proves impossible, struggling to simply find which way is up. I can't close my eyes, won't close them, withstanding the sting of salt in hopes of seeing her. I know we—the water and I—have reached land when I fly past tree trunks and nearly miss slamming into cars. My lungs start to fill with water. My arms hurt with attempts to swim upward, to find air, to find Sara. When I reach out, desperately, I realize I've been swimming downward this whole time. I touch concrete, what used to be a road. I panic.

This is the end.

I have eight months to live. No, there was no dramatic diagnosis of a tomato-sized tumor in my brain. There was no tragic scene in a doctor's office, complete with a nurse placing her compassionate hand on my shoulder and telling me to "hang in there." I do not have a terminal illness, unless you consider humanity itself a terminal illness. In any case, you shouldn't feel sad for me. I deserve to die. You'll see.

I didn't know I was going to die until I went to see the curiously named Dr. Bitterman. He's not the type of doctor you're assuming he is. He's a psychologist. Or psychiatrist, rather—he doesn't just listen and nod; he can dispense drugs to take away your problems. That's what I figured I needed. Google revealed lots of his kind near me, but I chose him based on the name. When he shook my hand, I fixated on his royal blue cuff links—who wears *cuff links?*—and thought about walking out. But then I saw the Stanford diploma on his wall, next to a framed picture of a happy family that appeared to be his, and figured maybe he was worth the $225 for forty-five minutes of wisdom.

Dr. Bitterman sat in an oversized chair designed for grandfathers who enjoy cigars in front of fireplaces. I sat on the couch across from him.

"I'm not here because I want to be psychoanalyzed," I told him.

He tilted his head to the side like a curious dog in response to the rising inflection of its owner's voice. Then he wrote something on the notepad resting on his knee, seemingly already ignoring my request.

"Then why have you come to see me?" His voice was calm, soothing, the type of voice parents use with children when they want them to behave: *Now, Billy, why don't you sit at the table like a big boy?*

His blue-framed glasses sat on the very tip of his nose, ready to slip off with just the slightest sneeze. Watching them, anticipating their fall, caused me almost as much anxiety as my reason for making this appointment. I wondered if I should leave, if he'd charge me a prorated amount for the five minutes of his time. I felt like a schmuck for coming, for thinking he could help me. His wealth—visible in the wood beams of his ceiling, the Zen water feature in the corner—relied on schmucks like me. That's what he should have called his practice: Schmucks for Bucks.

"I keep having this dream," I said, figuring *What the hell?*

The damn tsunami dream. I must have had it a hundred times in the last several months. It feels so terrifying, so real, that I've started to adopt a lifestyle of insomnia just to avoid it. Whenever I do slip into slumber, it's like I can feel my lungs filling with water. When I wake up, gasping for air that is in plentiful supply, I'm wet, drenched in sweat—or evidence of a parallel universe.

"What is this dream?"

I told him about it—the receding water, looking for Sara.

"Who is Sara?"

"My ex-girlfriend."

"When did the dreams start?"

"About eight months ago."

"When did the relationship with Sara end?"

Ten minutes in and he was already going for the easy explanation. I wanted to tell him that it's not all that simple, but I figured he should work for his money, go down the rabbit hole of my life and try to find his way out.

"Right before Christmas."

"So, about eight months ago?"

"Yes."

He paused a moment to write in his notes.

"Did you break it off, or did she?"

A good question.

"She did, I guess. But it's my fault."

"Do you want to say more about that?"

"Nope."

He did the dog-head-tilt again.

"Look, I'd just like to stop drowning every night," I told him.

"Fair enough," he said, showing me his palms, the way criminals do with cops when they don't have any weapons. "What do you think the dream *means*?" He squinted his eyes, hard, when he said "means."

"I don't know. That's why I called you," I said. "Can't you just hypnotize me out of having this dream? Or give me a pill so I can sleep dreamlessly?"

He smiled a tight-lipped grin that did not bare any teeth, a grin that said *Sorry, asshole, that's not how it works.*

"I think dreams are meant to share information with us, information that we're repressing from our consciousness for some reason." He crossed one corduroy-pant leg over the other, slowly and deliberately. Corduroy and cuff links. Sara would find this hilarious.

"Well, if this dream is telling me that my swimming skills need work, I'm not so sure I have time to address this. I'm very busy."

He sighed. "Jonathan, do you think you're depressed?"

"If I say yes, will that get me a prescription for a pill to make me sleep dreamlessly?"

He rested his chin, precariously, on the top of his pen. "You are very evasive," he said.

"Maybe, but I'm not depressed, so let's just get that out of the way."

"Do you get enjoyment out of the things you used to enjoy?"

I'm hard-pressed to remember the things I used to enjoy. The idea of a future with Sara was one. In its nonexistent state, it's rather impossible to get enjoyment out of it.

"You sound like a commercial," I said.

He ignored my quip. "How about you tell me about a typical week for you lately?" He gave his pen a shake, encouraging the ink to move down to the tip.

"I've been at the office quite a bit."

"What do you do?"

"I'm in advertising. For Radley and Reiser."

He hadn't heard of R&R, but he knew some of their clients—Spiffy brand paper towels, Woofers dog food, and Wave, which, like Tide and Surf, seems to be named on the assumption that customers like to think of the salty ocean when they wash their clothes. Having endured my tsunami dreams, I do not understand this.

"I'm a copywriter. I come up with headlines, write radio scripts, TV spots—that kind of thing."

"Are you happy as a copywriter?"

"Happy enough. I wanted to be a real writer, but turns out that does not pay the bills."

"What's a 'real writer'?"

"Like a novelist."

"You said you've been at the office quite a bit. Like, how many hours a week?"

I rolled my eyes up into my head, in search of my mental calculator. I've been getting to the office as early as seven, leaving as late as nine. That's fourteen hours. I multiplied that by seven—the number of days I've been working per week. When the total revealed itself, even I was a little shocked.

"About a hundred. More or less."

I watched him underline this figure in his notes. Twice, with enough force that the indents would be visible ten pages into his notepad.

"Does this seem excessive to you?"

"I suppose."

He sighed again. "Jonathan, do you think you can keep doing this?"

I shrugged.

"How would it make you feel if I said you had to take a week off?"

In that moment, it felt like the couch was tilting, like it was a seesaw and I was going to slip right off.

"I don't think I could do that."

"I think you could."

"I'm not sure my boss would agree."

"I can write a doctor's note," he said, reaching for his prescription pad. "What's your boss's name?"

"Look, fine, let's just start with taking tomorrow off. And this weekend." This was Thursday when I went to see him.

"And you'll come see me on Monday? To tell me how it goes? I bet your sleep improves."

I nodded, but I knew I'd never see Dr. Bitterman again.

He pressed his palms into the armrests of his chair and stood. I took this to mean I'd used my forty-five minutes, blown through a couple hundred bucks faster than a drunk in Vegas. When I got up from the couch, I was light-headed and stumbled a couple steps. He put his hand on my shoulder to steady me. I said something asinine about how I hadn't eaten since breakfast, how I could really go for a cheeseburger. I'm not sure why I wanted this Dr. Bitterman to see me as a normal guy whose greatest problem was waiting too long between meals. He shook my hand and told me he'd see me soon.

"Good luck," he said, opening the door for me.

And the next morning, Friday morning, I went straight to work.

R&R occupies three floors of a high-rise in a "revitalized" part of downtown Los Angeles. There are still drugs, guns, and gangs on most corners; they just say "revitalized" to increase property values. Like most "cool" advertising agencies, R&R abides by the rule that the more ceiling light fixtures and air-conditioning ducts showing, the better. Visitors are supposed to think "*Oh, how progressive! How cutting-edge!*"

R&R has a factory motif, complete with hard hats hanging on pegs outside each office, along with levers and pulleys that serve no purpose, like staircases that go nowhere in houses built by crazy people. You can't walk more than a few feet without running into a random cog or wheel leaning against a wall. I guess it's supposed to be very "artsy" to have these pieces just lying around, like a sculpture garden. But I think it looks like an automotive plant in Detroit exploded and some parts landed, inexplicably, on the West Coast. If the goal was to make these factory pieces an organic part of the R&R world, I suppose it's successful because employees sometimes gather around them to chat, since there are no water coolers. People are known to leave their coffee mugs on them. And, if one of the folders carrying our works-in-progress goes missing, the first thing the project manager says is "Did someone check the wheel upstairs?"

When I asked Rick, the creative director, about the factory motif, he said it's supposed to represent that all of us at R&R are part of an "idea factory." I said, "Oh, good, because I thought it was implying that we're all just replaceable assembly-line workers who should wear jumpsuits and hair nets and form a union." He didn't laugh.

I've gotten into a habit of working late on Fridays. People are usually gone by five. Lights go off. Quiet reigns. It's peaceful. This particular Friday, though, Kevin was working late, playing his heavy metal at a volume just barely audible. Kevin is my work neighbor, the art director who takes the words I give him and makes them look right on ads. I consider him a "friend," mostly because we have a forced intimacy. We can hear each other's every phone call, every fart, every "fuck" muttered when a deadline gets accelerated. See, at R&R, there are no actual "offices"—if, like most people, you define an office as an enclosed space. The offices at R&R have no ceilings (how progressive!), so they're really just like cubicles with very tall walls. Over the summer, I was privy to the drama of Kevin's job offer from a rival agency. He tried to be discreet, but I couldn't help but hear the negotiations back and forth, the offers and counter-offers. It was like my personal soap opera. Would R&R match the $100K salary the other agency was offering him? Turns out they would. And now we're convinced Kevin has a meth problem. He's lost thirty pounds in about two months. Given the pay raise, I suppose he can afford rehab at one of those oceanfront places with D-list celebrities.

This Friday, he was wearing shorts that I'm pretty sure were actually swim trunks and a tie-dyed shirt that looked to be purchased from a nearby Goodwill after sitting in a bin since 1986. This wasn't just "casual Friday" attire; this was everyday attire for Kevin. We don't have a dress code at R&R, for better or worse. The account people have to look "business casual" for client meetings, but not the "creatives." We get to wear jeans, flip-flops, anything really (as long as nothing is exposed that would alarm HR). Kevin wore pajamas and slippers on Monday, for example. I suppose the lax dress code is supposed to communicate "Look—we can wear jeans *and* think! So progressive! So *brilliant!*"

"You're still here?" Kevin said, sticking his head inside my not-really-an-office.

"I've been swamped." I nodded toward the job folders on my desk. Most of those folders were retired jobs, jobs long ago completed. All these hours at the office, I've been writing headlines for ads I haven't been asked to create, on behalf of clients we don't have. For example, *What if we represented the Beverly Hills Tennis Club?* I asked myself. And I spent a good week coming up with ideas, settling upon this as a line to sell lessons: "Give your wife a great backhand."

Kevin doesn't know of this charade of mine. He doesn't need to. We all like to enforce the idea that we're busy, to rationalize our paychecks—and our very existence.

"I thought only people who hated their families were workaholics," he said, with his stoner laugh. "You're a free man. You should be out on the town."

The thing is that Kevin doesn't know much about being free.

"Nightlife doesn't get going for a few hours. You know that," I said, like I was just like him, one of the guys looking forward to weekend bar- and bed-hopping.

"Take it easy, guy," he said, giving "knuckles" to my doorjamb before leaving.

It was just before midnight when I finally left the office, eyelids capable of staying open just long enough to make the short drive to Eagle Rock, to the rickety little house in the neighborhood the real estate agent swore was "up and coming." Sara and I had picked out the house together. I'd signed on the dotted line, but we were in it— the mortgage, the life—together. We overlooked the old appliances and the coming-up floorboards because we were sold on the small yard—if that's what you call a four-by-four-foot square of grass. We thought it might be good for a dog. We had dog aspirations.

I hate this house now. It's small—just eight hundred square feet—with a tiny kitchen, a bedroom barely big enough for a queen bed, a bathroom with a sink that belongs in a high school locker room, and a living room just large enough for a couch, a television, a bookcase, and a desk. But, for just me, it seems too large. It echoes with the sound of my own breathing. Then again, a closet would seem too large. I long for someplace small, cramped, where my thoughts only have so much room to wander, where my options for passing time are limited—my only choice being to sit with my knees to my chest and stare at the ground.

It's like this house is haunted by false hopes and failed plans and unrealized visions: Sara and I cooking pasta over the stove, playing with a puppy out back, wrapping ourselves in a blanket while watching a movie on a cold winter day (the place doesn't have heat). I wish we had settled on renting an apartment for a while, something temporary and easy to abandon, with plain white walls and cheap carpet that they change out after every tenant. This house, with the old porch out front, the hundred-year history in the walls, the now-dried-up garden and flowerboxes on the windowsills, feels too much like a home. They say "Home is where the heart is." Whatever happens when the heart of a home is gone, that's what this place is now.

The moment I lay down in bed, I was no longer tired. This is how it goes most nights. I stared at the ceiling, in fear of sleeping, of the waves crashing over me. I thought of what Dr. Bitterman had asked: "Jonathan, do you think you can keep doing this?"

What is "this"? Working hundred-hour weeks? Not sleeping? *Living*?

I fell asleep at some point. And in the dream, as I was running out of oxygen and dodging debris in my underwater purgatory, I relaxed, suddenly. This had never happened before. Everything went quiet, and it occurred to me that I didn't have to struggle. I could just let go. Drown. Would Sara see that as pathetic? No, I think she would understand the fine line between giving up and giving in. That's what it is—surrender. I stopped swimming and closed my eyes, letting the water take me wherever it willed. Pretty soon, I knew, it would be over. And when I woke up, drenched as always, I was not terrified for once. For once, I was relieved.

Spate of "detergent suicides" hits Japan
CNN.com

TOIKYO, Japan (CNN)—A 24-year-old Japanese man killed himself by mixing laundry detergent and cleaning fluids, releasing noxious fumes into the air and forcing the evacuation of hundreds of people from their homes.

The man mixed the chemicals in his home in Otaru, on the island of Hokkaido, and was found dead shortly after midnight Wednesday.

Around 350 people were forced to flee their homes to escape the poisonous fumes, thought to be hydrogen sulfide.

The man's mother fell unconscious after inhaling the fumes and was taken to a hospital, where she later recovered, a Hokkaido prefectural police spokesman said.

The latest death comes after a 14-year-old Japanese girl killed herself using the same method last week. Ninety neighbors were sickened by fumes and had to be treated in the incident in southwestern Japan.

In the week the girl died, a 31-year-old man outside Tokyo killed himself inside a car by mixing detergent and bath salts, police said.

I wonder why that fourteen-year-old Japanese girl had felt the need to end her life. The twenty-four-year-old seems unjustifiable too. True disillusionment does not occur until after the age of thirty.

I'm thirty-four.

二

When it comes to suicide, leave it to the Japanese to be the real innovators. They've had to get creative since guns are illegal there, something that would outrage Ted Nugent. Hanging and jumping in front of commuter trains are popular ways to go. They've actually put up guardrails on some lines to keep people from leaping on the tracks and disrupting rush hour. Those hard-working Japanese don't appreciate "snafus" interrupting their commute. Rail companies will even charge the families of those who commit suicide a fee, depending on the severity of the disrupted traffic. On some platforms, giant mirrors have been installed so a jumper has to look himself in the eye before doing the deed.

I'm fairly certain a vision of myself would only strengthen my resolve.

❋

Sara and I were going to take a trip to Japan together. I was going to propose on that trip, maybe at the top of Mount Fuji or while having drinks in a fancy hotel restaurant high above Tokyo. I had a plan. And as part of that plan, I'd purchased a Japanese culture book. I like to be an educated tourist, not just some white American jackass who expects everyone to know English.

It turns out that suicide is a part of Japanese culture. There's a whole section in the book about it. I kept the book, put it in a box with other "Sara-related stuff" that I could contain, compartmentalize—pictures, mostly. Turns out most things in my life are Sara-related, but I can't contain them. My own face in the mirror, for example. Just looking at it sometimes reminds me of her bizarre assertion that I look like that guy in *Office Space*. "Who, *Milton*? The fat guy who can't find his stapler?" I teased her. "No, silly, the main guy. With the dark hair and kind eyes and dopey smile."

The fact is that nearly seven hundred Japanese people commit suicide every week. That's almost a hundred people per day. Impressive. If there's a "suicide fad," they'd be the ones to start it. Since the internet came to life, their creativity has flourished. Now the downtrodden gather online to share their ideas, like housewives share recipes. One of these ideas strikes me as, well, brilliant.

Apparently, a few years back, the Japanese started committing suicide by mixing laundry detergent and other chemicals and inhaling the hydrogen sulfide gas. Don't mistake me for a science nerd. I have no idea what chemistry is involved, but I've done enough research to know the exact recipe. The message boards say it's "relatively painless."

While it's unlikely that those message board opinions are actual user reviews from The Beyond, I've come to trust the "relatively painless" bit and decided that this laundry-detergent concoction is the best way to go. I've considered the other conventional options. I don't think I could pull off a gunshot to the head. My palms get sweaty when I'm nervous. And Sara was very anti-gun. Slitting my wrists is not appealing. I don't like the sight of blood, and I don't want someone to have to clean up that mess. I'm intrigued by the notion of sticking my head in an oven, but this seems a bit too insane, like I might laugh as the oven got warm and decide to make a pizza instead. I've heard way too many horror stories of bridge jumpers surviving and spending their remaining years as mute vegetables, unable to speak in response to their loved ones' pained question: *How the hell could you do this to us?* I've done the whole car-running-in-the-garage/carbon monoxide poisoning before—not for myself, mind you, but for my parents' thirteen-year-old diabetes-ridden cat. This did not cause me much mental anguish because (1) the cost of euthanasia in a veterinary office is ridiculous and (2) I don't really like cats. Anyway, I have a very "been there, done that" feeling toward that method. Hanging seems so archaic, and I can't seem to find solid information regarding how long you actually hang there, suffocating, before death comes. I'm fairly certain I would screw up the pills thing. Someone would find me in a puddle of piss and vomit and I'd wake up in a mental hospital with concerned psychologists hovering over me, asking if I remember my name and the day of the week before showing me the way to group arts-and-crafts therapy. Behind closed doors, they would talk about my "cry for help." Holy fuck, the last thing I want to be is a pathetic cry for help.

This—the laundry detergent thing—is the way. I'll be respectful about it. I'll leave a note on the door warning people of the dangerous fumes within. I live alone in a freestanding house, so I don't expect I'll poison anyone nearby. By the time anyone finds me, the fumes will have dissipated. That's my reasoning. Yes, this laundry detergent thing is the way.

I can see the blurb now, in the metro section of the paper:

- Headline: "Los Angeles suicide: Man washes hands of life."
- Subhead: "34-year-old Los Angeles man makes a clean break."

The reporter will likely write something like "Did Jonathan Krause have dirty laundry to air? We may never know." Americans expect suicide to be rooted in scandal.

Here, suicide is taboo.

In Japan, it is righteous.

The Japanese have a ritual called *seppuku* that is part of the sacred samurai code. Rather than fall into the hands of enemies, the samurai plunges a sword into his abdomen to die with honor. The Japanese are big on honor—living and dying with it. Here in America, we think suicide is for nutty people who want to go to hell. In Japan, suicide is an expression of self-sacrifice, a way to fulfill a perceived duty to the larger society. With seppuku, that duty is to deny enemies the satisfaction of a kill. The duty is to die by one's own hand to escape opposing forces. Perhaps my "enemies" are self-made. Perhaps they are even imaged, illusory. But I will escape them nonetheless.

A few years ago, we—the collective "we" of R&R—were contacted by a well-known Los Angeles mortuary to put together their marketing campaign. Yes, apparently even mortuaries need advertising. Even death is an industry. We didn't get the business, but I delivered the perfect tagline nonetheless: "Because it's not a matter of *if*—it's a matter of *when*."

So when will I make my exit? It's all up to me, after all. That's the beauty of this. The better question is what I want to do before I leave the world. The project determines the timeline. That's what Creative Director Rick always says. He also says I thrive with deadlines: "Jonathan," he booms, "that's when you come alive."

The morning after the night I let myself drown in the dream, I sat in bed, laptop resting on my thighs, fingertips primed at the keys, more inspired than I'd been in months. I decided that my list of things I want to do before I die will not include "Skydive" or "See the Taj Mahal." I'm already committing suicide, so I don't think skydiving would give me much of a rush. And I don't think I'd *feel* much standing in front of the Taj Mahal. I've seen it in pictures. I don't want to drive the Autobahn, swim with a dolphin, kiss the Blarney Stone, ride in a hot-air balloon, or find God. I don't want to jump off anything, climb something, or run a great distance. I have no desire to test the limits of my body. I figure the laundry-detergent inhalation will be a good final exam.

Sara claimed not to have a bucket list. I found this out on one of our first dates, at a hole-in-the-wall Mexican restaurant that got a good write-up in *LAWeekly*. We were sitting at a little wooden table that looked to have been taken from a farmer's kitchen in the heart of Rosarito. We sipped from margarita glasses so huge that when she bent her head forward to lick the salted rim, her face nearly disappeared. While waiting for our fajitas, we took turns asking each other questions about our childhood, our fears, our dreams, the usual things you ask in the hopes of establishing what all those online dating sites promise in their lame commercials—a connection.

"What's on your bucket list?" I asked.

She scrunched her nose, as if she'd just discovered a roach floating in her drink.

"That's so morbid."

"Well, life is short and all that. I guess people like to have goals. I want to write a novel, for example."

She took a big sip. "But the minute you put something on a list, it becomes this... *thing*. Like an obligation."

I supposed this was true—about the novel, at least.

"What about grocery lists?"

"I don't make them," she said, readjusting the cloth headband that was holding her hair behind her ears. "I just go to the store and get what I want in the moment."

"Oh, god, are you a *hippie*? Do you go to the grocery store in *Birkenstocks*?"

She reached across the table and swatted my hand jokingly.

"Pray to the moon? Make your own deodorant?" I pressed.

"You act like not making lists is crazy."

"It is."

She dismissed me and asked, "What's the worst that could happen if you're without a list?"

"You're *listless*." I gave an exaggerated guffaw. She sucked on an ice cube from the bottom of her glass, as if she wanted to get the last of the tequila off of it.

"Seriously, though, if I forget milk or something, it's not the end of the world," she said.

"What would be the end of the world for you?"

"Wait, isn't it my turn to ask a question?"

"You can ask me two in return. Tell me—what would be the end of the world for you?"

She thought for a moment, biting her lip, her eyes downcast before fixing on me.

"I can't think of anything, short of the actual end of the world."

"So, apocalypse aside, you're just a happy person."

She shrugged, casually, like she didn't realize how lucky she was. "I guess."

I titled my document "Things to do before the end." My list includes the following, in no particular order:

- Take that trip to Japan
- Visit my parents
- Get the complete collection of *Seinfeld* and watch all episodes
- Give my clothes to the Salvation Army
- Take all my loose change to a Coinstar machine

I don't give a shit about writing a novel anymore.

I'm undecided about visiting Sara's parents, or Sara for that matter. I always liked her parents, Rhonda and Ted. I like to think they would want to see me. They said I was like a son to them. Maybe it will be weird for them, though. I'll have to think about this.

If I'm going to go to Japan, it will be worth my while to take a language class. We—the collective "we" of Sara and me—talked about taking a class. The house is just a few miles from a local community college filled with overambitious high school students and wayward twenty-somethings. The catalog still comes in her name—one of the many ways the universe continues to torture me. Taking a class could help the trip mean something. After all, I don't want to walk around clueless, with a baseball cap, a fanny pack, a camera, and an upside-down map. It will be a nice bookend to my life—to visit the land of my chosen suicide technique. And, hey, if I learn enough in a class, perhaps I can conclude my suicide note with a properly written "sayonara."

So I updated my list with one addition:

- Take a Japanese class

We had this before-bed routine, this mundane, boring ritual that I would have ridiculed in my twenties. The two of us, backs pressed up against the headboard on our respective sides of the bed, reading our respective books. Occasionally, a rogue foot would cross the imaginary boundary, a mischievous toe would rub against an unsuspecting calf. That night, she was engrossed in one of those trendy vampire tales she professed to hate when we got caught in conversations at dinner parties. I'd seen her take off the book jacket when reading at the little bistro table on lunch break at work. That—the removing of the book jacket—was one of the few times I saw her as really vulnerable, affected by what people think.

"In Japan, when men are asked to identify themselves, they give a job title and company name first," I said, reading aloud from the Japanese culture book.

"So, I would be 'Graphic Designer, R&R, Sara Mackenzie,'" she said with her best Japanese accent.

Yes, we worked together.

"There, what you do is who you are," I said, thinking highly of myself for this deep thought.

"Not too different from here, I suppose." She always one-upped me.

I scribbled our little exchange on the corner of a notepad next to the bed, then put the paper in my drawer with the rest of my random thoughts.

"Are you just going to keep putting papers in that drawer until a novel writes itself?" she asked.

"That's the hope."

She slid down so only her head was sticking out from under the sheets and adjusted her glasses. She wore them only at night, to read. I liked them and looked forward to us growing old together, when she'd have to wear them all the time. I'd started to think of this often—the years we would spend together. It was a fantasy of mutual absorption—discovering each other's every habit, every preference, every pet peeve and fetish.

I'd been with plenty of girls before Sara, but I'd never cared to know them like I cared to know Sara. Sara was the first girl whose morning breath didn't bother me, for instance—not because it didn't smell bad (it did), but because it was just part of her and I'd rather kiss her, first thing, than demand preparatory teeth-brushing. She wasn't perfect by any means. She pulled all the sheets to her side at night. She left her fifteen-year-old retainer on my nightstand more times than I can count. She had a habit of clipping her toenails while watching TV, sometimes failing to retrieve all the clippings so they would stick to the bottom of my feet when I didn't wear socks. Most of the time, I teased her about these things. And she teased me about how I sounded like an elderly person with emphysema when I cleared my throat, or about how my heels were so rough that they felt like sandpaper, or about how I made no attempt to bury my dirty boxers beneath other clothes in the laundry basket. We weren't resigned to each other. We weren't settling. We were just accepting, finally, of the meaning of togetherness.

She closed her book, using her glasses as a temporary bookmark, and rolled over, putting her hand on my thigh. This was something that would have excited me when we first met. But her touch had become something expected, normal, everyday. Of course, I chastise myself now for these things taken for granted.

"So what do you think happens if you're a guy in Japan without a job?" I asked her.

She leaned her head on my chest. "Then—poof—you don't exist."

Today is an otherwise ordinary Monday, made extraordinary by the fact that it is the beginning of my eight-month countdown. I am now a human with an expiration date.

Why eight months, you ask? It's all basic math.

According to Citibank records, I have $26,782.33 to my name. Consider the following expenses:

- Mortgage for the Eagle Rock house: $1,900/month. I can't be bothered with selling the thing. I want my last months to be relatively hassle-free.
- Utilities (water, gas, phone, internet, cable, electricity): $300/month.
- Food: $600/month. I'm a grown man, after all.
- Gas: $200/month. This is Los Angeles. Nothing is nearby or convenient.
- Other (cell phone, Netflix subscription, car repairs, etc.): $300/month. Initially, this "Other" category was

priced out at about $600/month because I was taking into account health insurance, my annual physical, the every-six-months dental appointments. But those things don't really matter anymore, do they?

That's $3,300/month.

Starting today, after I quit my job, that $26,782.33 will be a fixed figure. I could run up a bunch of credit card debt, but I don't want to go out that way. I'm a little fuzzy on what would happen to the thousands left on those balance sheets. I don't need my parents dealing with grief and phone calls from unsympathetic Capital One employees based in India. I figure they'll have to deal with selling my house; that will be enough of a headache. So $26,782.33 it is. Considering my expenses, basic division skills (my third-grade teacher would be so proud) determine my fate. Eight months. It will work out well. I will get to go to Japan in spring. If you're wondering how I'm going to pay for the trip, you have a valid concern. Airfare alone is a grand. The rail pass is another grand. And the damn dollar is so weak now compared to the yen. However, I have tucked away about ten grand in my 401(k). All those years, I thought I was saving to live at an old age, when really I was saving to die at a young one. There are penalties for using the money "early," but it should be enough to cover the trip. It has to be enough. I'm going. In spring.

This morning, the morning of my last day as an employed person, I slept straight through to the alarm for the first time in months. No tsunami dream, no sleep-deprivation headache, no dark circles under fatigued eyes. I've been in the habit of waking up before the alarm and then staring at the ceiling until it beeps. It's like I want to avoid beginning the day startled. Such is life—constantly warding off bad things.

Today, though, when the alarm beeped three times at 7:25 a.m., I hit snooze, like the good old days. I used to love to snooze. Sara never understood it. She couldn't understand why I didn't just get up. I told her snoozing is a sophisticated mind game. I knew I could stay in bed until 7:50 a.m. and still make it to the office by the "official" R&R start time of 9:00 a.m. There was something rewarding about defying the authority of the alarm, especially knowing that workdays do not allow for much defiance. There are meetings to attend, smiles to fake, small talk to conduct, boredom to endure, clients to please, bullets to dodge, hoops to jump through, and many other clichés—unless you just up and quit.

My morning work routine, designed to take an hour, goes like this: Walk down to the kitchen for coffee, black. While waiting for the pot to fill, chat with the receptionist, who is a dedicated fan of those reality TV shows featuring celebrities dancing. When coffee is ready, pour Cheerios and milk into Tupperware container, brought down from my office, where it is kept in a drawer to avoid coworker contamination. Breakfast could easily be eaten at home, but it's more enjoyable on work time. While the coffee cools and the Cheerios become just soggy enough, check personal email, visit CNN.com, and look for weird things on eBay, which is something I started doing after someone sold a grilled cheese sandwich with the profile of Jesus seared into it for $300.

As I take my first spoonful of Cheerios, a meeting invite appears in my in-box, with a red exclamation mark next to it. This is a disruption. My cereal becomes too soggy as I read what is apparently so important: Rick wants to call together the creative team to discuss an "urgent matter" in regard to Spot-Free, which sounds like a window cleaner but is actually an acne medication that's been around since 1988 even though it doesn't work. Every year, it's a mad rush to come up with fresh ideas for the Back to School campaign ads to run in *Seventeen, Girls' Life*, and the like.

It's a silly world I'm leaving.

"Okay, I know you're all busy, so let's make this quick," Rick says once we all congregate in the conference room, noticeably disgruntled and bleary-eyed. Meetings before 10:00 a.m. are not standard. I try to enjoy my coffee, but it just isn't the same outside the confines of my personal space.

"The issue at hand is that the client thinks 'Send your acne to detention' is too condescending," he explains.

"To whom?" I ask.

"To the acne."

"To the *acne*?"

This is what my existence has become: worrying about insulting zits.

"I know, I know. But at the end of the day, it's just too strong," Rick says.

At the end of the day—one of my favorite agency phrases, to be used interchangeably with "bottom line." In modern society, that's all we care about—the outcome, the result.

"The problem is that they want to stick as closely as possible to the detention visual we have," Cherie says, drawing our attention to her rendering of pimples sitting in a classroom looking...detained. Cherie is the art director with the most seniority. She does not like me because I thought her name was "Cherry" for the first year I worked here. If that appalled her, I wonder what she would think if I confessed to my assumption that, with a name like Cherry, she had a past in porn.

Everyone is quiet until Jake, the new guy, suggests "Get your acne expelled." He's just a kid, twenty-something, convinced that contributions like this somehow earn him points in a game that will end with him rich and happy. It takes passive Rick ten minutes to get around to telling Jake that his suggested line, while clever, presents the same problem as the other line. In those ten minutes, I decide to make a list of all the agency phrases that bother me:

- *Going forward*, as in "Going forward, I'll be sure to send you weekly updates." The subtext here is "Oops, I fucked up, I'll do better next time."
- *Perspective*, as in "From a client perspective." This word is interchangeable with "standpoint" and can be applied to people ("From Jane's perspective"), inanimate objects ("From a trade show booth perspective"), or abstract concepts ("From a logistics perspective").
- *Shoot*, as in "Why don't you just shoot me an email with that info?" Apparently, highly efficient workers do not merely send emails, they shoot them.
- *Recap*, as in "Let's meet tomorrow to recap" or "Just to recap, Jane will contact the client about the deliverable." Recap really means "Let's waste more time together reminding people of what they're supposed to do because work makes people incompetent idiots."
- *Assets*, as in "We're going to need all assets before proceeding with development of collateral." Sorry, but every time I hear the word "assets," I think of giant boobs.
- *Collateral*, as in SEE ABOVE. It's so militaristic. Then

again, agencies are battlegrounds.

- *Per*, as in "Per our conversation, I've included the follow-ing attachments." I don't know why this bothers me, it just does. It's pretentious.
- *Shelve*, as in "Let's shelve that for now and revisit it another time." The subtext here is "This idea is bullshit. Never mention it to me again."
- *Parking lot*, as in "That's an important issue, but it's taking us away from our main focus. Let's put that in the parking lot until our next meeting." Again, like "shelve," this is another way of saying "Your idea blows." I think this phrase should be expanded upon, as in "Let's put that on the third floor of the parking garage" or "Let's put that in the basement of the parking garage, behind the security guard's '86 Jeep Cherokee."
- *Off-line*, as in "Let's take this discussion off-line." The subtext here is either "I fucked up and I'd rather not admit it in front of a bunch of people on this conference call" or "You fucked up and I don't want to embarrass you in front of a bunch of people on this conference call."
- *Bandwidth*, as in "I'm not sure I have the resources or bandwidth to cover this project." I want to take this phrase a step further and start measuring my capacity in terms of hertz, as in "I'd need another five hertz to take on this project right now, and I just don't see that happening."

By the time I return to the conversation, there is still no resolu-tion to the condescended acne.

"Why don't we just put a spin on it and say 'Get out of acne detention'?" I say. "That way, you're saying the acne is detaining *you*. Put kids instead of pimples in the classroom

seats—because that seems more visually appealing anyway—
and have some standards on the chalkboard. Something like 'I
will have clearer skin' written over and over again."

They all look at me.

"That's brilliant, Jonathan," Rick says.

That was brilliant?

"Cherie, let's get this moving," Rick says.

Cherie looks visibly irritated—maybe with the idea, but more
likely with the fact that I was the one who came up with it.

"Let's touch base on this later today, everyone," Rick
concludes.

That's another one to add to the list—*touch base*. Where the
hell did this phrase come from? Is it a baseball reference? That's
my best guess. After a foul ball, the runner has to go back to the
base and the game resumes. If it is a baseball reference, "touch
base" is in tight competition with "tackle" as the most annoying sports-themed workplace term.

It's at this point that I start to conceive of my resignation
letter. By lunchtime, I have a draft that pleases me:

Dear _____: (I don't know who to address the thing to.
I report to Rick, but Rick reports to Theresa, which means
Theresa is technically my boss, even though I never talk to
her. I wonder if "To Whom It May Concern" is appropriate
in this case?)

I wish I could start this by saying "It is with great regret that
I must leave Radley and Reiser," but that would be dishon-
est. It is not with great regret that I must leave. It is with
relief. I am happy that I have been able to contribute to the
work done here, but I don't believe the work done here is

congruent with who I am anymore. If a person truly needs something—whether it's acne medication, paper towels, or Jesus Christ—I believe the person will find it without coaxing by us "advertisers." I am not someone who should be influencing the decisions of others. I don't want that power.

My last day will be today. We all know that if I gave two weeks' notice, I wouldn't actually do anything in those two weeks, so let's just cut the crap. It's been swell.

Sincerely,
Jonathan Krause

The whole bit about my not wanting "that power" makes the letter a bit lofty, but I'm satisfied nonetheless. I decide to email it to Rick and Theresa, because all communication at R&R is electronic and passive-aggressive. I get an automated "out of office" response from Rick, something about how he will be working from home for the remainder of the afternoon. Creative directors (and people with small children or certain medical conditions) seem to get this privilege. I wait to hear from Theresa.

When she calls me into her office, she seems mad. Then again, Theresa is one of those women who always seems mad. It's something to do with her stature. She's about four feet, ten inches tall, which may or may not classify as a midget. She seems to overcompensate for her height (or lack thereof) by holding her chin very high—almost too high, like a dog picking up on the scent of nearby food—and puffing out her chest, making everyone within her general vicinity aware that she must buy bras from the children's section.

"Jonathan, what is *this*?" she asks, waving my printed-out email in front of my face.

"It looks like a printout of my resignation email."

"You can't resign."

"I think I can."

"Are you angry at someone here? We can restructure the teams if that's the case."

"I'm not angry." But I do wonder how far she's willing to go to keep me. Would she fire people? How important *am* I?

"Well, your little email sounded angry."

I know why. It's the end of the message that does it, the "It's been swell." Theresa and I both know that people only use the word "swell" sarcastically. Like "dandy."

"I'm not angry," I repeat. And I'm not. Bitterly aware of the stupidity of daily work life? Yes. Angry? Not really.

"Well, I'm not sure I *understand* your decision then."

Theresa wouldn't, couldn't understand. She is the type who would have a complete crisis if she was without work to define her. We've never really understood each other—Theresa and I. There was that Christmas Eve when I was pissed about having to stay late. Sara had found these snowman mugs at a flea market and wanted to drink hot cocoa—she called it cocoa, not chocolate—out of them while watching that National Lampoon's Christmas movie. I hated the idea of her on the couch alone, waiting, probably wondering if I was in training to be an always-at-the-office husband. When Theresa finally dismissed me, I said, "Well, you have yourself a Merry Christmas." She said I "sounded angry." I told her I meant it genuinely, and she said, "Jonathan, you know I'm Jewish." And I suppose that's true—I did know she was Jewish. It's hard not to know she's Jewish. She talks about Temple frequently and is a big fan of the lox during morning meetings.

She hands me the printout. "Here, take it back. We won't tell HR about this. Think it over. Take a few days off. You probably need a few days off. You haven't taken a single day off since—"

"I don't need time off," I say, giving the letter back to her.

She takes a deep breath and puts her head in her hands, which is rather dramatic if you ask me.

"Will you freelance for us?" she asks, almost desperately, like a forlorn lover requesting "friends-with-benefits" status after a breakup.

Has she not *read* the letter? Haven't I made it clear that I am categorically opposed to advertising, as an industry?

"I don't—"

"Hundred and fifty an hour. You'll freelance for us. You'll keep some accounts as a freelancer."

A former version of myself would have thought freelancing was equivalent to living the dream: waking up at noon, forgoing a shower, finding some sort of happiness in working for three hours on an ad headline, billing for ten, then laughing merrily all the way to the bank. But now, when Theresa suggests it, I just can't find the point. I don't need the money. I've done my calculations.

Even if I did need the money, if I did freelance for these remaining months, the checks would arrive, in their some-what-obscene amounts, and I would be stuck with this distressing question: Is *this* what life is about? Mindlessly making money to spend on things that enable the perpetuation of existence (food, shelter, clothing)? Sure, there may be funds left over for a nonessential. People call this disposable income, which I've come to understand as money to help me enjoy things before I dispose of myself. But, see, that's the problem—what is enjoyable when it has a price attached to it? A movie costs $15. I find very few films able to live up to $15. Consequently, mindlessly making money enables never-ending disappointment. I don't want money now. I'm happier without it, happier knowing that the $5 In-N-Out meal should be savored because it means I am $5 closer to the end of my time here and, hey, I may eat In-N-Out only thirty-two more times (assuming a once-a-week visit). It all *means* something now.

"I'm sorry, Theresa, but I can't do it."

She backs away from me, slowly, the way women back away from husbands who have just confessed to cheating.

"Did you get another job? Did that fucking Mike Keller try to steal you from us too?"

Mike Keller at Keller & Fleishman poached a copywriter two years ago. Theresa seems incapable of letting it go.

"No, I don't have another job."

"So you're just taking some time off?" She seems confused.

"I guess you could say that. I don't plan on working, that's for sure."

She laughs a New York socialite laugh—she came to R&R from a big agency in Manhattan—until she realizes I'm serious.

"Oh, well, right. You feel that way now, but you'll get back out there."

I hate this phrase—*get back out there*. I hate it in reference to people who are unemployed, and I hate it in reference to people who have just had their hearts extracted from their chests and pummeled by the one person they swore they'd always love. "Out there" is not comforting. "Out there" is exactly what's terrifying.

"So what are you going to *do*?" she asks.

"I'm thinking about taking a Japanese class."

She laughs her laugh again, as if I've said I intend to become an astronaut. "I've heard it can take a lifetime to learn that language."

"I bet I'll get pretty far in eight months."

I head for the door, already making a mental list of everything I want to take home from the office. In advertising agencies, copywriters and art directors manage to accumulate a collection of useless stuff: tchotchkes from trade shows—ballpoint pens with flashlights at one end, digital clock key chains, those rubber balls you squeeze to exercise your hand muscles; gifted coffee mugs (everyone assumes we need caffeine, almost intravenously, along with multiple mugs); various toys, figurines, bobbleheads. All that really matters to me is my CD collection—Led Zeppelin, Pink Floyd, Bob Dylan. Yes, I still own CDs. I hate iTunes. I don't trust the Cloud.

"Jonathan, wait," Theresa says, just when I think I am free. She stands from her chair and approaches me, looking concerned. She puts her hand on my forearm.

"Are you sure it's not just that you need time off?" She gives my arm a squeeze. She has quite a grip for a little person.

"I'm sure."

"Because if this has something to do with Sara..."

It's been months, and I am still getting this pity routine. They say it takes half the time you were with someone to get over them. Maybe it takes that long for other people to get over the idea of the two of you together too. Sara and I were a "we" for a few years, so I have a while to go.

"No, this does not have anything to do with her."

I retract my arm from her trying-to-be-comforting grasp. She smiles softly, as if to say, *Okay, Jonathan, believe what you want to believe, you poor, lonely soul.* It takes everything in me not to tell her to go fuck herself.

I walk out of R&R at four o'clock, with my work bag slung over my shoulder and a stack of CDs under my arm. I have a framed picture of Sara and me, too. I'd forgotten about it, stored beneath a stack of "old clients" folders in my bottom drawer. There is no reason to leave it at the agency, to be thrown out with the tchotchkes. I tell Kevin, casually, that I will see him later. I don't feel like explaining. Advertising agencies are like high school campuses: word will get around. It always does. It did with Sara. They—the R&R drudges—knew we were "an item" before I did. I figure everyone will know I've quit by the close of business today. And, if Theresa has anything to do with it, the reason will be heartache over a former coworker romance. It makes for a good story, I guess. Rick always tells us copywriters that's all people want—a good story.

In a survey of international students, 86 percent of young Americans believed that the twenty-first century offers them hope. Only 34 percent of young Japanese agreed.

My conclusion from this is that Americans are blissfully ignorant morons. Especially the young ones.

Hope: the feeling that what is wanted can be had, or that events will turn out for the best. It's like faith, which you realize is ridiculous only after you've had it far too long. Faith in the tooth fairy, faith in the president, faith in the woman lying next to you, faith in humanity—the stakes get progressively higher over time, and reality starts to do a number on what you come to see as mere illusions. The Japanese choose not to mollify themselves with optimism. They look down the barrel of tomorrow and wait for the backfire of today— global warming, economic collapse, heartbreak, whatever.

And then they kill themselves, in great numbers.

Would it be wrong of me to assume that a whole nation understands me?

四

I met Sara at a planter—installed as part of the beautification of Los Angeles, no doubt—outside the high-rise that is home to R&R and a number of other big-dollar companies. She was just sitting there, on the edge, with a cigarette hanging out the side of her mouth. This was my spot, my planter, the place I came whenever I needed silence or space to think. My first impression of her was that she was imposing. I was annoyed until I realized how pretty she was. She had the kind of long blond hair those of us in the advertising business look for when shooting commercials for conditioners, and the kind of perfect, sparkling smile we want in toothpaste ads. Her eyes were a purple-blue color that you'd think would be available only in manufactured contact lenses, and it seemed doubtful that her skin had ever seen the sun. She jumped from her seated position when I approached.

"Oh, hi," she said, startled. The cigarette fell out of her mouth, and she caught it in her hand. That's when I realized it wasn't lit.

"You do know how to smoke a cigarette, right?" I said.

"No, not really, no." She seemed guilty and nervous, eyes darting side to side, as if on the lookout for a parole officer to haul her back to prison.

"Well, usually a lighter is involved, though a match would work too."

"I know that," she said with an amused roll of the eyes.

I stationed myself at my usual corner of the planter, deeming her uninterested in conversation.

"Sorry. I'm on edge," she said. "I just started at this company. I already got caught once taking one of my random breaks. I was in my car, listening to music, and, of course, the guy who hired me happens to pull up right next to me. I can't afford to lose this job."

"Where do you work?"

"Radley and Reiser. It's this advertising agency," she said, with a dismissive wave of the hand.

"Do you like it?"

"I've only been there one day. I've freelanced at a lot of agencies. This one is no different, really. Weird interior design. Pretentious people."

I knew then that I liked her.

"What do you do there?"

"I'm a graphic designer."

I could have guessed that. She had the "look" of a graphic designer—vintage-looking jeans, well-worn ballet slippers trying to pass off as shoes, and a fake-flower clip in her hair, above her ear.

"So, what's with the cigarette?"

She took the thing out of her mouth and twirled it between two fingers, the way middle school girls do with their glittery pens.

"Well, about half the people at the agency are smokers, which is typical, in my experience. I've calculated that they take an eight-minute break every hour to get a smoke. In an eight-hour day, that's about an *hour* of break time. That doesn't seem fair for the nonsmokers, does it?"

I shook my head and let her continue.

"So I'm pretending to be a chainsmoker. I take a half-hour break at eleven and a half-hour break at four because those are my hit-a-wall times of the day. I claim to need to smoke four cigarettes in a row at those times. With such a story, I need props."

"That's kind of an expensive non-habit, isn't it?"

"Nah, I just use the same ones over and over again."

"And how long do you plan on keeping this up?"

"Oh, indefinitely," she said, smugly. "I've been doing this for years. Haven't been caught yet."

I just nodded.

"Well, I should probably go back," she said.

"I guess that goes for me too." We started walking back to the business park quad.

"I'm Jonathan, by the way," I said, offering my hand. She shook it. She had a firm grip, the kind people reserve for interviews, when they actually care about the introduction and want to come across as "commanding."

"Sara," she said.

When she realized we were going to the same building, she said, "You work here?"

"Yep. Third floor."

She paused a second before the realization drained the color from her face. Her naturally smiling mouth fell into a frown. "Radley and Reiser?"

"Yep."

She play-hit herself in the forehead. "God, I'm such an idiot." I laughed and then promised I wouldn't say anything. "In fact, I may just start nonsmoking too."

She relaxed. "Well, Jonathan, I guess I'll see you again then."

"Eleven and four, right?"

"Of course. I have an addiction, after all."

That was how it started. Within a week, I was taking twice-daily "smoke breaks." It got to the point that I would reschedule meetings just so I could see her. I knew we didn't really need an elaborate, trick-the-boss scheme; advertising agencies assume creative people need breaks. Many come furnished with Ping-Pong and pool tables and minibars for this very purpose. Still, nonsmoking became kind of a "thing" for us. Within a month, she was hired on full time and we developed more "things." We sent each other one-liner emails, telegram style, with company gossip: "Auto-flush toilets going into bathroom #3 because unknown employee has problem with not flushing. Stop." We played "Hide the Tupperware" with people's lunches to see whose anger would lead to a company-wide email: "To the person who is stealing my lunch, please stop. I have low blood sugar, and I was looking forward to my tortellini." Our best prank was planting a tote bag in the women's restroom with strange items inside—a child's bubble wand, a Bible, dog treats, a framed picture of Justin Bieber. See, lost items always end up at the receptionist's desk, and then she does an all-agency announcement, like the ones from the principal that used to interrupt class in middle school: "Employees, a lost bag was found in the women's restroom, containing the following..." Nobody knew it was us.

One Friday afternoon, she came by my office, looking shy and tentative, and asked, point-blank, if I wanted to go pick up trash with her on the beach.

"I'm pretty sure that's reserved for people in orange jumpsuits," I said.

"Mine is more of a coral tone," she said. "But, seriously, do you want to come? Make a day of it?"

I'd never made a day of trash before, but I went with her because, in those beginning stages, you'll do almost anything to impress someone. In my dating history, I have gone to a figure skating competition, ridden a horse bareback (not recommended), watched *The Way We Were*, visited a butterfly garden, attended a poetry reading where we snapped our fingers instead of clapping, consumed spicy pho noodles that gave me the shits for two days, pretended to like cats, and wore a kilt (not for sexual purposes, to be clear, but to fit in at a girl's Scottish family reunion).

I would come to learn that volunteering was a "thing" for Sara. She considered it fun to be a part of something, as she put it. She walked for various causes—AIDS, breast cancer, MS. She spent a year after college in Costa Rica as part of Habitat for Humanity. I've seen pictures of her in paint-covered overalls standing with groups of grateful-looking brown people. At Thanksgiving and Christmas, she took days off from work to help at homeless shelters and food banks. On some Saturday mornings, she read to kids at the downtown public library. Randomly, she planted trees at parks, walked dogs for the Humane Society, donated blood, and led yoga class at the senior center. Oh, and she played chess once a week with Mr. Sacramone. In the demented nooks and crannies of my mind, I used to wonder if she cared more about Mr. Sacramone than she cared about me. I wondered if they had a secret bond. Mr. Sacramone is ninety-two years old. He has no teeth.

Before I met Sara, I assumed that do-gooders were motivated by a selfish need to see themselves as better than everyone else. I didn't give much of a shit about those worse off than me. I thought my cynicism made me wise. I said things like "Homeless people are homeless for a reason" and "Isn't it strange that people bring their clothes to the Salvation Army in *trash bags*? I mean, people aren't motivated by charity. They're motivated by tax write-offs."

Sara showed me that sometimes do-gooders are motivated only by the desire to do good; and sometimes doing good isn't a waste of time. It took me a while—months—for this not to intimidate me. For a long time, and sometimes now, I wondered if I was a project to her, just another humanitarian mission. After all, what would someone like her, someone who picked up trash *for fun*, see in a prick like me? But that's the thing with Sara. She saw the best in everyone, a trait that made her father worry she'd get mugged while putting coins in the hands of a homeless man.

"You do this every weekend?" I asked her, picking up an Arrowhead bottle filled with what I guessed to be urine. I held the cap, gingerly, between my thumb and index finger.

"Not every weekend, but whenever I can." Like the other trash collectors, we wore plastic gloves. As Sara put it, you could pick up a dirty diaper, touch your mouth later, and get infected by *E. coli*. It was romantic.

"Ever find anything really weird?" I asked, stuffing my second sticky Capri Sun of the day into my garbage bag. I was intent on filling that bag with as much trash as possible. At the very least, I had to get more trash than Sara. If need be, I would take garbage out of trash cans and put it in my bag when she wasn't looking.

"I find weird shit all the time," she said. "Lots of used condoms. I guess that's not so weird, though."

With used condoms scattered on the beach, you would think *E. coli* would have been the least of her concerns.

"I find a lot of Barbie doll heads. Just the heads. I don't know what happens to the bodies."

"Sharks eat 'em," I said. "That's where the meat is."

We went to a shack on the beach selling date shakes and hot dogs. They also sold "veggie dogs." Sara got one of those. She said she was a vegetarian, had been since she was twelve.

"What the hell is in a veggie dog?"

"I don't really care what's in it," she said. "It's what's *not* in it that matters to me."

"Pig intestines don't appeal to you?"

She shrugged. "I just don't eat anything that used to have eyes."

This *eyes* thing bothered me, but not enough to make me stop eating meat in the years I was with her. I wonder now if that would have made her happier—if I'd pledged to join her in this mission to not eat anything that used to have eyes.

We took our shakes down to the beach and sat in the sand as

the sun began its descent. It was one of those moments that you learn not to expect as you get older, one of those moments you think is confined to teenage imaginations. She pulled her arms inside her sweatshirt, hugging her body for warmth while the empty sleeves flapped in the breeze. I put my arm around her, pulled her close to me. Just two humans trying to stay warm—that's the rationalization that hung in the air for a good ten minutes until I broke the silence.

"Sara?" I said.

She was looking out at the ocean, giving me the privilege of admiring her profile—the sharp definition of her nose, the rise of her cheekbones. She kept shaking her head, trying to get strands of hair out of her face.

"What?" she asked, seemingly startled, as if I'd disrupted a movie playing in her head.

I used a finger to comb the flailing strands behind her ear and took her chin in my hand, forced her to look at me. She closed her eyes, and I had that instant to see what hope looked like on her face—eyebrows slightly raised, lips barely parted. Then I closed my eyes, and I kissed her—not long, but long enough for the balance to shift, to feel that she was the one kissing me. Her hair tickled my face as she put more of her weight into me. When I pulled away, her eyes were still closed and she was smiling. With her arms still in her sweatshirt, she fell into my lap, as if what had just happened had disturbed her center of gravity.

After the age of twenty-five, I had abandoned the idea of "the bases," or at least the idea that each base was some kind of event—kissing, tonguing, fondling, licking, fucking. I had come to assume that adults progressed from that first kiss to rounding home in the course of a night or two. We'd all done this before, hadn't we? We'd all played the game, knew how it all ended, saw no need in prolonging the inevitable. We'd all accepted that it would never be like it was the first time, like it had been when we were younger, with the thrill of anticipation, discovery, sin. Adulthood was about coming to terms with this, lowering expectations, resetting standards, going through the motions, and just appreciating an opportunity to get off every now and then. Love and "the one" were created by Hallmark, sex was driven by biology—we all said these things as if they were novel, as if they were wise, as if we were superior beings, one step ahead of every urge and illusion.

I did not get the sense that Sara shared any of these beliefs. If I hadn't known better, I would have guessed she was a virgin— though I would learn, in that somehow-mandatory discussion of past relationships, that she'd been with four guys. She kind of blushed, as if she was embarrassed, as if this number was somehow pathetic. "I've really only had long relationships," she said, as means of explanation.

With her, it was slow, but not the type of slow that certain girls mandate to express their heightened sense of morality. It wasn't slow because she wanted it to "mean something." It was slow because she wanted to savor it, enjoy it—"it" being the physicality, the buildup, the suspense. For this reason, I can remember, distinctly, the night we made out for hours, the way you do when you're fifteen, when you realize your tongue is actually a muscle because it gets so fucking sore. I can remember, distinctly, the night I unbuttoned her jeans while watching *The Shawshank Redemption*—she had never seen it, which I deemed unacceptable—and slipped my fingers inside her. I can remember, distinctly, the first time I saw her naked. She swung her hair over her shoulders, coyly, so that the ends just barely covered her nipples. She probably lamented the size of her breasts, thought men wanted more to grab, spent stupid sums of money on bras with the latest innovations in realistic padding. My palms had no complaints though. The normally unexposed skin of her stomach, the skin only a handful (or two) of men had been privy to touching, was almost translucent. Her arms, from where her shirt sleeves ended to her fingertips, were just a shade darker. Calling them tan lines on someone so white would be a misnomer. She had this birthmark on her hip, at that place some girls get fairy tattoos. I kissed that place first. Then I followed the path of neon-blue veins, visible just beneath the surface, until my lips had traversed her entire body. She made me believe it was possible to forget all the times before—the softness of every other girl's lips, the predictable ear-sucking, the roll of every other girl's hips, the feeling of skin adhering to skin, breasts pressing against chest, with nothing but a sweaty film in between. It was like she possessed some magical power to erase memory or induce time travel back to adolescence, when everything I knew about women was from my father's hidden *Playboy*s. You would think I would hold on to this possibility, hold out hope for finding it again, with someone else. I don't, though. I'm convinced it was only possible with Sara.

The night we slept together for the first time, she was drunker than I would have liked her to be. I've never liked sleeping with a girl when she's drunk. There's always this worry that I'm taking advantage of her. I told Sara that, because I'd decided I would tell her everything.

"I think you have self-esteem issues," she said, with a laugh that made her burp. It smelled like the gin and tonics we'd had at the bar. She'd had too many, an error that, when made by others in the past, caused me to lose respect. With Sara, though, it only made her more human, likeable.

She took hold of my shirt collar and pulled me close to her until we both fell backward onto her bed.

"Meaning?"

"You're afraid that I'm only going to sleep with you because I'm slightly drunk, like I wouldn't sleep with you otherwise."

"Maybe."

I kissed her neck because I knew she both hated and loved it—that strange duality of tickling. She squirmed and maneuvered her body out from underneath me.

"Let me assure you that you are very sleep-with-able," she said, sitting on top of me, straddling me. She pulled my shirt over my head and helped me out of my pants without the awkwardness that sometimes comes with undressing. She even managed to remove my socks in a timely manner. It was the only indication I'd had up to that point that she'd done this before, that I wasn't the first guy she'd ever tried to love, that maybe I wasn't as special as I wanted to be. But then she rolled onto her back, pulling on my side to encourage me to put my weight on top of her. I liked her that way—innocent, unsure, trusting.

Whenever I first slept with a girl, I could never actually sleep. Whether it was her bed or mine, there was just something unsettling about sharing that small space. All that body heat, those sprawled-out limbs—it felt intrusive, demanding. *This is what people do, Jonathan*, I'd tell myself, in attempts to coach myself into feeling comfortable enough to doze off. In times of desperation, I relied on Tylenol PM. With Sara though, this wasn't necessary. I must have just fallen asleep effortlessly, deep enough to not notice until the morning that her leg was tangled up with mine. Sometimes, these days, when I wake up, I expect Sara to be there. All those years unsure how I'd share a bed with another for any length of time, and now I'm left wondering how I can sleep alone. It's like that phenomenon of phantom limb experienced by amputees after the removal of a leg or arm. They claim to still feel the limb, attached. I guess I have phantom Sara.

When she woke up that morning after the night we slept together, she didn't run to the bathroom to fix her makeup. She couldn't be bothered, seemingly assured that I would see her like this—pillow-creased cheeks and puffy eyes—at some point anyway. There was this unspoken understanding that we would be in each other's lives for some period of time, a significant period that neither of us wanted to define in exact terms.

"Those aren't real, are they?" I asked, nodding toward a vase at the side of her bed holding branches with cherry blossom blooms on them.

"Of course not," she said, like I was stupid. She never had a problem with indicating my stupidity. She was never careful that way, never accepting of the idea that the male ego is a land mine. "Cherry blossoms bloom and then die within days. It's one of nature's greatest tragedies." She said this with an exaggerated sadness.

"So they're fake."

"The branches are real. I made the flowers out of tissue paper. Something I read in a magazine."

"How very Martha Stewart of you."

"Don't get any ideas," she said. "I can't cook for shit."

I liked that she was telling me not to get any ideas, that she was assuming we would have a future together in which such ideas would apply.

"Well, they look real."

"I think so. I love cherry blossoms."

It struck me as an odd thing to love, these flowers that die too soon.

In the few years of being with Sara, I would develop an entire archive of these oddities, these tidbits that defined her: she liked sunrises better than sunsets, hated tomato seeds (not tomatoes, just the seedy part), took off heeled shoes when she drove, slept on her right side, thought people lived under the streets to control the traffic lights when she was a kid, cried over roadkill, underlined paragraphs she loved when reading, bought tickets to bad movies because she said movie theaters had the best napping conditions, marveled at how she was littering the Earth with her DNA every time she pulled out and discarded a loose strand of hair, never went to gyms because she said they make humans look like hamsters—running on contraptions, but not really going anywhere.

I don't know what to do with the archive now. I find myself searching through it, like my own personal Sara microfiche (yes, I'm old enough to remember microfiche), even though it would be better for this information to be cleared, to free up space for something, anything else. Maybe, though, the information is saved for a reason. Maybe I'm supposed to hold on to it, let it feed masochistic tendencies that remind me of what an asshole I am for watching her go.

In the kitchen, I have a calendar stuck to my fridge with a magnet that says "Life sucks." It was sarcastic, funny, when it wasn't true. My mother gives me a calendar every year, as if she's afraid I'll forget the damn date without her thoughtfulness. The theme of this calendar is "Inspirational Places." It features photos of glaciers and snowcapped mountain ranges and rolling green hills. These inspire me to get another calendar. I never actually used calendars for anything other than cheap wall art until I met Sara. She was the type to take note of important birthdays, to care about full moons and the official start of seasons. She got tickets to concerts and plotted out three-day weekend adventures months in advance. She jotted down release dates for movies and books and albums. For her, the calendar provided joy of anticipation, excitement for things to come. Since I've been alone, there isn't much to come that's worth anticipating. Sure, there is my impending suicide, but that's in the spring. Next year. I don't have a calendar for next year yet.

Sometimes I find myself glancing at the calendar, expecting to see her scribbles there. It's like when I roll over in bed in the morning, in that fuzzy just-awake time when disbelief is suspended. I'm always confused—for a split second—when I don't see her on her designated side of the bed. These are the little things that torment me. Daily.

Months ago, before my laundry-detergent resolution, I started marking off days with big X's, like I was counting down to Christmas. When I'm gone and my calendar is found, maybe the X's will explain everything. Maybe that'll be enough of a suicide note, each X representing an annoying errand run, an obligatory parental phone call, an oil change. I've come to think it's an accomplishment just to survive the monotony of being alive.

Today, however, I have something to remember—the first night of my Japanese class. Enrolling was easy, not like it was when I was in college. Everything is online now, no face-to-face communication necessary. The class itself cost me around a hundred bucks. Only twenty bucks a unit at a community college. The parking permit cost me another thirty bucks. Yes, it costs more to park on campus than to receive a unit of education. The books and other materials cost me just under seventy-five bucks. All of this fit nicely in my category of "Other" expenses. It was thrilling, almost, to use my credit card, to know that the end is coming nearer with every purchase. A week from today, class starts. It's on the calendar.

Japan suicides near record high in 2007
Reuters

Over 33,000 people took their lives in Japan last year, topping 30,000 for the tenth consecutive year despite a government campaign to reduce what is one of the highest suicide rates in the world.

A report issued by the National Police Agency on Thursday showed that 33,093 people killed themselves in Japan in 2007—the second-largest number on record after 34,427 in 2003—mostly because of debt, family problems, depression, and other health issues.

There was also a leap in the number of suicides involving toxic hydrogen sulfide gas made from household detergents, a previously obscure method that is spreading rapidly as Internet messages tell victims how to produce the poison at home.

"This extremely regrettable situation has been going on for a long time," chief government spokesman Nobutaka Machimura said of the data.

"It's a very hard problem, but we want to do as much as we can."

五

I should have known I'd feel like this, stepping onto a campus at the age of thirty-four. By "this," I mean a loser. I'm surrounded by teenagers looking to accumulate credits that will look impressive on their college applications, young adults who could not get into regular college, and adults who are either bored or seeking a career redo.

In my backpack, I have the *Integrated Course in Elementary Japanese* textbook and workbook (which I purchased used, so it already has all the correct answers marked in it). I also have a *Random House Japanese–English Dictionary*, a grammar bar chart, and a vocabulary bar chart. These bar charts make it seem like learning Japanese is virtually impossible, like maybe it should be taught along with Egyptian hieroglyphics on a reality show called *So You Think You Can Learn Something?*

The class is in a bungalow, an afterthought classroom crammed in next to the soccer field. I take a seat in the back row, trying to be as inconspicuous as possible. Within five minutes, the room fills with about twenty-five students—five rows, five chairs to a row. There's another older guy in the class, who sits next to me, of course. He's overweight, almost too big to fit in the little chair. His hair is either very greasy or he likes his styling gel a bit too much; I'm going with the former. He's wearing a polo shirt with a name badge still pinned to it, something he forgot to take off after his shift at whatever lowly retail job he has. He turns to me, gives a forced smile, and offers his gigantic hand. I shake it tentatively as it dawns on me that he thinks we're friends.

"Jonathan," I say. "And you're Bob?"

He looks at me like I've just rocked his entire world with my psychic skill.

"Your name badge," I say, pointing at it.

He nods and unpins the badge. The teacher calls us to attention. She's Japanese, unsurprisingly, and short—maybe just under five feet tall—but intimidating nonetheless. She strolls through the classroom, looking at each of us intently, as if storing our faces in her memory bank. Her posture is perfect, so perfect that I wonder if they made her walk with books on her head in whatever strict schoolhouse she attended in Japan. A pink cardigan is pulled tight around her tiny body, penny loafers (with the pennies inserted) on her child-sized feet.

After one lap around the room, she returns to the front, points at her nose, which is the cultural equivalent of pointing at one's chest in America, and says, "Miyagi Meiko *desu*." She tells us this means "I am Meiko Miyagi." Miyagi is her last name, her family name. The family name comes before the given name in Japan, which makes sense when I think of all those stories I've heard about Japanese people dying for their kin, in the name of dignity and honor. Some dumb kid in America would never die for his family. Here, we even have people with *just* first names, like Madonna. And Sting. And Rihanna.

We are told to call her Miyagi Sensei. In Japan, *sensei* is used for teachers, doctors, politicians, basically anyone of relative importance. I wonder if it's considered humorously sarcastic in Japan to greet a janitor with *"Konnichiwa, sensei."*

After explaining that we can download the syllabus online (though the way she says it sounds like "downlord"), she tells us she wants each of us to introduce ourselves as she did and say why we are taking the class. The first kid is so distracted trying to "downlord" his syllabus on his laptop right then and there—the world has changed so that patience is no longer a virtue—that he just repeats "Miyagi Sensei *desu.*" A few students laugh, but not as many as I think should laugh in response to this obvious display of stupidity.

"No, no, you introduce *yourself*," Miyagi Sensei says, with a few quick jolty nods.

The kid understands, and the utterly dull introductions commence. Aside from a couple in the front row who say they are taking the class "to bond" (I would think there are better activities for bonding—sex, for example—but I'm no expert on relationships), most of the students are trying to get some elective units to graduate or are learning Japanese for mysterious "business purposes." We all know the United States is the dying superpower. Asia is next in line, they say. But what these idiots don't realize is they should be learning Chinese, not Japanese. Hasn't anyone told them not all Asians are the same?

Miyagi Sensei points to the girl sitting in front of me.

"Asahi Rihoko *desu*," she says in a small voice. Her Japanese is rehearsed. She's done this before. I am fascinated by this, and by the fact that she shares her last name with a Japanese beer I have consumed on numerous occasions.

"I'm learning Japanese because I am Japanese. Obviously."

I can't see her face, only the tightly knotted bun of black hair on top of her head. She has no trace of an accent. She sounds as white as me. Several students in the first few rows crane their necks to look at her, as if she's some exotic zoo animal. They are curious, dying to ask all the wrong questions:

- "Are you really good at math?"
- "Do you play sudoku?"
- "Do you own a kimono?"

"My parents want me to know their language," she says, sitting up straighter in her chair. She has a strangely long neck, like a ballet dancer.

This pleases Miyagi Sensei. She turns to the teacher's assistant, a white guy named Todd who looks like he learned Japanese so he could hit on Asian chicks and find out if they really have sideways vaginas (as the urban legend goes). They carry on a quick conversation as if none of us are here. Finally, she turns back to the Japanese girl who doesn't know Japanese.

"We think this is a great idea!" Miyagi Sensei says. I have no doubt that Miyagi Sensei's children already know Japanese. They might know Chinese too, just because. They probably play the piano and study calculus for shits and giggles.

"My parents do too," the girl says. The students laugh good-naturedly. They're all young enough to have a collective annoyance with pesky parents. My parents live in the Bay Area, a good six hours away by car. They're hard-pressed to get me to call them on holidays, let alone take a language class to connect to my family tree. Then again, my roots are British, so I'm told. Very little about me is interesting.

"Sir?"

It takes me a moment to realize that Miyagi Sensei is talking to me. Christ, I've become a "sir."

"Uh, what?" I say, as if I'm shocked, as if I don't know what's expected of me even though I've been sitting here listening to twenty other students and their torturous introductions for the past fifteen minutes.

"Tell us your name," Miyagi Sensei says. She talks to me like I'm a four-year-old. Turns out learning a new language as an adult makes you feel like you did when deciphering Dick and Jane stories in kindergarten.

"Uh, Jonathan Krause... I mean, Krause Jonathan *desu.*"

Necks are craning to look at me now, the idiot stumbling over his words and flunking the very first assignment. I lock eyes with the Japanese girl who doesn't know Japanese. They—the eyes—are brown, almond-shaped, adorned by lashes seemingly blacker than her hair. She has beautiful skin, with light-brown distinctive freckles stretching across the bridge of her nose and her cheeks. She is proof that not all Asians look alike after all. It's the freckles. I wonder if Asians think all white people look alike?

"And why have you signed up for Japanese class?"

Suddenly, I'm nervous, uncomfortable with this Japanese girl who doesn't know Japanese staring at me.

"Sir?"

"Uh, well, I want to take a trip to Japan."

Miyagi Sensei looks amused. "Some people in Japan know English," she says, as if English is a simple nursery rhyme every toddler there learns. Maybe it is.

"I just thought it would be better to know some of the language, to enrich the experience."

This appears to satisfy Miyagi Sensei. The Japanese-girl-who-doesn't-know-Japanese turns back to face the front.

"Okay, then," the teacher says, "the first order of business is choosing a Japanese name."

She passes out a list of choices. Nothing really seems to suit me. I narrow it down to these:

- Kazuki
- Takumi
- Kaito
- Naoki

I like "Kazuki" best because it sounds like either a high-end motorcycle or a martial arts move that could kill a small child.

Unfortunately, there are consequences to sitting in the back. I've been out of school too long to remember this. The two guys in the first row take "Kazuki" and "Kaito," respectively. One of the guys in row two lays claim to "Takumi," and a guy in the third row snags "Naoki." With all my preferred options gone, and the teacher pressuring me for a choice, I settle for "Daichi," which sounds like the make of a cheap car: "What do you drive?" "Oh, I drive a Daichi."

The females make the choosing of names a complicated procedure that takes a good twenty minutes. They bargain with each other, they trade. "Reina" and "Asuka" are much-desired. Just as I'm getting bored, the teacher comes to the Japanese-girl-who-doesn't-know-Japanese.

"I don't need to pick a name," she says. "I'll keep what I have."

Miyagi Sensei smiles. It's obvious she has already selected her pet.

"Rihoko, then?"

"I go by Riko for short, actually," she says. Miyagi Sensei makes a quick note on her class list and then continues until everyone has a name they don't feel comfortable saying out loud (except for this Riko girl).

Perhaps to boost our confidence, Miyagi Sensei tells all of us to get in pairs and make a list of the Japanese words we already know. Students turn quickly to their preferred partner and, fearing Bob will try to partner with me, I tap Riko on the shoulder. She is also partnerless. In her case, it's because she scares everyone with her already-Japanese name and an actually noble reason to be here. In my case, it's because I'm old and I already fucked up.

"I hate to ask this of you, but would you like to be my partner?" I ask, feeling as if I'm burdening her, placing an oppressive weight on her frail shoulders.

She laughs. "You sound like you're asking someone for a kidney."

She turns her desk around to face mine and takes out a notebook and a mechanical pencil.

"What's your name again?"

"Daichi," I say. "But my friends call me Jonathan."

She laughs again. She's an easy laugher. It's a trait of the young.

"Okay, well, I'm sure both of us know the word *sushi*," she starts, writing it down. This relaxes me, immediately. I had feared she'd start with some kind of complicated Japanese greeting, something her parents made her memorize right after she uttered "mama."

A few minutes later, this is our list:

• Sushi

- Karate
- Karaoke
- Origami
- Konnichiwa
- Anime
- Sashimi
- Sake
- Teriyaki
- Ninja
- Sayonara
- *Domo Arigato, Mr. Roboto.* You know, from the song.

"This list makes me realize how often America ruins things," I say. "We turned *kamikaze* into a girly alcoholic beverage."

She adds "kamikaze" to our list, excitedly.

"Well, the Japanese butcher American pastimes too," she says, with an air of intelligence. "You should see what they do to pizza there."

"Have you been?" Maybe she can give me some pointers.

"Oh, no, but I've heard stories." She leans close, like she's sharing something clandestine, a secret that could change the Western world as we know it. "They put mayonnaise on their pizza."

"No way."

"It's true."

"You know, if your parents want you to learn Japanese so bad, perhaps you should talk them into an educational trip to Japan."

She shifts in her chair, uncomfortably. "I don't think they'd go for that."

"Well, you could go on your own sometime," I say. It occurs

to me that maybe she can't go on her own. Maybe she's a teenager. It's so damn hard to tell with Asians.

"I'd like to."

"I'm going," I say, a bit too excitedly, like a kid in the short bus on the way to Disneyland.

"I know. You said as much in your little introduction," she says. She has more sass than I expect from a stereotypically demure Asian chick. "You know, most people planning a trip to a foreign country just get a 'learn while you drive' CD or app or whatever. It's a little extreme to take a semester-long *class*."

"I'm an extreme kind of guy." I say this in reference to my plan to die by laundry detergent, but I realize she's thinking I'm someone who rock climbs without a harness and jumps out of planes on weekends.

"I guess I see your point," she says, like she's not entirely sure. "May as well make the most of things."

"You only live once and all that," I say, bored with my own assertion.

"Not if you're Buddhist."

Miyagi Sensei calls us back to attention. By the time all the groups have shared their predictably similar lists, class is over. Miyagi Sensei passes out an inch-thick booklet with common phrases for us to review "in our spare time."

With a courteous bow, she dismisses us.

"See you next week?" Riko says, shoving her notebook into her oversized purse.

"Probably."

"Scared off after one class?"

She gives me a little jab in the arm, something playful and adolescent, before swinging her purse over her shoulder and leaving. I rub my arm, as if it's been wounded. It occurs to me that this is no time to collect acquaintances. If there's one thing that disturbs me about this whole inhalation-of-laundry-detergent endeavor, it's the aftermath, the finding of my body, the phone call from the police to my clueless parents, the gasps around the office at R&R. I don't need to be making promises to people, even promises as benign as "See you next week." I don't need to add to the list of people who will have to hear the news of my bizarre death. It's better that I leave without loose ends. I know what it feels like to be the one left to tie them.

Unsure of what is expected of a suicide note? Google it. There is a site that compiles suicide notes gathered at coroners' offices, supposedly for the purpose of psychological analysis, though I bet it's more to satisfy curiosity among those who cannot fathom taking their own lives.

Single female, age 21
My dearest Andrew,

It seems as if I have been spending all my life apologizing to you for things that happened whether they were my fault or not. I am enclosing your pin because I want you to think of what you took from me every time you see it. I don't want you to think I would kill myself over you because you're not worth any emotion at all. It is what you cost me that hurts and nothing can replace it.

Single male, age 51
Sunday 4:45 PM. Here goes.

To whom it may concern,
Though I am about to kick the bucket I am as happy as ever. I am tired of this life so am going over to see the other side.

Good luck to all.
Benjamin P.

Married male, age 48
Elaine, Darling,
My mind—always warped and twisted—has reached the point

where I can wait no longer—I don't dare wait longer—until there is the final twist and it snaps and I spend the rest of my life in some state run snake pit. I am going out—and I hope it is out— Nirvanha, I think the Bhudaists (how do you spell Bhudaists?) call it which is the word for "nothing." That's as I have told you for years, is what I want. Imagine God playing a dirty trick on me like another life!

The neighbors may think it's a motor backfire, but to me she will whisper—"Rest - Sleep."

Albert

P.S. I think there is enough insurance to see Valerie through school. She is the only one about whom I am concerned as this .38 whispers in my ear.

Divorced female, age 61

You cops will want to know why I did it. Well, just let us say that I lived 61 years too many.
People have always put obstacles in my way. One of the great ones is leaving this world when you want to and have nothing to live for. I am not insane. My mind was never clearer.

Married male, age 74

No more I will pay the bills.
No more I will drive the car.
No more I will wash, iron & mend any clothes.
No more I will have to eat the leftovers cooked the day before.
This is no way to live.
Either is it any way to die.

W.S.

To the undertaker: We have got plenty money to give me a decent burial. Don't let my wife kid you by saying she has not got any money.

Give this note to the cops.
Give me liberty or give me death.

Married male, age 45

Dear Claudia,

You win, I can't take it any longer, I know you have been waiting for this to happen. I hope it makes you very happy, this is not an easy thing to do, but I've got to the point where there is nothing to live for, a little bit of kindness from you would of made everything so different.
P.S. Kid, disregard all the mean things I've said in this letter, I have said a lot of things to you I didn't really mean and I hope you get well and wish you the best of everything.

Cathy – don't come in. Call your mother, she will know what to do.

Love,
Daddy

Cathy, don't go in the bedroom.

Single male, age 13

I know what I am doing. Annette found out. Ask Cara. I love you all.

Bill

Widowed female, age 52

Everyone seems so happy and I am so alone. Amy. I wanted to visit you but I am going around in a dream. Alice I wanted to help you paint but how could I with a broken heart. And my head aches so much, my nerves are ready to break and what would happen if they did? You will say I am crazy and I can't go on this way just half living. I loved this house once but now it is so full of memories I can't stay here. I have tried to think of some way to go on but can't. Am so nervous all the time—I loved Ron too much. With him gone I have nothing. Oh I have the girls and family but they don't fill the vacant spot left in my heart. I'm so tired and lonely.

Mother Love, Louise

Married man, age 52

Dear Joan,

For 23 years we lived happy together. Our married life was ideal, until two years ago when I witnessed Kristy die in the hospital something snapped in me. You remember when I returned from the hospital I broke down. That was the beginning of my illness. Since then my condition was getting progressively worse, I could not work or think logically. You have been through "Hell" with me since then. Only you and I know how much you have lived through. I feel that I will not improve and can't keep on causing you and the children so much misery. I loved you and was proud of you. I loved the children dearly and could not see them suffer so much on account of me.

Dear Children: Please forgive me.
Love, Frank

Divorced female, age 37

To No-one and Everyone:

Because of a growing conviction that a hereditary insanity is manifesting itself beyond my control, I am taking this way out—before mere nuisance attacks and rages against others assume a more dangerous form. Because I am an agnostic and believe funeral fanfare to be nonsense—I ask that it be forgotten. I hereby bequeath 1) To Mark B. all personal effects—to be divided as whim decrees—with Dr. Lois J., L.A. and to each—a deep fondness and love. 2) To Joe A. the greatest devotion—the kind that "passeth all understanding." 2a) And my life.

Anita R.

3) To my father, Vincent M., the sum of one dollar ($1)

My first thought is that these notes make people like me, people who take their own way out, seem slightly off their rocker. My second thought is that we probably seem this way because we are.

六

hardly ever call my parents. It's not because I don't give a shit about them. It's just that they ask so many questions— *How's work? Have you been writing? Are you dating anyone?*— that remind me, and them, that something is "off" with me. Behind chitchat about the forecast and whether or not the Giants will make it to the postseason (Dad's a big fan), I can sense their disappointment, their worry, their curiosity as to how it is that I am their offspring.

The inescapable fact of suicide is that you do not just dissolve into the cosmos. Your body is left, for someone to find. My parents won't be the ones to find me, unless there is a parental psychic power of which I am not aware that compels them to make a trip to Los Angeles on the day I do the deed. A neighbor will find me, most likely. I'll emit an odor. This is an unpleasant, but inevitable reality. My parents may have to identify me though. Even if I just tape my birth certificate to my chest, along with a Post-it that says "Please don't trouble my family," they will be called to the morgue. I imagine there are rules about this type of thing, sections of manuals dedicated to the protocol. They are my next of kin. They will have to bear the responsibility. There is nobody else.

When I was a kid, I used to beg my parents to give me a sibling. Brother, sister—it didn't matter. I wasn't picky. Once I learned in fifth grade about the mechanics of sex, I begged them to make a baby. I would walk into their bedroom on weekend mornings, when they were still under the covers, and tell them that they should do it, right then and there. I told them I would watch cartoons, maybe make myself breakfast, make *them* breakfast, as if this was some kind of fair trade: *you make a baby, I'll make Eggos.* I was persistent about this for months, until my father finally sat me down, with a sternness in his face I'd never seen before.

"Jon, you have to stop with this baby stuff," he told me. "You won't be having a brother or sister. I'm sorry, but that's just how it is. We live in a neighborhood with plenty of kids. You'll see as you get older that friends can be just like brothers and sisters."

"Well, why can't I have a real brother or sister though?"

"You just can't. It's not possible."

And then he proceeded to tell me that he'd been "fixed," asking me to recall when we had Pooh, our dog, "fixed," telling me that it was the same thing. For years, I thought my father just didn't have balls, like the dog.

Some years later, he would explain that he was "fixed" because my mother had had a miscarriage when I was just two years old. In my father's words, "It killed her." She couldn't take the chance of that loss again. Besides, he'd said, "How could we do any better than you?"

What my parents didn't understand was that I never really cared about having a playmate—I was always kind of solitary—but I knew, even at a young age, that I would be expected to fulfill whatever dreams they never managed to fulfill themselves, and that was a tall order. There would be nobody else to share the load. Everything would be dependent on me. If I fucked up my life, there would be no brother or sister to compensate, to keep balance and sanity. Now, with my end looming, I have to consider that I am leaving my parents with nobody in whom they can entrust their hopes, their future. When I'm gone, there will be nobody else to have a wedding where they give toasts. There will nobody else to make them grandparents. There will be nobody else to take care of them when they're old, make sure they are treated well in whatever old-person facility they come to call home. It's sad, really. It makes me an asshole, I guess. But, then again, I didn't ask to be an only child. I didn't ask to be born.

"Jonathan, it's so good to hear from you!" my mother says.

There's the usual click of my father picking up another phone. They have landline phones in nearly every room. They like to have family conference calls. It works out fine unless Dad gets too close to Mom with the portable, creating interference that makes it completely impossible to understand what anyone is saying.

"Is that who I think it is?" he says. He always says this; sometimes, I want him to think it's Ed McMahon.

When I was with Sara, I used to call more. We used to call more. At least once a week, she would say, "Have you called your parents? We should call your parents." And I'd oblige. With her, it's like my mind jumped ahead—to marriage and kids and all those usual things—and I thought that maybe it'd be a good idea to have my parents involved, rooting for us, offering to babysit, helping with down payments. I found myself caring to know them again, beyond just a holiday visit and a birthday card in the mail.

Now, I call about once a month and, when I do, I'm pretty sure my mother cries. Her voice gets shaky with an emotion that she says I don't understand because I'm not a parent.

"How's it going, Jon?" My father is the only person who calls me Jon.

"Things are good, things are good." It's best, I've realized, to keep it short and sweet, and to repeat key phrases.

"How's work going?"

Here come the questions. I start to pace the short length of my galley kitchen. I don't plan on telling them I quit my job with R&R. I don't see the point. My mother loves to tell all her friends about her son who writes advertisements. She says "advertisements" in the pretentious way, the way that sounds like "advertissments." It seems like it would cause her unnecessary pain if she knew I was unemployed. And my father would be tortured about my stalled retirement account.

"Work is good." This isn't a lie. Work is good, in that it is nonexistent.

This is an appropriate time to divert the conversation away from me: "What are you guys up to?"

"Your dad's golfing a lot," my mother says, with an undertone of resentment. She hates the hours he spends on eBay buying clubs, let alone the hours he spends on the courses. She complains that he always forgets to put sunscreen on his cul-de-sac of baldness. She says he's going to get skin cancer one day, that she's going to have to take him to radiation treatments.

"Your mom's getting her eyes done," my father says, with a long sigh. They are like children, really, tattling on each other.

"The doctor calls them *eye hoods*, Jonathan."

They're talking over each other, like all married people seem to do after a few decades. It's like part of the contract—*in sickness and health, in good times and bad, in muddled conversation, as long as we both shall live.*

"She thinks she looks like a bassett hound."

"So, what? You're having plastic surgery?"

"Oh, Jonathan, everyone is doing it," she says. It's funny how parents chastise you for using this phrase in adolescence but fall back on it when old age approaches.

I used to assume that this superficial ridiculousness, this vanity, was an American thing. But my Japan book tells me that the "everyone is doing it" rationale is alive and well there too. In Japan, the "in" thing is double eyelid surgery. Most Asians have flat eyelids, so they have surgery to put in a crease. That way, their eyes can open wider and look bigger, more "Western," like the eyes they see in all the movies and TV shows we send their way.

People are never happy.

"Do you really think that's necessary?" I ask her, stopping my pacing to empty the dishwasher. I multitask on almost every parental phone call.

"I just want to have my old face back. The doctor says I could look ten, maybe *twenty* years younger."

A while back, we did this campaign at R&R for this "rejuvenating" wrinkle cream. That's a marketing term that refuses to die—*rejuvenating*. Slap it on a bottle of anything—face cream, conditioner, nail polish, bubble bath—and you're guaranteed to sell upward of 40 percent more product. People like my mother are that desperate to believe. And I suppose people like me have fed the desperation with every ad, every false promise.

"Gloria Steinem had her eyes done, you know. She had eye *bags*, but it's similar," my mother says. "And insurance is covering it. The flaps of skin may affect my peripheral vision." She states this with such resolve, convinced that the actions of a famous feminist and the agreement of an insurance company mean more than disapproving hesitations from her husband and son.

"When are you having it done?" I ask, hoping it's long after I'm gone. I don't want to see my mother altered.

"Next week," my father says.

"So the next time you see me, I'll look so much younger!"

"Well, I wanted to talk to you about that, actually. I was thinking of driving up for a visit soon."

I can hear my mother clap her hands together in excitement about this.

"For the holidays?" my father asks.

"No, before then. Soon. I don't really want to celebrate the holidays this year."

There is silence on their end. They are not sure what to do with this information. They've come to see me as weirder and weirder recently. They seem afraid of my weirdness, unwilling to challenge or even question it. It's like I've scattered a bunch of eggshells on the ground and nobody wants to walk on them.

"That's fine, dear," my mother says, gently. "Whenever you want to come, we'll be here."

Like most parents of grown children, I guess they figure they'll take what they can get.

"All right, well, I'll call again when I know the exact dates."

"Looking forward to seeing you," my father says.

"We love you," my mother adds.

"You too."

✳

It's best to see them sooner rather than later. If I see them right before the end, I may have more doubts, more second thoughts about my decision. And, when I'm gone, their memories of me will be much too fresh, still at the forefront of their minds, left over from our visit. It will make the pain worse. This way, they'll see me for the last time months before I die. In the time in between, we'll settle back into our routine of estrangement and limited contact. It'll be better for everyone this way.

They are going to want a note though, an explanation. So much will be expected of it, me being a writer and all. Without a creative brief, it turns out I'm rather lost. If I were to create a creative brief for a suicide note, it would include these directives:

- Explain motive. Make this succinct.
- Emphasize sanity (i.e., "I am not crazy").
- Apologize.
- Provide instructions for practical matters like the funeral, money, etc.
- Say something poetic. Make sure it is exceedingly vague and cryptic, leaving loved ones attempting to decipher it for years to come.

The trickiest part is the apology. It has to be done in a way that doesn't elicit anger. I mean, after all, how sorry can you be if you go through with something so drastic? They will ask that question during the phase of grief that involves getting pissed off at the dead.

The logistics are the easiest part. I jot down some notes:

- Don't worry too much about the house. Even in this shitty market, it's worth more than it was when I bought it. You will have a nice profit.

- My car is paid off.
- If you want to do a funeral (I concede funerals are more for the living than the dead, so I'll keep mum on any preference I have), keep it simple. No priest. No "Amazing Grace." No black. Just have some drinks and try to say nice things about me, because I may be listening.

There is the matter of what to do with my body. According to the way-too-casual-sounding website FuneralDepot.com, a traditional, low-end funeral costs $6,000. Six grand to put me in the ground? No, thank you. Burn me, please. Cremation almost always costs less than two grand. I'll take that option. That's what 99 percent of Japanese people choose, and I've already concluded that the Japanese are on to something. According to the Yamaguchi Saijo Funeral Parlor and Crematorium in Sapporo, it takes about an hour and a half to cremate an adult body. That's nothing—just the length of a typical romantic comedy. I don't give a rat's ass what's done with the ashes, as long as they're not put in an overpriced urn to be placed on a fireplace mantel. I'll just want them scattered somewhere—preferably not the ocean with everyone else's ashes. Is this the type of wish I should express? I wonder if my mother would consider it too frivolous if I request that Kansas song during the scattering—*All we are is dust in the wind*. My mother loves Kansas. In high school, our marching band did a rendition of "Carry On Wayward Son" during Friday night football games. She used to bounce in her seat, for which I scolded her every time. She embarrassed me, I told her. I would never forgive her, I told her. I wanted another mother, a cooler mother, I told her. Once the teenage years passed, she probably thought the worst was over. I hate that this can't be true.

I sit on the toilet, seat down, confined to this small, six-by-three-foot closet of a bathroom. I figure the smaller the space, the greater concentration of gas, the quicker my end. I take a deep breath, let the poison fill my lungs, envision it irritating the lining, burning my insides. When I close my eyes, I feel dizzy, like after a night of too much drinking. "You've got 'the spins,'," Sara used say, ordering me to sleep with one foot hanging out of the bed, touching the floor, "for stability," she said.

Everything goes quiet, the kind of eerie quiet, like when I'm lying in bed with my earplugs at night, staring at the ceiling. A while back, I started wearing earplugs to sleep. It's not that I have noisy neighbors, the fighting or the fucking kind (or the combo) who are up at all hours. It's not that I like to sleep during the day when the gardeners have the leaf blowers working full force. It's not that there is a compulsive vacuumer living upstairs. But I started wearing earplugs. I get the cheap kind, the squishy ones that fit to the contours of your inner ear and come out looking yellow in the morning. On the box, the listed uses are loud concerts, motor sports, shooting ranges, and activities involving power tools. I just wear them to sleep. I forgot to put them in one night, and that's when I realized why I wear them: it bothers me to hear myself breathe.

In these last moments, I can hear my breath ever so faintly. In and out. I cough, my body's attempt to rid itself of the gas. It's too late, though. No amount of coughing can save me now. I take one final breath, hold it, like I did when I was a kid, going down for a dive in the swimming pool on a summer day. Consciousness leaves me. There is nothing now but peace.

ad I known Japanese class would involve so many partner activities, I would not have signed up. I just want to learn the damn language, not interact with human beings. Apparently, Miyagi Sensei thinks one cannot be done without the other.

When Riko asks me to be her partner again, I can't think of a rational reason to say no. So I say, "Uh, sure," and we open our books to the section on greetings.

"'Good morning' is the easiest," Riko whispers. She's read ahead. She points to the word in the book. It's pronounced "Ohio." This *is* easy. When I go to Japan, I will say "Ohio" to every person I meet, no matter the time of day. Other things like "Thank you for the meal" are so complicated that I don't plan on ever thanking someone for a meal, which is a shame. I'm usually very polite.

Miyagi Sensei and the creepy teacher's assistant go through an exchange that she says we are supposed to be able to mimic by the end of class. What sounds like gibberish to me translates to "Good afternoon. How do you do? Nice to meet you." They bow back and forth to each other, like little windup toys on the fritz.

"I'm fairly certain that the only part of that routine I have any hope of mastering is the bowing."

"Don't be too cocky," Riko says. "I read that there are a couple dozen cases of people either being killed or receiving serious skull fractures while bowing to each other with the traditional Japanese greeting."

"This doesn't bode well for me."

"Don't worry," she says, "I'll help you."

Miyagi Sensei tells us to go wherever we want to practice and return to the classroom in fifteen minutes. Riko says, "Come on," and I follow her.

She stops at an empty student lounge at the end of the hall. It seems like it used to be a janitorial closet; it has that musky, industrial odor to it. There is a mismatched furniture set comprised of a couch that looks like it came from someone's lawn and a couple of upholstered chairs, one with a floral print and one plaid. There's also a coffee table with several stains and etchings from students past—"Beth hearts Jim," "Fuck your mom," that type of thing. Against the wall, by the door, is a vending machine stocked with drinks that I thought were no longer made anymore: Orange Crush, Pibb Xtra, Welch's soda, Hawaiian Punch in a can. Riko stuffs a crumbled-up bill into the machine and, after it spits it back out to her two times in a row, a Coke is finally dispensed.

"Third time's the charm," she says. She's an optimist, this young girl. She pops the tab on her soda and takes a sip, then sits on the couch, feet on the table, like this is her living room.

"Okay, so you start," she instructs.

"*Konnichiwa*," I say. I remember this much.

"It's seven o'clock at night."

"So?"

"*Konnichiwa* is 'good afternoon.'"

"Well, that's what the teacher said."

"Let's impress her with 'good evening.'"

"I don't have it in me to overachieve," I say. She looks astonished. "And I don't know how to say that anyway."

"Konbanwa," she says. "Kon-ban-wa."

"You don't need to say it that slow. I'm not an idiot."

She crosses her arms over her chest. "You were implying otherwise."

Within the next ten minutes, almost against my will, Riko has coached me to memorize the sounds that are required to come out of my mouth. That's all they are to me—sounds.

"So, aside from learning Japanese, what do you *do*?" she asks, looking at her watch, noticing the few minutes to kill. I don't want to do this, engage in small talk. I decide to keep it short, courteous, but nothing more.

"I work in advertising. As a writer." But I'm somehow incapable of letting this lie linger. "Well, that's what I used to do."

"Used to? And now?"

"I'm not really doing anything."

She looks me up and down, and I'm suddenly self-conscious. I suppose I've "let myself go" a bit. I haven't shaved this week, for one. At first, it was laziness, but now I'm rather committed to seeing myself with a beard before I die. I suppose I should add "Grow a beard" to my list of things to do before I go. Maybe I'll resemble Jesus when I inhale laundry detergent. Maybe I'll acquire postmortem followers.

"How long do you plan on doing nothing?" she asks.

"Until April or so."

"So you have a plan in mind."

I shrug and nod, and we sit in an awkward silence.

"And you? What do you do?" It's not that I care; I'm just passing time, trying not to be a disinterested jerk. When I first met Sara, during those meet-ups by the planter, she said I didn't ask enough questions.

"I work at the independent movie theater over by the college," she says. By "the college," she means the one that is an actual university, not this silly institution we are currently attending.

"Make popcorn, tear ticket stubs?" I say. "I did that when I was in college."

She looks insulted. "I'm a projectionist." This is the upper echelon of movie-theater jobs. Whenever there is a problem—the film stops, the sound goes out—the audience turns around and looks up for that person, as if looking for the Lord hHimself.

"And it's not some silly college job. I get paid pretty well, actually." I've managed to offend her. It only took a couple minutes.

"Right, sorry. I just thought you looked like a college student." Actually, she could pass for a high school student, easily.

"I'm twenty-two," she says, deadpan. I'd thought nineteen, tops. I'm sure an advertiser somewhere has used the line "Get the skin of a Japanese goddess," while promising a blend of natural ingredients straight from a spring at the base of Mount Fuji.

"That's a good age," I say, which is just about the stupidest thing you can say in response to someone's age.

"Is it?" She laughs, which puts me at ease.

The truth is that twenty-two is a horrible age. You've just finished college, brainwashed with the idea that you can make a seamless transition to a dream job and a spouse and a home (or at least a freaking condo) and a sense of completeness and meaning. At twenty-two, you're starting to see that you were tricked. You're wondering if it's possible to go back, to get a do-over. You want to prolong those days of smoking weed and losing track of time and working at jobs that don't require you to actually care about them. Like movie-theater jobs.

"And how old are you?" Riko asks.

"Thirty-four."

She doesn't comment on this, like it's of little importance to her. All she says is "We should get back."

I've given a number of presentations in my time. I've exuded confidence, arrogance even, while standing in front of tables lined with executives, sets of critical eyes fixed on me, to explain creative concepts and provide my "expert insights" (Creative Director Rick's embellishment) into the "messaging needed to meet tactical objectives." After years of this, I stopped getting nervous, stopped sweating, stopped loosening my tie, stopped worrying that I would suddenly forget English. I didn't need to picture them naked or taking a shit or whatever other strategies those speaking coaches tell you to employ; I was in my element. It's sad to think that spouting BS to rooms full of clients was "my element."

Standing up here with Riko, though, exchanging this Japanese dialogue, the fears from high school speech class return. Suddenly, I'm overly conscious of the fly on my pants, wondering if I got pen on my face while taking notes earlier, convinced that my voice sounds funny. We make it through, though; witnessing my level of relief after, you would think I'd just survived bungee jumping. I haven't done anything like this in a long time, something with the potential to make me look stupid, expose me as not having it all together. There's something exhilarating about that vulnerability. Riko gives me a little high five.

For the remainder of class, Miyagi Sensei starts reviewing the Japanese writing system. Actually, it is incorrect to say "system"; there are three of them. Three systems. Most of the students seem to interpret this to mean "The Japanese are nuts." I interpret this to mean "Americans are morons." We have a single twenty-six-letter alphabet and people still can't spell.

In Japanese, there are two phonetic-type systems, the hiragana and the katakana, with forty-six symbols each. The hiragana is for any words native to Japan. The katakana was developed for the sole purpose of accommodating words from other countries, like "burrito" or "ménage à trois." Then there's the third system, the kanji. There are more than five thousand symbols in the kanji. When Miyagi Sensei sees our jaws drop at this fact, she affirms that kanji is "fun" but that we won't be doing it this semester.

"We will, however, learn the first twenty hiragana symbols tonight," she says.

"Tonight?" I find myself saying out loud. A few of the students giggle.

"Yes, Daichi," she says, taking to my lame Japanese name like a slab of raw fish to a sushi platter.

To the rhythm of Miyagi Sensei's clapping, we go through the sounds of the twenty hiragana symbols: *a, i, u, e, o, ka, ki, ku, ke, ko, sa, shi, su, se, so, ta, chi, tsu, te, to.* There's something very Third Reich about her pacing. I feel like I cannot pause, cannot miss a beat. It's like my life depends on it.

After we have the sounds forced into our skulls, we practice drawing the symbols. Apparently, to write Japanese, you also have to be somewhat of an artist. There is a specific method to the madness, specific strokes you are supposed to make, in a specific order. For most of the sounds, there is no easy way to remember the accompanying symbol. This is "a," for example:

And this is "sa":

In the columns of my notebook, I write ideas for weird mnemonic devices. For example, "shi" (pronounced "she") kind of looks like a chick's ponytail:

And then there's this one:

"I have an easy way to remember that one," Riko says, peeking over at my scribbling. She's already done with her practice, waiting for Miyagi Sensei to dismiss us.

"What's that?"

"Well, it looks like a wave, doesn't it?" she says, seeming very proud of herself.

"I suppose so."

"It's *tsu*, as in *tsunami*."

And, in the column of my book, I write, "Like the dream," the dream I haven't had since making my laundry-detergent decision. If that's not affirmation, validation of a good choice, I don't know what is.

It's raining when we leave class, one of those Los Angeles nights when the air smells like a wet towel—moist, mildewed. I don't have an umbrella, so I'm walking fast to the parking lot. I hear footsteps picking up pace behind me.

"Hey!"

I turn around. It's Riko, running after me, an oversized hoodie covering her head. My best guess is that she wants to suggest a study session.

"I forgot to ask you," she says, now walking at a fast clip to stay parallel with me. She reaches into her purse and retrieves a sort-of-crumpled flyer, the kind people pass out at the mall when they want you to buy something stupid, the kind they jam under your windshield wiper because you refuse to take it from their hands.

"My friend's band is playing at this bar Friday night," she says, waving the flyer at me until I take it from her. "I told him I'd invite people. It'd be awesome if you could come."

I'm reminded of what it's like to be twenty-two, to have friends, to have friends in bands, to have friends in bands that play at bars, to use the word "awesome."

"I don't know...," I say, continuing walking.

"Oh, come on. They're just starting out. Maybe you could give them a few advertising pointers. Some kind of grassroots campaign, you know?"

Ah, yes, the twenties, when possibilities seem endless.

"I don't know."

"Well, you don't have plans on Friday night," she says.

"How do you know?"

"Because you would have already said so. It would have been the easiest excuse in the book."

I take the flyer from her. It's amateur. They're called Wild Horses, a Rolling Stones cover band. Their tagline says "We'll take you for a ride," which sounds like it's better suited for the escort section of the classifieds.

"Riko, I appreciate the invitation, but this really isn't my scene."

"Come on, it's just one night. I'll let you cheat off me on the next quiz."

"You are persistent."

"You're, like, one of the only people I know in Los Angeles. Just come so I don't look like an idiot going alone."

"You are almost as good with the guilt trips as my mother."

"Is it working?"

We're at my car. I unlock it and open the driver's-side door. She's just standing there, raindrops staining her sweatshirt, looking sad, almost destitute.

"Look, if I go—and that's a solid *if*—I won't stay long."

She smiles, an overly grateful and toothy grin, like a home-less person who has just panhandled her way to another fix.

In Japan, there's this cultural phenomenon of men in their twenties and thirties becoming recluses and spending years in their bedrooms, unwilling to face the world. They're referred to as hikikomori, literally meaning "pulling away, being confined." They choose isolation, an existence of nonexistence, instead of striving to meet the education and career standards and expectations of Japanese culture. Psychologists there have found no way to classify this. They shove it in the category of "adjustment disorder," but they admit this is inaccurate. Hikikomori is new and peculiar. They say it's specific to Japan. I disagree. There are young adults in America like this, those who run up against the realities of the world and decide they'd rather play video games. I used to join society in lumping people like this, along with people who commit suicide, into a category labeled "weirdos." Freaks. Failures. Losers. Now I get it. It would have been better, maybe, if I'd decided at a younger age to disregard the notion of "making it" in the world and dedicated myself to mastering Grand Theft Auto, stealing computer-generated vehicles, running over computer-generated old ladies, carousing with computer-generated hookers, shooting up computer-generated enemies. Perhaps this is a better way to escape than death by laundry detergent.

I haven't been to this part of Los Angeles in months, the trendy, young part of Los Angeles. Los Feliz, to be specific. This is where all the twenty-somethings come with the hoops through their nostrils and tattooed sleeves up their arms and jeans so tight that the metal-studded belts are obviously just for show. I thought I would feel safe in the bookstore, but this is not your usual chain bookstore with old ladies browsing the gardening section. This bookstore is an "independent" bookstore and, with this designation, it has attracted the very people I hoped to avoid, the people who cling close to dreams of being poets and novelists, the people who consider themselves legitimate writers. They have not yet realized that they will need legitimate jobs, that the working world will strip them of their fanciful dreams until, one day, they wake up at the age of eighty and lament their failure to tell "their story," as if it's unique. They'll die maintaining that the next Great American Novel is hiding within their brains. They just don't know this yet. And even though I do, even though I'm a step ahead in this respect, they still make me feel old and boring and on the outskirts of some circle of enlightenment. Their very demeanor implies I'll be doing them a favor by inhaling laundry-detergent fumes.

I buy a newspaper and take it next door to an "independent" coffee shop. Riko instructed me to meet her here, in this strange place where everyone has a Mac laptop and glasses that I can't believe they need for eyesight purposes. They all seem at work on something, likely a screenplay, even though it's eight thirty on a Friday night. They must not have day jobs that require them to seek reprieve at home or a bar.

In the half hour I have before Riko's friend's band's show starts, I scan my horoscope (which says I should try adding plants and flowers to my inside space, confirming my suspicion that horoscopes are not for straight men), check out the weather (little sunshines every day), and then immerse myself in an article about how there aren't enough dead people for medical students to cut open in anatomy class. This strikes me as a shame.

According to a world-renowned doctor in the article, "If we want to advance medicine and find cures for cancer, we can't do that using plastic or synthetic materials: we need human bodies." I have one of those. I could do something with my suicide. I mean, aside from killing myself. Perhaps I would have a little afterlife pride while thinking "What did I do with my life? Not much. But with my death, I cured cancer!" There is a cost-savings benefit to this way too. When the body goes to a university or tissue society (that's what they call them, which makes me picture a bunch of organs sipping wine, eating cheese and crackers, and discussing literature), that institution is responsible for cremating the body and getting the ashes back to the family. This would be so much easier on my parents. Of course, the research I've done indicates that I do not get to choose how my body is used. My head could get lopped off and put in a turkey pan so future plastic surgeons can use it to practice eye-hood surgery, for example. I'm not sure my mother will be comfortable with this.

"You actually showed."

I look up to see Riko standing over me, her eyes heavily shadowed with blue, her lips a sparkly purple. She's wearing what I think are called "booties," boots truncated just above the ankle. There are safety pins holding together the straps of her black shirt. It amuses me that people pay money for clothes that make them look like they don't have a dollar to their name.

She sits in the chair across from me. It's a tall, round table so small that there is barely room for my newspaper, let alone our elbows. I put my hands in my lap, but that feels awkward, like I'm jacking off under the table or something. I drop them down to my sides.

"I didn't know anyone read the newspaper anymore. You are hip." She exaggerates the "p" on "hip," making fun of me.

"Just passing time. I got here early."

"Well, me too. I'll be right back," she says, jumping up. "I'm going to get a hot chocolate."

She skips into line with an energy I don't understand and returns a few minutes later, blowing a cooling breath on her drink. She sits across from me again, eyeing my newspaper, still lying on the table folded open to the body-donation article.

"Cadaver shortage, huh?" she says, referencing the headline. "Are you considering doing something about this?"

I try to look humored, instead of caught. "Seems like a valid way to go out."

She waves her hand over her hot chocolate, shooing away the steam. "That's a weird thing to say."

"They cremate you when they're done with you."

"That's a weirder thing to say."

"Would you want to be cremated or buried?"

She looks at me as if she's just now realized I'm crazy, though I've tried to suggest this all along.

"Um, neither, thanks. I'm only twenty-two."

"We're not talking next week here. I mean when you die, when you're old," I say, because people are only comfortable discussing death in the context of "old," if they are comfortable at all.

"I don't know. Cremated, I guess. Seems like less of a hassle."

"Agreed," I say. "Did you know that in Japan, after they cremate you, the loved ones pick through the ashes with chopsticks to put the bone fragments in the urn. They start with the feet and end with the head, so you're not upside down in the urn."

"Why the hell would you know this?" she asks. "Never mind. I'm not sure I want to know." She hops out of her chair and waves for me to follow her.

The venue is a hole-in-the-wall place that you'd think is a whorehouse from the outside. The entrance is one of those big, metal doors that always leads to a dead body on TV crime shows. We walk through a long hallway, lined with flyers promoting bands, selling IKEA furniture, requesting roommates, asking if I've seen a missing schnauzer named Daisy. It smells like cigarette smoke, even though smoking isn't allowed. The floor is concrete, as if the owner figured it wouldn't be worth it to put down anything nice since it would just get trashed. And it *is* trashed. It's sticky and wet in places, making me wonder how some of these girls are wearing sandals. It's packed with people, which wouldn't be hard to accomplish given it's the size of a typical master bedroom. There's a blue lighting effect on the stage, highlighting the particles in the air—the supposedly forbidden smoke, the dust, the dirt.

About two minutes into the Wild Horses set, I regret coming. When Riko said they were a Rolling Stones cover band, I imagined fun renditions of "Satisfaction" and "Brown Sugar," with people my parents' age in the audience recapturing their youth. Maybe there would be some pot smoking in the name of nostalgia. This is not the scene at all. Aside from the fact that all the band members bear some resemblance to Keith Richards, you would not know that this band has anything to do with the Rolling Stones. Perhaps if I could decipher the lyrics, I would be able to spot the songs to which they are paying homage (if "homage" is even what they're paying; I don't think Mick Jagger would agree). But they are just mumbling and moaning, slowly, like they are all doped up on heroin. I don't even know what to call it, but Riko leans over and whispers, "Sorry, I didn't know they'd be so emo."

So I guess it's "emo."

Whatever it is, it's testing my patience with my suicide plan. Given a razor, or just a toothpick, I'd slit my wrists right here and now.

I take my last swig of beer from my plastic cup. No bottles allowed (perhaps because the sharp edges could be used for the aforementioned wrist-slitting). I don't know what kind of "grassroots" campaign I could possibly concoct for these guys. I might first suggest a name change more in line with their musical offerings: Rolling Stoned?

"Which one is your friend?" I ask, practically yelling over the din. I remember these nights. I already know that I will go home with my ears ringing and my throat dry.

Riko points at the guy with the bass guitar. She leans in close to say something, so close that her nose collides with my cheek. "I guess he's not really *my* friend," she says. "He's my ex's friend."

It makes sense to me now. She was hoping to see him, the ex, here. And she wanted him to see her with me. I would be that other guy, that unstylish douche with his hands in his jeans pockets.

"Do you want to get out of here?" she asks.

There's this surreal feeling when you leave a music club, like the rest of the world has been on pause while you've been in there. The air seems crisper, clearer than you remember it. The sounds of traffic on the street are distant, foreign.

"That was bad," she says. "I feel terrible for making you come."

"You didn't make me do anything."

"Pancakes?" She nods in the direction of a diner with a neon sign flashing "OPEN 24 HOURS."

"I don't know...."

"Oh, come on. They have this thing called the Hunka Hunka Burnin' Love Pancake with peanut butter and chocolate chips and caramel. I'm hungry. Please?"

And, in spite of my hesitations, I find myself sitting in a little booth with red vinyl seats, watching Riko and her Hunka Hunka Burnin' Love. Nearly all of the other tables are full, mostly with college-aged kids and a sprinkling of guys my age who are dressed like they want to be college-aged. There are a couple loners who look to be transients, but then again it's really hard to tell with fashion these days. There's an energy to the restaurant, that Friday night, going-out-to-party energy. Yes, this is the beginning of the night for most. A stop for pancakes is an opportunity to fuel up for the dancing and drinking to come.

"I can't believe you just got plain pancakes. You're no fun," Riko says, soaking up some of the caramel sauce with the piece of pancake on the end of her fork.

"I don't think I ever said I was fun." I say it seriously, but she seems to think I'm joking, perpetuating this false belief that I'm funny.

"I really shouldn't have dragged you along tonight. I thought they would be good. He's always saying they're amazing," she says. "The three of us—me, the ex, and the bass guy, Steve—all used to live in this place together, so we were pretty tight. Now, I just live with Steve. He's nice enough to let me crash until I figure out a new situation. It's odd, I know."

"Were you hoping to see him there tonight?"

"Who? Steve?"

"No, your ex."

"Oh god, no," she says, shaking her head so emphatically that it's clear she's overcompensating for a lie. She busies herself with the pancake-eating.

"When did you two break up?" I ask, figuring I may as well make conversation if I have to sit here eating breakfast food at ten o'clock at night.

"Five and a half months ago," she says, so precisely. She offers the information eagerly, like she wants to talk about it. Why she's choosing me as her confidant is a mystery. Perhaps she's misreading my apathy as nonjudgmental understanding.

"We moved here from San Francisco last year. I don't really know anyone here besides him, ya know?"

This explains why she's latched onto me like a hungry leech.

"I guess I'm going through a—what do they call it?—quarterlife crisis?" She forces a laugh, trying to make it seem like it's silly even though it's clearly not.

"You're from San Francisco, then?" I ask, begging to change the subject. I didn't sign up to be Riko's therapist.

"Yep, born and raised."

"My parents live up that way," I say. "I'm driving up to visit sometime soon."

"Maybe I could tag along," she says, again with that uncomfortable laugh.

I decide the previous subject was better.

"So, you and the ex—how long were you together?"

"Since high school." She's more wistful than she should be for twenty-two, like being with this guy aged her in some way.

"High school. Wow. That's a long time."

It occurs to me that Riko has probably slept with only one person in her life.

"It's dangerous to be with the same person during those years," she says, with a wisdom that irks me. "You get so used to the way things are that you forget you'd be better off with someone else or, in my case, alone."

"You think you're better off, then?"

"I *know* I am," she says, with an infusion of confidence. We all like to think we're empowered after goodbyes with the people we love. We like to think that the experience makes us stronger, wiser. We like to think there are better opportunities ahead. There *must* be, we say. We like to think it all happens for a reason. I've come to believe that *nothing* really happens for a reason, though we are alarmingly good at creating reasons for the things that happen. When I die, someone will say "Well, God needed another angel." If death is just related to God's angel needs, then I'd say God is a greedy bastard.

"Don't get me wrong," she continues. "I still care for Ben, I do." Ben is his name. Ben is a very nice-guy name.

"No regrets, though?"

"No. We grew apart," she says. Because that's what we say in order to put a nice bow on our breakup package.

"That happens." I let her have her flimsy rationalizations. They comfort her at night, I'm sure, like a security blanket comforts a child.

"What about you? Do you have a girlfriend?"

"Nope."

Do I seem like a guy with a girlfriend? If I had a girlfriend, wouldn't I be with her tonight instead of with some quarter-life-crisis-having girl from my Japanese language class?

"Who was your last relationship?" she asks, very talk-show style. She thinks her questioning is a fair trade—her listening ear for mine. She's not picking up on my hints that I'm not interested in this reciprocation.

"This girl I worked with," I say. Sara would hate me for referring to her so flippantly. She would especially hate being called "this girl."

"Sara," I clarify. I have to clear my throat when I say her name. It catches in there, almost.

"When did you guys split?"

"I don't know; a while ago."

"Like more than a year?"

"No, less than a year."

"You're still hung up on her, I can tell."

"That isn't news to me."

"You should get her back." Her eyes are wide, excited with all the romantic possibilities. Riko is the type of girl to envision boom boxes below bedroom windows, red rose petals strewn across king-sized beds.

I just shake my head.

"You can't just give up."

This is the one thing I'm convinced I can do. "There's no getting her back. Trust me."

She rolls her eyes. "You men are so dramatic."

I stab my pancakes and shove three bites' worth into my mouth, figuring the sooner I finish, the sooner we can get out of this place.

"What's Sara like?"

"I don't know," I say, hoping this works for me as a conversation-ender the same way it works for guilty parties on the witness stand in criminal trials.

"I'm sure you know. You think about her 24/7. It's obvious."

"Jesus, Riko, what do you want from me?"

She leans back in her seat, like dangerous flames have just erupted from my mouth and singed the ends of her beloved black hair.

"I'm just making conversation, dude."

She says it in that way that implies I'm out of line, maybe even a little insane, like she's the calm cop and I'm the drugged-up junkie waving a gun in the air. Perhaps now Riko sees me for who I am. Perhaps she will tire of my rudeness, stand from her seat, throw her napkin on the table, and stomp out of the restaurant, leaving me with an apology to craft (and the bill). You would think this would relieve me—to be left alone, albeit at this crappy diner—but it unnerves me a bit. And the fact that it unnerves me unnerves me even more.

"She's a graphic designer," I offer, regretting immediately that I've chosen her occupation as the first way to describe her. *Graphic Designer, R&R, Sara Mackenzie.* "Blond hair. Blueish eyes. Very sweet. I wanted to marry her."

"Ben's a graphic designer too. Those artist types are so tricky."

"I guess."

"You miss her so much."

"And the sky is blue. Let's stop stating the obvious."

There I go again, being an asshole.

"You know, you're just thinking of her as perfect. It's selective memory."

"It's not selective. There's nothing about her I didn't love."

She looks at me, skeptically. "It's just that phrase—you don't know what you have till it's gone."

"Well, I suppose that's true."

The waiter comes to the table, not soon enough, to drop off the check. I reach for my wallet and take out a ten-dollar bill for my half. I'm not paying for hers. The last thing I need is for this girl to think we're on some kind of date. She doesn't hesitate to take out her own wallet. It's "retro," I guess, with a Velcro strip to stay closed. When she rips it open, I flash back to being twelve, to beginning ownership of cash, to flaunting Swatch watches as if they were Rolexes.

"I should be going," I say, just in case she has another destination in mind.

"Past your bedtime?" she jokes, but this is, in fact, the case.

"It was past my bedtime when I met you at that coffee shop."

She slides out of the booth and motions for me to stand.

"Come on, old man," she says, offering me her hand. I don't take it. Instead, I use the table to push myself up.

❊

We walk down the sidewalk together, in silence. I have to slow down to keep even pace with her. Unlike me, she is in no rush. She is the type to stroll through life. She puts her weight on her heels, like she has trust in the world that she just shouldn't have, like she thinks it will catch her if she falls backward.

"This is me," she says, stopping in front of a banana-yellow Mercedes-Benz, one of those cars from the late seventies that takes diesel and chugs along with the same sounds as the cars in Autopia at Disneyland. It has an old blue-and-yellow California license plate.

"Thanks, again, for coming out," she says. "I appreciate it."

"No problem," I lie.

She lowers herself into the bucket seat and says, "*Oyasuminasai*, Daichi."

I have no idea what this means, and she reads the clueless-ness on my face. She smiles, mischievously, like she knows more than me—about Japanese, life, whatever—then says, "That means good night."

In Japan, saying "I love you" is very unusual. There is not even a direct translation in Japanese for this overused English phrase. The Japanese think just sitting together is enough, especially in a love relationship. They talk with silence, expressing affection wordlessly.

They even have a word for this—haragei, literally meaning "belly talk." For the Japanese, intuition is the driver of interaction. They listen "when their belly talks." The slightest nuances in facial expression or tone tell them everything necessary. Westerners, particularly marriage therapists and followers of Dr. Phil, could not even fathom the intricacies of this communication. They would consider the Japanese repressed, emotionally stunted. They would chuckle while predicting the very collapse of Japanese society. And, yet, the divorce rate in Japan is half that of America's. Not that a statistic means much, but it has to mean something.

九

When people talk about love, they like to think that theirs is magically different. They like to think that their connection, their private gestures, their shared hobbies, their secret confessions are somehow unique. Sara and I had none of these romantic notions. It's not that we didn't believe in love. We did. We were in it. However, I wouldn't modify "love" with silly adjectives like "deep" or "profound." We didn't exchange cards and chocolates on Valentine's Day. We didn't insult each other by conversing in baby voices. Our love came with little pressure to be something. It just *was*.

Before Sara, I'd told two women that I loved them (and, no, I'm not a freak who counts his mother as one of these women). With those two women, it was made into an event, a marker in the relationship, as in "From this point forward, these two people mean something to each other." It wasn't like that with Sara. She meant something to me the first time I met her at that planter. And I can't even remember when I first told her I loved her.

There was lots of talking in that first year or so we were together, that manic getting-to-know-you phase full of proclamations, spoken in generalities to protect our dreams: "When I get married, I hope the man, whoever he is, does not mind that I want to keep my name," she said, for example. "I mean, I'll slap his last name after mine for social purposes, to let people know I'm married or whatever, but I don't want to actually change it."

(I liked the sound of Sara Krause, but I appreciated her resolve more.)

There were conversations like this one:

"I think monogamy is possible," she said, "but not at all natural."

"You're in the 'spread the seed' camp?"

"I don't know. I don't think it's just biology that makes monogamy unnatural. It's more than that."

It was obvious she'd given this some thought.

"People get drunk on love. And when they sober up, they want the buzz again. When it comes down to it, we'll always want something new. We'll always want that thrill of the beginning. We're infatuation junkies, aren't we?"

I didn't know the "right" answer to this question, so I gave the honest one. "Maybe. But I think we're also infatuated with the idea of finding someone who keeps us interested."

"That's probably true."

"Just please don't tell me you believe in 'open relationships.'"

"Oh god, no," she said. "But I understand cheating. I don't think it's right. But I get it."

Her saying that, admitting to a universal truth we all like to deny, let me know I could trust her.

"It's like that line—satisfaction is the death of desire," she said. "Once you have what you want, you don't want it anymore. I guess that's what scares me about marriage."

"But you want to get married?"

"Sure," she said, as if it made no sense to avoid something just because of fear. Then she went and added, with the slightest smile, "When the right guy comes along."

And this one:

"I don't think I want to have kids," she said.

This surprised me. If anyone would be a good mother, it would be Sara.

"I'm too sensitive for it," she explained. "If my kid was sick or bullied or heartbroken, I don't know if I could *handle* it."

Now, in retrospect, I wish I'd said "That just means you know how to love." Instead, I said "Maybe you'll change your mind."

She rolled her eyes at me. "Everyone tells me that. And then they say 'But don't you want to see what they'd look like?' and 'But who will take care of you when you get old?' As if procreation is just a vanity project resulting in future caretakers. Isn't that selfish?"

I shrugged. "I guess so."

"Well, my husband, whoever he is, will have to be okay with how I feel," she said, again careful not to stray from the generality, not to imply that I might be the one to have to accept this childless life. If I'm honest, I was disappointed, a little. I'd never even thought about kids before. I mean, I'd thought about them in that I was aware of their general existence and the fact that most people had them eventually. But I'd never thought of my own. Sara's refusal to have them made me wonder what they'd be like.

Those were the big ones, the potential minefields—marriage, family. But there was more to the manual of living happily with

Sara Mackenzie, like she wanted a dog (and a yard for the dog), and she wanted never to worry about money, and she wanted to travel and put pushpins on a map—red ones to remember the places she'd already been, blue ones to mark the places she wanted to go. She wanted to put a blue one on Japan.

"Why Japan?" I asked.

"I want to see the cherry blossoms," she said, as if this was a common reason for people to trek to the other side of the world.

"What about you?" she asked. "What do you want?"

The honest reply would have been "I just want to be with you," but it was too soon for such sentiment, so I just said I would have to think about it.

There are all those little things you think you can't tell anyone, but you hope, one day, to find someone who will hear them. And each time you fall in love, you are convinced that that person is that someone, and you divulge just a little bit more than you had the last time. Sara and I had a frenzy of confessions, testing each other's limits, looking for that breaking point when the other says "You horrify me." There was nothing she could say that horrified me, though, and it seemed to be a rare vice versa situation.

She told me she hadn't lost her virginity until she was twenty-one, somehow sidestepping the drunken hookups of college. But, she added, she'd probably kissed at least fifty guys. "I'm a kissing slut," she said.

I told her how I had a strange, one-time-only (fingers crossed) bout with mouth herpes. It happened when I was nineteen, while on a summer trip through Europe, one of those trips every young guy takes, complete with a backpack and two college buddies. Her response was just "How cliché."

She told me that whenever she drove on highway overpasses, she thought of how just one little jerk of the steering wheel could send her careening to her death. She told me how she pictured this and how it made her feel more alive.

I told her I didn't always shower every day.

She told me she didn't either.

I told her I had this fear of developing sudden Tourette's in a meeting and shouting "Fuck you" out of nowhere.

She told me she'd done mushrooms once, and ended up in a bathtub crying for what seemed like an entire day. She also told me she'd tried cocaine, and all it did was compel her to vacuum her apartment obsessively.

I told her I'd never even seen cocaine before—in person, I mean. She quipped, "Not even on your cliché Europe trip?"

She told me that even though she cared about the environment, she wouldn't consider buying a Prius because they were ugly.

I told her "If fate had arranged for us to meet at a stoplight and you were driving a Prius, we probably wouldn't be here right now."

She told me she'd snooped through my nightstand drawers once and had discovered the little scraps of paper I stored in there with random thoughts that I hoped to turn into a novel one day.

I told her I didn't think I'd ever really write a novel.

She told me "I think you will."

There wasn't much to say after all this conversation. The "thrill of the beginning" passed, and we realized it gives way to the comfort of the known, if you let it. From that time forward, we expressed our love in silence, mostly. With belly talk, as they say.

I don't remember when we bought the house, exactly. There are all these events that exist in a jumbled-up mass. I know when we moved in; it was summer, a typical Los Angeles weekend day when the smog and heat collect in the valleys and driving through Malibu Canyon to the beach takes at least two hours. It wasn't the best day to be lifting furniture out of a U-Haul truck, a truck which seemed to have a bad wheel, like those grocery carts that go all cockeyed. But we were committed to a goal of getting the truck back to the lot before closing and then enjoying White Russians with extra ice while watching *The Big Lebowski*.

I'd lived with someone once before. I'd been in my early twenties and it was for all the wrong reasons, as move-ins at that age usually are. We talked like we were mature enough for such a thing, used phrases like "consolidating expenses" to rationalize our idiocy. Her name was Angie. Within a month, any affection I'd had for her was reduced to petty arguments about whose turn it was to wash off that pink gunk in the shower. I couldn't stand the way she got coffee grounds all over the counter and reused dental floss and left her bras strewn across the floor and recited hip-hop lyrics like she thought they applied to her: "*We be big pimpin', spendin' cheese.*" When we broke up and went our separate ways, as they say, I blamed these things. Now, though, I understand it was just that I didn't really love her. I was probably too young to really love anyone.

Sara had never lived with anyone before, not even a roommate. She liked her space, she said. She didn't want to have to worry about what someone else felt like for dinner, or take into consideration someone else's TV viewing habits, or adjust her schedule to accommodate someone else's waking and sleeping hours. Some nights, she wanted to eat ramen in her pajamas and watch a *CSI* marathon until two in the morning, for instance. I told her she never had to worry about what I wanted for dinner. I'd been subsisting on Hot Pockets for a number of years. I said I would get earplugs if she decided to stay up late, singing at the top of her lungs or whatever else, and we would have two televisions, so neither of us would have to give up our guilty pleasures.

The combining of our possessions was a mess. Before meeting each other, we had each purchased complete furniture sets— the expensive kind, the kind you get when you realize you're a grown-up and it's no longer appropriate to eat at a hand-me-down kitchen table that has crayon etchings on it from when you were five. When we decided to move in together, we took inventory of everything and were forced to confront a nagging question: *What the hell are we going to do with all this crap?* We had two sets of eating utensils, two washing machines, two leather couches, two king beds—all this evidence of our respective, stubborn commitments to a fully formed single life.

"Maybe we should get a storage unit—for the overflow," she said.

"Why don't we just sell it?"

She started biting her nails. I would come to know that Sara's state of mind was evident in the state of her nails. All this talk of moving in together had them splintered and bleeding.

"I don't want to sell it. I want to keep it."

"Why?"

She shrugged one shoulder, evasively.

"In case we split up?" I ventured.

She looked at me, ashamed. "I'm sorry. I know that sounds awful."

I understood, though, or I tried to. When you're with someone at the age of twenty, it's easy to give yourself away, because you don't have much of a self to give. At our age, there was more to lose.

"It's not awful. I'd rather you freak out now than be a runaway bride."

That was the first hint I'd dropped that I intended to marry her.

So we got a storage unit, ten feet by ten feet, and filled it with evidence of our former selves. Canvases of her old artwork leaned up against the craps table I hadn't used in years. The walls were lined with boxes of rejects, items that didn't make the cut for inclusion in the home we called "ours"—my coffee machine (hers was better), her framed Sarah McLachlan album covers (I can't stand Sarah McLachlan), my collection of green Jägermeister bottles (no explanation necessary), her paisley sheet set (we compromised with a gender-neutral teal). With the assortment of appliances, an old mattress, a dresser, and various electronics, someone could have taken up residence there. We could have charged rent. I suppose if anything represents the complexity of merging lives with another human being, it was that storage unit.

It was something of a revelation to me when we didn't argue about the pink gunk in the shower. It turns out we took mutual responsibility for our filth. We took turns scrubbing the shower: "If I get cancer from these Comet fumes, you better too," she said. It was the first time in my life I'd understood what my parents had—a partnership, an agreement to take on life with all its annoyances and chores and requirements, together. She made dinner; I did the dishes and took out the trash. She dusted and polished; I vacuumed (she had no patience for the multiple attachments). There was a harmony to it, an ease. We didn't so much argue as we expressed complete amusement at the other person's way of seeing something. Like this:

"Must you leave these half-empty soda cans everywhere?" I'd said, throwing away yet another one of her Mountain Dews, consumed when she wanted to stay up late drawing.

"I'd say they're half full."

"Of course you would."

I'd decided I wanted to marry her soon after I met her, but it was more than a year after we'd been in the house together before I was ready to actually undertake the logistics of it.

She always wore this turquoise stone on the ring finger of her right hand. I took it from her jewelry box one day and crammed it in my wallet, into that little pocket with my driver's license. She was notorious for fiddling with her rings—for taking them on and off, for losing them—so she didn't think much of it when it disappeared. I told myself that when the time was right, I would take it to a jeweler. I would tell him to use that turquoise ring for size. I would tell him I wanted a square-cut diamond, something antique-y, because Sara had mentioned liking a ring like that when she dragged me to the flea market one weekend. I knew she wouldn't want me to spend thousands of dollars on it. That, more than anything, would persuade her to reject my proposal. She wasn't one for pomp and circumstance. She wouldn't want a fancy wedding, complete with a hundred drunk people doing the chicken dance in our honor. She would want something quiet, just between us. She would want the proposal to be the same way.

And that's when I got the idea to take her to Japan. To see the cherry blossoms.

Sakura is the Japanese name for cherry trees and their blossoms. In Japan, as early as a.d. 794, cherry trees were planted and cultivated for their beauty, to adorn the grounds of the nobility of Kyoto.

Every year, the Japanese Meteorological Agency and the public track the sakura zensen, or the "cherry blossom front," as it moves northward. There are nightly forecasts following the weather segments of news programs. The blossoming begins in Okinawa in January and typically reaches Kyoto and Tokyo at the end of March or the beginning of April. The Japanese pay close attention to these forecasts, knowing how short the blossoming time is, and turn out in large numbers at parks, shrines, and temples with family and friends to hold flower-viewing festivals. These hanami festivals celebrate the beauty of the sakura and what they represent—the transient nature of life.

By the end of the first month of Japanese class, we are able to perform skits utilizing our limited conversational skills:

- How are you?
- My name is _____.
- Nice to meet you.
- Good morning.
- Good afternoon.
- Good evening.
- Good night.
- Yes.
- No.
- What time is it?
- Are you a student?
- What is your job?
- What is your hobby?

- Where are you from?
- I am American.
- How much does that cost?
- This is _____. (We can fill this blank with select items, including a hat, book, notebook, bag, pen, pencil, tape, fish, pork cutlet, meat, menu, vegetable, shoes, wallet, dictionary, bicycle, newspaper, tape, watch, and jeans. This is how you say "jeans" in Japanese: *jinzu*).

We can also count to 99,999, but none of us seem to be able to incorporate this into a dialogue.

Riko and I have become skit partners. We do not even ask each other "Do you want to be partners?" anymore. We are just partners. It's understood. We have played all the usual roles in our required skits—shopkeeper and customer, teacher and student, student and student. As you may have guessed, our skits are incredibly dull.

Miyagi Sensei has started giving us fifteen-minute breaks after the first hour of class—probably because we are putting her to sleep with the same overly enthusiastic introductions, greetings, and repetitive discussions of hobbies. It comforts me to know that Miyagi Sensei is human, that she feels something as mundane as boredom. In her compact, efficient body, with that tight-lipped almost-frown on her face, I'd been thinking of her as an emotionless robot, manufactured in her homeland and sent to the United States to collect data.

"The usual spot?" Riko says as we leave class for our break.

The empty student lounge with the weird furniture and the vending machine has become our "usual spot," where Riko always gets a Coke. So close to my departure date, it was not in my plans to have a "usual spot" with someone, but Riko is just

Riko. She might try, unknowingly, to dissuade me from my exit plan, to convince me that life is worth living, but I can't take her seriously. She's just a kid.

"What'd you get on the numbers quiz?" she asks, taking her seat on the couch.

This is exactly what I mean—she's just a kid, concerned with such things as grades in a community college Japanese class.

"I got a B."

"Jonathan! A B? I thought you studied!"

"I did study."

The fact of the matter is that I don't really do much studying. I'm not here to get impressive grades. I'm here to learn some Japanese for my trip. In my downtime, I'd rather continue my journey through season four of *Seinfeld*, not make flash cards. Her disappointment is evident, though. I feel the need to explain.

"I confused number seven and number four."

She just shakes her head at me. "Seven is *nana*, or *shichi*, if you're talking about time," she says in a rehearsed way. This is true—the Japanese have different words for numbers depending on the context in which you use them.

"And four is either *yon* or *shi*," I say. "I know. I just screwed up."

She continues shaking her head.

"Did you know *shi* also means death?" I ask her. "In hospitals, no rooms are numbered '4' so the patients don't get freaked out."

"You are so bizarre," she says. "Why do you know this stuff?"

"Why does anyone know anything?"

"Never mind. Let's just settle on you being bizarre."

She pulls her knees up to her chest. "So, what are you up to this weekend?"

She has taken to asking me this every week since our little concert outing, and I always give a generic answer that makes it sound like I am occupied: "I have some odds and ends" or "Chores, errands—the usual." It's just that I'm not much interested in seeing terrible cover bands and talking about breakups over dessert-style pancakes. This weekend, though, I don't have to dodge potential invitations because I won't even be in town; I'm driving to the Bay Area for the parent visit.

"I'm headed up to see my mom and dad."

"Oh, right, you said you were planning that." She taps the lid of her soda can, bending the metal tab back and forth the way you did in elementary school while reciting the alphabet, hoping it would break on the first letter of the name of your crush.

"I'm leaving Friday, back on Sunday, so it'll be a quick trip."

"What's the occasion?"

It's to say goodbye, essentially. But this wouldn't make sense to Riko, so I say the opposite, the socially appropriate: "Just to say hi."

"Would it be totally weird if I wanted to come along?"

"Yes." The word just comes out of my mouth, like a hammer-to-the-knee reflex. Is she actually serious?

"I would be a quiet passenger. I'll bring headphones and just listen to audio books. And I'll help pay for gas."

"I don't know, Riko," I say, hoping she'll take that as a no, not force me to be an asshole.

The Japanese have a phrase created exactly for these situations—*chotto*. It's equivalent to "No, but I don't want to be rude" or "Not so much, I'm very sorry." It's a mild rejection of whatever has been suggested. In our language book, when Takeshi tries to ask Mearii on a date, she says "*Chotto*," as opposed to "Yeah right, suck it," for example. The Japanese are very passive.

"I've been wanting to go home for a while now. I have some business to attend to," she says, too formally, like she's going up there to execute a will or testify in a trial. I mean, what business could a twenty-two-year-old possibly have to attend to?

"Please?" she says. "I don't know if my car would make it all that way. I guess I could figure out how to take a train."

She's laying it on thick. We both know taking any kind of public transportation in California comes with a fair chance of ending up either totally lost or mugged. Sara and I took the Metro once "for fun" to see the Los Angeles Philharmonic at the Disney Concert Hall. I was pretty much shocked when neither of us got stabbed.

"Let me think about it, okay?" I say.

"Think about it? But you're leaving *tomorrow*."

She's pushy, this one.

"I'll let you know by the end of class."

For the second half of class, Miyagi Sensei has set up a slide carousel and projector—technologies that I would expect a Japanese person to have long ago retired in favor of something computer-based. She says she wants to talk to us about climate in Japan and teach us the words for the different seasons while doing so. She tells us that Japan, from top to bottom, mirrors the Eastern Seaboard of the United States. Hokkaido, the northernmost main island, has a climate similar to Maine, while Kyushu, the southernmost main island, has weather like Florida.

I raise my hand, feeling stupid doing so. It gets tired, hanging in the air, waiting for Miyagi Sensei to turn around and acknowledge it. I remember back to the days when I'd use my other arm as a prop, a support for the raised hand, as if being in class was so tiring. How little I knew about what life had in store.

"Yes, Daichi?" Miyagi Sensei says, with her signature double-nod.

"If I plan to be in the central part of Japan in March, what will the weather be like?"

She puts a finger to her chin, thoughtfully, tilting her head from side to side.

"It can be cold, or sometimes spring comes early and it is warmer."

"Will I see the cherry blossoms?"

I've already researched this question myself, concluded that it's a crapshoot. But, somehow, I want Miyagi Sensei to tell me otherwise. I want her to give me hope.

"This is a difficult question, Daichi," she says. "The cherry blossoms come and go so quickly. Very easy to miss."

She explains to the class what I already know about the *sakura*, the cherry blossoms. I zone out, then set my mind to conjuring up a reason for why I need to do the drive up north solo, without Riko.

I guess Sara was my last passenger. This startles me almost as much as the time I realized I hadn't left the house in a week because there were no dirty socks in the basket when I went to do the weekly laundry. I only wear socks with shoes. And I only wear shoes when I leave the house. What can I say? It was holiday break. We were off work at R&R, and Sara went to visit her best friend in Seattle. I didn't know what to do with myself.

Another thing—I've never gone up north with anyone other than Sara before. We did that drive probably a half dozen times in the few years we were together. We always took the scenic route, all the way up the Pacific Coast Highway to 101. Every time, she pressed her face to the glass, staring out at the ocean as if she'd never seen it before, as if she were a hick from the Midwest who had been trapped on a farm shucking corn for the first three decades of her life. We stopped to take pictures so often that the voyage took us nearly ten hours. Ventura, Santa Barbara, Solvang, Carmel—I could create an entire photo album for each of those stops.

The first time we did the drive, we stopped at the Madonna Inn in San Luis Obispo for the night. It's this kitschy hotel with themed rooms, popular with the type of honeymooners who do shotgun weddings in Vegas while drunk on Popov vodka. I picked the "Oriental Fantasy" room based on her love of cherry blossoms. And there were cherry blossoms—in the printed wallpaper, the gold accent pieces, the oriental screen, the bedspread. But all she could do was laugh.

"I think the word 'tawdry' is reserved for just this type of place," she'd said, using a stuck-up British voice.

"The website description said 'elegant,'" I told her.

"Well, I think you may need to suggest some new copy."

We made the best of it, though. Sara was good at that, could have listed it as a skill on a résumé: *Experienced in making lemonade out of lemons.* We went to dinner downtown, split a bottle of wine, and then came back to the room, where I undressed her and she said, lying naked on the bed, "Jonathan, do you love me?"

I said I did.

Maybe that was the first time I'd said it.

We got to my parents' house the next day, in the late after-noon. I'd never brought a girl home to meet my parents before. It had never occurred to me. Sara told me to relax, that she was great with parents. And she was. She hugged my mother like they already knew each other's deepest secrets, like they'd spent hours gossiping on the phone. She manned the grill with my father, making room for her veggie kabobs and these burg-ers that looked like she'd put a salad in a Cuisinart and shaped the result into a patty. Even my father liked them. We all drank too much of my mother's homemade sangria and laughed at pictures of me from junior high. There was a silent, mutual understanding that this was the first of many visits. We were sure we'd all be family one day.

Miyagi Sensei claps her hands together once when she dismisses us. We file out of class, Riko so close behind me that if I stop suddenly, she'll face-plant into my backpack.

Once we get outside, she says, expectantly, "So?"

I suppose it won't affect me one way or the other if I have a passenger. Or it shouldn't.

"I'm not stopping once the whole way, so your bladder better be ready. And I'm taking the fast route, the trucker route, not the scenic route."

She nods along.

"And I'm just your driver. I'm dropping you off and picking you up. You can't meet my parents. That would confuse the hell out of them."

"So, I can come then?"

"If you must. Bring your own snacks. And bring those head-phones of yours. I'm not big on car chatter."

There has been a dramatic increase in suicides in Japan since the 1990s, leading the government to spend billions of yen on suicide-prevention strategies. In 2007, the Japanese government released a nine-step plan, a "counter-suicide White Paper," in the hopes of slowing down the suicide rate. To better understand suicide, the National Police Agency revised its categorization of motives for suicide into a division of fifty reasons, with up to three reasons listed for each suicide. Job loss was blamed for about 65 percent of suicides. Life hardships were blamed for 34 percent. Depression remained at the top of the list.

It's an American idea that money leads to happiness. The Japanese prove that idea wrong. Japan is number two in national wealth (behind the United States), but it doesn't crack the top fifty happiness-wise. There are more suicides in Japan than in some of the poorest countries on the planet.

Some say that suicide is just a part of Japanese culture. Americans have baseball games and muscle cars and Bruce Springsteen and barbecuing; the Japanese have *seppuku*, which I've already mentioned—the ritual suicide by samurai to avoid being captured; and *kamikaze*, flying one's plane into the enemy during war; and *banzai*, charging into the enemy with a fearless death wish. From the seventh-century *Book of Northern Qi*: "A true man would [rather] be the shattered jewel, ashamed to be the intact tile."

It's simple, really. In their minds, suicide is the best action in certain circumstances. It is the noblest choice in the face of disgrace. It balances the scales. Perhaps I agree with this because I want to think of myself as courageous instead of cowardly.

ust before midnight on Friday night, I pick up Riko at the
movie theater where she works. She'd said she had to man
the projector that night, begged me to wait for her shift to
end. I figure we'll drive through the night and get there bright
and early Saturday morning.

She's waiting outside, dressed in black pants, a white button-
down shirt, and a blue scarf that she's wearing like a tie. Her
theater uniform, I presume. She has a rolling suitcase next to
her, the kind people take on business trips.

"Hi," she says, settling into the passenger's seat.

She runs her hands over my BMW's wood trim and leather
seats. Yes, I got a BMW, back when I believed something like
a nice car, evidence that I'd "made it," would complete me.
You'd think I'd be immune to the effects of advertising, but this
is not the case. I don't think it's the case for anyone desperate
enough to be "happy."

"Nice car," she says, in a way that makes me think she sees through advertising. Maybe she can see through me entirely.

For the first couple hours of our trip, Riko does exactly what she said she'd do. She sits in the passenger's seat quietly, with her headphones on, listening to an audio book—*On the Road* by Jack Kerouac, she tells me. It takes everything in me not to roll my eyes at this cliché choice of literature. She has placed a hundred-dollar bill in the cup holder of the center console for gas, and she has informed me that there are potato chips, licorice ropes, and chocolate chip cookies in the back seat if I so desire.

Somewhere outside Bakersfield, I decide that perhaps I should utilize her presence to make the drive go by faster.

I tap her headphones and she flails, startled, as if she's forgotten I'm there, as if she thought the car was driving itself.

"Are you hungry?" she asks, plainly, seemingly unable to conceive that I'd disturb her for any other reason but to retrieve snacks.

"No, I just thought I'd ask how you like the book."

"It's okay. Not quite the road trip book I was expecting, though."

I nod.

"How's the driving?" she asks.

"Pretty uneventful."

"You're not getting tired already, are you?"

"No, I'm fine."

She sits, headphones now in her lap.

"I wonder if truckers fall asleep at the wheel a lot," she says. That is who we are sharing the road with, mostly.

"Let's hope not."

"You know, I still don't understand why you don't just buy a CD to learn Japanese. Or download an app. You could be practicing, like, right now. No class necessary."

"I don't learn well that way. Besides, a class better prepares me for conversation. For my trip."

She sighs. "Right. The all-important trip. Are you going there to find a wife or something?"

"No," I snap. "For the cherry blossoms."

She sighs again. "The cherry blossoms. Right. Okay. Don't take this the wrong way, but what is your deal with cherry blossoms?"

I suppose she has a right to ask. I suppose my enthusiasm for this flower, as a heterosexual man, is rather peculiar.

"Aren't there cherry blossoms in the United States that you could see?" she asks.

"There are, but they're here because the Japanese gave them to us."

Sara had explained this to me when I asked her the very same question. Japan gave over three thousand cherry blossom trees to the United States as a gift in 1912. These trees were planted in Sakura Park in Manhattan and on the shore of the Tidal Basin in Washington, DC. In 1965, the gift was renewed with another three thousand or so trees.

"They're only indigenous to East Asia," I say.

"Well, thank you, Wikipedia."

"You can make fun," I say. "It's just something on my bucket list." I don't feel like explaining beyond this.

"Fair enough."

"What about you?" I ask, diverting attention away from me.

"What about me? I never really thought twice about cherry blossoms."

"No. I mean, what do you want to do before you die?"

She gives me that too-familiar "You're a fucking weirdo" look.

"I'd like to live a long time first, for one."

It's strange to me that people have this goal of living a "long time." What is there to do with all those years, besides lament the loss of hair, dexterity, vision, hearing, brain cells, bladder control, and dreams? It's depressing. And nobody likes old people. Nobody gives one shit about them—in America, at least. They are just in the way. They take twenty minutes to pull out of parking spots, an hour to find coupons in their wallets at the grocery store register, and what seems like three years to cross a street. Plus, they remind us that we will someday be like them, and we really hate that. In Japan, they appreciate their elders. They even have a national holiday called Respect for the Aged Day. Many families have several generations living under one roof. Here, we just shove them into nursing homes. It's no wonder elderly people in Japan live so long. There are actually more elderly people than young people in Japan.

"Like how long do you want to live?" I ask Riko.

"I don't know. A hundred years? That sounds fun."

"*Fun*? Why?"

"Just to see how the world evolves," she says, casually, as if she's never heard of global warming and is not aware that all of us here in California will be under water while those in Kansas will suddenly have beachfront property.

"I think it'd be so cool to see my children, grandchildren, even great-grandchildren grow up."

So far, I know that Riko's list of things to do before she dies includes:

• Have babies

It's fair to assume that it also includes:

• Get married

I wonder how much we will have in common from this point forward. She will figure out soon enough that I don't want what convention tells me to want—a wife, some kids, a life span of more than thirty-four years.

"You don't want kids?" she says. It must be obvious on my face.

"No," I say. "I would screw up a kid, for sure."

"I'm sure everyone thinks that. Your parents probably thought that and, look, you're fine."

If she only knew.

"Plus, there are all these things that could go wrong," I say. "Diseases, accidents, you know."

"So you would call yourself an optimist?" she says, sarcastically.

"I would call myself a realist."

She shakes her head and shifts in her seat so she's sitting with her legs bent underneath her.

"You're not a realist. If you were, you would know that *realistically* those things wouldn't happen."

"But they very well *could*."

"A lot of bad things *could* happen. A meteor could fall from space, somehow make it through the Earth's atmosphere without burning up, and come crashing down on us right here and now in this car."

That wouldn't be so bad, actually. Quick and dirty.

"If you live your life in fear, what's the point of living at all?" she says.

"You have a point."

There's this comedian, Doug Stanhope, who does this bit where he says something like "Life is like a movie. If you've sat through some of it and it's sucked, it probably isn't gonna get great right at the end and make it all worthwhile. No one should blame you for walking out early."

"All I'm saying is that you can't predict life. You can't control it," she adds.

What she doesn't know is that you *can* control life. You can walk out of the movie, metaphorically speaking. You can inhale laundry detergent.

"So, back to your list," I say.

She fills the next ten minutes with these spontaneous plans for her future:

- Go to an Olympics, preferably Summer
- Have someone paint a picture of her
- Be an extra in a movie
- Jump over a waterfall
- Visit the place she was born
- Donate money and get her name on a park bench
- Watch all the Oscar-winning movies
- Fall in love
- Give birth
- See a Broadway show
- Get a tattoo

When I ask her what kind of tattoo she wants, she says she has no idea, which makes me think I can take nothing she says seriously.

"What about you?" she asks. "What do you want to do before you die?"

"Go to Japan."

"Yes, I know. We've covered this one. Anything else?"

"That's the big one."

"Okay, so if it's so big, when are you going? It seems like with this mission of yours you should already have your tickets."

"I want to finish a semester of Japanese first."

"Okay," she says, impatiently, "so after you do the class and the trip, then what? If that's your sole life goal, what are you going to do once you meet it?"

"Move on to something else."

I'm not sure what I expect from the "afterlife." I don't believe there is a God standing at some majestic gate, tallying up all our sins and good deeds to determine our destination. I don't think there is a destination—a heaven where you meet up with your long-lost loved ones on puffy clouds and play with unicorns pooping rainbows, or a hell where you toil and sweat and regret all those times you took the Lord's name in vain. I think humans, like animals, just die. When our brains stop, when neurons cease firing and all those chemical reactions we call "emotions" come to an end, we just die. It can't be that complicated.

I would tell all this to Riko, but I'm pretty sure she would ask me to pull over so she could hitchhike the rest of the way to San Francisco. Then she would end up on an episode of *48 Hours* and I'd feel like a dick.

"I want to go to Japan sometime," she says, wistfully. "I think it'll be weird, though. I'll look like everyone there, but feel so out of place."

"I feel that way almost every day," I say. "And, yes, it's weird."

"Do you mind?" she says, putting her headphones back on her ears. I take this as a dismissal of my morbid conversation topics.

Five minutes later, her head is resting against the window, her neck bent awkwardly. She sleeps like that the rest of the way.

According to Riko's scribbled instructions, her parents live outside of San Francisco, in the notoriously foggy city of Pacifica. It's a detour, way more of a detour than I'd anticipated. Just as the sun is coming up, we pass my usual turnoff to where my parents live in Piedmont and cross the bridge into the city and then take I-280 to California 1 into Pacifica. When we pull off the freeway and stop at a light, I lean over and shake her awake.

"Are we here?" she asks, rubbing her eyes. Only truly content people can sleep so peacefully.

"We're here."

She takes in her surroundings, then guides me through the neighborhood streets. They live in a nice area, near the beach. The houses are older, but big with nice yards. It's the type of place where kids sell lemonade at wobbly stands their dads built and play handball against the garage door after school and jump rope in the street because cars know to look out for them. She says we're really close now; it's just up the street a ways.

"What's your 'business' here, anyway?" I ask.

"Just some personal stuff." She reaches into the back seat, organizing her things. She looks at herself in the mirror, finger-combing her hair and pinching her cheeks—the lazy woman's blush.

"If it's okay with you, can you just drop me off? I don't want to have a big introduction thing."

"Trust me, I don't want that either."

She gives me a satisfied nod, then points. "It's right here."

"Right here" is a two-story house surrounded by full-grown trees. There are some of those ceramic geese in the front yard. I pull up along the curb. An older white guy is mowing the lawn in a pair of khakis and a collared shirt.

"Not to be politically incorrect, but your parents must be really well-off to have a white guy in golf attire for a gardener."

She smiles awkwardly, then opens the door to get out. In my rearview mirror, I watch her go to the trunk to get her suitcase. The gardener guy approaches her and lifts the bag out for her. He's like a butler too, apparently. Then he gives her a hug, a tight one, and a kiss on the cheek. I watch her eyes finding mine in the rearview mirror. She looks like she's been caught. In what, I don't know. She waves me off. Who is this guy? A relative? Riko is not a halfsie, so this is not her father. Maybe he's an unusually affectionate neighbor. He starts to come around to my side of the car, to introduce himself, I'm sure. But she takes hold of his arm and pulls him toward the house while saying something I can't hear or make out via lipreading. As I pull away, I watch her go up the flower-lined walkway to the front door, this man at her side, arm around her waist.

I don't think I'm the only one with secrets.

In 2004, three Japanese humanitarian workers who had been held hostage in Iraq returned home after nearly three weeks in captivity. They were not greeted with smiles and hugs; they were greeted with a sign at the airport that read "You got what you deserve." To top it off, the government billed them $6,000 for airfare, a decisive "fuck you." In counseling, when asked to list the three most stressful moments during their ordeal, they said the following:

1. When they were kidnapped, on their way to Baghdad.
2. The day when they were broadcast on TV, with knives to their throats.
3. Coming home.

Despite what they say, no matter your circumstances, coming home is never easy.

十二

Piedmont is a small, quaint town, what real estate agents call a "bedroom community." It's got tree-lined streets, good schools, a low crime rate. My father likes to remind me that *CNNMoney* magazine named it one of the best places to live. Growing up, I remember a history teacher telling us that in the Roaring Twenties, Piedmont was known as the "City of Millionaires" because it had the most resident millionaires per square mile of any city in the United States. Some of the mansions built then still stand today. My parents don't live in one of those, but their house is nice—"classic contemporary," my mother says. She watches quite a bit of HGTV. I suppose it goes without saying that my suicidal tendencies are not to be blamed on my upbringing. Clint Eastwood grew up in my town. I could have made something of my life. I just didn't.

✳

It always feels strange to knock on the door and wait on the stoop of the home where I spent the first eighteen years of my life. Like I'm just another visitor, someone selling Girl Scout cookies or magazine subscriptions or Mormonism.

"Jon!" my father says when he opens the door. "How the heck are you, kid?"

In addition to being the only person who calls me "Jon," he is the only person who calls me "kid." Coming from anyone else, it would sound like a sarcastic jab.

"I'm good, Dad," I say, almost getting the wind knocked out of me when he hugs me. Most men are taught to give very short hugs, with minimal chest-to-chest pressure applied. My father does not seem aware of this convention.

He looks older to me every time I see him. His hair is more receded, almost completely gone except for some stubborn white hairs still clinging to the sides and back of his head. He's wearing a Tommy Bahama shirt, as if he lives on a cruise ship.

"Is that him?" my mother's voice calls from inside. I can hear her fast-approaching footsteps on the hardwood floors.

"It's him," my father shouts over his shoulder before turning to me and whispering, "Beware of her eyes."

That is not adequate warning, though. They aren't even "eyes" as I understand them; they are slits in her face, surrounded by swollen, red, puffy skin. When she'd said she was having surgery, I didn't expect it to look like this, like she'd been in a gang fight.

"Jonathan, sweetheart, it's so good to see you," she says, standing on her tiptoes to get her arms around my neck. I'm almost afraid to kiss her cheek, to make any contact with her face.

"Jesus, Mom, are you sure you can even *see* me?"

If I could see her eyeballs, they are probably rolling.

"You look like you got beat up," I tell her.

And maybe she did, in a sense, by the realities of aging, mortality. Her only defense is dyeing her gray, thinning hair brown and having her eye hoods snipped.

"It's not so bad," she says, acting like I'm freaking out over a paper cut on her finger.

"She's going to look amazing in just a week or two," my father adds, with just the slightest mocking.

"Enough about me, though. Look at you!" she says, standing back like I'm a work of art to be admired. If only. "What *is* this?"

She touches my beard, tentatively, like she thinks nesting birds will fly out of there and attack her. I suppose I have progressed from looking like I've been camping for a weekend to looking like I live in the Alaskan wilderness and hunt caribou for food.

"It's hair on my face. Some people call it a 'beard.'"

She gives me an "Oh, you!" nudge.

"You look like Charles Manson," my father says with a chuckle.

"I'm much taller than Charles Manson. He was, like, five foot two."

"What are you now? Six foot two? I swear you're taller," my father says, standing beside me, noticing the few-inch advantage I have over him. I don't have the heart to tell him that their spines are compressing under the weight of gravity, that they are, in fact, shrinking.

"Come in, come in," my mother says, waving me inside quickly, as if she's rescuing me from a snowstorm outside.

They sit on the couch in the living room and mute the TV—a golf tournament. My mother pats the cushion next to her and I sit, obligingly.

"How was the drive?" my father asks. Our conversations tend to revolve around practical matters—how my car is running, the status of my retirement account, who I'm voting for in the next election, that kind of thing.

"It went by fast."

"I can't believe you drove through the night," my mother says, putting her hand to her chest, like my drive-by-night stint has taken her breath away.

"Less traffic that way."

"Well, we're just so glad you came to visit," she says.

"Work still going well?" my father asks.

"Great."

"And what are you doing for fun?"

It's like an interview, really. I'm just hoping they don't ask me where I see myself in five years.

"Well, I decided to take a Japanese class."

"A Japanese class?" my father says.

"Why would you take a Japanese class?" my mother adds.

They're both befuddled, maybe slightly concerned, like I'm a wayward offspring suddenly committed to a career of making birdhouses out of toothpicks.

"I'm planning a trip to Japan. I thought some language skill would come in handy."

Most parents would be impressed with such an endeavor, but my parents are looking at me the way people look at transients singing to themselves on street corners.

"By yourself?" my mother asks.

I nod. They glance at each other with matching furrowed brows.

My father clears his throat. "Do you think that's a good idea?"

"I wouldn't be going if I didn't think it was a good idea." Or

I suppose I would, but they do not have intimate knowledge of my masochistic tendencies.

"When?" my mother asks.

"In the spring. March, probably."

"But what are you going to *do* there?"

It's like I've told them I'm going to Greenland, someplace where daily activities are somewhat of a mystery.

"Travel around. Hopefully see the cherry blossoms."

"By yourself?" my mother asks again.

I want to express my annoyance by pointing out that she has already asked this question, but I'm afraid she'll think I'm suggesting she has early-onset Alzheimer's. My mother is what I call a "spinner"; she gets an idea in her head and then googles and spins herself into a frenzy about it, unable to sleep for days.

"I'll be fine," I tell them. Apparently, they need to hear this.

My mother stands from the couch, almost angrily. "You always say that—you're fine, you'll be fine. Fine, fine, fine."

She goes to the kitchen, drops a tea bag in a mug on the counter and fills the mug with steaming water from a kettle on the stove. She returns, using two hands to clutch the mug, as if it's heavier than it is. She hands it to me. I don't drink tea, but I hold it anyway.

"You don't have your tickets yet, do you?" she says, wrapping a knit blanket tightly around her shoulders.

"Not yet."

"Then there's still time to change your mind."

I don't dare tell them how unchangeable my mind is, how committed I am to my plan.

"What else have you been up to?" my father says, distracting my mother from her horrible visions of her son traipsing about the Orient, alone.

"Nothing, really."

What do they want to hear? What do parents want to know from their grown children? What would assure them that they've done a good job with the whole child-raising process? What would help them sleep better at night?

"Have you met anyone?" my father asks.

My mother gives him a warning look, scolding him without words for asking the question, for prying. I'm sure they've talked among themselves about how I should "get out there." After all, every human needs companionship. A girlfriend, a wife—yes, that is what would assure them that they've succeeded as parents. That is what would act as a lullaby for them as they lie in bed at night, wondering about my existence 350 miles away in Los Angeles.

"I've met lots of people," I say. "I met this sixteen-year-old kid at the grocery store checkout. I met this nice Indian guy at the gas station. I—"

They both laugh, grateful for the comic relief.

"You know what I mean," my father says, serious again.

"There is someone," I say to appease them, to grant them their wish. It's the least I can do.

"Oh?" my mother asks, with an interested arch of the eyebrow.

"Her name's Riko. She's in my Japanese class."

"Riko?" my father asks, but he says it like "Rick-o," like she's a fifty-something, overweight detective working vice on a 1970s cop show. Sergeant Ricko.

"Reek-o," I enunciate. "She's Japanese."

"How interesting," my mother says, which isn't quite the right thing to say in response to someone's nationality. It implies there are others that are uninteresting. Maybe there are.

"Is *that* why you're learning Japanese? To impress a girl?" my father asks, with a wink.

"Sure," I say, because his wink is begging me to relate to it. And maybe I *am* learning Japanese to impress a girl. It's just that the girl is not Riko.

Satisfied with the status of things, my mother moves on to present the itinerary for my stay, which begins with brunch. My parents love brunch. They talk about it like they discovered the concept. They can't get over the wonder of combining breakfast foods and lunch foods in one grand meal. Oh, the mix of salty and sweet, savory and saccharine! They take me to a place they refer to as "their spot." I miss having a "spot" with someone. Sara and I used to go to this place called the Filling Station. It was a gas station at one point, maybe a hundred years ago, converted to a breakfast joint. We made the hour drive on some weekend mornings, just for their huevos rancheros.

We sit in a booth, and my parents peruse the menu like it's new to them—oohing and ahhing over omelets and french toast, discussing the viscosity of the hollandaise sauce. They share a pair of reading glasses, which may seem kind of cute in theory but is completely obnoxious in practice. They pass the spectacles back and forth clumsily, getting impatient when the other is taking too long.

The waitress takes our orders, one of which is a plate of hash browns to "get us started." Only my father would request a brunch appetizer. She brings them to the table a couple minutes later, making me wonder how long they've been sitting out, ready, under those heat lamps. My father digs right in, shaking salt generously on the portion he's deemed his.

"Watch the sodium, Paul," my mother says, clicking her tongue like a boarding school headmistress.

My father, a devotee of the "happy wife, happy life" philosophy, says, "Okay, Bernie." My mother's name is Bernice, but my father has always called her Bernie, or Bern. I feel for him, living under the reign of her fears, trying to sneak in a shake of salt away from her ever-watchful, hoodless eyes.

"I have to use the ladies' room," my mother says, excusing herself. When she's gone, my father squeezes ketchup on a corner of his plate.

"Don't pay too much attention to her," he says, with a patience that must come with four decades of marriage. "I think it's some kind of midlife crisis."

"I didn't know women had those."

"Ever since...with what happened..." he starts, in search of words he doesn't seem to want to find. He sighs. "Well, you know, she just frets more now."

When my mother returns to the table, our food arrives. After drooling over cinnamon-apple pancakes, she orders oatmeal (and makes my father do the same). It's got little black specks in it that look like ants. She says they're flaxseeds. She says they make for a "cholesterol-lowering power meal." This triggers a discussion of omega-3s and the benefits of walking at a pace of four miles per hour for a half hour, at least six days per week. It occurs to me that she's made it a hobby for the two of them to defy what I want to embrace.

After we finish eating, my father says he may as well use the restroom. "Too much coffee," he says.

When he's gone, my mother leans across the table like we're teenagers trading secrets and says, "Sorry about earlier, when Dad was asking you about your dating life." Her tone implies she would never have asked herself, though she most definitely would have.

"It's okay. That's what parents do."

"It's just that we hardly ever talk to you anymore. You've been so distant. We worry, that's all."

"I'm fine, Mom."

"You always say that—*I'm fine, I'm fine.* But I don't see how I could believe you," she says, laughing uncomfortably. "You're in advertising. You lie all the time."

"Well, if you keep bugging me, I won't be fine. Is that what you want?" I add my own uncomfortable laugh.

"Of course not," she says. "It's just that with what happened... Well, that must have been hard, but you never talked to us about it at all and—"

I'm wondering now if they planned this—these tag-team bathroom trips—in attempts to get me to talk to them about "what happened."

"Mom, I'm fine. Really."

"If you say so."

When my father returns, we pay the bill and head back to the house, where my mother says she has "a little something" for me—"since you won't be visiting over the holidays." My mother is, in effect, giving me a farewell gift. She doesn't know this, but maybe it will comfort her when I'm gone.

Gifts from mothers are always to be feared. They are of two varieties: the nostalgic variety and the self-improvement variety. The nostalgic variety includes framed family pictures or—for the creative types like my mother—photo calendars, photo mugs, or photo key chains. Yes, she once gave me a picture of the two of us that I am expected to let hang with my keys. It conflicts with her desire for me to get her a daughter-in-law. The self-improvement variety includes hygiene-related products like Crest whitening strips or toenail clippers, button-up shirts suitable for yacht owners, and cologne.

Here are my top five guesses:

- Socks. My mother is a big giver of socks.
- An electronic toothbrush.
- Vitamins—a big tub from Costco.
- A book called *Why You Should Stop Masturbating and Start Dating*.
- The DVD series *Planet Earth*. This would fall into the self-improvement category, if you're wondering. At least once every couple of obligatory phone calls, my mother asks if I've seen it yet. She says it will "expand my horizons." I tell her my horizons are good as is.

"It's nothing big. Just something I wanted you to have," she says, sitting across from me on the love seat. Dad is reclining in his favorite chair.

As I start to open it, though, I realize this gift is of the nostalgic variety. I see what appears to be the back of a frame. I must have about twenty framed pictures at my house. I keep them in a box in my closet, next to a stack of dress shoes I sort through only for job interviews and weddings and funerals—the important events in life. When my parents visit, I make sure to put the pictures on display. I can't imagine them *always* being there—my mother and father, long-gone pets, younger versions of myself, all staring back at me.

This isn't a family photo, though. It's a picture of me with Sara.

"What is this?" I ask.

My mother reaches for it. "I don't know. I've had it for months. I thought you might like it, and—"

"Why would you give this to me?"

"I'm sorry," she says quickly, taking back the picture.

"She didn't mean to upset you," my father adds.

"I'm not upset." This must be a lie, because my face feels very hot.

There is a moment of silence, maybe to remember what it felt like to have a daughter-in-law on the way, along with some grandkids to occupy their retirement. It's like my parents' future is somehow contingent on mine. If they knew the future I had in the works, perhaps they could adopt a new kid, get a large dog, make alternate plans.

"I asked Rhonda if she thought it was a good idea. She seemed to think it was okay."

The name rattles around in my head. *Rhonda, Rhonda, Rhonda.*

"Sara's *mom*?" I finally ask.

My mother eyes my father, who just shrugs in his "Oh, heck" way.

"You still talk to Sara's mother?"

"Sometimes. Just on the phone."

Thoughts race: What do they talk about? Eye hoods and hot flashes? Or more than that?

"But you only met her, like, one time," I say. It was when they visited for Christmas. All of us went to see this *Nutcracker* play, then drank way too much wine at dinner. My mother told the story of how I peed in my footie pajamas when I was a kid.

"I can't help it that we bonded." I detest this word. *Bonded.* Like they adhere to each other with some kind of super-strong glue, the kind you have to special-order on the internet.

I want to know if they talk about me, but it seems very adolescent to ask this. Does Rhonda ask how I'm doing? Does my mother say "He's doing just great"? Does she believe herself when she says that?

I stand and feel suddenly weird in my body, unsure if my

legs will hold me. My parents look at me, from their still-seated positions.

"I think I have to go," I say.

"Go? Go where?"

"I don't know."

"Right now?" my father says. He stands to talk to me eye to eye.

"Honey, let's talk about it," my mother says, sounding well-coached by a therapist during an intervention. Fuck, is that what this is?

"I don't want to talk about anything."

This is no way to say goodbye.

"I'll be back. I just need to get out for a while."

It's like I'm a kid again, fighting with them, making a dramatic exit out the front door, slamming it hard enough to express my anger, but not so hard that the little glass window insets shatter like they did when I was fourteen, when they grounded me for doing shots of Dad's whiskey with my friends at what they thought was an innocent sleepover involving video games and Doritos.

I get in the car and drive to the closest supermarket. They have the alcohol locked in a glass enclosure, and I have to ask one of the pimply faced employees to open it for me. Considering my overgrown facial hair and the fact that it's the middle of the afternoon, I'm sure it's assumed that I'm a homeless drunkard. There was a time when this assumption would have bothered me, but today I go through the checkout line wordlessly, making no attempt to explain my purchase. And the way the gum-chewing cashier swipes the bottle, apathetically, glancing up just long enough to give me her confirmatory "you look twenty-one" nod, I realize that nobody cares what I'm doing with my life. Nobody cares if I'm about to get in my car, park somewhere, and get drunk on a bottle of Grey Goose. Yes, I bought "the good stuff." I put that in quotes because anyone who works in advertising knows that's a crock of shit. Vodka is a "grain-neutral spirit," meaning it all pretty much tastes the same. Grey Goose was put on the top shelf of the best clubs. It was a marketing scheme, concocted by Sidney Frank. He wanted to introduce a "premium" vodka (read: expensive) to the market, and he did. All he needed was that elegant, frosty-glass bottle with the words "DISTILLED AND BOTTLED IN FRANCE" stamped on it. Lovers of luxury ate—or drank—it up.

I drive to one of my favorite lookouts of the Bay Bridge. I used to love the bridge as a kid, so much so that my parents were convinced I'd become an architect or an engineer. Every weekend, I begged them to take a trip to San Francisco—not because I loved the city, but because I loved the bridge we had to cross to get to the city. In fact, we could have just driven there and back for the entirety of a day and that would have been pure amusement for me. There was something exhilarating about it, driving over the water, no choice but to accelerate, trust the road beneath us. I played games in my mind, looking at the clock and telling myself "If we pass Yerba Buena Island by 11:03, there won't be an earthquake."

I kissed my first girlfriend here, at the lookout. I was sixteen, had just gotten permission from my parents to drive their car for purposes other than to school and back. Jessica was her name. I called her Jessie. I'd kissed girls before her, but she was the first girlfriend, the first to make that semantic jump and agree to deem herself "mine." We dated for four months, which is the equivalent of three years in teenage time. We used each other like practice dummies—testing each other's lips, feeling each other's bodies. I can't remember her last name. It was something Polish, long—Grabowski or Garbowski.

Considering my love of the Bay Bridge, it would be poetic to end my life by jumping off of it. But, as I've said before, I don't trust bridge jumps. People survive them. If I had to choose a bridge, the Golden Gate would be the one. I've done enough research to know that after a fall of just four seconds, jumpers hit the water at about seventy-five miles per hour. At that speed, the water is like concrete to the body. Most jumpers die on impact. Those who survive the fall usually drown or die of hypothermia in the water. It's the surest way to go if you're a jumper. About one person every couple weeks meets their end there, making it the most popular suicide destination in the United States. Japan's Aokigahara Forest is another popular destination. So many people take their lives there that the local government has stopped publicizing the numbers in an effort to de-sensationalize the place.

I unscrew the Grey Goose bottle cap and take a swig, taking note that this is the first time I have done such a thing. I'm not a swigger. I'm not even much of a drinker. If I was, maybe I'd consider pulling off a departure in the style of Nicholas Cage in *Leaving Las Vegas*. I don't think I have that dedication, though. I want it to be quick and easy. I've shown little tolerance for the act of living, and I feel just as little tolerance for the act of dying. My death—inhaling the fumes in the comfort of my home—will be fast, private, and, according to those message boards, painless.

Drinking is big in Japan, probably the closest thing to an escape you can get without jumping in front of a train. It's widely known that the Shinjuku Station at midnight is crawling with thousands of plastered commuters, stumbling onto platforms, vaguely sure of their suburban destinations. Well-dressed businessmen fall down stairs; women vomit into their own purses—this is what I envision. Officials of the Japanese Railway estimate that 60 percent of passengers are drunk.

After just three big swigs, my eyes are heavy, tired. I let myself sleep, parked there in my car, in a deserted, overgrown lot overlooking the Bay Bridge, a mostly full bottle of vodka as my passenger. If anyone were to find me here, I'd be exposed for exactly who I am—a thirty-something, scruffy-faced guy looking for a way out.

I wake up to a cold breeze whistling through the cracked-open window. The sun is setting. Whatever drunkenness those swigs gave me is gone, vanished as quickly as it came. I expected deep thoughts, epiphanies. Instead, I got sleep.

I drive back to my parents' house, through the streets I'd traversed on foot and bike years before. The front door is unlocked. They are sitting on the couch, watching something on the Travel Channel. Their heads turn in unison when I walk in the door, their faces showing a mixture of confusion and relief.

"Where have you been?" my mother asks, trying not to sound angry. I am, after all, a grown adult.

"I was just out. Driving around."

"Is everything okay?" my father asks.

"Fine."

With that, my mother offers me some of the spaghetti and meatballs she's made for dinner. I join them in watching a show about renovating a home in the heart of Tuscany—the retired couple's dream. We don't talk about my time by the bridge. We don't talk about the redness of my eyes. And we sure as hell don't talk about Sara.

Once the home in Tuscany is renovated and the white-haired husband and wife clink their wine glasses while a sun sets behind them, my parents say good night and I go to my bedroom, preserved as it was before I left for college. They could easily make it into a bonus room for the treadmill and my mother's sewing machine, but they have put those in the garage and persisted in sustaining the illusion that a sixteen-year-old still lives with them.

My bed has the same navy-blue comforter, my high school diploma still hangs above my dresser, and my desk is cluttered with books I read in my sophomore year—*The Catcher in the Rye, The Scarlet Letter, The Great Gatsby.* I remember this time of my life, when I was just a kid worried about his driver's test and an upcoming formal. It seemed stressful at the time. It's all relative, I guess. You never realize how simple life is until you acquire new complications.

Among all my old books is a tattered Bible. I used to pray at night and ask for toys and good grades and, occasionally, when feeling philanthropic, world peace. I was raised with the generic brand of Christianity, the one that comes with Santa Claus, presents, and days off from school. I believed in an all-knowing God, or wanted to, for the same reason I believed in fate. We want an omniscient man in the sky to take the reins of our lives. We shudder at the idea of everything being our choice, our fault, our responsibility.

I choose not to believe in God at all now. If I did believe, if I chalked up all my life experiences to God's plan, I'd have to consider him (or her or it or whatever) an asshole. They say it's bad to harbor hate, hold grudges. It's bad for the blood pressure. So I just don't believe. The Japanese don't believe, either. According to a Gallup poll, about a third of Japanese people say

they are "convinced atheists," while over half describe themselves as "not religious" or "atheist." The only other country in
the world with more atheists is China. The Asians, they get me,
they really get me. That's why I must visit. My mother would
never understand.

The Japanese have this phrase that's very popular in their culture, maybe as popular as "chill out" in our country. It's *shikata ga nai*, translated to mean "It can't be helped."

Dear Mom and Dad,

The first thing I want you to know is that my death was relatively painless. At least that's what those knowledgeable in my chosen technique promised it would be. The second thing I want you to know is that this has nothing to do with you. If you think you could have raised me better, you couldn't have. If you think you could have loved me more, you're mistaken. If you think you should have seen this coming, you shouldn't have. I find comfort in this finality, so don't worry about me. I prefer this to thinking about what has been and worrying about what will be. I don't ask you to understand me. I just ask you not to blame yourselves. Shikata ga nai.

Love,
Jonathan

P.S. Please donate my body to science. Mom, I know you always wanted me to go to medical school. This is the way.

十三

The next morning, over my mother's fresh-from-a-box blue-berry muffins and coffee, we say our goodbyes. Of course, they don't know that this is it—the final goodbye. They ask when they'll see me next, and I say I'll have to get back to them, that work has been busy. They say they'll still call, whether I like it or not. They ask if I want to take any food home with me. They ask me to consider shaving my beard.

"It was such a quick visit, but we're so glad you came," my mother says as they walk me to the car. My father is carrying my bag. He insisted.

"I'm glad I came too."

I hug them—Mom first, then Dad. I try to make it tighter and longer than usual, so that when they recall the last time they saw me, they'll smile.

I open the trunk, and my father puts my bag inside. He gives me a slap on the back and tells me to drive safe.

"I love you guys," I say. That will make them smile too.

They stand in the middle of the street, waving, long after I've pulled away. I can't help but look in the rearview mirror at them, my father's arm around my mother's waist, their heads cocked toward each other. They will be okay, I think, without me.

Riko is sitting on the curb, hiding inside an oversized black hoodie, Converse-sneakered feet pigeon-toed. She has that tired, hit-by-a-Mack-truck look to her, similar to the one I seem to have. I put the car in park and pop the trunk for her. She walks to the back of the car, slowly, like a hungover person struggling with every step. By the time she comes around to the passenger's side, I've opened the door for her. She slides in and immediately pulls her knees to her chest and puts her feet on the seat. There was a time when I would have been concerned for the leather, when I would have requested the removal of her shoes. I can't bring myself to care now.

"Hey," she says, exhaustion evident in her voice.

"Rough night?"

"Something like that."

She closes her eyes and crosses her arms over her chest. Then she pulls on the strings of her sweatshirt so the hoodie cinches shut around her face. It doesn't take a genius to know this isn't the time to ask her about the "gardener."

A few hours into the drive, she wakes up and pulls off her sweatshirt, revealing greasy hair. She starts rummaging in her bag of snacks and pulls out a licorice rope. She sucks on it absentmindedly, then she says, "I'm sure you're wondering about the man you saw at my house."

"She speaks!" I say with mock enthusiasm.

She bites off a piece of her licorice rope, somewhat violently.

"I don't have to tell you," she says. "I just didn't want you to get some weird idea about me and an old white guy."

"Well, I already got some weird ideas, so..."

"He's my dad," she blurts.

"He must have some pretty recessive Japanese genes," I say, still trying to keep it light. I'm not interested in becoming part of whatever family drama she is about to disclose.

"Would you stop?" She's angry. I've never seen Riko angry.

She pulls out another licorice rope but doesn't put this one in her mouth. She just twists it around her finger.

"I'm adopted, you asshole."

For some reason, I had not considered this. I thought he was either a stepdad or her mother's mister (is this the proper term for a male mistress?). In the not-so-recessed recesses of my mind, I considered that maybe he was her lover, that Riko likes aged men, has some kind of daddy complex. This all seems twisted now.

I wait for her to say more, to add to her confession. Without more, with just "I'm adopted, you asshole," I don't have much of a response. Anything I can think to say—like "Well, you've acclimated very well" or "So your last name really isn't that of a Japanese beer?"—just sounds wrong.

"I don't tell people, if I can help it," she says, finally.

"Why?"

She shrugs. "I feel like when I do that, I'm wearing a sign that says 'My real parents didn't want me,'" she says. "Plus, I don't want to answer all the questions—when I came here, why my parents gave me up, what I remember about Japan."

"I won't ask any of those things."

The truth is I don't want to know any of those things. I'm not someone Riko should be trusting with her well-kept secrets.

"I don't know a thing about the adoption," she says, telling me anyway. "I don't remember Japan, have no idea why my parents got rid of me. I came home to find the adoption records. I knew my parents had them."

"And?"

She takes a manila folder out of her backpack.

"Right here," she says. "My dad caught me going through the files. They're pissed at me, convinced that I'm opening a can of worms that is better left closed."

I want to tell her that she probably is, but this is not what she wants to hear.

"Why is it so weird to them that I want to know where I come from? Look at me," she says. I obey, looking into her determined, narrowing eyes before looking back to the road, tightening my grip on the steering wheel. "I've got these squinty eyes and black hair and a first name of Rihoko. And my last name is Smith. Smith!"

She's having a quarterlife crisis and an identity crisis—two crises.

"My parents think I'm just going through a phase of 'finding myself,'" she says, with dismissive, mocking air quotes.

"I'm pretty sure finding oneself is not a phase. It's just life."

"Wow, profound," she says with annoyed sarcasm.

"So, what now?"

"Well, the records have just my father's name."

"Are you going to try to find him?" I try to ask this with as little judgment in my voice as possible, disguising my belief that

I think she's an overly hopeful kid about to become like the rest of us disillusioned adults.

"I don't know," she says, dismissively. "His name's Hideo. Hideo Shimura. You know what Hideo means? I googled it."

Name meanings are silly. "Jonathan" means "God gives." It doesn't say what God gives. Just that God gives. White elephant gifts? A damn? A rat's ass? The shirt off his back?

Still, I play along and say, "What does it mean?"

"'Splendid man.'"

I make a grunting noise, confirming I've heard her, and we drive in silence for a few miles, until she says, "Do you think he's splendid?"

"I would have no idea."

"I can see the skepticism on your face. I mean, what father gives up his child, right?"

I look at her again, just like when she commanded me to notice her squinty eyes and black hair. There's something in me that wants to protect her—from her own hopes, from whatever life has in store for their destruction. "Maybe he didn't have a choice."

She shrugs. "Maybe."

And, for whatever reason, I'm compelled to tell her one of my secrets. It's something defensive in me, something in response to the judgment in her voice when she asked "What father gives up his child?"

"I got Sara pregnant," I say, squeezing the steering wheel so tight, my knuckles are white.

It's not so bad, actually, to do confessions like this—in a car, at the wheel, eyes fixed on the highway. There is no opportunity for awkward embraces of empathy. I don't even have to see the look on Riko's face—the shock, the pity.

"What do you mean?" she says. I can see out of the corner of my eye that she's leaned away from me, body pressed up against the passenger's side door, like she's not sure she wants to get close to this truth.

"What do I *mean*? I mean, I got her pregnant. Please don't tell me I have to explain the mechanics of this."

"No, I get that. But, like, *recently*?"

Riko thinks this is a case of regrettable breakup sex. A cliché "oops." Oh, to be young, when most of what you know about the world is from hour-long TV dramas.

"No, while we were together."

"Oh," she says, waiting a moment before asking "Is that why she left?"

"Sort of. I guess," I say. "It's complicated."

"Did she have the baby, then?"

"Do you think I'd be taking Japanese classes and hanging out with you if I had a kid to take care of?" It comes out mean. "Sorry," I say immediately.

"Well," she says. "*I'm* sorry."

We sit in silence a moment before she asks, "Is that what I'm supposed to say? That I'm sorry?"

"I never know what people are supposed to say."

More silence.

"Why are you telling me?"

"I don't know," I say, honestly. "Maybe to let you know that life is strange and there isn't always an easy explanation for the way things go."

"You don't have to get all paternal on me."

And that's how I feel in that moment—like her father, like I'm imparting wisdom to her that she's not ready to accept.

"You would be a good dad, I think," she continues after

a pause, as if she knows me well enough to make such an assertion.

I call her bluff: "What makes you think that?"

"Just a hunch."

She pulls her knees to her chest, forcing herself into a fetal position, though the seat is making it difficult. When I'm home in my own bed, I sleep like that—on my side, knees bent. It's like it's our goal, as adults, to somehow make it back to the warmth and comfort and safety of the womb. She falls asleep and I drive, not needing to put my foot on the brake once until we cross the Los Angeles County line.

When I drop her off, her old Mercedes is the only car in the movie theater parking lot.

"Thanks for everything," she says, shoulders slouched in submissive gratitude.

"It was nice to have you along." I almost don't want to admit this. It seems to contradict my conviction that life is just one shitty situation after another.

She looks up, smiles, then leans across the center console and gives me a loose hug.

"I owe you one."

I wave her off, and she shuts the door. I wait until she gets in her car and starts it before I go on my way. When I come to the first red light, sitting there with a Pearl Jam song on the oldies station (which makes me feel ancient), I have a strange sensation of loneliness. Not emptiness—that feeling of hopeless finality that comes when someone is gone completely—but loneliness, that feeling of want that comes when someone is there, but not *there*. The light turns green and, for a second, I wish Riko were here to give me her best youthful, naïve guess as to what this means.

Tomonaga Osada, a local official in Aichi prefecture, suggested that authorities distribute secretly punctured condoms to young married couples to help boost the birth rate. His unorthodox ploy did not garner much support, but it did reflect the growing concern about Japan's demographic plight. The fact is that there aren't enough babies being born to maintain the population.

Across the country, hundreds of towns are expected to disappear in coming years as young women migrate to bigger cities. And, once in those bigger cities, they aren't having babies either. Some women want to be stay-at-home moms, but they can't find men who can support a traditional family. It used to be that men had permanent jobs as part of shūshin koyō, Japan's system of "lifetime employment," which disallows layoffs (at worst, unnecessary workers were sent to "banishment rooms" with minimal work responsibilities until they became so disheartened that they quit). Now, since the prime minister has lifted restrictions on layoffs, "lifetime employment" is no longer a guarantee. More women have become focused on their careers and are all too aware of the childcare shortage. Even if women do have children, they often have only one because of the cost of raising a kid (upward of 60 million yen, apparently).

The Japanese government has stepped in to try to encourage childbearing. They've distributed a "women's handbook" with fertility education. There are even state-sponsored matchmaking events. It's hard to imagine such a thing being necessary in the United States, where the families with the fewest resources seem to have the most children (does stating this make me an asshole?). A possible solution: send our extra children to Japan. You don't have to say it, I know—stating that makes me an asshole.

十四

Everything would be different if I'd remembered to buy condoms.

It was a stupid thing to forget on the night you plan to tell your girlfriend you bought tickets for the two of you to go to Japan. To see the cherry blossoms she so loves. To fulfill a dream of hers, basically.

I knew she would kiss my face repeatedly, thank me over and over again, jump up and down, ask "Is this for real?", and then take me to the bedroom to show me how much she loved me. I knew it'd be a celebratory evening. I'd remembered to buy the champagne, just not the condoms.

We lay naked, her on top of me, pressing herself into me. We did this often—flirted with what most young couples consider disaster. She wasn't on the pill, said it screwed with her hormones, messed with her *chi* or whatever. It was more exciting this way. I'd rub against her, get myself wet with her, sometimes even go inside her for a moment, in search of that feeling you had when you were seventeen, when you got that rush of disobe- dience while bargaining with the first girl you ever loved: "Just for a second, I promise." We were always responsible when it mattered though—she more than me. She'd press her hands into my chest and say, "Condom, Jonathan," and I'd do the familiar arm-stretch to my nightstand drawer, where we kept our stash, surrounded by the confetti of my little scraps of paper.

Except we were out that night. The box was empty.

"Shit," I said, pulling out of her, despite everything in me telling me not to.

"What is it?"

"We're all out."

I sat up while she was still on top of me. She leaned forward, put her arms around my neck, kissed my ear.

"I can go to the store," I said, already envisioning the hassle of getting dressed, flattening my mussed-up hair, making the drive to the local pharmacy.

"Or you could just stay here."

She put me inside her again. I should have pushed her off, gently. She'd had a glass of champagne. I knew champagne made her instantaneously tipsy. It was while drinking cham- pagne that she giggled over the word "what" for a good twenty minutes while playing Scrabble: W-*hat*? W*h-at*?

"Sara, I don't know..."

"It's just one time."

It was the exact line they warn you about in those sex-ed videos in high school. Except in the videos, the guy is the one doing the convincing. As the woman, she was supposed to know better in these situations. Stupidly, I decided she did.

"Just one time," she pressed.

She was already moving up and down on me, making it nearly

impossible for me to access my better judgment. It's still my fault, though. I could have remembered the fucking condoms.

A few weeks later, she threw up. We blamed the previous night's Indian takeout. After all, she felt better by the afternoon. But then she felt sick again in the evening. And queasy most of the next day. And then again on Monday. We both knew what this could mean, but we avoided stating the possibility out loud. Instead, I brought her 7UP and saltines in bed and told her to take the day off.

She called while I was in a meeting with some stuffy businessmen from Hong Kong intent on proclaiming to the world that they made the best plasma television. "Better than the Japanese," they said. Even then, when I had yet to learn all about Japan's commitment to technological excellence, I doubted this.

"What do people want in a television?" As I posed this question, my phone vibrated on the table in front of me, flashing Sara's name. The clients looked at me expectantly, and I silenced the ringer.

"They want a clear picture. The clearest," I continued.

The phone flashed her name again. She never called me twice in a row. She hardly ever called me, period. She wasn't a phone person, used it mostly for practical reasons like "I'm stuck in traffic. Can you set the oven for 425?"

"So picture this: You show a guy watching a baseball game on TV. The screen is huge. The picture is so perfect that he becomes a part of the game, like he's there with all the other fans. Your headline: 'Be there. Without the drunk hecklers.'"

They nodded excitedly, repeating "drunk hecklers" to each other, confirming their understanding of this American term.

"Or, there's a woman watching a talk show. Something trashy like *Jerry Springer*. Your line: 'Make *Jerry Springer* a work of art.'"

They nodded again, and Creative Director Rick said he'd give them a few moments to talk among themselves. Once in the hallway, he shook my hand and said, "You have a great future ahead of you."

But then Sara called a third time and I knew, somehow, that Rick was wrong.

"I'm pregnant," she said, before "Hello," before chastising me for ignoring her previous calls.

"Are you sure?"

That's what the guy always asks, but when I asked it I felt like a prick, like I was calling into question her ability to pee on a stick and read the simple pictographic results.

"Yes. I'm sure," she said, appropriately annoyed. "I took three tests."

"Okay."

"No, it's not okay."

"We'll figure it out."

She sighed and said, "Whatever. I don't want to talk to you when you're at work."

And then she hung up.

For the record, "We'll figure it out" was not an empty promise. I really did think we would figure it out. The truly catastrophic accidental pregnancies happened to teenagers, college students, poor people. We were two gainfully employed adults. We had a home together. Neither of us had a severe mental illness or a drug addiction. And, if all went according to plan, I would put a ring on her finger. In Japan. We could still go to Japan, couldn't we? She'd be—what?—six months along or so? It would make for a good story for our child. It didn't occur to me that we wouldn't have the child. In my fantasies, we'd even enjoy being parents. We'd be optimistic with our choice of words, always calling the baby a "surprise," never a "mistake." We'd look back on Sara's anti-motherhood beliefs and laugh.

When I got home from work, Sara wasn't there. She hadn't left a note, contrary to her usual M.O. when she had to make a quick trip. I took a beer from the fridge, wondering if it'd be my last one for a while, if I'd join Sara in forgoing alcohol for the next nine months. When I'd finished it and sat through an hour of *Forensic Files* reruns and she still wasn't home, I called her cell phone.

"Where are you?"

Her voice was shaky, like she was running or crying really hard.

"You're going to think I'm crazy."

She blew her nose, not far from the receiver.

"What's wrong?"

"I'm at the storage unit. I don't know why. I just had to be somewhere alone. And I remembered that this blanket my grandma made me when I was a kid was in a box here."

"I'll be there soon."

The storage unit facility was dark. I couldn't imagine many people would transport their belongings after sundown, on an unseasonably cool night when the mist wants so badly to be rain. I pulled up to the gate and rolled down the window to enter our code. I still have that code on the little card the facility manager gave us back when we got the place. It resides between a long-expired library card and a Ralphs grocery store card.

The parking lot was empty, except for Sara's sedan, parked haphazardly across two spots. I took the elevator to the second floor. The halls were quiet, littered with moving carts and dollies, remnants of the frenzied activity of moving.

I could hear her crying before I even rounded the corner. When I got to our unit, the door was rolled up halfway. I pushed it up all the way so I could get inside, and she was just sitting there on top of the washing machine, wrapped in a blanket so often consulted for comfort over many years that the threads were coming out.

"Hi," she said, looking up.

"Can you even tell it's me through all those tears?" I asked, putting one hand on each of her thighs. "I could be a serial killer roaming the halls, looking for distressed women."

She laughed, which I took as a good sign.

"Hey," I said, ducking to put myself in her line of sight. "What's going on?"

"I'm freaking out."

"I can see that."

She pulled both hands through her hair. I'd never seen her like this.

"We'll get through this. It'll be okay."

"Will it, though?"

It was the most complicated, simple question I'd ever been asked. She started biting her nails, and I saw no choice but to give her an equally complicated, simple answer: "Somehow, yes. It will."

"How do you know?"

"I don't. But I'm sure you could take a survey to find out how people react to this type of thing and they would all say the outcome was just fine."

"They say that to rationalize their choices. You're only as happy as you tell yourself to be."

And maybe she didn't have it in her to tell herself to be happy as a mother.

"We just found out about this, okay? Let's take some time to think before we get too upset."

"We don't really have much time," she said.

I didn't know if she meant time to get rid of the kid or time to get a crib and figure out where the baby would sleep. I was afraid to ask.

"This just isn't what I pictured, Jonathan."

She hardly ever called me Jonathan. It was always "babe" or "baby." When she did call me Jonathan, she was angry—spitting it out like a curse word. I told her it was like she was using my own name against me.

She pushed herself up and off the washing machine and paced back and forth, making a winding path around the strewn-about boxes containing our previous lives.

"We'll make it work," I said.

"I don't want to just *make it work*."

It was a fair protest.

"I can make a crappy brochure design work. I can make overcooked pasta work. I can make frizzy hair work. But this? *This*?"

"You don't have frizzy hair," I said, trying to keep things light. It's a bad habit of mine—making jokes at the worst times.

"Can you be serious for five seconds?" she said.

That's an awful lot to ask is what I wanted to say. I refrained.

"I don't know anything about being a mother."

I considered this a subtle insinuation that she was considering keeping the baby. Obviously, that was my immediate choice—to keep the baby. Maybe it was an immature and selfish impulse. Maybe I imagined that keeping the baby would mean keeping Sara tethered to me, indefinitely. A baby was even better than a ring.

"Look, we will figure it out. Why don't we take a couple days to think things over? You always feel better after a good night's sleep."

I put my hand on her shoulder. It was the most sincerely consoling I'd ever been with a woman. This was the first crisis Sara and I'd had together, one that would quickly morph into the last. I didn't know what I was doing, felt like I was emulating a nice guy on a TV show. But she gave me a weak smile, which told me I was pulling it off.

"Trust me," I told her, with an earnestness to my voice that I wanted so much to believe. "It will all be okay."

I hugged her, tightly, to convince her I was right. But, in time, we would both see me as a liar.

Things to do before I die—updated:

- Go to Japan
- ~~Visit my parents~~
- ~~Get the complete collection of Seinfeld and watch all episodes~~
- Give my clothes to the Salvation Army
- ~~Take all my loose change to a Coinstar machine~~
- Learn Japanese
- Get rid of the damn storage unit

Turns out I had $65.37 in change sitting in one of those big plastic cups they give you in Vegas to hold your chips. I figured I could put that money toward hiring a company to come and haul away everything in the storage unit. But I'm kind of opposed to such a company. They make a living off other people's laziness. I suppose most companies function this way, but these guys (they call themselves "junkies") do it so damn blatantly. Besides, I remembered that Riko had said she would be moving into her own place. She might need some of the crap that's in there. And maybe what she doesn't need could be included with my Salvation Army purge. In any case, the storage unit will be gone soon enough. One less thing my parents will have to fret about when I'm gone. This is what I call end-of-life efficiency.

十五

We have learned all forty-six characters in the hiragana alphabet, and Miyagi Sensei is introducing us to katakana, a totally separate alphabet created to incorporate words from other languages. They take the word *"television,"* for example, and assign it symbols that match up to the sounds in their language: *te-re-bu,* in this case. There is no "L" or "V" sound in Japanese, but they make do. "L" becomes "R" and "V" becomes "B," which is why you might hear a Japanese person say "I rike the Rorring Stones" or "Happy Balentine's Day" (interesting fact: in Japan, the women are supposed to give gifts and chocolates to men, not the other way around). In any case, the phonetics may be screwy, but you have to appreciate their attempts to assimilate like the good Japanese people they are.

Miyagi Sensei has us repeat after her: *"Ko-n-pyu-ta."*

We say this three times, in unison.

"What is this word?" she asks us, with a smile, trying to prove to us that Japanese is not so hard to decipher after all. Unfortunately for Miyagi Sensei, we all look at her blankly. We have no idea what she's talking about until she points to a picture of a computer. Then it makes sense. *Ko-n-pyu-ta.* That's how katakana works.

When she's tired of this game of slow repetition and pointing, and we're tired of sounding like idiots, she tells us to write our names (our real ones, not our Japanese ones) using the katakana alphabet. I'm at a loss, and the confused look on my face invites the teacher's assistant to do his job and assist me. He takes my pen and writes this in my notebook:

ジョナサン

"*Jyo-na-sa-n,*" he says, slowly.

It makes me uneasy to have a man my age hovering over me, enunciating like I'm either deaf or very old. Nevertheless, I repeat after him, taking note of this as the first time I've felt lame saying my own name.

With the remainder of class, Miyagi Sensei tells us to practice writing the katakana characters and rehearsing their associated sounds. Katakana is no easier to remember than hiragana, but here are some of my favorite mnemonic devices:

- Ro: Round this is not. Square it is. I use a Yoda voice in my head for this one.

- Ma: Madonna's tit in the early nineties.

- Ho: Hos go to church to be forgiven for their skanky sins.

After class, Riko and I walk to the parking lot together, like usual. The campus is outfitted with extremely bright lights to scare away wannabe rapists, but I still feel the need to make sure she gets into her car safely.

"I have so many flash cards to make," she says, sounding flustered. "Do you think the katakana is going to be on the final? That gives us, like, two weeks to memorize all those characters."

"I'm sure it'll be fine," I tell her. Apparently, I'm a pro at making this promise.

"It's just that I have work, and the apartment move, and—"

"I wanted to talk to you about that, actually."

We arrive at her car right then, and she gets inside, leaving the door open for me to lean against it.

"Do you need furniture? A washer and dryer? That type of thing?"

"Well, yeah," she says, with that sassy look preteens use when they roll their eyes and say "Duh."

"You may be in luck, then. I have a whole storage unit full of stuff I don't need," I say. "And if you help me clean it out this weekend, you can have whatever you want from it."

"For free?"

"Sure. I don't need the money."

She looks at me like she's just won the showcase on *The Price Is Right*.

"You're serious?"

"It would be pretty shitty of me to be joking."

"I was planning to just use a sleeping bag and take my clothes to a Laundromat and get takeout and sit on the floor to eat."

"How very Japanese of you."

"You're a lifesaver. Just call me and tell me what time to be there."

"Will do."

She's about to pull the door closed when she says, "You're sure you don't need the stuff?"

"I'm positive."

Sara left me with our storage unit. When she told me she wanted to be on her own (I'm getting to that part), she threatened to make a new life with the contents of that storage unit. Somehow, I persuaded her to trust me a while longer. It wouldn't matter in the end. She would leave me anyway, and the stuff in the storage unit would become just that—stuff.

After we went to a doctor to confirm that she was, in fact, pregnant, we became the type of couple I'd never thought we would be—the bickering, resentful, fighting kind. I knew it was about the baby, but we argued about everything except that—my negligence with taking out the trash, my refusal to put my dirty socks in the laundry basket, my inconsideration when putting sticky fingers on the remote control. For the most part, I let her complain and criticize, thinking of it as necessary venting. We had a life change ahead of us. There were hormones involved. I had to pick my proverbial battles. But when she flipped out upon seeing an empty roll of paper towels, when she chastised me for not replacing it, when she asked "How can we have a kid if you still act like one?", I'd had it.

She had her hands on her hips, one foot turned out to the side, in stereotypical bitch stance. She opened the cupboard and pulled out a roll of paper towels, placing it on the counter with dramatic flair.

"See? Is that so hard? You just reach into the cabinet, you get a new roll, you throw away the empty roll. Done."

She looked at me in that way you hate to have someone look at you. The stare says, "Holy crap, you are not who I thought you were." The stare makes you wonder who you thought you were and, sometimes, it makes you wonder who you *are.*

"You don't have to say it like that, okay?"

"Well, I go to the trouble of trekking to the grocery store to make sure we *have* paper towels. All *you* have to do is take out a new roll."

"This isn't about the paper towels, is it?"

She made a sound somewhere between a grunt and a sigh.

"This is about the condoms. You're still mad I forgot to buy condoms."

"No," she said, holding a corrective finger at me, "this is about the paper towels." Then, under her breath, "Though, yes, I'm still mad about the condoms."

We'd been over this before, gone back and forth trying to place blame, as if determining fault would solve something. I forgot the condoms, she forgot common sense. But then, as she said, she forgot common sense because I remembered champagne. My only rebuttal was that she should have remembered that champagne turned her into a complete idiot.

"We're not getting anywhere with this," I said. "You're pregnant. We should probably talk more about the future, not the past."

She sat on the counter, arms crossed in front of her chest.

"Is it *me*? Do you not want to have a child with *me*?" I asked.

It was a question that had been nagging me ever since she called me, upset, with the news the pee sticks had told her.

"Jesus, it's not you. It's just a big fucking deal, period." She released a breath, so big that it made her bangs flutter.

"Okay, but here we are. Is it any comfort that it's with me?"

"I don't know, okay?" she said. She leaned back so her head rested on the cabinet door.

I didn't want to consider getting rid of the baby. I'd always called myself pro-choice, professing support of women's rights, mostly as a politically correct way of saying that I hoped any girl I knocked up would have an abortion. That was before Sara, though, when I couldn't imagine loving someone enough to have a child with her. Looking at Sara then, imaging the bean-sized human inside her, I was convinced that killing that bean-sized human would be the death of us.

Maybe, though, I had to let us die for Sara to survive.

"There are options," I said, tentatively.

She met my eyes.

"Are there?" Her inquiry was weak, barely audible.

"I'll support whatever you decide." I knew this had to be true, whether I wanted it to be or not.

"I'm just so confused," she said. She put her head in her hands. I approached her, with caution, waiting for her to scream at me again about the paper towels. She didn't, though.

She kept her head in her hands, and her shoulders started to shake as she cried.

"I think I need to move out," she said, the words trapped in that hidden place between her chin and her chest, shielded by her falling-about hair.

"What?"

She looked up. Her face was red, wet.

"I need space to think. There's too much pressure on me this way."

"I just said I would support whatever you decide. There's no pressure from me."

"Yes, there is," she said. "I know what you want, no matter what you say. I can feel that every time you look at me."

There was nothing I could say, because she was right.

"I'll just get the furniture and everything from the storage unit. We'll live apart for a while."

I didn't want her to resort to that, though, to needing the storage unit. The storage unit was reserved for a worst-case scenario, for the complete failure of our togetherness. I knew that once she rented her own apartment and filled it with our leftovers, that would be the end.

"There are lots of month-to-month rentals in this area," she said, as if she'd already researched it. That hurt more than anything.

"No," I said.

She looked confused. I'd never denied her anything up to that point, for better or worse.

"I don't think we need space to work through this. If you feel pressure, I think you need to feel that pressure. We're in this together. This isn't just about you."

If you'd come into the kitchen in that exact moment and seen the look on her face, you would have thought I'd just slapped her.

"Let's see a therapist, someone who specializes in this type of thing," I said.

The idea had come to me suddenly, inspired by some desperate attempt to believe in what people who like Oprah profess.

"A shrink?" She was just as perplexed by the suggestion as I was.

"We need a third party, someone objective."

She shrugged her shoulders half-heartedly, as if the weight they were holding was too much for her.

"If that's what you think is best, I'll give it a shot."

I kissed her forehead. She leaned into my chest.

"Why do they call it a shrink?" she asked.

I had no idea, but I said, "I think it's because they make your problems smaller."

"That sounds nice."

I put my arms around her and lifted her off the counter. She wrapped her legs around my waist, her arms around my neck, resting her head against my cheek. I rubbed her back, my hand going over and over the bumps of her spine.

"Will you take me to bed?" she said in a small voice.

And I did, convinced for the first time in my life that, maybe, I would be a good dad.

Japanese Turning to Suicide by 'Detergent Death'
NPR

In the past year, some 300 people in Japan have killed themselves by deliberately mixing bleach with other household cleaners and then breathing the toxic hydrogen sulfide fumes.

BBC reporter Chris Hogg says 50 people in one month alone have killed themselves that way. The Japanese have been alarmed both by the ease of carrying out a "detergent death" and by the way the toxic gas can seep out and affect people living around the victim.

Last week, after a 24-year-old man committed suicide with the deadly brew, authorities had to evacuate 350 people in his Hokkaido neighborhood. On April 24, the suicide of a 14-year-old girl caused 70 neighbors in the same apartment house to fall ill.

Hogg says authorities have linked the problem to Web sites and online message boards where people discuss ways to commit suicide. Some of the online recipes describe detergent death as relatively painless.

"What's happened in the last few days is that the

national police agency has urged Internet service providers to delete information from these Web sites about how to make hydrogen sulfide," he says. "For the first time, really, we're seeing authorities trying to act on this issue."

The ranks of detergent deaths come from the same demographic range as other types of suicides in Japan, Hogg says. Japanese people who kill themselves are often elderly and worried about burdening their families, but he says younger Japanese also turn to suicide.

"This is a society where this is enormous pressure on people," Hogg says. "And it's also not a Christian society. Because it's not a Christian society, in the moral code there aren't the same sanctions, if you like, against suicide. There is a long tradition of suicides in Japan, going right back to the samurai."

十六

The couples therapist was a middle-aged woman named Janet Bridge.

"Do you think that's her real name?" I asked Sara as we pulled into the parking garage next to Janet Bridge's office building.

"What do you mean?"

"It sounds too perfect for a therapist, *bridging* the gaps between couples and whatnot."

"Like how the Channel 7 weather guy is Dallas Raines?" she said.

God, this girl was my soul mate.

"Exactly."

Janet Bridge was an extremely petite, fifty-something-year-old woman with big eyes that seemed to take up half the real estate of her face. If I had to guess, she'd been a gymnast or a horse jockey in a former life. She flipped through our paperwork, humming to herself as she skimmed, then looked up at us with a smile and said, "So."

"So," I repeated back.

"You're pregnant," she said to Sara.

Sara nodded. "Almost seven weeks."

She was counting. I took this to be a good thing.

"And you're not sure about being a mother, is that right?" Janet Bridge said, looking down at our paperwork, then peering up at us again through her glasses.

"In a nutshell," Sara said. "I've always said I didn't want kids."

"Can you tell me why?"

"I don't know. It seems so all-consuming, having a child. I like to volunteer and I like to do my art and I like to travel. I just...how is any of that possible with a child?"

"Lots of people have children and still do those things," Janet Bridge said.

I got tentatively excited at the notion that Janet Bridge was on my side.

"Maybe they try...and they get very stressed out trying," Sara said.

"Maybe," Janet Bridge said.

Come back to my side, Janet.

"It just seems like a huge life change," Sara said with a sigh.

"It is," Janet agreed.

"What if I have this baby and I regret it?"

All I heard was "What if I have this baby?" I reached across the cushion separating us on the couch and grabbed Sara's hand.

"I suppose that's possible," Janet said. "Though most people don't seem to express regret over having their children, do they?"

"What if they're kidding themselves?"

Janet shrugged. "What if they are?"

"What if it's always in the back of my head that I shouldn't have become a mother?"

"What if it's not?" Janet said.

Sara just nodded a pensive nod, and Janet turned her attention to me.

"You want this baby, Jonathan?" Janet asked me. She had to look down at her paperwork to remember my name.

"I do," I said, infusing my voice with the confidence I thought Sara needed to hear.

"Why?"

"Sara would be a great mom. She really would. She's made me such a better human, so imagine what she could do with a kid. A kid is a blank slate. I want to spend my life with Sara— with a kid or without. We didn't expect this; but I didn't expect I'd meet Sara either, and that's worked out great."

Sara squeezed my hand. When I looked over at her, there were tears in her eyes.

"Sara, how does that make you feel?" Janet asked.

"Good," she managed, her voice small and squeaky.

"Sara, is it accurate to say that you're at least considering keeping the baby?" Janet asked.

"Well, yeah, of course."

Janet retrieved a box of Kleenex and passed it to Sara.

"What if we decided, for good, that you were keeping the baby? Right here and now," Janet said. "How would you feel?"

Sara dabbed at her eyes with the Kleenex. Several seconds passed, and I got nervous.

Finally, Sara said, "Relieved."

"Relieved?" Janet pressed.

Sara nodded. "Relieved to have the decision made."

"Interesting," Janet said. "You didn't say scared or anxious. You said relieved."

I turned to Sara and said in a quiet voice, as if this were a private conversation that Janet Bridge wasn't privy to, "Maybe we just need to go all in. Maybe we just need to say we're having a baby and let that be reality. The back-and-forth is killing both of us."

Sara looked at me with mascara-smudged eyes and said, "Yeah. Maybe."

"The fact is," Janet Bridge said, "none of us knows what's going to happen in our lives. Our paths meander. Nobody can tell you what's right or wrong. All we can do is use the information at hand to make the best decision possible."

I was—still am—fairly confident that this was a Christopher Walken line in *Wedding Crashers*. This is the type of wisdom health insurance pays for.

Sara never said outright that her decision was made, but her actions spoke for her. Used books started arriving at the house—books about pregnancy and labor and taking care of newborns. She collected them in a stack on her nightstand. She started reporting the baby's size to me—a raspberry, then a cherry, then a strawberry, then a lime. She poked me in the side when I said, "Are we having a baby, or a piece of fruit?"

The night before our first ultrasound, the twelve-week ultrasound, I caught her standing in front of the mirror, naked, analyzing her figure from the side.

"Look," she said. "A little belly."

I couldn't see what she saw. She looked the same to me. But I said, "Look at that."

I don't know what I was expecting at that first ultrasound appointment, but it wasn't an actual baby on screen. But, sure enough, there was an obvious head and an obvious body. Future arms and future legs were moving around.

The ultrasound technician was a thirty-something woman in pink scrubs. "You see that?" she said, pointing to the flicker on screen.

We nodded. It was like a loosely screwed-in light bulb flashing.

"That's the heartbeat," she said.

"Wow," Sara said.

The technician flipped a switch so we could hear the sound— like a horse galloping under water.

"That sounds like a good heartbeat if I ever heard one," I said.

"One hundred fifty-seven," the technician said. "Nice and strong."

When the technician left, and we waited for the doctor. Sara looked at me, smiling, and said, "I'm growing a human being."

After that appointment, Sara called her parents and her best friends to tell them the news. It had been our little secret until then. I preferred it that way, liked that there was this thing between us that nobody else could touch. Once they all knew (well, not all; we decided to wait to tell coworkers until she was showing more), they started bombarding us with questions— questions about our plans to get a bigger place (we didn't have any, figured our guest room/office would just acquire another "slash"—guest room/office/nursery) and our plans to get married (I had those, but Sara was unaware). It grated. "They're peeing all over our baby," I told Sara. She did her usual thing—poked me in the side.

When Sara started complaining that her clothes were getting tight, we made a trip to the mall and spent an hour in the maternity store. Typically, Sara wasn't a big shopper. In the time we'd been together, I'd seen her buy things here and there, but she never went out with the express purpose of purchasing clothes. She'd told me it was one of the many things I should be grateful for when it came to dating her: she just couldn't be bothered with fashion. But when she was pregnant, that changed. She wanted to show off her belly (which, at that point, was not really a belly, but she saw the potential). She bought stretchy, flowing dresses and long knit shirts and pants that had, in lieu of a waistband, extra fabric that stretched up and over the belly-to-be. After spending a couple hundred bucks, we walked out of the store and saw the strategically placed baby-things store. I knew she would want to go in. "Just to look," she said.

It wasn't just to look, though. Of course it wasn't. We walked out forty-five minutes later with enough baby outfits to attire five children. I asked her if she was planning on adopting, if she was aspiring to be Angelina Jolie. "It's good for me to start buying stuff for the baby. Makes it seem real," she said.

Except, turns out, it wasn't real. Or, it was. And then it wasn't.

We went for another doctor's appointment a month after the first one. Sara peed in a cup and stepped on the scale and got her blood pressure taken. Then the nurse led us to the exam room, where Sara lay back on the table and flipped through a magazine, waiting for the ultrasound technician.

"I think it's a boy," she said, not looking up from the magazine. "I just have a feeling."

The internet had said it was possible we'd find out the sex that day.

"We shall name him Ralph," I said.

She looked up, smiled. "No, we shall not."

When the ultrasound technician came in, Sara lifted her shirt and folded the bottom half of it beneath the underwire of her bra. The technician squirted gel on her bare almost-belly and started moving the wand around.

"Let's see the flicker," Sara said.

I was sitting in a chair right next to her. I leaned closer to see the screen in front of us.

It was obvious that something was wrong.

"I don't know what I'm looking at," Sara said, tilting her head.

At the previous appointment, the baby, our blob, had been swimming around the black sea of amniotic fluid. Now, there were just small pockets of black, the baby squished up between them, contorted.

"Well, the baby is in a bit of a funny position," the technician said. But it was obvious from her tone that "funny" was not the right word. "Heart rate is fine—160. I'm going to get the doctor."

She gave us a tight smile that was not at all reassuring.

Sara looked at me with terror in her eyes. "Do you think everything is okay?" she asked me.

I had no idea. How could I? But I said, "Yes."

It's hard for me to remember the doctor as anything but a prick. I know—don't shoot the messenger. I didn't shoot him. I just think he's a prick.

"The fluid is low," he said, as if we would know what this meant.

"What does that mean?" Sara said, asking the obvious. Her face had become suddenly devoid of color.

"Hard to say, exactly. There could be a deformity with the baby's kidneys or urinary tract, meaning the baby is swallowing the amniotic fluid, but not processing and excreting it properly. That's what amniotic fluid is, basically—fetal urine."

We nodded, though we still didn't understand.

"It could also be a problem with the placenta," he said.

"But, no matter what, it's a problem," Sara said. I could tell she wanted so badly for him to disagree.

"Well, yes."

"Is it common?" I asked.

He rolled his eyes up into his head, as if searching for a percentage. Then he said, "Not *common*. But I see it every now and then."

"What do we do?" Sara asked.

"I want you to rest, stay off your feet. We'll check the fluid levels again in two weeks, see if there's improvement."

"And if there's not?" she asked.

I winced. Did we want to know the answer?

"Well, as you can see, the baby can't move around much if there's not enough fluid. Growth is affected, at the very least. Organs get compressed. At worst, the baby would press against the umbilical cord, reducing blood flow and causing. . . "

He didn't say it, but we knew what he meant. *Death.*

He printed out the one ultrasound image he was able to get of the baby's face, the head turned out toward us, black circles of eyes seemingly saying "Help! I'm in trouble." Sara put it on her nightstand when we got home. I don't know how she could look at it. It still gives me occasional nightmares.

Sara was silent for the duration of the drive home. It was only when I put the car in park that she said, "I can't believe this is happening."

"I bet things will look better in a couple weeks," I said. Circumstances had turned me into a glass-half-full type. One of us had to be.

Sara googled her anxious heart out until well past midnight that night. She found some stories of women whose levels improved. They recommended drinking a gallon of water a day, eating water-heavy foods (like fruits), soaking in baths, and lying on the left side (which, apparently, gets blood to the placenta more efficiently).

She didn't go to work the next day—and wouldn't go to work for the two weeks until our next doctor's appointment. I went to work because it wouldn't do any good to sit at home with her, googling. Now, I wish I'd sat at home with her, googling.

That first day after the "your baby might be in trouble" news, I forgot I had to attend a new business pitch at a vitamin-manufacturing company. I was supposed to represent the copy department of Radley and Reiser. I should have told Rick that I wasn't feeling well. Instead, I attempted to fake enthusiasm and sound smart, which did not go well. After the meeting, Rick asked if I was high. We didn't get the business.

Two days later, I came home from work and discovered Sara lying flat in our bed, her almost-belly exposed and covered in gel. She had a small device in her hand, connected to a small version of the doctor's ultrasound wand.

"What are you doing?" I asked.

"I bought it online," she said, "to find the baby's heartbeat."

I wasn't sure if this was a good idea, but I couldn't resist saying, "And?"

"I found it earlier—159," she said. "I can't find it now."

She moved the wand through the gel, but there was only static. Then a whooshing noise came over the speaker.

"Is that it?" I asked, prematurely excited.

"No," she said. "That's the blood flowing in my arteries or something. That's what the girl on YouTube said, at least."

"Let me try," I told her.

I tried until there was no gel left, until her stomach was sticky and dry. Finally, she said, "The baby moves around a lot. The girl said that too. It's hard to find the heartbeat when they're so small. We're probably not doing it right."

The two weeks felt like a year. When we went in for the appointment, the prick doctor greeted us. We were pegged as problematic now, too advanced for the ultrasound technician in the pink scrubs.

"How are you feeling?" Dr. Prick asked Sara. "Any bleeding? Spotting? Cramping?"

"No," she said. "I feel fine."

We had convinced ourselves, during those two weeks, that everything was okay. There were no signs to indicate otherwise. Sara drank so much water that she was using the bathroom every twenty minutes. She was bloated with watermelon, her skin pruned from hours spent in the bath. She took the temperature of the bath to make sure the baby didn't overheat. She was so on top of it. Everything had to be okay.

Sara lay flat on the exam table, and her inhalation of breath was audible. I sat in the chair next to the table, reached out and clutched her ankle. We stared at the screen, awaiting the image of our baby.

It wasn't obvious at first if the situation had improved. The baby didn't seem as contorted as the previous time. I could tell it was, in fact, a baby.

But, before we could get hopeful, Dr. Prick said, "I'm not seeing a heartbeat."

My ears started ringing. Through the ringing, I heard Sara shriek: "What?"

Dr. Prick interpreted this as an actual question and went on to explain.

"The way the baby is measuring tells me the death occurred shortly after the last appointment."

Which explained why we weren't able to get a reading on the fetal Doppler.

"I'd guess a few days after the last appointment," he said.

I hated him. I hated him for telling Sara to rest for two weeks. I hated him for not checking on her sooner, for letting her sit around with our dead baby and all that irrational hope inside of her.

"Do you see how blood is no longer going to the baby?" he said, pointing to the screen.

Sara wasn't looking at the screen, though.

The medical interest on his face disgusted me.

"Can you stop?" Sara screamed. She was head-down, chin to chest.

Dr. Prick seemed disappointed, like he wanted to continue examining our mysteriously dead baby. He handed Sara a box of Kleenex, a robotic gesture if I ever saw one. I continued clutching her ankle, like it was a railing in a fast-moving subway car.

Dr. Prick said there were two options: they could induce labor if Sara wanted to give birth and see the baby, or Sara could have a surgery called a D&E—dilation and evacuation.

"I don't want to see the baby," Sara said.

I felt relieved, then guilty that I felt relieved. Should we want to see our baby? We looked up photos on the internet later, photos of gray, lifeless, very miniature but perfectly formed humans. I knew then we'd made the right choice.

"I don't do D&Es, but I'll call a doctor who does," Dr. Prick said.

The fact that he didn't do the procedure made us aware of how uncommon our predicament was. Less than 1 percent of babies die in the second trimester.

"We'll get to the bottom of this," Dr. Prick said. "We'll do testing on the fetus."

I hated—still hate—that word: *fetus*.

He said we could stay in the exam room as long as we needed and then left us alone.

"This is going to fuck me up," Sara said, sobbing.

A prophecy.

"I just can't believe this," I said, because I couldn't, and I didn't know what else to say.

Dr. Prick came back quickly with a business card for another doctor, with an appointment time for the next day written on the back. It was obvious by the way he lingered there that he needed us to leave, that other patients were waiting.

"I don't want to walk through the waiting room," Sara said.

Doctors' offices really should have a secret back exit for people who get bad news.

"I've got you," I told her.

I ushered her down the hallway, then through the waiting room packed with women and their bellies full of healthy babies, like a security guard protecting a pop star. When we got outside, her knees buckled and she fell to the ground, burying her head in her hands and crying so hard that she couldn't catch her breath. A man passed us, staring. I gave him the finger.

❃

That night, we passed a beer back and forth between us—Sara's first beer in months.

"I feel guilty drinking this," she said. "What if they made a mistake? What if the baby's still alive?"

I didn't respond, thought it best if she realized her denial and delusion on her own. She took bigger sips.

"Are we going to survive this?" she asked next.

Her eyes were red and puffy, pleading.

"Of course we are," I said.

I really thought we would.

The diagnosis on the surgery packet: *fetal demise*. I can't imagine a more depressing pair of words. I sat in the waiting room, the packet in my lap, waiting for a nurse to tell me she was all done. They'd said it would take only an hour.

When they brought me back to see her, she was reclining back on the gurney, looking woozy. She gave me a weak smile. When she sat up, blood saturated the sheets beneath her.

"That's normal," the nurse said, before I could ask.

I had a plastic bag with her clothes and shoes. I pulled out one thing at a time, helped her get dressed. The nurse gave her a giant pad for her underwear. I tried not to think too much about the blood, afraid I'd pass out. I did once, in college. I sliced my finger open while chopping something, and I woke up on the floor. In my defense, I'd been drunk before the slice.

The nurse helped Sara into a wheelchair and gave her a cup of ice chips. I left to get the car, pull it around front so she wouldn't have to walk far. The drive home was mostly silent. At one point, I asked if she was okay, and she said, "How could I be?"

At home, I walked her to bed, my hands on her hips. I fluffed the pillows to feel like I was helping somehow. I asked her too many times if she needed anything, and she said no. She said the pain wasn't bad, but she took the Norco pills anyway. To zone out, I guess. Her speech became slowed and slurred. When she fell asleep, I took two of the pills myself. I wanted to zone out too.

The next morning, she was inconsolable. The internet warned me of this, the hormone crash. To be honest, and I know this makes me an asshole, I couldn't be around her like that. It was too hard to see her that way. Sara was always the better, stronger one of the two of us. Seeing her reduced to that...I just couldn't handle it. I went to work like normal, fitting the stereotype of the emotionally unaffected man. I told everyone she had pneumonia and I wasn't sure when she'd be back. "Well, take good care of her," they said.

She called me in the middle of the workday, while I was in a meeting, pretending to pay attention.

"I talked to the HR person at work to see if I could get bereavement leave because I'm almost out of sick time," she said. It was hard to understand her because of the tears and the Norco.

"That's a good idea," I said.

"No it's not," she shouted. "She said losing a baby in the second trimester doesn't *qualify* for bereavement leave. Like, our baby wasn't a real person or something."

She was furious.

"I'm sure you can take medical leave. We can talk to the doctor," I said. Another stereotype: man, the fixer.

"That's not the point," she said. "The point is that our baby was a real person."

"Babe, I know that," I said. "It's just a dumb policy."

"*You're* a dumb policy," she said and hung up. When I tried to call back, she didn't answer.

I stayed at work later than usual that night. Again, I'm an asshole. When I finally came home, she was sitting up in bed watching HGTV. She looked awful—her face pale, eyes swollen slits of their former selves, hair tied in a messy knot on top of her head.

"Hey, babe. How you doing?" I said, the eggshells cracking under my feet.

"I feel completely alone," she said. "I'm the only one hurting. You're fine, apparently."

"I'm not fine," I said. "I'm just trying to move forward."

"Well, enjoy that. Must be lovely to have that ability," she said. Then: "My boobs started leaking milk."

"Sara…"

"Fuck you," she said.

A few days later, she was calmer, but we still weren't right. We were awkward with each other in a way we'd never been before, sounding formal when inquiring about each other's days, saying "excuse me" when bumping into each other in the bathroom. I'm familiar with the stages of grief. I know there are five of them. But she seemed to be aware of only one: anger. I let her be, made myself the sacrificial punching bag.

I went with her to her postsurgical checkup, resenting that people who have lost babies need to share a waiting room with people having them. I could see the hate on Sara's face as she watched those pregnant women flipping through celebrity gossip magazines without a care in the world. I knew if I reached over and touched her, she would flinch like a startled animal.

The doctor said she was healed, everything was back to normal. Physically, at least. That's all doctors concern themselves with.

"What about the tests done on the baby?" I asked him as Sara closed her legs and removed her feet from the stirrups.

I thought if we knew what had gone wrong, we would have what everyone wants after a loss—closure.

"You'll have to take that up with your regular doctor," he said.

Dr. Prick.

We did take it up with Dr. Prick. Well, we took it up with his nurse, because he was far too busy with more important things.

"I'm very sorry to tell you this," the nurse said, her voice overly saccharine and fucking annoying, "but it appears the products of conception were not sent for testing."

Products of conception—like something sold alongside the condoms in a brightly lit aisle of Walgreens.

"What do you mean?" I asked.

"They should have been sent. It's standard. We can see if the lab still has the sample, but it's doubtful at this point."

Our baby, the sample.

Any small, nonphysical improvements Sara had been making were voided by this news.

"They threw away my baby without ever figuring out what happened," she screamed through tears.

She'd started saying "my baby," not "our baby."

"I know, sweetie. It's terrible," I said.

"That's all you're going to say? It's *terrible*? You're not going to *do* anything?"

"What do you want me to do?" I kept my voice calm, even.

"We should sue him."

The vengeance in her eyes, I'd never seen anything like it before.

"Okay," I said. "I'll look into it."

I had no intention, of course. I just wanted her to stop crying.

I returned all the baby stuff and maternity clothes while Sara was napping one Saturday afternoon. She was always napping. When I came home, she was awake, sitting up in bed.

"How you feeling today?" I asked.

I'd read some message boards online, and they said the general question of "How are you?" was far too overwhelming for the bereaved. It was more manageable for them to report on their feelings that day.

"You returned everything?" she said.

It was immediately obvious that the favor I'd thought I'd done had been a mistake.

"I thought all that stuff would make you sad."

"What's sad is that you clearly don't want to try to have another baby. You're already over it. Moving forward or whatever."

She wasn't totally wrong. I hadn't even thought of trying to have another baby. This had gone so horribly awry. I was concerned only with going back to normal, the way we'd been before all this. I'd started fixating on the Japan trip, thinking that would be our reset button.

"Sara, of course we can have another baby," I said. "I just thought having the stuff around would upset you. We can buy it all again."

"You could have just taken it to the storage unit," she said.

"I didn't think of that."

She rolled her eyes. "Of course you didn't."

I resorted to calling my mother, remembering that she'd had a miscarriage once too, a miscarriage so traumatic that she didn't want to try for another child. I'd been enough.

When I told her what had happened, my mother was quiet. I thought the call had dropped, but then I heard her sigh.

"Oh, Jonathan, she's going to need time," she said finally, her voice shaky and sad.

"How much time?" I asked.

"Your father asked the same question when this happened to us," she said, with a pitying sigh.

"So I just have to wait it out."

"That's how it works, I'm afraid."

I'd never find out how much time it would take.

Sara was gone a week later.

In Japan, women who experience miscarriage often find comfort in Jizo statues. These stone figurines line temples and cemeteries across the country. They have childlike faces and are adorned with red caps and bibs. They're believed to be protectors of unborn babies, babies who did not have a chance to build up good karma on earth. The Jizo helps smuggle the children into the afterlife in the sleeves of his robe.

I wish I'd known about this Japanese tradition when Sara was with me. I would have bought a Jizo statue online (they have them; I've checked). I would have put it in the corner of our bedroom. I would have encouraged her to crochet outfits for it and bake cookies for it. Maybe it would have helped. Maybe she'd still be with me.

十七

When I roll up the door of the storage unit, Riko gasps.

"Holy shit," she says, putting her hand over her mouth in astonishment. "You didn't accurately convey the amount of stuff."

"I don't think I accurately remembered the amount of stuff."

She walks around the best she can, considering there is barely any ground visible beneath all the crap, withdrawing her hands from the pockets of her oversized coat to keep balance. She lets out a deep breath and puts one foot on top of a box labeled "Kitchen" in Sara's messy handwriting. With hands on her hips, knee bent, vision forward, she looks like a mountain climber set on a summit.

"So, where do we start?"

"I have no idea," I say, because I don't. There really is more than I remembered. Boxes stacked from floor to ceiling, furniture pieces crammed together. There is no organization, no method to the madness, probably because Sara and I both thought—hoped—there wouldn't be any reason for organization or method. I, for one, envisioned us coming to terms with just purging everything one day, when we realized that neither of us was leaving the other, when we signed on for "forever" with naïve confidence.

"What do you need for your apartment?" I ask.

She surveys her options. "I don't know. The basics. A bed. This bookcase would be nice," she says, examining it, taking out the removable shelves as if inspecting the quality of the wood, like she has a right to be choosy.

"Let's divide everything into categories," she continues: "what you want to keep, what I can use for my apartment, what can be donated, and what's headed for the dumpster."

"I don't think there's anything I want to keep."

"Are you sure?"

"Yes. Let's just do your apartment, donations, and dumpster."

She shrugs, says "You're the boss," and gives me a mock salute.

"How am I supposed to know what to throw away?" she asks, opening one of the boxes. She takes out a squeezed, nearly empty toothpaste tube and turns it over in her hand. It's usually assumed that the man is the one who squeezes the toothpaste tube impulsively, irresponsibly, while the woman rolls it neatly from the bottom. Sara and I reversed this assumption.

"I mean, this is obviously trash," Riko says, tossing it, "but what about the other stuff?"

"Use your best judgment," I say. "I just want to get this over with."

With that, she goes to work. We are quiet for a good hour. Aside from furniture and appliances for Riko, most everything else is going into a trash pile. There are some things that Riko does not need, but someone might. She has stuck pink Post-its on these that say *donate*. She works faster than me, probably because this is all a bunch of shit to her and she can treat it as such, objectively.

There are things I consider keeping, before telling myself it's silly, especially because I won't be around much longer to be appropriately sentimental and nostalgic. There are Sara's high school yearbooks. *You didn't even know her then, you idiot.* There are cassette tapes Sara had saved, for some inexplicable reason—Pearl Jam, Nirvana, Tori Amos. *Do they even make tape players anymore?* What the hell would you even do with these? There are shoeboxes filled with cards Sara had collected over the years—from her parents, grandparents, old boyfriends, friends. I open one:

Dear Sara,
Welcome to your twenties. Keep that optimistic spirit of yours. And don't drink too much.
Love,
Dad

I open another:

Dearest Sara,
I live to play chess with you. Please thank that boyfriend of yours for sharing you with an old guy like me.
Happy birthday, sweetheart!
Love,
Mr. Sacramone

Mr. Sacramone, the ninety-two-year-old Sara called a friend. There's a whole photo album with pictures of the two of them.

"What the heck is this?" Riko asks from the back corner of the storage unit. She holds up something unrecognizable. "It looks like an old apple or something." She brings the brown, shriveled thing up to her nose.

"Where did you find it?"

"In here," she says, holding up a box of tampons.

I know what it is. It's a star squash.

The thing with the star squash started before Sara and I moved in together. She was staying at my apartment almost every night, in that phase of experimenting with all-out togetherness. One Saturday morning, she sent me to the grocery store so she could have some time to herself. She had just gotten this charcoal set and was making a mess of drawings all over the living room. I felt proud, husbandly, running errands for her, for us. I got everything on her list: cottage cheese, corkscrew pasta (she was very particular about the shape), apples, cilantro. I don't spend much time in produce sections, so when I spotted the star squash, I was intrigued. What was it? How did one consume it? I put it in the cart, for kicks. When she unpacked the groceries—she loved organizing the fridge and pantry—I heard her laugh all the way from the bedroom.

"What the hell is this?" she yelled.

"It's a star squash. I thought you'd like it," I yelled back, as if I were talking about a piece of jewelry I'd gotten for her.

That night, I found the star squash in my medicine cabinet. The next morning, I put it in her purse. Over the course of a week or so, it resided in my box of Raisin Bran, in her car's cup holder, in my pillowcase, in her running shoe, and in my boxers drawer. Sometime right before we moved, I put it in a box of tampons. And apparently that's where it had stayed.

"I want to keep that," I say as Riko starts her throwing motion toward the dumpster pile.

"*This?*" she says, referencing my squash with disgust.

"Yes, that."

"You don't even know what it is."

"It's a star squash."

"Okay?" she says, tossing it to me. It's about a quarter of its original size. It fits nicely in my pocket.

At the end of a few hours, Riko is in possession of a bed, bookcase, small desk, coffee table, refrigerator, washer and dryer, television, and a variety of kitchen appliances. I have made her day, maybe her year.

"I feel guilty taking all this," she says.

"Why? Someone should have it."

"I guess I don't understand...."

"Understand what?" I ask.

She's looking at the ground when she says, "Why do you still have so much of her stuff?"

"I'm some kind of masochist, I guess."

"No, I mean...why did she leave all this with you? Did she just up and disappear to travel the world or something?"

"Riko," I say, as a statement unto itself. She doesn't appear to hear me, though, doesn't notice the warning in my tone.

"Won't she want this stuff at some point?" she goes on.

"Riko," I say again.

"Some of it is personal—photo albums and things."

"Riko," I say again.

She looks up with mischief on her face and says, "Maybe you should get rid of it. Just imagine the look on her face when she finally comes back for it and you tell her it's gone."

"Riko," I say again.

I'm going to have to tell her.

"Huh?" she says, finally hearing me.

I sit on a footstool and take a deep breath.

"Riko," I say. "Sara's dead."

I'm not sure I've said that out loud to anyone who didn't already know. Maybe I've never said it out loud to anyone at all. Even myself.

Riko takes a step back, nearly tripping and falling over a rolled-up rug.

"I should have said something before, but I don't like to talk about it."

She disregards my dislike of talking about it and asks, "What happened?"

"Car accident," I say. "That typical situation where the other guy survives with the customary minor cuts and bruises."

That's all I want to say about it.

"Jesus," she says.

"I tried calling for him. He was no help."

She is incapable of appreciating a joke. I suppose I can't blame her. It's been months, and I'm still fairly incapable of appreciating a joke myself.

"I can't believe I grilled you with all those stupid questions about her. Why didn't you stop me?"

"I don't know. Sometimes it's nice to talk like it was just a breakup, like she's still alive, just not *with* me."

She nods.

"I can't even imagine," she says. "Are you okay?"

When people ask me this, I always say yes. I've never understood the question. It seems unnecessary, like asking someone drenched after standing in the rain for hours, "Are you wet?"

How could I possibly be okay? Who could lose the person he loves more than anyone or anything in the world and still be okay? Being okay seems like an unrealistic goal, an impossibility. The only certainty I have is that I can end the non-okayness. It's in my power to do that, at least.

"Do I seem okay?" I decide to ask her.

"I have no idea," she says.

We are quiet again, chins pressed to chests as if mourning her right then and there, before Riko says, "Well, now I feel really weird taking this stuff."

"It's not all hers. Some of it is mine. We mixed and matched," I say. "She would want you to have it. She was that kind of person."

Riko runs her hand along the edge of the bed frame, collecting dust on the tips of her fingers.

"You have to keep some of this stuff," she says. "You can't throw all of it away."

"What am I going to do with it?"

"Save it, for years from now, when you're able to smile looking at it."

But Riko doesn't know that "years from now" does not apply to me.

"Some of these are family photos and things," she says, pawing through a box labeled *pics*. "Won't her family want these, at least?"

I hadn't thought of that. As already acknowledged, I'm an asshole.

"Maybe. That could be a good idea."

"Do you still talk to them? Her family? Friends?"

She's going to hate me for what I have to confess.

"I haven't seen them since—"

"Since the funeral? It's probably too hard, huh?"

She's taking more pity on me than I deserve.

"Riko, I didn't go to the funeral."

Another long-held breath leaves me with this confession. Riko's mouth drops into an elongated "O."

"What?"

She crosses her arms over her chest and looks at me like I've just called her that word you're never supposed to call women. Sara used that word liberally, joked that we should name our future dog that word just to see the looks on people's faces: "Come 'ere, Cunt!" Her backup dog name of choice was Dammit: "Sit, Dammit!"

"I just couldn't bring myself to go. I can't see her parents. It's just going to make it harder."

"You're an idiot," she says.

"Noted."

"Funerals are for closure. That's why we have them."

"What if I don't want closure?"

"It's not just about you. Her parents probably wanted closure. Then you had to go and upset them by just not showing up, making them wonder what the hell is wrong with the guy who loved their daughter. You left them with this big, open-ended mystery. It's cruel."

"Don't hold back," I say.

"You need to take this stuff to them, at least," she says, struggling to lift the pics box and dropping it in my unwilling arms.

"What am I going to say? Sorry I missed the funeral, but here are some pictures?"

"You're the wordsmith," she says. "You'll figure it out."

She grabs one of the moving carts from the hallway and attempts to lift the washing machine by herself.

"You don't have to pull a muscle just to prove a point," I say, helping her. "I'll go. I'll visit them."

"Good." She doesn't look at me.

"Will you come with me?"

I feel stupid asking, like an insecure five-year-old requesting an elder to hold his hand on his way to the bathroom, even though he should be a "big boy." It's just that I figure Sara's father is less likely to shoot me if I have a demure Asian woman in tow.

"Come with you?" she says, seemingly shocked by this expressed need for her company.

Before I can rescind the request, she quickly says, "I guess. I mean, yeah. Sure."

Three hours later, the moving van Riko rented is full and the storage unit is empty. There are a few things I take with me—mostly the pictures and photo albums. And there's this one box, wrapped in red-and-green striped paper, labeled "For Mom and Dad" with a sealed card on top of it. We didn't really celebrate Christmas. We watched Christmas movies and partook in Christmas cookies at work, but we didn't do gifts. Sara said she felt wrong giving gifts because there were better things to do with money, like donate to charities. Since the time she'd been a teenager, she'd been instructing her parents to give the money they would spend on her gift to different foundations—the Clean Water Fund, the Salvation Army, the Red Cross, the ASPCA. I joked that her real issue was that she hated malls.

I figure the least I can do is give this gift, this anomaly, to her parents, belated as it may be.

"So that's it," Riko says as we stand in front of the empty unit.

I pull down the door and say, "Yep, that's it."

One thing crossed off the to-do list, I tell myself. Though I fear Riko has inspired the addition of two more:

- Visit Sara's parents
- Visit Mr. Sacramone in the old-people's home

Sara and I used to play this game, if you want to call it that, of thinking of unacknowledged "momentous events." Here are some we came up with during car rides, on walks, or while staring at the ceiling on a Saturday morning:

- The last moment on Earth when nobody was talking on a phone
- The last moment on Earth when nobody was watching a television
- The last moment on Earth when nobody was having sex
- The last moment on Earth when nobody was online
- The last moment on Earth when nobody was talking
- The last moment on Earth when nobody was being born
- The last moment on Earth when nobody was awake
- The last moment on Earth when nobody was asleep
- The last moment on Earth when nobody was driving a car
- The last moment on Earth when not a single light was on

I wish I could remember more, because we thought of hundreds. I should have maintained a written list. In any case, it's strange that society evolves without anyone recognizing these moments. Before we know it, the present is the past and the future is here.

Here's a "momentous event" to ponder:

The last moment on Earth when nobody was dying.

十八

The funeral was the week after the accident. I'd been holed up in my—our—house, ignoring concerned phone calls. People left casseroles and chilis and lasagnas on the doormat. I retrieved them but didn't eat them. There were cards too, full of the usual condolences: *So sorry for your loss. Can't imagine your pain. Thinking of you.*

Sara's parents, Rhonda and Ted, left messages. They started off unimposing: *We know you loved our Sara so much. This is all such a shock. Please call us when you are ready.* But, as the week went on, their tone turned perplexed:

Hi there, Jonathan. We don't want to bother you, but the funeral is tomorrow, as you know. We haven't heard from you. We're wondering if you have all the information. It's at Forest Lawn, ten o'clock. We were hoping you'd put together something. Sara always said you were a great writer, good with words. And we know you loved her so much. Anyway, we'll see you tomorrow.

My initial response was astonishment—how could they expect this of me? But it was fair of them, really. I knew her better than anyone—something that turns out to be a torturous burden when it's time to say a collective goodbye. They would expect me to divulge memories, to share secrets, to make them laugh and cry. They wanted me to help them remember her accurately so that they could eventually move on, forget. That's what funerals are, aren't they? Venues in which we remember for the purpose of forgetting?

In any case, I didn't skip out on the funeral because I hadn't written anything. I did write something. I still have it, long-hand, on the back of a flyer advertising pizza specials that some bored teenager affixed to my doorknob with a rubber band. It's in the nightstand drawer with all my other writings that have never seen the light of day:

Sara reused Ziploc bags. She never left a light on. She turned off the water while she brushed her teeth. She cared about something as large and abstract as the planet, as the future. I've always found caring for myself all-consuming.

Sara possessed a determined optimism. In a world of billions of people, she thought she mattered. And when she loved you, you became intimately aware of how much she thought you mattered too. Sometimes, when she held you, you may have even thought *"She's right."*

She found joy in watering plants, painting her toenails, a new hummus dip. Her eyes got big with excitement when a puppy crossed her path, when a just-ordered book showed up in the mail, when the sun rose. Gratitude was easy for her; despair was impossible. She wanted to see the world. She wanted to do things. She was on a mission to prove to herself, and to you, that life was only boring if you allowed it to be.

If you had the occasion to simply meet her, or if you were lucky enough to know her, or if you had the profound good fortune to love her, your understanding of life will be forever changed. A world that concedes to losing Sara is a world that no longer makes sense. You may be left to wonder if it will ever make sense. You may be left to ask yourself what happens to hope, trust, will, and purpose, when the one who gave them birth dies. You may be left to wonder if you will ever meet someone like Sara again, and you may grieve a good long while when you realize the answer is probably no.

I practiced it a few times in front of a mirror. When I got to "She wanted to see the world," my eyes started tearing up, no matter how many times I repeated it over and over in an attempt to desensitize myself. In short, I skipped the funeral because I don't like how I look when I cry. I hate the Elvis snarl of my mouth, the flaring of my nostrils, the contortion of my face, the saline, the snot. And I especially hate hugs from strangers, offerings of tissues, and looks of pity that only confirm how much everything blows.

At ten o'clock that Friday, when everyone else was gathered to honor her, I was on my computer, commencing my obsessive Japan research. It started innocently enough—I just wanted to know how they did funerals in Japan. What I learned was that the Japanese are not a hard-core religious folk, for one. Lots of atheists. For those who are believers, religion is something of a smorgasbord. They are in support of "dabbling," picking and choosing from a variety of rituals and superstitions—from Buddhism and Shintoism, mostly. They steal some holidays from China. They decorate their streets for Christmas. They choose Christian, American-style "white weddings" because they're pretty, while they generally trust Buddhist rites for funerals. It's all very willy-nilly. There is no one understanding of "right and wrong." This intrigued me, coming from a culture in which the generally accepted idea is that if you were not baptized, if you did not make the choice to select the Lord as your savior at the ripe old age of zero, you are going to burn in hell for all eternity. The Japanese seemed less serious, less condemning, more humble to the fact that life itself is willy-nilly. There is no single belief, no single ritual, no single God who will save us from the crapshoot that is existence.

I've been told the ceremony was beautiful. It was closed casket, for reasons I still hate to ponder. According to my parents, who sat in the front row with Sara's parents, there was a good turnout, which makes sense considering the type of person Sara is, or was (tense still trips me up). My mother said "An old man spoke," which I assumed meant Mr. Sacramone. Kevin from R&R told me later that everyone from the company was there—even Theresa. If my absence perplexed him, he didn't show it. He never asked why I wasn't there. Nobody asked. Once my mother said, in a small voice, "It would have been nice to have you with us." There was no trace of curiosity or condemnation. It was like they wanted to avoid knowing my reasons, didn't want intimate knowledge of what anguish would keep me at home on my computer instead of saying goodbye to my girlfriend one last time. That's the thing with grief—people want to know you appreciate their casseroles and chilis and lasagnas; they don't want to know that your appetite, your taste for anything, died with her. They want to know they are consoling, helping you through the hard time. They don't want to know that you're so torn up inside that you want to kill yourself.

✳

The last time I saw Sara's parents was a week before Sara went on bed rest, the week before everything started unraveling. I visited them then to ask for their daughter's hand in marriage. I know it's customary to ask just the father, but Sara was so close to both of her parents; it seemed strange to exclude her mother, to presume that this was a business deal between men. I had the ring and tickets to Japan in my pocket, as evidence of my intent, when I knocked on the door.

Sara's mom answered, wearing sweatpants and a ratty old T-shirt.

"Oh, Jonathan. What a nice surprise. I was just doing some cleaning," she said. Ted came up behind her, gave me a loose hug with a back slap for good measure.

"Did we forget you were coming by?" Ted asked.

"No, I didn't call. I guess I should have."

I had my hands behind me, cracking and recracking my thumb knuckle anxiously. There was no real reason to be nervous. I knew they liked me.

"Is something wrong?" Rhonda asked, putting her hand to her chest, suddenly concerned.

"Is Sara okay?" Ted asked.

It's then that I realized I had the appearance of an undertaker in my just-from-work suit and my just-from-work exhausted frown.

"Oh, god, yeah, she's fine, she's fine."

"You had us worried there a second," Rhonda said. "Thought there'd been an accident or something."

And we all laughed to break the tension, because there was no accident—not then. Sara was fine, then.

"Sorry, I guess I'm just a little nervous," I said, using the cuff of my jacket to wipe beads of sweat from my forehead. "Can I come in?"

They opened the door wide for me, invited me to share a bottle of wine with them. I told them my reason for coming, said I wanted to make Sara my wife. Ted said, "It's about time," and Rhonda cried tears of the happy variety, fanning her face in a vain attempt to dry them. I showed them the ring—a square-shaped diamond, antique-looking. Ted slapped my back again, called me "son," as in "Nice going, son." Rhonda gasped and said, "Sara is going to be so happy." Then I took out the trip tickets, put them on the table. They didn't even have to get their glasses and lean in close to see the destination. They knew.

"Japan?" they said, in unison.

We all knew she wanted to go.

I nodded. "To see the cherry blossoms."

In Japan, it is a tradition for literate people to write a death poem—called a *jisei*—near the time of one's own death. The most famous death poems are written by Japanese Zen monks and haiku poets. My favorite, though, was written by Ōta Dōkan, the builder of Edo Castle, who met his end in 1486.

> Had I not known
> that I was dead
> already
> I would have mourned
> the loss of my life.

I'm not sad about my impending death, my inhalation of laundry-detergent fumes. I'm not scared. Like Ōta Dōkan, I am all too aware that I'm dead already.

十九

The final exam for our Japanese class falls on the anniversary of Sara's death, almost to the hour. I decide not to tell Riko this because I don't want to disturb her pretest studying. Or maybe I just don't want to talk about it.

She is taking our final exam very seriously. When I find her in our usual spot, it smells like popcorn and tuna and burnt pizza, like she's been consuming meals in here for days. She is sitting at the far end of the couch, shuffling through a massive deck of flash cards, nodding her head and confirming answers as she goes. Sometimes she does not even need to flip over the cards to confirm; she just knows. I don't feel particularly concerned about the exam or my grade in the class, for obvious reasons. It's liberating, actually, to flirt dangerously with failure.

"*Konnichiwa, tomodachi,*" I say, which means "Good afternoon, friend."

She looks up and smiles. "*Konnichiwa.*"

"You're studying too hard," I tell her.

"I want an A."

"*A* is for Asian."

She takes a rubber band out of her hair and stretches it around her stack of flash cards, then looks at her watch and says, "We better get going."

The halls are filled with students attempting to walk and review textbooks at the same time. Some of them have Number 2 pencils and Scantron forms in their hands, worried looks on their sleep-deprived faces.

"Do you know how rich the Scantron company must be?" I say to Riko.

"Hmm?" she says. She is walking while flipping through flash cards. I peek over her shoulder. She's reviewing age, time, cost.

"The Scantron company. They must be a billion-dollar company. Think about it. They produced one Scantron form and one machine. The same form has been around since I was a kid, so at least twenty-five years, right?"

"You're old," she says, distractedly.

"Every school across the nation requires students to use those silly forms for tests. Let's say they cost fifty cents—that's fifteen bucks for a classroom of thirty students. Multiply that by the number of classes, and that's a pretty good sum for just *one* campus. Multiple that by the number of campuses and—"

"This is fascinating, really, but we're about to take our Japanese final and I don't think there will be math on it."

"I will be doing math to calculate how many questions I can miss and still pass."

She stops suddenly and gives me the look of a stern mother. "You *better* pass."

I shrug. "Does it matter?"

"Of course it matters. If you don't pass, you can't take the next Japanese class."

I didn't know I was going to take the next Japanese class. According to my plan, I will be around only until April, which is the middle of the semester.

"You are taking level two, right?" she says, folding her arms in front of her chest, like she's bracing herself for potential disappointment.

"Am I?"

"Yes, you are." She pounds her little, Asian fist against my chest with unexpected force. "You're not allowed to leave me here by myself."

The exam is fairly easy, even for me. There's a written part in which we have to translate English sentences into hiragana. This is not too difficult, being that our vocabulary is so limited. We can do very little involving verbs, for instance. We can say "I am American" or "She is twenty-one years old" or "He is a teacher," but we cannot say "I like America" or "She drinks sake" or "He wants to be a teacher." And we know only whole numbers. We can say "It is nine o'clock," but we can't say "It is 9:18." This simplifies things.

The oral exam involves reciting basic, memorized sentences, the types of sentences that make asses of all people learning foreign languages, as they are delivered with too much pride to native speakers who try not to laugh: "Hello. My name is Jonathan. I am thirty-four years old. I am a student. I am American. It is six o'clock. Nice to meet you." The teaching assistants must be very bored by these exchanges.

"How did you do?" Riko asks me. She is waiting outside. She finished her test about ten minutes before I finished mine.

"Fine, I guess. I don't think I have to ask how you did."

"No, you don't," she says confidently.

We walk to the parking lot and stop in front of her car.

"So, do I get to see you over Christmas break?" she says.

"Actually, I was going to ask you about that."

She arches one of her eyebrows.

"I think I'm ready," I say, "to see Sara's parents. It would help, I think, if you were, you know, *there*."

"Sure. Okay," she says, slightly flustered. "But are her parents going to think it's weird if I'm there? They don't even know me."

"They're going to think it's weird that *I'm* there. They'll be too distracted by that to notice you. No offense."

"None taken."

"So, I'll call you?" I say.

"Sure. Whenever."

She opens her car door and I mock bow at her. "*Arigatou*," I say.

She laughs. "Why don't we know how to say 'You're welcome'?"

"Good question."

"Every conversation we've learned ends with '*doozo yoro-shiku*,'" she says. (In case you've forgotten, that means "Nice to meet you.")

"Well, in this case, that works too," I say. "*Doozo yoro-shiku*, Riko." I stick out my hand.

"*Doozo yoroshiku*," she repeats, shaking it.

These days, most communities in California consist of tract homes. Every house looks alike. They're not identical, mind you. The contractors go to great lengths to create the illusion of variety and character. For example, they choose three paint colors, usually neutral shades with names like "Adobe Dust" and "Olive Branch" and "Mojave Sand." Then, on House A, they make the exterior walls "Adobe Dust," the trim "Olive Branch," and the front and garage doors "Mojave Sand." Next door, at House B, the exterior walls are "Olive Branch," the trim is "Mojave Sand," and the doors are "Adobe Dust." And so forth. Oh, and sometimes they make House B the mirror image of House A—the garage door and front door switch sides, for example. That gives you "individuality." Still, the windowpanes are made of the same cheap white plastic, stucco reigns supreme, and everyone has the same landscaping—homeowner's association-approved grass, perfectly cut by Mexicans, along with a healthy hedge and yellow flowers lining the quaint walkway. That is most Californian neighborhoods: mass-produced sameness.

But Rhonda and Ted Mackenzie live in this secluded community by the sea where no house looks like it belongs with the next. They are all just thrown together, expected to get along. One house looks as if it were imported from a little town in France, with cobblestone and out-of-control ivy. Another looks uprooted from New Mexico, with its red tile roof and mud-looking walls. The house next to Rhonda and Ted's appears to have come from the year 2056, with its sharp edges and concrete walls and round windows cut out in random places, like the portholes on a ship. As for Rhonda and Ted's house, it looks to have come straight from the English countryside, complete with bricks from the ground up, a wood thatched roof, and tall chimneys. You would think the people inside call cigarettes "fags" and have terrible teeth.

"I didn't even know this neighborhood existed," Riko says, staring out the window as the houses pass by.

"I think they prefer it that way."

"Some people still have their Christmas decorations up," she says, pointing at the twinkly lights and plastic Santas with the excitement of a four-year-old. "What did you do for Christmas, anyway?"

"Nothing. I don't like Christmas."

She gives me an exaggerated roll of the eyes and a sigh that informs me I'm a hopeless case.

We pull up to the curb in front of their house, and I let out a deep breath.

"Ready?" Riko says.

"Not really."

I have come with their wrapped gift, the one labeled "For Mom and Dad," along with the card. I brought some other miscellaneous things too—photos, mostly. There's some jewelry, too, that Riko insisted I not throw away—a few pendants, a silver chain, some rings, a bracelet that Riko says is a "tennis bracelet" (to be worn during tennis?), and some earrings that I can't, for the life of me, remember if I ever saw Sara wear. I can't even remember if her ears were pierced. I mean, they must have been, since she owned earrings. Why don't I remember her earrings? This is another reason I don't want to stick around—I'm afraid of what else I'm capable of forgetting.

I spent all of last night looking through photographs in search of her earrings. But, in most pictures, her hair covered her ears. It was always falling in her face. She cursed the hair dresser who had cut her "front layers" too short, so they wouldn't join the rest of her hair in the ponytails she loved. I think I'd said something like "It's just hair, it'll grow back," which was an insensitive thing to say. Still, in my defense, I couldn't have known she'd have those too-short "front layers" for all eternity.

The front door opens before we've even approached it, as if they've been glued to their front window, anticipating my arrival.

"Jonathan," Ted says, as a statement, like he's confirming that I'm there, that I didn't disappear into the same void as his daughter.

"It's so good to see you," Rhonda says, hugging me for an inordinately long time.

"It really is great to see you," Ted confirms, wrapping his arms around his wife and me, so the three of us are hugging. I seem to be the only one uncomfortable with this. Well, Riko seems uncomfortable too.

The display of affection seems genuine, though. I search for bitterness in their eyes, in the tightness of their facial muscles, but there is none.

"It's been a while," I say, and I mean it's been a while since I've seen them, but Rhonda responds with " Sometimes it feels like just yesterday she was here." I assume Sara's death will be their reference point—the central dot of their life compass, around which all other events will occur—possibly for the rest of their lives.

"This is my friend Riko," I say, motioning for Riko to come forward. She's been hovering in a corner. They don't seem to know what to make of her, but they smile politely.

"I'm his mule," Riko says, noticeably struggling to hold the box of stuff we've brought from the storage unit.

"Shit, sorry," I say, relieving her. "This is the stuff I was telling you about."

They smile and nod. I'd warned them that I was coming with "a few things." I wanted them to know I'd been selective, that

I hadn't just put everything Sara-related in a pile to dump on them. I'd done my best to decipher value, so as not to overwhelm them with more crap in the already-crappy situation of losing their only child.

"Well, come in," Rhonda says to us.

The inside of their home is lived-in. They have not "tidied up" for my visit, which puts me at ease. A blanket is draped over the couch haphazardly. Magazines are strewn across the coffee table—*Newsweek* and *Marie Claire* and *Travel + Leisure*. It makes me feel better to know they think about things like travel and leisure now. Mugs sit on coasters. The TV buzzes at low volume—an episode of *Everybody Loves Raymond*. This, this space of theirs, is proof that life carries on, in all its usual ways, even when we would prefer that it not. I'd had the preposterous notion that there would be some kind of Sara shrine, complete with an enlarged portrait perched on an easel, flowers, and those tall candles people leave next to wooden crosses on the road. There is no shrine. There are pictures of Sara here and there, arranged in such an unspecial way that a visitor would have no idea she was gone. In my quick assessment of the living room, I see flattering pictures of her (a stylized college graduation photo, a studio portrait done when she must have been in high school) as well as those not-so-flattering candid pictures we all have— one with her tongue out and eyes crossed, another of her displaying gleaming braces, and another with a bad perm and feathered bangs. It's as if they think making a point to "honor" her, to move the "nice" pictures to a display case while tucking the goofy ones in an album somewhere, will confirm the reality that she is gone, a person to be remembered fondly, perfectly.

Their old golden retriever, graying around his chin and ears, strolls in on rickety legs to see what all the commotion is about. I'm grateful I remember his name.

"Hey, Buster," I say, patting his head. He seems to remember me, and I'm grateful for this too.

"Can I get you two anything?" Rhonda asks as we take our seats in the living room.

"We're fine," I say, speaking for Riko.

"So, how have you been?" Ted asks me. I am tense, shoulders up near my ears, bracing for some assault, some firing of questions like "Whythehellweren'tyouatthefuneral?" and "Didn'tyoucareforSaraatall?" He seems kind...too kind. I can only assume a surprise attack is in my future.

"I'm fine," I say. Then I wonder if this is the wrong response. Maybe I should say I'm "not fine." Does being fine indicate that their daughter didn't really matter much to me?

"I mean, I'm doing okay. I miss Sara," I say. These words burst into the air, lively and energetic, like they've been released from solitary confinement.

"Your mother tells me you freelance now," Rhonda says, making small talk. It's like we're trying to show we can talk about things not related to Sara, go on like normal. It's all a sham.

"Yes, I am now free," I say. We laugh, as if to prove to each other, to ourselves, that we can.

"We take a Japanese language class," Riko says, making herself part of the conversation.

"Is that right?" Rhonda says.

"Sara's probably happy to hear that," Ted says. He speaks of her so casually. Her name just rolls off his tongue. There is no crack in his voice, no change in his facial expression or demeanor. He must talk about her often if he is immune to her name like this. I wonder if she is, in fact, listening in on us, as he implies. Does he go about his life, thinking she is always there, omnipresent? Does this make it worse or better?

"Sara really wanted to go to Japan," Rhonda says to Riko.

I can almost see the metaphorical light bulb going off above Riko's head: *ding*.

"I didn't know that," she says.

"She was an artistic type," Ted says. I want to correct him, clarify she was an "artist," not a "type," but I let it go.

"She just loved cherry blossoms, thought they were so beautiful," Rhonda says.

Riko eyes me, smiles. She gets it now, all of it—my reasons for taking the Japanese class, my obsession with Japan and these flowers that die too soon. It's embarrassing, almost, to be this transparent.

"I'm planning to go to Japan in the spring," I say.

Rhonda and Ted nod. It's the first time today I've seen them solemn.

"That will make her happy," Ted says, looking down, clearing his throat.

I clear mine too, then Rhonda saves us from inevitable breakdown by changing the subject.

"So, what did you bring for us?"

I set the box on the floor in front of me, sort through it.

"Well, there were a ton of photographs," I say, handing over a few of the albums and stacks of the loose and disorganized singles. Rhonda and Ted lean in close together, to review. They flip through them, faster than I expected. Granted, many are of sunsets, random birds, rolling waves—Sara appreciated these things. But still, when I looked at these, I spent a good minute or so on each picture, wondering what she saw in each sunset, each random bird, each rolling wave. What possessed her to take the picture?

"Oh, this one is cute," Rhonda says, showing Ted. It's one I took. It's a close-up of Sara's profile. She's laughing. I took it on her thirtieth birthday, as she was unwrapping gifts. She just seemed so fucking happy. I was sitting right next to her, at Buca di Beppo, a family style Italian restaurant. That's why it's so close-up. It's almost blurry.

"Do you want any of these?" Ted asks me.

I shrug. I look at Riko, like she's supposed to tell me what to want, but she just shrugs too.

"She was your daughter. I mean, I don't—"

"We remember what she looks like, son," Ted says bluntly, but not coldly.

"Jonathan, if you'd like some, just go ahead," Rhonda says, taking her husband's cue.

I flip through a stack, pretending to assess each picture, even though I already know my favorites.

"Can I have this one?" I say.

Both of our faces are in the shot, together, cheek pressing against cheek. We're lying on the floor of our tent. We're in Joshua Tree. You wouldn't know it looking at the picture, but we're naked, our legs all tangled up together. It was her idea to grab her camera, to capture us in that moment. I want this picture not just because of how it makes me remember her, but because of how it makes me remember myself. There was a time when Jonathan Krause hoped for things. There was a time when Jonathan Krause thought life was somewhat fair. There was a time when Jonathan Krause believed in the ridiculous notion that two people could be happy together, forever. This picture is proof of that time, that Jonathan.

"Thank you," I say.

"Fact is, many of these probably mean more to you than they do to us. We don't know the stories behind all of them like you do," Ted says.

"And Sara's probably glad for that," Rhonda says, managing a laugh.

"Ain't that the truth," Ted says, his eyes rolling upward like he believes Sara's up there, not on a cloud in heaven, but, like, in their attic.

"Ted's right, Jonathan," Rhonda says, decidedly. "Please, take the pictures." She pushes them toward me. The tone of her voice implies she'd be sad if I didn't. Maybe she doesn't want them for the same reason I don't want them—it's too hard to remember. I hand the photos to Riko. She can deal with them.

"I also brought some jewelry she had," I say, handing over a jewelry box and its contents.

When Rhonda lifts the lid of the box, the little ballerina inside starts to turn in circles as music plays. Rhonda gets misty-eyed.

"I didn't know she still had this," she says. "I must have gotten this for her when she was ten years old."

"Guess they make those ballerinas to last a long time," Ted says, putting his arm around his wife and pulling her into him. He kisses her head. We all know the ballerina in a jewelry box should not outlive its owner. This is a grave injustice.

Rhonda starts to look over the jewelry. She shakes her head.

"I don't remember these," she says.

This relieves me; I don't remember them either.

"We didn't bury her with any jewelry, did we?" Ted says.

Rhonda shakes her head. "She probably bought these from a homeless peddler on a beach somewhere because she felt bad for him."

"That sounds like Sara," I say.

And we have our first laugh in memory of her. Riko smiles but doesn't join in, like she's acknowledging that what we know of Sara is sacred to us, and not for her to understand fully.

"There was this that I found too," I say, pulling out the wrapped gift.

"For Christmas?" Rhonda asks, high-pitched and confused.

I nod and hand it to her.

"That's weird. She stopped doing Christmas gifts with us when she was a stubborn teenager," Ted says.

Rhonda tears off the paper to reveal a wooden box. Sara had been taking a woodshop class. On Wednesday nights. At the community college.

Ted takes it from Rhonda and turns it over in his hands. They both look perplexed.

"Oh, there was a card on top," I say, handing it to them.

Rhonda opens it. I watch her eyes scan the contents. She looks up at me with something—pity, maybe—in her face.

"Jonathan, I think this is for you."

She hands it back to me and I read:

Sorry, babe, I had to write "To Mom and Dad" on it so you wouldn't open it. Then I remembered I could just hide it in the storage unit. Brilliant! It's nothing big, and I know we don't do gifts, but I'm tired of seeing you put all your writing ideas in that nightstand drawer. Maybe this will help. Plus, it will fill up faster, so maybe you will be more motivated to actually do something with the ideas. No pressure. Haha. I put a few of my ideas in there to get you started. I love you.

Riko is peeking over my shoulder, reading along. She leans back when she realizes what it means. Rhonda, Ted, and Riko talk among themselves, marveling, I guess, at this gift from The Beyond. Their voices morph into something unrecognizable, just background noise. I open the wooden box and, just as the card specifies, it's full of little white scraps of paper. I unfold one and read, reluctantly. It's a quote: *Love is laughing at jokes when they're not so good and listening to problems when they're not so bad.*

I unfold the others, carefully, as if each might contain a fortune I may not deserve:

- *Only someone who truly loves you will tell you when you have food on your face.*
- *Till death do us part, I will buy you star squashes.*
- *Wrinkling isn't so terrible when there's someone to do it with.*
- *Two strange peas in an irregular pod.*
- *In the exploits of this life, how about I am Bonnie and you are Clyde?*

This one knocks the air out of me:

- *If you die first, ask if you can bring a friend.*

And this one too:

- *Even when it's no longer just you and me, even when baby makes three, we'll never forget you and me.*

I start to choke on my own saliva. Riko must see me go white, struggling for air.

"Are you okay?" she asks, patting my back like I'm a baby that needs to be burped.

"Yeah, I'm fine," I say.

Rhonda and Ted look at me and say, simultaneously, "Are you sure?"

"I don't know," I say, catching my breath again.

"She really loved you," Rhonda says, her hand on my knee. "I know that doesn't make anything easier."

"It doesn't," I say.

"Please don't be so hard on yourself," she says.

How the hell does she know to say this? It's exactly what I need to hear, though I can't take the advice.

"I need to go," I say, standing quickly. It's abrupt. I don't know if they had a meal planned for us. I don't smell anything cooking. Rhonda and Ted eye each other. Ted nods once.

"Son, you know we love you, like one of our own," he says.

"You can come by any time, to talk," Rhonda says. "It helps us too, you know."

I just keep nodding. I don't feel like my throat will relax enough to enable me to speak.

After a few moments of my incessant nodding, Riko says, "Thank you," like she's my enlisted mouthpiece, my PR assistant. She is carrying the wooden box and the photos. We are leaving with things. This was not what I intended. Rhonda hugs me, and I feel sad when she lets go.

Before I know it, I am outside, winter sun shining on me. They close the front door, reluctantly.

"Do you want me to drive?" Riko asks, cautiously. My mental state must not seem too stable at this point.

"That would be good."

She takes my keys and I get into the passenger seat, staring at the wooden box she's placed in my lap.

"You okay?" she asks, starting the car.

"Not really."

"They're nice people."

"I know."

"Rhonda's right—Sara must have really loved you."

"Don't say that."

"Would you feel better if I said she must have really hated you?"

"Yes, that would be great."

She allows silence for several blocks. She breaks it with "So, she wanted to go to Japan?"

I am leaning my head against the window, enjoying the feel of the cool, hard glass.

"Yes, she did."

"So that's why you're going? For her?"

"You make it sound like I'm going to find her there."

"Okay, then, you're going for her memory."

"I don't know. What do you think?" My response is regrettably snarky, rhetorical. Part of me really wants to know what Riko thinks, wants her to set me straight, tell me that the trip won't mean what I need it to mean. I still want to believe it will, though. I want to believe I can get everything I desire—pre-suicide absolution, resolution—with the simple sight of cherry blossoms.

I sit on the toilet—seat down—confined to this small, six-by-two-foot closet of a bathroom. I figure the smaller the space, the greater the concentration of gas, the quicker my end. I take a deep breath, let the poison fill my lungs, knowing that in just a few moments, I'll be gone.

What the message boards did not mention is that these few moments would feel like an eternity, my own personal hell of atonement. Somehow, in these few moments, I will feel years of pain, come to understand the very definition of agony. I feel the gas flowing through me, igniting fires throughout my body, burning me from the inside out.

My mind and body are not in unison. What my mind wants—the end, my end—is not accepted by my body. My body fights, instinctively, for life. I fall to my knees, so hard that my head whips forward, my forehead banging on the wall. My hand, almost in defiance of me, wanders to the doorknob, turning it frantically, searching for clean air outside the confines of this room. I'd planned for this, jammed the door into a locked position to save myself from myself—or that's what I thought at the time. It does not feel that way now.

My throat constricts, taking in less and less air. It's almost time. I flail about the bathroom, yanking the towels off their racks, creating a mess I did not want to leave. I fall backward against the shower door, and that's when it happens—I go out, just like that, with a final thwack. It's less climactic than I'd hoped. The frenzy, the terror does not dissolve away, but it is knocked out like a tired boxer in the last round. There is a piercing ringing in my ears, then nothing. It all goes black.

二十

The Japanese have this alleged custom called *ubasute*, in which an elderly relative is carried to a mountain or other remote, isolated place and left there to die. People gasp at this, say it's heartless, brutal. Even the Japanese wave it off as a practice that's long dead, as if they're ashamed of it, as if it's embarrassingly archaic. But really, how much is it different from what we do today in America? We still drop off our old people so we can go about our daily lives. We just don't trek to mountaintops; we go to nursing homes.

The cruelty of life is right there in the name—"nursing home." We're all just infants in the end, as helpless as we were when we arrived in the world. Turns out the circle that is life is way less joyous than *The Lion King* would have us believe. The only way to avoid the cruelty is to die in your peak years. Like Sara. Like me.

It's not just the helplessness that's cruel—sitting around in diapers, spitting up on yourself, eating pureed vegetables that don't require teeth for chewing. What's cruel is that everyone dotes on babies, yet nobody gives a shit about old people. Sara gave a shit, which is why she visited a nursing home on a regular basis to hang out with an old man who wasn't even her grandpa. She wasn't his next of kin, guaranteed a prime spot in the will, with a handsome inheritance. She just liked to make this man's day.

I've never been to an old-people's home. My grandmothers—two very stubborn creatures—refuse to go. There's Grandma Edna, who would chain herself to the pillars of her front porch before she'd move to "a home" (that's what old people call it, with a tone of doom). She claims to love her small, one-story Craftsman in Oakland, though she complains that all her neighbors are "illegals." I don't think it's the house she loves as much as her routines, her lifestyle. She's got her herb garden. And her vitamin regimen. If you went to her house and saw the bottles occupying her kitchen counter, you would guess this regimen occupies a minimum of three hours of her day (possibly four hours, being that she's ninety-two years old and moves very slowly). She likes things her way. She's got her couch with the plastic protective covering, and her television set, even though she can't see the picture. It's not that she's blind; it's that the screen died years ago, and now she just likes to sit and listen to the television. There is no use in explaining that this is, essentially, a radio.

Then there's Grandma Bea, who won't go to "a home" because she likes to think she's still twenty-three years old. In the past two years, she has been to Niagara Falls, some supposedly famous stalactite caves in New Mexico, and Alaska to kayak with orcas and see the northern lights. I would guess that Grandma Bea is operating off a very long "Things to do before you die" list. I have a stack of postcards from her, most of which I can't read because her penmanship resembles that of someone who has had several strokes. Grandma Bea has never had a stroke. Grandma Bea claims to be healthy as a horse. This is in spite of the fact that she has a strong affinity for Kentucky Fried Chicken. She has a dog, Sadie. She expresses her love for Sadie with KFC, and Sadie has over one hundred pounds on her golden retriever frame to show for it. Grandma Bea washes her own dishes with Sadie's dishes—it's that kind of love.

From the outside, the home looks like a dreary, concrete medical facility. I was expecting something more residential, with better landscaping.

"So who are we here to see?" Riko asks as we pull into a parking spot.

I've brought her with me again, feeling like Linus with his tension-easing security blanket. I didn't tell her much about what we would be doing. I just asked if she'd come with me, to play a friendly game of chess with a resident in a Pasadena nursing home. She said, "I'm better at checkers, but sure."

"His name is Mr. Sacramone," I say. "I've never met him." She doesn't ask the obvious, which is why I like Riko.

When we go inside, it smells like peas. I suddenly understand why my mother is trying to delay aging with flax seeds. I approach the nurse at the reception desk, a young woman in magenta scrubs. She looks bored. I assume not much goes on here, except for chess and the occasional death.

"Hi, I'm here to visit someone," I say.

She nods at me impatiently, as if thinking *"Right, well, why the fuck else would you be here?"* Truth is, I could come up with many alternative reasons for a human's visit to this facility. I could be delivering a truckload of Depends or those meal-supplement shakes. I could be a dentist, on call for an emergency denture repair. I could be a balloon-animal artist, here for afternoon entertainment. I could be a lawyer looking to finalize someone's will. I could be selling coffins. I could be a talent scout, wanting to cast the next "I've-fallen-and-I-can't-get-up" commercial.

"His name is Mr. Sacramone," I say.

She brightens. "You're here for Mr. Sacramone?"

"Yes."

She slides some visitor information paperwork my way and lets me use her pen, which has a little globe at the end of it, acting as the clicker.

"He hasn't had a visitor in quite some time. I'm sure he'll be so happy to see you." She leads us down a hallway, ponytail swinging with each bouncy step. The corridor is lined with abandoned elderly in wheelchairs, seemingly parked there against their will. Riko follows so closely that she steps on my heel twice.

"Are you family?" the nurse asks.

"No, I'm a friend."

We pass by many rooms—some with doors closed, others open—and try not to gawk at the stale lives inside. Some residents have pots of flowers by their beds. Some have hearty plants, indicating they've been here a while. There are pictures in old chrome frames on nightstands, televisions on at full volume. Food trays are stacked by the doors, awaiting pickup by some poor soul whose job it is to scrape remaining Stouffer's meals into trash cans.

We stop in front of a room with a closed door. The nurse taps lightly.

"Mr. Sacramone?"

"If he's sleeping, we don't want to wake him," I say.

"Mr. Sacramone doesn't sleep."

"Ever?" Riko asks.

"Not since 2004," she says. Judging by her nonchalant expression, this is supposed to make sense. I search my brain for insomnia-causing events in 2004 and don't find any. That was the year Janet Jackson exposed her tit during the Super Bowl halftime show, wasn't it? Like a good advertising peon, I remember Super Bowls.

From behind the door, we hear the shuffle of slippers on lino-leum. The doorknob turns slowly, and a small man's wrinkled face appears in the crack he allows for us. His eyes droop like a bloodhound's and his cheeks sag like they've given up in their fight against gravity. He's wearing a plaid robe with several stains on the front.

"Yes?" he says. He doesn't have his teeth in.

"Mr. Sacramone, you have visitors," the nurse says happily.

"Who is it?" He speaks with a significant lisp, but I can understand him. He's clearly practiced at speaking without teeth.

"It's Jonathan," I say.

"And Riko," Riko says quietly.

"I don't know any Jonathan and Riko," he says, cringing at the oddity of Riko's name. The nurse looks at us quizzically. There is no way around revealing the reason for my presence. This man obviously has the potential to be gruff.

"I knew Sara," I say.

Riko nods, understanding that I have dragged her into my "process." That's what they call mourning, right? A "process"?

"Sara?" Mr. Sacramone says.

The nurse is pitying me now, with those damn "I'm-sorry-for-your-loss" eyes I can't stand. While still looking at me, she says to Mr. Sacramone, "You remember Sara."

We watch him as he racks his brain. I imagine him mentally riffling through a Rolodex, calling up names and faces from the past, doing his best to prove that his memory is intact, that old age hasn't gotten the best of him.

"Of course I remember Sara," he finally says. He smiles, opens the door a bit more. "She was very good at chess."

I never knew Sara was particularly good at chess. I knew she was good at dominoes and Scrabble and Jenga. But I never played chess with her. This is when I wonder what else I don't know about her. This is when I wonder what I used to know but have already forgotten—like the earrings. Just brushing my teeth in the morning, something so mundane, causes me angst because I can't remember what brand of toothpaste she used. It was either Crest or Colgate—one of the Cs—but I can't remember.

"Well, we're not very good at chess, but would you mind if we play a game with you?" I ask.

He wrinkles his nose, skeptically. I fixate on the large, deep pores.

"Doesn't that sound nice, Mr. Sacramone?" the nurse says. She talks to him like he's a kindergartner reluctant to play tag with the rest of the kids. "Welcome your visitors inside. You three can have a nice chat."

She gives us a little nudge on the smalls of our backs, and just like that, we are in Mr. Sacramone's room.

If the nursing home smells like peas, Mr. Sacramone's room smells like peas that washed down the sink two days ago and have not yet been mashed up by the garbage disposal. It's dark, and there's a strange dampness. It would be the perfect environment for fungus growth.

He shuffles over to a small table, on which sits a chessboard. I wonder if it is always out on display like this, if maybe he plays games with himself, if maybe he has multiple personality disorder to keep it interesting. Sara never said much about him. Then again, I never asked. All I know is she met him while visiting her grandmother in the nursing home. After her grandma passed, she just kept coming. I used to think it was silly, this dedication of hers to a chosen stranger. On more than one occasion, when she woke me up early on a Saturday while getting ready to go see him, I cursed him in my head, even wondered "When is that guy gonna croak?"

"Well, then, have a seat," he says.

There are two chairs at the table. He takes one of them. I offer the other to Riko, but she waves me off and sits on the edge of the bed, uncomfortably, hands clasped in front of her like she doesn't want to touch anything, especially the bedsheets he wraps around himself at night.

"I don't have much time left, so don't waste it," he says as I sit in the chair across from him. "Why the hell did you kids come to visit me?"

Age is all relative, I suppose. To a teenager, even to myself, I am old. To Mr. Sacramone, I am a kid.

"I know how much you meant to Sara," I say, considering this a sufficient answer to the question.

"That girl meant a lot to me too," he says. "But, if memory serves me—which it sometimes don't—she passed quite some time ago."

"A year ago," I say.

He smiles his toothless smile. "You'll grieve faster when you lose more people," he says, as if this evolution is a good thing.

We are silent for moment. Then he turns to Riko and asks, "And who the hell are you? Did you know Sara?"

"I'm Riko. And, no, I didn't know Sara."

"Well, then, that's too bad for you." He says it like he's mad at her.

"I'd love to hear more about her, though."

He stands from his chair, which seems to require effort and concentration. I can almost hear his joints cracking, berating him for the demands he places upon them.

"Lucky for you, I have this," he says, but he has not made his way to the "this" yet and we are left to wait awkwardly. He approaches his desk and opens a drawer. He pulls out a picture frame and brings it back to the table with him. He seems like a different person now that he has this under his arm. There is a pleasantness to him now, defying the grumpy-old-man stereotype from before.

He motions for Riko to come to the table. I can almost hear his elbows creak like the rusty hinges on a door. He doesn't offer her his seat; he just wants her attention. Chivalry probably does not get the toothless anywhere.

"I look at this every so often," he says, showing her the picture.

There is Sara beaming, cheek to cheek with Mr. Sacramone. He looks about as happy as his worn face will allow him to look.

"She was beautiful," Riko says, looking up at me. I've heard this often since Sara died, as if it was more of a tragedy because she was conventionally attractive.

"She was more beautiful on the inside, if you can believe it," Mr. Sacramone says.

I can believe it.

"Actually, I have something for you," I say, taking out a

photo album from my backpack. It's the one I found at the storage unit. His arthritic hands—knuckles swollen, fingers bent at weird angles—reach for it, coveting it before they have a chance to hold it.

The album is full of pictures of the two of them, but my eyes go right to Sara on every page: Sara holding a winning Bingo card. Putting up red, white, and blue streamers. Standing over a birthday cake. Holding a dozen balloons. Hovering over a salad bowl full of ice cream. Doing the limbo, with the bar so low that the residents must have been nostalgic for their youth. She was always in a good mood when she came home from her visits to the nursing home, but I'd had no idea about any of this. She was part of this community. I can't imagine that the place smelled of peas when she was alive. I imagine it smelled like her perfume, or, rather, her "body spray," as she considered perfume not her style. It was a fruity scent, one of those strange concoctions like raspberry–cucumber or mango–citrus. I can't remember the name, exactly. I wish I could. I would buy a lifetime supply and use it as air freshener.

"That's Ruth," Mr. Sacramone says, pointing to an old lady dancing with Sara in one of the pictures. "She died just last month." He does this with other residents in the pictures—points out who is sick, who is deceased. He seems invested in our understanding who is still around and who is not. I suppose when you are old, this is rather important to track.

"You must have been very close," Riko says.

"She came to visit, to play chess, because she knew I didn't have anyone else," he says. "'Course, it wasn't just chess. We talked. I guess you could say Sara was the closest thing I ever had to a daughter. My wife and I, we never had kids. Either her plumbing was faulty or mine was, if you catch my drift."

"Did your wife know Sara too?"

"Oh, no. She would have liked her, though. Janet passed some years ago now. In '04."

I understand his insomnia now. Years have passed and he's still sleepless. This lends more necessity to the laundry-detergent fumes.

"When I heard 'bout the accident, I think I cried harder than I had since Janet died. God sure don't make a lick of sense sometimes." He fiddles with one of the chess pieces in his palms.

"Well, if it's any consolation, Sara cared for you quite a bit," I say.

He laughs, revealing those lonely gums again, and says, "You don't gotta tell me that. Sara made sure I knew that every time I saw her."

I pick up a chess piece and tap it on the table, nervously. Mr. Sacramone seems in no rush to fill this silence. I suppose patience comes with age.

"You're him, aren't you?" he says finally, pointing an accusatory finger at me.

"Who?"

"Sara's boy," he says. "You're exactly as she described you."

"She described me?"

"Of course," he says with a laugh that catches in his throat, causing him to cough up a disturbing amount of phlegm. "She talked about you quite a bit."

"Good things, I hope."

He lifts one eyebrow. "Would she have reason to say otherwise?"

I shrug. "I don't know anymore. My memory tells me I did and said everything wrong."

"Well, you probably did," he says, "but that girl still loved you."

Somehow, this helps, when he says it.

"It hurts, doesn't it?" he says, not sorrowfully, but factually.

I nod. I feel them, the tears, pressing on the backs of my eyes, like a rioting crowd behind the doors of Walmart on Black Friday.

"You're not here to play chess, are you?" he says, looking from Riko to me. He's on to me. I had worried I'd have to at least pretend to play chess to get to talk to him a bit. And I know nothing about chess besides this:

- There is a board with black-and-white squares.
- There are kings and queens and some other things that appear on Pepperidge Farms shortbread cookies.
- "Checkmate" is a good thing (for you, not your opponent).
- In the movie *Searching for Bobby Fischer*, this little kid has a "gift" and some adults ruin it for him.

"I don't have any words of wisdom," he adds, "if that's why you came."

And maybe that *is* why I came. I don't say anything, though, fearing that if I try, my voice will crack and I will be revealed for the sad mess I am.

"You young people always think old folks know the secrets to life," he says. "The real secret is that there is no secret."

I'd figured as much.

He smiles in response to some thought in his head, then says, "I knew Sara loved you because she started asking me all these things about Janet, how I knew Janet was 'the one,' if I believed in love lasting a lifetime."

I can't tell if this makes it worse or better. The terms seem interchangeable, like if I were to forgo laundry-detergent fumes and go on living, the only choice would be better *and* worse.

Good times would forever be tainted by the fact that I couldn't have them with Sara.

"Sometimes," I admit, "I wish I could remember us as not really in love, you know? Like I think that would make it easier."

Couldn't she have been "just a girlfriend"? A blip on the radar? Like all the others before her? I'd forgotten all of them, their faces, like you forget the face of your dental hygienist or your third-grade teacher. The features just dissolve in time. And yet, in this year that's passed, Sara's face is right there, in abusive detail, whenever I close my eyes.

"Sorry, kid," he says.

"You know, Janet used to love dresses," he says, asking us to trust that he is going somewhere with this, fashioning a story that imparts the wisdom he claims not to possess. "She had a different one for every occasion. I used to get so mad at her for spending money on them. What woman needs a hundred dresses? 'A princess,' she said; then she asked me, 'Aren't I your princess?' Women know how to say these things just right, don't you?" He winks at Riko. She smiles.

"When she died, I looked at each of those dresses and remembered the day she wore it. The funeral home asked me to pick out one, for her burial dress, and I just stood in front of that goddamned closet for hours." He shakes his head, the way people do when they are trapped in a memory.

"What did you pick?" I ask, luring him out of the confines of his private sadness. He looks up at me suddenly, startled almost. Years later and remembering her still makes him forget himself, his very surroundings.

"I didn't pick anything," he says with a shrug. "I couldn't choose. Now, I think I was just selfish. You know, didn't want to have one less dress to look at."

I glance toward the door of the closet in his room, wondering about its size, its ability to hold all these dresses of hers.

" 'Course, didn't know then that I'd get old, have to sell my house and come here. There ain't room here for a hundred dresses. I took four. Janet's buried in somethin' the funeral home picked out, and I got four dresses left."

I don't know what to say to this, so I say nothing. I imagine the dresses in his closet, in those plastic hanging bags. I imagine him unzipping each bag, smelling each dress, with the scent of time past. I imagine this as a nightly ritual. I imagine the agony of coming here, having to give up more of her.

"Why weren't you at Sara's funeral?" he asks, looking at me with scolding eyes. Riko stands behind me now, unwilling to serve as my shield.

"You couldn't pick a dress, and I couldn't stand to see Sara in whatever dress they picked for her," I say. This sounds poetic. I feel momentarily proud.

"It was a closed casket," Mr. Sacramone says.

And now I just feel like an idiot.

We sit in silence. He sets down the king he's been fingering and adjusts the other pieces so they sit on their squares in a way that is perfect to him.

"It would have done you good," he says, and my advertising mind immediately thinks of the milk campaign: "Funerals, they do a sad soul good."

"Funerals make it real in a way that it needs to be real," he continues. "That's why we have them."

"That's what I told him," Riko says, quietly. Mr. Sacramone winks at her again. They're ganging up on me.

"I just couldn't go."

He nods. "Knowing Sara, she wouldn't have wanted you to

go if you didn't want to.'"

He uses this phrase—*knowing Sara*—with such enviable ease, the way Sara's father did, like memories of her no longer bring acute pain. I don't feel capable of obtaining this skill, if that's what you'd call it.

"Did she ever tell you about the time she dropped my teeth in the toilet?"

He is back to smiling, his emotions as transitional as I wish mine could be.

"No, she didn't tell me," I say. And why not? Fake teeth in a toilet is amusing. Did she think I wouldn't care? Would I have cared? Maybe, that day, I came home to find the house dark. Maybe I turned on the bathroom light and heard her groan and roll over from one side to the other. She hated when I came home late. She hated to have her dreams interrupted. Maybe, by the next day, she'd forgotten about the teeth in the toilet, or replaced the story with a new one. Sara took funny anecdotes from each and every day. She found teeth-in-the-toilet stories all the time. Or they found her, confident that she would validate them with warm laughter.

"She went into the bathroom to get them for me and I hear this 'plunk' and then that laugh of hers, like Julia Roberts's in *Pretty Woman*, when the jewelry box snaps shut on her hand. She asked if she should fish them out, but we both thought that wasn't such a swell idea, being that I am one to believe 'if it's yellow, let it mellow.' Catch my drift?"

Fake teeth in a pee-filled toilet? How could I not have been a worthy recipient of such a story?

"So that's what happened to your teeth?"

He nods. "I could get new ones, but don't see why I need 'em. I have nobody to impress anymore."

I have this refrain for almost everything—buying a new pair of shoes, going to the gym, getting up in the morning, existing.

"Gosh, she would have made a great mother, don't you think?" There's a twinkle in his eye. I can't tell if he knows, if she told him. Riko squeezes my shoulder.

"She would have been a great anything," I say.

"Right. Well, only the good die young."

Did he just quote Billy Joel?

"Can I tell you something?" I ask.

He moves his tongue over his gums at the same rate he rolls his eyes. "Do I look like a priest waiting for confessions?"

A toothless priest, I think.

"Well, go ahead," he says, resigned.

"I haven't been to her grave."

He chuckles, and I think he must not have heard me correctly, because what I've said is, well, not amusing.

"What?" I say as he persists in chuckling. He stands from his chair slowly, still chuckling.

"You haven't been to her grave?" he says. He puts his bare feet back in his slippers and moves toward the door.

"No, I haven't." I follow him into the hallway, not sure where we're going. Riko is on my heels.

"You're visiting me, and you haven't visited *her* yet? I think you have your priorities wrong."

I stop at this, but he is still shuffling down the hallway. He makes a right into a room with couches and a couple televisions. It is empty, though a TV is on. Riko and I stand in the doorway and watch him move to a windowsill with a small pot of baby pink roses sitting on it. He looks one way then the other, like he's crossing a street, and then he takes the pot and hides it inside his robe. He comes back to me, a journey which seems to take an hour. I wonder if it seems to take an hour to him or if the entire world just slows as you approach your eventual stop. He hands the pot to me.

"When you go," he says, "leave this for me."

Things to do before I die—updated:

- Go to Japan
- ~~Visit my parents~~
- ~~Get the complete collection of *Seinfeld* and watch all episodes~~
- Give my clothes to the Salvation Army
- ~~Take all my loose change to a Coinstar machine~~
- Learn Japanese
- Get rid of the damn storage unit
- ~~Visit Sara's parents~~
- ~~Visit Mr. Sacramone~~
- Visit Sara
- Get a nice gift for Riko

The list grows. If I wasn't so intimately aware of my own resolve, I might think I was procrastinating this death thing. I just want to do it right. Nothing is worse than someone leaving the world suddenly, abruptly, without preparations made.

The idea to get a gift for Riko came to me after I finished a bottle of cabernet sauvignon I'd saved for years, for a "special occasion." I don't know what I'll get her, but I should get her something. She's helped me cross off a few things on my list, after all.

二十一

I t's just a couple minutes until our second-semester Japanese class is supposed to start, but there's no sign of Riko. I've placed my textbook on the chair in front of me, saving it for her, like I used to do for friends in junior high. The book's placement embarrasses me, exposes the fact that I'm waiting for someone, expecting someone. Voices in my head tell me "She's not coming back."

But then she walks in, looking rushed and frazzled, right ahead of Miyagi Sensei. She doesn't thank me for saving the seat for her; it's assumed I would.

"My stupid car wouldn't start," she whispers, then turns to face the front.

Miyagi Sensei has her usual rolling bag at her side and her usual pleasant smile.

"*Konbanwa*," she says, with a hurried bow. The class responds in turn.

"How was your *ba-re-ku?*" she asks us. She enunciates the katakana—*ba-re-ku, ba-re-ku.* I see the characters in my head:

This must mean I'm learning.

Still, it takes me a moment to realize she's asking us about our "break." Is there no word native to Japan that means "break"? I guess that could make sense, considering the Japanese are notorious for their work ethic. Many Japanese companies mandate six-day workweeks, for example. And the government wonders why the suicide rate is so high. Interestingly, a word that *is* native to Japan is *karoshi*, meaning "death by overwork." The first case was reported in 1969, upon the death from a stroke of a twenty-nine-year-old man in the shipping department of Japan's largest newspaper company. In the 1980s, during the bubble economy, several high-ranking business executives died suddenly. If you ask me, *karoshi* is just a type of suicide.

We spend the first twenty minutes of class telling Miyagi Sensei how we spent our winter breaks. Every now and then, Miyagi Sensei translates a word into Japanese for us.

- Vacation is *ya-su-mi*
- Christmas is *ku-ri-su-ma-su*
- Tree is *ki*
- Ski is *su-ki*

There is a very low probability any of us will remember these words. Well, Riko might.

"Okay! Let's start something new," Miyagi Sensei says, with an enthusiastic clap of her hands. "*Ganbatte!*"

That means "Go for it." In response, we all say, as we have been trained, "*Ganbarimasu*," which means "I go for it." I can only hope it sounds less lame when coming from a native speaker's mouth. It's probably similar to our phrase "You rock." I imagine English-language students have trouble with this one, thinking perhaps we encourage someone by calling them a stone.

"We are going to do verbs," Miyagi Sensei says.

Verbs. The cornerstone to any good sentence.

In the next half hour, we learn a few basics:

- To go
- To return
- To come
- To eat
- To drink
- To sleep
- To wake up
- To watch
- To read
- To study
- To do

An interesting selection.

In English, we would be paralyzed without the verb "to be." Back in high school, that was the first verb we learned in Spanish too. In fact, as I recall, Spanish has "*ser*" as "to be" for somewhat permanent states and "*estar*" for temporary conditions. So "I am a happy person by nature" would utilize *ser*, while "I am happy in this moment, but it probably won't last because happiness never does" would utilize *estar*. I was a big fan of this convention.

I suppose "*desu*" is "to be," in that it's tacked onto the end of sentences describing what something is. *Watashi wa Amerikajin desu* means "I am American." The funny thing is that native speakers often don't bother with the *desu*; it's implied. I can only conclude that the Japanese are not too concerned with *being*. Judging by the "key verbs" presented to us, they are concerned with *doing* (and all the things required for a body "to do"—eat, drink, sleep). And they are also concerned with studying.

Perhaps if they formally introduced "to be" into their vocabulary, there would be fewer laundry-detergent suicides. Or perhaps there would be more. After all, "being"—while empowering and exhilarating at first—can become burdensome.

You would think that, given the three alphabets, conjugating verbs in Japanese would be unnecessarily complicated. It's not, though. As Miyagi Sensei explains, there is simply one thing to worry about—whether something is done, or whether it is not. In Japanese, verbs have absolutely nothing to do with the person to whom they apply, which makes sense considering that individuality is apparently so unimportant in Japanese culture that they couldn't be hassled with "to be." An example: In English, we have five forms for the verb "to go," depending on *who* is going:

- I go
- You go
- He/she goes
- We go
- They go

In Japanese, I, you, he/she, we, they all take the same form of the verb *"iku"*—*"ikimasu."* So either someone *ikimasu*-es or they don't (in which case it's *"ikimasen"*). Doesn't matter who.

All of this reminds me of the Japanese phrase "The nail that stands out will be struck down." Individuals are trumped by the collective. To further hammer in this idea (pun intended), the word for "wrong" in Japanese is the same as the word for "different." This belief system is obvious in advertising (as most cultural conventions are). A jeans campaign in America had this copy: "Dare to be different." The Japanese version was "Fit in with the group."

Another interesting thing about Japanese grammar: they only have past tense and present tense—no future. So "I will inhale laundry-detergent fumes" is written the same as "I inhale laundry-detergent fumes." In a sense, the present is the future, and the future is the present, which may explain the innovative, ahead-of-their time electronics in Japan.

After filling our brains with verbs, Miyagi Sensei tells us to "go forth and conjugate." It sounds sexual to me—but judging by the lack of smirks in the classroom, I'm alone in this.

"Do you want to get dinner?" Riko asks as we file out of the room. "I want to ask your advice about something."

Before this invitation, my plan for the night included separating my pants into jeans and non-jeans for Salvation Army donation purposes. I can't think of an excuse fast enough, so I say, "Sure, I guess."

We go to a hole-in-the-wall Chinese place that smells like MSG, if MSG has a smell. It's one of those places that has a dingy curtain between the dining area and the kitchen. I try to peek underneath it, checking for small dogs running around frantically, in fear for their lives.

Riko breaks apart the wooden chopsticks in front of her and

starts fiddling with them in her hands, rubbing them together like she's trying to create a fire.

"So, what could possibly require my advice?" I ask. I say this with wholehearted self-doubt. I'm quite sure I'm ill-equipped to advise anyone on anything.

"I can't stop thinking about my adoption," she says, putting her chopsticks down with dramatic deliberation.

The waitress, an awkward teenage girl probably recruited by her parents to help out and earn a few bucks, places two glasses of water in front of us. Riko orders on our behalf—moo shu something.

"My parents, in Japan, gave me up when I was three years old," she says. "It's not like I was an infant when I came here. I mean, three years old is a *toddler*."

"You don't remember Japan, though?"

She looks at me like I'm an idiot. "Do you have memories from when you were three?"

Sara and I talked about our first memories once. She said hers was riding in the car with her dad, listening to Neil Diamond. They were going to check on a rental property he was managing at the time. She remembered running around the backyard of the property and falling, scraping her knee on the cement. One of my first memories is getting squirted in the face with a juice box. In kindergarten, I think.

"Sorry, I guess I just thought—hoped—you'd have some memory of it."

"Well, me too." She's still looking at me like I'm an idiot. "Anyway, that's the thing that keeps getting to me—why would they give me up after *three years*?"

I can see what she's doing—going down a rabbit hole of *why* and *what if*, searching for an explanation that will counteract her suspicion that she wasn't worthy of love from the very people who gave her life. She wants to understand, to replace question marks with periods, to put to rest her doubts and fears. We all want the same thing.

"I have no idea, Riko."

"I mean, it couldn't be as simple as they didn't want a baby in the first place, because they kept me—for *three years.*"

I imagine the fabrications taking up residence in her mind: Maybe she was the cast-off child of a royal emperor. Maybe she was taken from her parents by a black market adoption agency looking to make a few bucks. Maybe she was taken into protective custody because her parents were descendants of expert samurai swordsmen with many enemies.

"I always wondered why my parents didn't have baby pictures of me," she says. "They have a few, but they're probably from my birth parents. Do you think they kept any for themselves?"

"Probably," I say, because I know that's what she wants to hear.

"Why would they give me up?"

"I really have no idea. What do the adoption records say?"

"They just list my father's name, like I told you before. Hideo Shimura. There is no reason stated for the adoption, nothing like that."

"So, what advice do you need?" I ask, cutting to the proverbial chase.

"It's obvious, isn't it?"

I shrug, and she rolls her eyes at me, impatiently. "Should I write to him? Would that be weird?"

I let my head fall back and stare at the ceiling. Someone has thrown a pencil up into one of the panels, like a dart at a board. I wonder how long it's been up there.

"I don't know, Riko. Like your parents said, you don't know

what kind of worms are going to come out of that can."

I feel like a douche referencing her parents, like I'm on their side.

"Informative worms, maybe," she argues.

"I just think looking for closure could be a bad idea." The condescension in my voice continues to annoy even me.

"Like you should be talking. You're going all the way to Japan for closure."

I wait a second for her to apologize, but she doesn't.

She continues, "And besides, I'm not looking for *closure*. I'm looking for a beginning."

This is where we differ. She seeks a beginning—of what, I don't know—and I seek an end.

"Will you at least read the letter and tell me if I should send it?"

"You already wrote it?"

"In hiragana," she says. "It reads like a four-year-old wrote it, but that's probably how he remembers me anyway, right?"

I'm not sure if she means this to be funny or sad, so I don't laugh or sigh or make any sound at all. She slides the paper across the table covertly.

I unfold it to see that she has managed to construct a short letter based on the basic grammar and vocabulary that we now have at our disposal. This is what it says, translated into English:

Father,
Often, I think of you. There are many questions, but there is also time to answer the questions. Today, I say thank you. I speak a little Japanese. I am in a Japanese class. I like to read books. I like to go to the beach. I love cats. I am sorry my Japanese is not good. When I learn more, I will write.

She is right; this reads like it was composed by a four-year-old, a precocious four-year-old placing a personal ad. I don't know why she wrote that she liked the beach and cats. Because she can, I guess. It's amazing what limited vocabulary inspires you to share.

"So?" she says.

"What does *ai wo komete* mean?" This is how she's ended the letter, before signing her name.

"It means 'with love.'"

She loves this man she's never met?

"I looked it up online. I guess 'with love' is not a common way to end a letter in Japan. They don't even say 'I love you' there like we do," she says. I'm aware of this.

"Do you think I should take out the love thing?" She answers herself before I can. "No, whatever, to hell with that. I'm American, and my dad can deal with it."

She calls this man "Dad" already?

The waitress arrives with our food, and Riko distracts herself by dividing it up for us.

"I'm sure he'll be happy to hear from you."

She smiles, confirming that I have said the right thing, and hands me my plate.

"I'm going to send it," she says.

"You know where he lives?"

"Like I said, I've done some research." She takes a bite of her food, swallows. "He lives in this little mountain town outside Toyko. Nikko. It's worth a try, right?"

"It sounds like the try is worth it to you, yes."

"And if he doesn't write back, I'll just have to let it go."

I nod, though I doubt her ability to do this.

She uses her finger to pile the last bit of rice onto her fork and says, without looking up at me, "If this blows up in my face, you're not allowed to say 'I told you so.'"

I feel bad for travel agents. Thanks to the internet, they've become rather obsolete, like the tailors and blacksmiths of yesteryear. I've created my Japan itinerary based on reading some guy's travel blog titled "Have a blast in Hiroshima!" I appreciated the humor, so I stole his itinerary:

- Day 1: Arrive at Narita Airport, and wander around Tokyo.
- Days 2–5: Spend time in Tokyo. Towns like Kamakura or Nikko make for "easy day trips." I'm a little apprehensive about what the Japanese consider "easy."
- Day 6: Take the bullet train (they call it the shinkansen) from Tokyo to Kyoto and wander around Kyoto.
- Days 7–10: Spend a couple of days in Kyoto and one day in Nara and/or Osaka, "easy day trips" from Kyoto.
- Day 11: Travel from Kyoto to Hiroshima. Take the blogger's advice and have an ironic blast. I imagine I'll visit the Peace Park, where there will be horrific stories about charred children. I will probably wear a shirt with the Canadian flag on it and say "eh" in the presence of natives. If the vibe is bad, that's okay, because the itinerary tells me to leave for Miyajima and spend the night there.
- Day 12: Wander around Miyajima. It's an island, I guess. From there, leave for Himeji and visit some castle. Then back to Tokyo.
- Day 13: Depart Japan from Narita Airport. I may upgrade to first class, depending on my funding situation. This will be my last plane flight, after all.

It's a general plan. It could change. On the map, the general plan looks like this:

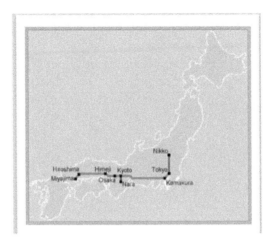

I figure I'll send postcards to Mom and Dad, Riko, Rhonda and Ted, Mr. Sacramone, maybe even Miyagi Sensei. I'll say cryptic things like "I think it is possible to have monk-like peace" and "Now that I've tasted authentic sashimi, I can die a happy man." That way, when I make my grand exit shortly after my return, they'll have something to support the comforting idea that everything happens for a reason and we're all pleasantly involved in a big master plan.

二十二

The reason the phrase "easy day trip" concerns me is that the Japanese seem to think many things are easy that are not, by normal-person standards, easy. Like calculus and structural engineering. And kanji.

Miyagi Sensei persists in describing kanji as "fun," while I would describe it as "a bitch." Kanji is a bitch. It's the third Japanese language system, created to distinguish the educated from the uneducated. At one time, only the elite, and mostly men, were "privileged" enough to learn kanji, with all its complicated pen strokes. Women communicated only with the hiragana alphabet. Their lack of knowledge of kanji's complex pictographs kept them inferior. This little history lesson pissed off Riko and made her profess determination to learn every character in the kanji alphabet. To this I raised an invisible glass and said "*Kampai*," the Japanese version of "Cheers."

To give you an idea of how ridiculous kanji is (and how ridiculous Riko's mission is), this is how you write "o'clock," as in "three o'clock," in kanji:

Yes, all that for the ":" in "3:00."

It is said that the most complicated kanji have upward of thirty pen strokes. This one is a doozy:

What does it mean, you ask? It means "mythical bird." It's almost like the kanji-creator was laughing at all of us, saying, "Ha, go ahead, work 'mythical bird' into a sentence. See how bad your carpal tunnel gets."

According to Miyagi Sensei, there are thousands of characters; and when these characters are paired with hiragana, there are thousands of different meanings. It is enough to make one (or me, rather) wonder why one (or, I) should even bother attempting to learn this language. As far as I can tell, the Japanese have created this communication system so that nobody can understand them. Sort of like the Morse code on German warships. When America falls, which it will, these pesky Japanese, with their pesky language, will plot and scheme and take over the world. They will forbid us all from speaking until we adopt their language, meaning we will all be silent and, therefore, much easier to manage.

This is where the world is going.

So far, Miyagi Sensei has taught us only the kanji numbers:

This is enough to render us dumb and drooling. Miyagi Sensei tries to help us with various mnemonic devices, but there is simply no way my mind can make sense of any of the numbers past three. Some kid in class says, "Well, it takes *five* pen strokes to make the character for five." But this is not helpful because (1) this rule does not apply to all the other characters ("8" has two pen strokes, for example) and (2) there are many shapes I can make with five pen strokes that don't come out looking like the kanji character "5." This is when I check out. Miyagi Sensei starts sounding like Charlie Brown's teacher, and I doodle, which is something I haven't done since my days at R&R during status meetings.

This has five pen strokes, one stroke shy of a swastika. When I was a kid, we had some Indian neighbors put a design like this on their iron gate. People were outraged. The India people just thought it was pretty.

The English alphabet is kinder. "S," "C," "O," and "U" have one fun pen stroke, for instance. We are big fans of curves because we are too damn lazy to lift our pens and complicate matters. Again, this is why I worry about the "ease" of my planned Japanese day trips.

Halfway through class, we're all pretty much brain-dead. Miyagi Sensei looks at her watch and says, "I have idea!"

She does this sometimes—leaves out particles. I can't blame her. English has no rule for particles. We say "I'm going to school" (not "I'm going to *the* school"), but we say "I'm going to *the* hospital" (not "I'm going to hospital"). Rule-based Asians must hate us. Miyagi Sensei also thinks "Skitpresentation" is one word, which makes her so much less intimidating to me.

"Let's take a field trip to Nakada," she says.

Nakada is a Japanese restaurant in a strip mall. I've seen actual Japanese people come out of there, which is usually a good sign if you are looking for "authentic" cuisine. To be honest, as a sheltered white man, I am not looking for this. I prefer foreign food to be Americanized. I don't go to English pubs and order kidney pie. I tell the waitress I'll have the pie, hold the kidney. I'm aware that this approach to food means I could starve in Japan (which would be far less exciting than inhaling laundry detergent), but I'm also aware that the corporate tentacles of McDonald's reach very far. (On a side note, do the Japanese eat tentacles? If they do, it's a pizza topping, no doubt.) After all, one of the first words we learned to write in katakana, after our first names, is "McDonald's"—Ma-ku-do-na-ru-do. This picture even appears in our book, alongside text of a conversation between "Takeshi" and "Mearii," our Japanese language heroes (similar to Dick and Jane) who decide they want to eat a hamburger for lunch:

"Who would like to ride with me?" Miyagi Sensei says.

I'm ashamed that my first thought is that choosing to ride with an Asian (a female, no less, who is relatively "fresh off the boat" in that she doesn't always use particles correctly), is some kind of death wish. And while I have one of those, I'm quite particular about it, as I've made clear. A casualty in the passenger's seat of a Honda (I'm guessing) is not how I want it to be fulfilled. Thankfully, a few kiss-asses agree to ride with the teacher, and Riko and I decide to take my car.

"I hope she doesn't make us speak Japanese to the waiter," Riko says as we follow Miyagi Sensei's car. There is a line of students, cars in procession, and I wish we had fluorescent stickers on our windshields that said "Sushi Field Trip," like the ones that say "Funeral" when everyone is on their way to a graveyard. It would be beneficial to slap a "Funeral" sticker on at all times, now that I think about it. Nobody would cut you off. You wouldn't get the finger as often. A cop would be highly unlikely to pull you over. People would generally leave you alone. Grief to humans is like deet to mosquitoes.

"I'm just going to point at things on the menu," I say. This has always worked for my father in Mexican restaurants. We live close enough to the border for him to know that the double "L" in "*quesadilla*" makes a "Y" sound, but he cannot get his mouth to cooperate with his brain. So now he just points, and that's fine.

"Let's get sake," Riko says, excitedly. Her youthful enthusiasm makes me forget I'm in my thirties.

Our procession of Japanese language students pulls into the Nakada parking lot. We get out of the car, and Miyagi Sensei gathers us in a huddle like we're sixth graders and instructs us to say "*Konbanwa*" and bow to the hostess. I hate the bowing thing. It's never a half-assed deal. To be done right, a ninety-degree angle must be achieved. For me, this is exercise.

Miyagi Sensei's plan quickly goes awry when we venture inside and see that the hostess is a sixteen-year-old blond girl with a nose ring, wearing a kimono with the same sense of discomfort as a punk in a dolphin costume at Sea World. Also, the proper way to wear a kimono is with the right side tucked in with the left side over it. This hostess has the left side tucked under the right. In Japan, this is only done for burial attire on corpses. Trust me, I've researched.

"*Konbanwa!*" Miyagi Sensei says to the hostess. A few of the kiss-asses, the daredevils who agreed to ride in the same car with her, mutter this "good evening" greeting as well.

And this is what the hostess says in response: "Huh?"

We are given a table near the back of the restaurant. Miyagi Sensei advises us on some menu options, recommending:

- Tempura udon: Noodles in broth topped with shrimp and vegetable tempura
- Unadon: Teriyaki eel (eel!) over rice
- Katsudon: Pork cutlet with egg over rice
- Miso soup: For something "light," she says

Despite her suggestions, six people choose the California roll, three people pick the teriyaki chicken bowl, and one idiot, Vernon, insults Miyagi Sensei's very being by selecting a wayward special called the Mexicali roll, which involves carne asada wrapped in seaweed and rolled in Spanish rice, topped with salsa. Maybe he makes this choice to purposely offend Miyagi Sensei. After all, she is always calling him "Bernon." Remember, in Japanese, the difference between "V" and "B" is like the difference between "R" and "L"—nonexistent. I would advise anyone to take a minute to consider the amusing consequences of this:

- Bictory
- Biolence
- Bagina

Riko and I both order the *katsudon*, which seems to please Miyagi Sensei. Perhaps I will get "extracredit" (which she also thinks is one word). Riko whispers to the waiter that she'd also like sake, two glasses. I don't know why she whispers. We're all adults here, after all. Of course, she gets carded anyway. I don't. A depressing chain of events.

When the sake comes, she pours my cup first, then hers. We are somewhat detached from the conversation at the rest of the table, which is fine by me.

"Isn't that the same Pink Floyd shirt you were wearing the other day?" Riko says, pointing at my attire disapprovingly.

"Yes." I offer no further explanation. Riko does not need to know that I've given away almost my entire wardrobe—save for a few T-shirts, jeans, and a jacket (for Japan)—because I plan to die soon.

"So," she says, "it's been two weeks."

"Two weeks since…?"

"Since I mailed the letter," she says. "No response."

"I'm sorry, Riko," I say. I'm genuine about this, a surprise to me and probably Riko too.

"But, get this—I found out the name of his inn, where he lives. Or, well, I'm assuming he owns it."

"Okay?"

"It's *Rihoko no ie.*"

The speed with which I translate this amazes me. Rihoko's House.

"He named it after you?" I say.

"I guess."

I admit, I get that warm, tingly feeling in my scalp upon hearing this. It's poetic, his naming the place after her. Makes me think he loved her, even if he gave her up for whatever reason.

"He must care for me, right?"

"He must."

"Why won't he write back?"

"Maybe he didn't get it," I say, reaching for an excuse she has likely tried to grasp herself.

"I just want to know him. Is it too much to want that?"

"I don't think so," I say, leaving out another truth: *but the universe might.*

Our food arrives. It looks edible.

"Anyway," Riko says. She blows a cooling breath on her food. "Enough about me."

"If you say so."

"Have you thought about what Mr. Sacramone suggested? Visiting Sara?"

It's almost like she's taunting me: *I'm confronting my demons. Now you confront yours.*

"I've thought about it, yes."

"And?"

"I don't know if I'm ready for that."

"You'll never be ready. Who would be ready for something like that?"

Maybe she's right.

She takes her first bite and says, "This isn't as spicy as I thought it'd be."

I give her my best dad look and say, "Riko, nothing is ever what we think it will be."

Here is a finalized list of people I want at my funeral or remembrance ceremony or whatever it is:

- Mom
- Dad
- Riko

That's it.

I don't want to bother Rhonda and Ted with more tragedy. Same goes for Mr. Sacramone. And I don't want Miyagi Sensei to feel guilty that I chose a suicide technique developed by "her people." There's nobody else in my life, really. For a moment, this makes me sad, but then I remember: having nobody in my life was the goal. The fact that Riko is on the list means I have failed.

二十三

When I was a kid and my parents used to take me to "visit" my grandpas, I'd wander off, looking for the graves with the piles of fresh flowers, the ones with the recently unearthed soil and the over-green grass attempting to meld with the surrounding less-green lawn. I wondered if the recently dead were lingering to see who would visit, who their true loved ones were, who would bring the nicest bouquets. I don't believe in the afterlife now. No ghosts. No spirits. No heaven in the sky where Sara and my gramps can frolic, jumping on rainbow slides to get from one cloud to the next. There are parts of me that are still childish, though. As we step carefully from one row to the next, I find myself scanning the grave markers, doing math subconsciously, subtracting birth years from death years, looking for answers like six or eleven—real tragedies. I find one with just a single date and can't help but say, "Hey, Riko, come look at this one."

She is not as sadistic as me. The sight of the plaque in the ground marking some poor child's birthday and deathday makes her overwhelmingly sad.

"Poor baby," she says.

She is holding the pot of baby roses from Mr. Sacramone in one hand and a bouquet of daisies in the other, a piece of foil wrapped around the cut stems. When I'd asked her to come with me, she'd insisted on bringing flowers to place on Sara's grave. She asked me what kind of flowers to get, and I said cherry blossoms. She laughed and said, "I'm pretty sure that's a tree not native to California." Then I snapped, "Jesus, I don't know," and she showed up twenty minutes later with daisies.

My parents and I visited the grandpas' graves annually, on Father's Day. There was Grandpa Hank, who died right before I was born (oh, the circle of life), and Grandpa Floyd, who provided my sole funeral experience. Almost every time we came to the cemetery, we spent at least twenty minutes walking the graveyard, searching for the right resting spots, feeling as stupid as you do when you can't find your car at Disneyland: "Did we park in Goofy or Minnie Mouse? Or was it Pluto?" We could have asked, could have gone to the little office and said, "Hello, we can't find the graves of our beloved relatives." We could have received clear directions. Graveyards are like parking lots, after all, plotted out by a letter and a number coordinate—A3, B6, H10. It's simple, really. But we couldn't stand admitting that we didn't know. It's the equivalent of flagging down an attendant in the Disneyland parking lot to drive you around in a cart: "Oh, there it is!" So we wandered, pretending we were just a family out for a leisurely cemetery stroll, ignoring the suspicious glances of proper mourners.

Riko and I had no choice but to go to the little office to ask where Sara was buried. Even if I'd had the nerve to call my parents or Rhonda and Ted, I imagined they'd have given unhelpful instructions like this: "You're just going to pass three oaks, hang a right at the Ackerman family plot, and then look down."

The lady in the office was nice enough. She looked up Sara's name in the computer and said "Aha! C3." She gave us a map and pointed out the location. "It's a beautiful area." Her eyes lit up, like she was excited to show us a house for sale.

Turns out C3 *is* a beautiful area. Lots of trees and shade. It's pressed up against a hill marking the end of the cemetery grounds. Riko is scanning the tops rows of graves; I'm starting at the bottom. We've almost met in the middle when she says, "Found it."

The plaque is simple. It just says "Sara Lu Mackenzie, our beloved daughter, August 4, 1984–December 20, 2015."

"Her middle name was Lu?" Riko says.

"It was her grandmother's name, short for Luanne." Somehow, I've managed to retain this fact.

Riko places Mr. Sacramone's roses and her daisies next to the grave, in the convenient hole in the ground. The death industry thinks of everything. I wonder how long Sara's grave has been flowerless, forgotten. I feel like I should have been here for it, for her.

"You okay?" Riko asks. We stand, hip to hip, looking down at the ground.

"I don't know," I say. "What am I supposed to feel?"

"No idea," she says. She turns around, squinting in the face of the setting sun. I crouch and touch the grass. The lawn in this area is all uniform—no new graves.

"Do you ever talk to her?" Riko asks.

"To who?"

"Sara. Like, when you're lying in bed at night, do you ever talk to her?"

Riko sits on the grass next to me, runs her fingers through the blades.

It would be normal for me to talk to Sara, before bed, in the darkness, the way most people talk to God. I could confess my flaws, state my apologies, profess my love, share my plans. I don't, though. I can barely say her name without my voice cracking.

"I think I'm afraid to."

"Is there something you'd want her to know?"

That I'm sorry. That I miss her. That I'm inhaling laundry-detergent fumes because I can't imagine life will ever mean anything again.

"I don't know."

"You don't want to talk about it. Sorry."

"It's okay."

She tugs at a handful of grass blades, pulls them out of the ground.

"Ben called," she says.

I get the distinct feeling I'm supposed to know who Ben is.

"My ex," she clarifies.

Oh, him.

"Says he misses me."

"Do you miss him?"

She shrugs. "Of course. I mean, everyone misses something that used to be around, don't they?"

"I guess."

"Not sure that means I should be with him again."

"I don't know much about 'shoulds.'"

"I have no idea what I'm doing with my life. Do you ever

have moments when that reality hits you, like a cartload of bricks?"

"Every day." I should say "Every day, until recently, when I decided to just end it all."

"Is that normal?"

"I don't know much about 'normal.'"

"And still no word from my dad."

I don't want her to dwell on this, so I ask, "Are you hungry?"

Maybe the question is inappropriate. Maybe this gravesite visit was supposed to be more climactic. Maybe I was supposed to have lost my appetite in the midst of all the emotional upheaval.

"I'm starving," Riko says, which relaxes me.

With that, we leave the cemetery. I don't say anything to Sara—out loud or in my head—because, like I said, I just can't. Maybe I'm supposed to cry, but I don't. If anything, I'm relieved that all I am is hungry. Maybe that relief is what Mr. Sacramone meant when he said "It'll do you good."

We get a large cheese pizza and take it back to my house, where Riko has suggested we watch the Japanese movie *Shall We Dance?* It's one of our homework assignments. I agree because I can't think of anything else to do. In addition to giving my clothes to the Salvation Army, I also donated all my DVDs and CDs. Options for entertainment are limited.

The basic plot of the movie is this: The main character is a *kaishain*. That means "office worker." We learned this word early on, before we learned words for the seasons or colors or other "basics." He has a bleak, R&R-type job, and his existence is consumed by performing this job and commuting back and forth between this job and a tiny home in the suburbs. And by tiny, I mean the house looks like a slightly enlarged dollhouse, something in a Tim Burton movie. The hallways are too narrow, the ceilings too low. Once again, is it any wonder the Japanese are killing themselves in such large numbers? Anyway, our protagonist decides to add some excitement to his dull life by going to a dance studio.

This—when he starts dancing—is when I stop paying attention.

"Your people are so repressed," I say.

Riko takes a bite of pizza and pauses the movie. "I don't think you're one to talk."

"I'm not repressed."

"Right," she says dismissively.

She resumes the movie and watches intently. As the *kaishain* does the waltz and confronts his mundane existence, Riko takes diligent notes. When the credits start rolling, she rattles off the worksheet answers for me. I write them down, halfheartedly. I could give a shit about homework assignments at this point, but I know it matters to Riko that I show some enthusiasm.

"Thank you," I say.

"Oh, whatever, don't even worry about it," she says. "That assignment was easy. And it's the least I can do."

She puts down her mechanical pencil and gets a too-serious look on her face that unnerves me.

"You've helped me a lot," she says. "You're a good friend."

Oh, god—I don't need this type of sentiment at this juncture.

The DVD has returned to the main menu. We stare at the screen, as if entranced.

"I guess we're both in weird life phases," she says.

Or end-of-life phases.

"I guess," is all I say.

"I had this kind of crazy idea," she says, putting down a piece of crust. "What if I came with you?"

My first thought is: to the afterlife? I start to panic.

"To Japan," she says.

I am momentarily relieved and then slightly panicked again. I hadn't pictured anyone with me on my farewell tour of Japan. She must sense my hesitation, because she starts countering all the possible problems with such an arrangement: "I'll pay for my own airfare, of course. We can get separate hotel rooms. Or hostel rooms, whatever you're planning on doing. You don't have to change your itinerary for me. I saw Nikko listed as a possible side trip on your itinerary. If you don't want to go, I'll just head there on my own. I'm totally fine traveling alone. I went all over Europe after high school. I won't get in your way. Promise. I just thought it would be fun. But if you—"

"Okay," I find myself saying, mostly out of guilt. She thinks I'm a good friend, and here I'm going to leave her by way of laundry detergent. This Japan trip will be my parting gift to her. I have money left to buy her ticket. She will say it's too much. She will protest. I'll insist.

"Really? I don't want to impose on your trip. I know it's important to you. I just feel like we both have reasons to go, so why not go together?"

"Riko, it's okay. You don't need to convince me," I say. "Besides, you can be my translator. We both know you're way better with Japanese than I am."

She nods. "We do both know that."

"So you're going to visit your father?"

She tries to play it cool, says, "I don't know, I'll see how I feel when I get there." I know that's her plan, though. She has no other reason to go all the way to Japan. I fear for her, knowing that whatever scene she has in her head is unlikely to play out in life.

"I'll bring my professional camera. I'll take a lot of cherry blossom pictures for you," she says, knowing already what scene I have in my head.

That's when I wonder if I should also fear for myself.

Dear Mom and Dad,

I want you to know that I'm happy this way. I thought about it for a long time, and it's for the best. But I know that's selfish. This isn't just about me. It's about you too. I'm sorry for leaving you in this way. I know how it feels to be left. My car is paid off, and the house is worth more than when I bought it. I don't need a formal funeral. Please donate my body to science or have me cremated. I wish I could express my love for you adequately, instead of just reviewing these boring logistics. I do love you, and my leaving this world shouldn't imply otherwise. Thank you for always being there for me—that is, when I allowed you to be there for me. I am at peace.

Love,

Jonathan

P.S. Please give the accompanying note to Riko Smith. I've included her address.

Dear Riko,

I know what you may want to believe—this was some kind of horrendous accident, a laundry mishap. This was the odd, fateful *result of Comet dust flirting with bleach, having a detergent three-some. But, no. I planned this, Riko, well before I met you. I have to say, you did your damned best—unknowingly, of course—to persuade me to stay here, to give life another chance. You have been such a wonderful, unexpected friend. I sure as hell (don't shudder at that word, please) don't want you to think I didn't give a shit about you. I'm hoping you won't think that, because you're a fairly smart person and you know that's not true. You're probably even smart enough to figure out that giving a shit about a person, deciding to care in spite of all the reasons out there to save yourself the trouble, is what leads to "laundry mishaps" like this. Thank you for reminding me that while the world, in general, disappoints, not all the people in it do. You have optimism. You have dreams. I've envied that. I gave up too long ago. I hope all that you want comes to you.*

Ai wo komete,

Jonathan

二十四

By March, I've cleared out much of the house—donated most everything. Strangers I don't know, somewhere, are sitting on my furniture, wearing my clothes, incorporating my possessions into their lives. I still have the box of Sara photos on my nightstand. I don't know what to do with it besides torture myself with the memories it contains, use it to strengthen my resolve.

There's one of us at a Dodgers game, wearing the blue visors they were giving away with admission that day. Sara went to baseball games solely for the 1950s-era malts with those wooden tongue-depressor–like spoons. There's one of us at the Santa Anita racetrack. When all bets were in, Sara selected the horse least likely to win—the underdog, or underhorse in this case. On the drive home, she made a list of the most ridiculous horse names: Smashed Moon Rocket, Bully Fully Loaded, Push the Cocktails, Lord of the Loot.

In summer, we went up to Idyllwild some weekends to hike the same trail—the Ernie Maxwell Trail. There's a photo of Sara in front of the sign. She'd googled the hell out of Ernie Maxwell's name, trying to find out who he was, why this stretch of dirt was named after him. It turned out he was the founder of a local newspaper, which was not nearly as exciting a story as we'd hoped. There's a photo of us in Joshua Tree—lots of them, actually. We climbed all over the rocks, like little kids in a jungle gym. Sara sought out the formations that looked like objects—a shelled peanut here, a ballet slipper there.

There's a picture of us on Halloween. I dressed as a hobo and wore a sign around my neck that said "Will work for a girl-friend." Sara went as her charitable self. Before Thanksgiving one year, we volunteered at a soup kitchen together. Sara's idea, of course. We dished out a mysterious stew that smelled like over-microwaved vegetables, but the line was still out the door. One woman introduced herself as Fredda and said to me, "You have a beautiful wife." She looked at Sara lovingly, then moved along, clutching her bowl. Sara said, playfully mad, "You bastard. You never told me you were married." I wanted to think Fredda could see the future.

Many of the pictures are on random days, "unimportant" days, forgettable days. Most are indistinguishable close-ups of me or her or the two of us. Reminds me of a study I read about. Japanese and American people were given cameras and told to photograph their best friend. The Americans took close-ups, zooming in so that the face occupied most of the photo. The Japanese stepped back and took photos that featured the people as just part of a background. In America, self trumps surround-ings. In Japan, the person is nothing without context. Sara and I were, so obviously, American. And maybe that's why I'm inhaling laundry-detergent fumes—all I can see when I close my eyes are faces. Sara's smile. My former smiles. The proverbial big picture is lost on me, out of focus to the point of not existing.

I still think of the pictures that could have been. I think of us going to Japan. I fantasize so often about how I would have proposed that, sometimes, in the wee hours of the morning when my thinking isn't entirely clear, I'm convinced it actually happened. I got down on one knee at the top of Mount Fuji. I can see her face. The wind is blowing strands of hair in front of it. She keeps pushing them away to see if the ring in front of her is real. There are tears in her eyes as she says "Yes, yes, yes" over and over again.

Maybe the reason I don't "talk" with her now is because I don't want to consider what she would say. She might tell me that going to Japan will make it hurt more. And I will have to argue that all I have left of her is her desire to see Japan. That's part of her that's still mine, in a sense. And going there may be the closest I'll ever come to being with her again. I'm afraid if I admitted that to her, I'd hear her whisper in my ear: "I'm not there, Jonathan. I'm not here either. I never will be."

Miyagi Sensei has assigned an end-of-semester project for us. We are told to do a report on an aspect of Japanese culture we find interesting. Riko and I partner up, predictably. I'm in charge of the written report; Riko is in charge of putting together a visual presentation.

"Why don't we do it on sushi chefs and the training they undertake?" she says.

She sits in her chair with her legs bent underneath her. I'm always mystified by how she bends that way. The students next to us are talking about doing their report on Japanese game shows, like the ones where people play human Tetris, contorting their bodies to fit through different shapes. Riko would be good at that.

"I read that sushi chefs used to undergo *ten years* of training before working in a restaurant," she says. "Now they're so in demand that they can start working after only two years. But still—can you imagine? Ten years? We let people become doctors in less time than that, don't we?"

"Probably."

"It takes, like, a year just to learn how to make the rice."

"Miyagi Sensei said to choose a topic we find interesting."

"And?"

"I'm not that interested in sushi chefs."

Riko unfolds herself and stretches her legs out into the aisle between the chairs.

"Well, what does interest you?"

She's annoyed, as she should be.

"Kamikaze pilots," I say, not skipping a beat. "The brave dudes who crashed their planes into enemy ships."

"The suicide bombers of yesteryear?"

"Right."

"You really are so weird."

When I get home from class, I decide to start packing for the trip. True, I haven't bought my ticket yet—been keeping my eye on flight prices for weeks—but I want to pack, to keep my hands and mind busy if nothing else. I'm limiting myself to one large backpack. My understanding is that everything is smaller, cramped in Japan—including overhead compartments and space between seats on trains. The last thing I want is to be another tourist with an obnoxious rolling suitcase and superiority complex. I don't want to be the final annoyance that compels a well-dressed businessman to jump in front of a bullet train.

This way, I won't have to check a bag, which is good considering I have a history of luggage disappearing. Airlines end up giving me a sum of money to cover my losses, but that's never what I want. What I want is my clothes back, because I hate shopping. When I die, I may find the void containing that suitcase that never made it to New York for that one client pitch. There's a great tie in there, and a sports jacket so comfortable I used to wear it around the house on weekends.

The phone rings, and I know it's the only person who still calls me:

"Hi, Mom," I say.

"What are you up to?" There is always hope in her voice when she asks this, like she wants me to be up to something that gives her faith that my future will be happy.

"I'm packing, actually. For my Japan trip."

She doesn't say anything for a moment. I assume it's because she's gulping away some disbelief.

"So you're going, then? For sure?"

This is when Dad comes on the phone, and Mom informs him that I'm going to Japan.

"Tonight?" he says. Because that's how my Dad is.

"No, soon," I say. "I don't have my ticket yet, but soon."

"You don't have your ticket yet and you're packing?" My mother seems so perplexed by this that I have no idea how she'll possibly understand the laundry-detergent inhalation.

"I'm just getting prepared."

"Like the Boy Scouts taught you," Dad says. This is a joke, or my father is losing it, because I was never in Boy Scouts.

"You know, they have earthquakes in Japan," my mother says.

"I'm aware."

"Just remember—earthquakes don't kill people; buildings do."

"Are you being serious right now?"

"I'm just being a mom," she says, which reminds me of how much she loves me, which makes me very uncomfortable. "They say you should stay indoors to avoid falling debris outside. And crouch next to a pillar or a supporting wall, and protect your face from shattering window glass."

She says all this like I have not spent my entire life in California, where earthquake readiness is part of the curriculum up through high school. "Duck, cover, and hold" was ingrained in us as thoroughly as "Say no to drugs."

"Are you sitting in front of the computer right now? Looking this up online?"

"She is," my father says, with a sigh. "She always sits in front of the computer."

"Rhonda sent me an email the other day about the Big One hitting Orange County," she says. Rhonda's name comes out tentatively, like she's still not sure I'm okay with her relationship with my dead girlfriend's mother. I'm not, really, though I guess they can console each other when I'm gone. I wonder how often they email. They probably send forwards to each other, ones with dogs wearing human clothes and inspirational quotes about life. Their emails are probably multicolored with elaborate fonts. That's how mothers are.

"Okay, I'm going to get back to packing," I say, cutting this all short.

Dad says his goodbye and hangs up. Mom is still there.

"They say it could be any day now," she continues. "The earthquake."

"Well, it's a good thing I'm going to Japan, then."

Packing takes me all of twenty minutes. I've already thinned out my wardrobe, so my options are limited. I decide that, given my exit plan, I should do my half of the final project for Japanese class, and I should do it now. It's not that I really care about the class, but I know Riko has a greater chance of hating me posthumously if I leave her stranded on an assignment in addition to leaving her stranded, generally.

I don't even need to do much research. I start writing.

Japan is infamous for kamikaze—suicide attacks by military aviators toward the end of the Pacific campaign of World War II. Kamikaze pilots would intentionally crash their aircraft into enemy ships—planes often full of explosives, bombs, torpedoes, and full fuel tanks. Essentially, the planes had been converted to manned missiles; lives were sacrificed in the name of greater accuracy and chance of success.

For the first kamikaze unit, Commander Asaiki Tamai asked a group of twenty-three talented student pilots to volunteer. All of the pilots raised both of their hands. The names of the four subunits within the Kamikaze Special Attack Force—Shikishima, Yamazakura, Yamato, Asahi— were taken from a patriotic poem:

Shikishima no Yamato-gokoro wo hito towaba, asahi ni niou yamazakura bana

Translated to:

Asked about the soul of Japan,
I would say
That it is
Like wild cherry blossoms
Glowing in the morning sun.

It is said that Japanese pilots painted cherry blossoms on the sides of their planes before embarking on their suicide missions, or even took branches of the trees with them. The government encouraged people to believe that the souls of downed warriors were reincarnated—in the blossoms.

Maybe, in some way, this report will offer Riko vague insight into my death.

I click over to the travel website. It's a Tuesday. They say that's the best day to buy airline tickets.

Sure enough, they're at $1,300, which I'm supposed to consider a bargain. I exhale a breath that's been held for too long and hit the "Buy" button.

"This isn't due until May," Riko says when I hand her the report, neat and bound the way I did in high school, when I'd wanted to kiss ass.

"I know. I wanted to get it done."

She looks skeptical.

"Okay, weirdo," she says, tentatively, shaking her head. "You must really have no life."

"I really don't."

She flips through the report, stopping when a paper falls out of the middle of it. I've strategically placed this paper.

"What's this?" she asks, retrieving it from the floor. She unfolds it, looks at me.

"I hope the dates are okay with you, because the tickets are nonrefundable," I say. "It's spring break, a little earlier than I wanted to go, but we'll still see cherry blossoms if we're lucky and—"

"You bought my ticket?"

I nod.

"You didn't have to do that," she says. She looks almost angry, like I've disobeyed her insistence that she not be a burden on this adventure of ours.

"Yes, I did," I say.

"No, you didn't."

"For me, I did."

She lets it be, after a long sigh that is more like a defeated huff.

"I don't know what to say." She holds the ticket between us, like she's considering giving it back but knows this would be pointless, as I've already spent the money and the ticket has her name on it. You can't just exchange airline tickets these days. I think a "terrorist alert" goes straight to the White House if you even attempt such a thing.

"I mean, really—I don't know what to say," she says, now holding the ticket against her chest, like a schoolgirl with a love letter.

"I've heard 'thank you' is popular."

She bows deeply, past the recommended ninety-degree angle, and says, "*Arigatou.*"

"How come they still haven't taught us how to say 'you're welcome'?" I ask.

She comes up from her bow and laughs.

"Maybe you're never welcome in Japan," she says.

"Let's hope that's not the case."

DANGEROUS JAPANESE 'DETERGENT SUICIDE' TECHNIQUE CREEPS INTO U.S.

Wired.com

A suicide technique that mixes household chemicals to produce a deadly hydrogen sulfide gas became a grisly fad in Japan last year. Now it's slowly seeping into the United States over the internet, according to emergency workers, who are alarmed at the potential for innocent causalities.

At least 500 Japanese men, women and children took their lives in the first half of 2008 by following instructions posted on Japanese websites, which describe how to mix bath sulfur with toilet bowl cleaner to create a poisonous gas. One site includes an application to calculate the correct portions of each ingredient based on room volume, along with a PDF download of a ready-made warning sign to alert neighbors and emergency workers to the deadly hazard.

The first sign that the technique was migrating to the United States came in August, when a 23-year-old California man was found dead in his car behind a Pasadena shopping center. The VW Beetle's doors were locked, the windows rolled up and a warning sign had been posted in one of the windows. Police and firefighters evacuated the shopping crew before a hazmat crew in chemical suits extracted the body and began cleaning up the grisly scene.

Then in December, emergency workers responding to a call at Lake Allatoona in Bartow County, Georgia, found a similar scene. Inside the car—along with the body—were two buckets containing a yellow substance. A note on the window said "Caution" and identified the chemical compound by name.

Nobody connected the cases until last month, when a Texas surgeon realized that a new and dangerous suicide method was making the rounds. Dr. Paul Pepe, chief of emergency medicine at UT Southwestern Medical Center, warned emergency workers that they could become innocent casualties of the technique if they're not careful. Other experts agree.

"The normal response for an EMS, is they're going to break open the window," says August Vernon, assistant coordinator for the Forsyth County Office of Emergency Management, who was consulted by the Department of Homeland Security on the danger this week. "And that's a pretty normal call: someone unconscious inside the car. Fortunately, those people left notes, which is pretty unusual and a good thing."

"Eventually," he adds, "someone isn't going to leave a note."

The American version of the method substitutes a common insecticide for the bath sulfur used in the Japanese recipe; bath sulfur isn't available in the United States. But the tweak does nothing to make the gas less dangerous for people nearby. In one of the Japanese cases last year, 90 residents in an apartment building were sickened when a 14-year-old girl used hydrogen sulfide (H2S) to take her life.

The so-called "detergent suicides" in Japan sparked considerable and ongoing interest on the Alt.Suicide Usenet groups, where people considering suicide share tips and tricks. This week, one depressed man wrote of his plan to release hydrogen sulfide gas in his car while driving, in the hope that he'll lose consciousness and crash – making it look like an accident.

"I got the idea to use hydrogen sulfide poisoning by reading of the tremendous success (for lack of a better word) that the Japanese people have had with it," he wrote on Monday. "It is their most common suicide method. I understand that the method smells but I have found the stench of failure in my life as well."

When other newsgroup denizens pointed out the recklessness of his plan, he gave it up as too risky to innocent bystanders. After exploring other techniques, the man announced on Wednesday that he decided he'd rather live.

"With months of research I have discovered that there is no 'easy' or 'painless' or 'quick' way to die," he wrote. "So, from here on out I am going to pick up the pieces to my life! Maybe you should too."

二 十 五

hate airports. There is anxiety in the air, along with germs ejected from sneezing noses and coughing mouths. Nobody is happy—not the security people, not the bored storekeepers selling the neck pillows, and certainly not the passengers. Even if you are looking forward to wherever you are going, you are either (a) agitated because you arrived early and must entertain yourself with celebrity gossip magazines and overpriced coffee or (b) stressed because you arrived just a tad late and have to sprint to your gate. I suppose there is the chance that you arrive at the airport with impeccable timing—you check in, go through security, and arrive at your departing gate with, oh, ten leisurely minutes to organize yourself. But this involves an unlikely chain of events—cooperative traffic on Southern California freeways, no long lines or other snafus while checking in, and minimal drama in the security line.

Riko and I have arrived early. I blame this on her being overly prepared and, well, Asian. We stand in the security line, with nearly two hours remaining before boarding time.

"They better need to take me into a secret room and strip-search me, because I have no idea how else I'm going to pass the time," I tell her.

She hops around on her left foot, passport and boarding pass in her mouth, both hands gripping her black boot, pulling it off her right foot. It's an interesting dance. If she did this for two hours, I might not be bored.

Going through airport security requires a near-complete disrobing. Walking through the metal detector—shoeless and coatless, having deposited my keys and belt and watch and coins in a little dish—I feel as if I'm about to enter prison. If these airport employees had any sense of humor, I would say "Okay, you have my valuables, give me the orange suit and shackles." But they don't have a sense of humor, a fact that doesn't stop me from saying to Riko, a bit too loudly, "I've never understood this liquids rule. I mean, you're allowed liquids less than three ounces. Well, what if there are four terrorists on the flight. That's twelve ounces of badness, more than enough for—"

"Shut up," Riko demands, conscious of the scolding eyes upon us.

"What?" I say, innocently.

"Do you *want* us to get detained?" she whispers as we wait for our possessions to come down the conveyor belt.

"Yes, I already said that," I say. "What else are we going to do with the next two hours?"

We put on our shoes and coats, concluding the American security charade. A guy had a bomb in his shoe once, and now we have to smell stranger's feet in airports for all eternity.

Don't they realize that someone smarter will come up with a better idea, not involving a shoe? We're always a step—pun intended—behind.

"I bet the Japanese don't have these ridiculous security measures," I say.

"Would you just shut up?"

Riko pulls my arm and we make our way to the gate. Of course, we are the first passengers there. Our flight isn't even listed on the board yet.

We wander into one of the newsstand stores they have every hundred feet or so. The way Riko browses the trail mix packages and scans the magazines, you would think she just stepped off a plane *from* Japan and is entranced by the American goodies. She flips through a crossword-puzzle book before putting it back on the shelf, as if she is displeased with the clues, unimpressed with the vocabulary involved. Then she defies her own pretentious demeanor by picking up a stuffed monkey and saying, "Look, how cute!"

Who would want to purchase a stuffed animal, add to their things-to-carry, before boarding an airplane? Maybe children placed on planes by their divorcée parent to cross the country and visit the other parent want something soft and fuzzy to keep them company.

"Aren't you going to get anything?" she says, standing in line. She has two bottles of water, peanut M&M's, the monkey, a thousand-page paperback, and a random Red Delicious apple. The armful of items tumbles onto the counter the moment she gets to the register. The lady looks at her and says, with absolutely zero sarcasm, "You need a bag?"

We wait at our gate, Riko staring out the large windows at the planes coming and going. She looks like a five-year-old. The monkey doesn't help appearances. I ask her if she's ever been on a plane before, like a big girl. She asks me why I'm such a prick.

"Do you think this trip is a good idea?" she says, out of nowhere. She stretches her legs across the empty seats and tears off the corner of her M&M's bag with her teeth.

"For you or for me?"

"For both of us. Or either of us. Or whatever."

"I don't know," I say. "Don't expect me to know things like that."

"Can we go to Nikko early on? I want to get it over with."

She speaks of it like a root canal.

"Don't see why not."

"There will be so much to see," she says excitedly, popping an M&M in her mouth. She rambles—about karaoke booths and belting out songs until the wee hours of the morning; about the Shinto and Buddhist temples and shrines and enviably peaceful monks; about the bright lights of Tokyo, the futuristic arcades, the Harajuku girls; about the infamous "pod" hotels, "rooms" reduced in size to a plastic or fiberglass block roughly six by three by four feet, providing just enough space to sleep.

"Or suffocate," I interject.

"Hmm?" she says.

"It sounds like a coffin."

This does not stop her. She goes on—about the Bunraku puppet theater, the kabuki, the sumo wrestling, the Imperial Palace, the anime movie theaters, all the gardens. Two things occur to me: Sara would like Riko, and Riko is trying very hard to pretend that this cross-Pacific voyage isn't all about finding her family. She's just another American tourist with a checklist of things to see, that's all.

"I really hope we see the cherry blossoms," I say, aware that

I'm interrupting Riko, but unaware of what, exactly, she's in the midst of saying.

"Yeah, me too."

Then we are quiet. She listens to music, little buds in her ears compelling her head to bob and her lips to move every now and then. Normally, I would pass the time with a newspaper or a book or something, but I just sit there, waiting, staring at nothing in particular. Other passengers start to arrive— Japanese, mostly. A man comes on the loudspeaker, welcoming us to Flight 891 and telling us that boarding will begin in nine minutes.

The plane is a big one—three seats on each side, five in the middle. When we board, we pass a staircase leading up to first class, where I imagine rich businessmen sip champagne, preparing to fully recline their seats for the twelve-hour flight. I haven't seen a plane like this since I was ten years old, when my parents took me to Hawaii.

Riko takes the window seat, her face pressed up against the plastic, her breath fogging up the space around her mouth. Again, I ask her if she's ever been on a plane before. She pulls down the shade, wedges her monkey between the seat and the window, and rests her head against it, eyes closed, arms crossed. Of course she's been on a plane before—maybe a plane just like this one—when she was three years old. Maybe her father bought her a monkey then too, not that she'd remember.

When the stewardess (or air hostess or whatever the hell they're called these days) comes around with the customs card, I find out that the silent woman to my left is a Japanese citizen. I am given the visitor form, while Riko is asked "Japanese citizen?" She shakes her head and mumbles, "I'm with him."

"Oh, family?"

We look at each other, thinking "Do we *look* like family?" then realize, seemingly simultaneously, that she's asking if we're married.

"No," we say, at the same time.

"Connecting to Bangkok?"

She thinks we're a couple, this lady-of-the-sky. And she thinks that, as a couple, we would choose a conventionally romantic getaway like Thailand over Japan.

"No," we say, together again.

She smiles and moves on.

Sometime during the first of four movies being shown, with the fuzzy picture and the dialogue barely audible over the roar of the plane's engines, I fall asleep. I miss lunches #1 and #2, which Riko informs me were terrible. She eats her apple and says, "You should have gotten something at the airport."

The plane touches down in Tokyo at 4:00 p.m., which is something like 9:00 a.m. of the same day back home. My body is confused. It is sure of only one thing—it is hungry. We stand in line at immigration, mixed in with people from all over the world—Mexico, Finland, Spain, according to their passports. When it is our turn to make our foreign presence known, we are told to place each of our index fingers on a little scanning pad while a camera snaps our photo. I think to myself: "This is the photo they'll use if I'm wanted for a crime while I'm here," and I smile a goofy grin. Somehow I manage to screw up the fingerprinting. As the officer is trying to explain that I must do it again, I have my first in-Japan revelation: English is not a universal language.

Fingerprints and photos on record, we proceed to customs, where the agent seems either surprised or worried (hard to tell) that we have only backpacks with us. It takes us five minutes to figure out that he is trying to ask us how long we are staying. Finally, we say, "*juu ni*," meaning twelve. He smiles and we are on our way. We get our Japan rail pass—our means of traveling the country—and we board our first train, the Narita Express, bound for Tokyo.

"Can you believe we're here?" Riko says.

I look out the window, at the landscape racing by. Green, lush countryside and farming land turns to a concrete jungle—neon signs and power lines and metal-clad factories, blocking views of mountains and rivers and forests. Institutionalized-looking apartment buildings are packed together. Racks of clothing crowd balconies. The living spaces here must be too small for closets, or at least too small for dryer units.

"No, I can't believe it," I say.

Billboards and building names flash by. I recognize hiragana and katakana here and there, almost none of the kanji. We are going much too fast for me to convert characters to sounds, to decipher words.

"The next stop is Shinjuku Station," the voice says.

Announcements come in Japanese and English, thankfully. The English woman's voice sounds exactly like the one on the tapes Miyagi Sensei uses for our listening exams. Maybe there is one woman in Japan, getting rich by crossing a language barrier as tall and wide as Mount Fuji.

"This is where we get off, right?" Riko says. She's not really asking me; she's telling me. She's already lifting her backpack, tucking her monkey underneath her arm.

Shinjuku Station is the busiest in all of Tokyo. We arrive around six, perhaps too early to see the rumored swarms of drunkards. There are swarms of briefcases, though, and black suits. People rush by us, fast and furious. It is like New York, except that I don't fit in here, being tall and white with this backpack on my shoulders and dazed look on my face.

We make our way up the street. Our hotel is supposedly close to the station, but we've been walking a few blocks now with no sign of it. A bitter wind blows; a few snow flurries flutter past my eyes. It's much colder than I'd anticipated. I don't imagine the cherry blossoms will want to reveal themselves in weather like this.

We are going against the crowds. We are in the business district, after all. A broken dam of people floods the station. They are all focused on getting home to their families in the suburbs. We are in their way. They seem to have even less patience for Riko than for me. I am obviously American, dumb. She is supposed to understand them.

"What's with the surgical masks?" Riko asks. She doesn't whisper. At this point, we've both realized that English is unlikely to be understood here, especially at the pace we speak.

"I have no idea."

About half the people coming at us are wearing white surgical masks over their faces. I saw them on the immigration and customs officers at the airport, but I'd assumed they had something to do with fear of contamination by foreigners. I wasn't even insulted by this; we *are* dirty. Then I wondered if they feared a terrorist attack, biochemical warfare breaking out in the departures lounge. But, honestly, aren't the Japanese smart enough to know that a little paper mask won't protect against that?

On the train, the attendants wore them. Passengers too. Now, on the streets, there are masses sporting them. I feel like I am in a Will Smith movie about the coming of the apocalypse. There is probably an advertising agency representing the company that makes these things. Hell, there are probably several companies competing to have the best mask. But what's the selling point? Could it be a weird fad, like when we put safety pins on jean jackets in the eighties?

"There it is!" Riko says. She's spotted the high-rise hotel. The moment we step beyond its sliding glass doors, we are warm.

"Welcome," a woman says, in the best English we've heard thus far. It's a nice hotel; English is probably a prerequisite for working here.

"*Konbanwa*," Riko says. Show-off.

"Can we take your bags? We are sorry it is so cold for this time of the year."

This is our introduction to the Japanese service industry— our bags are removed from our tired shoulders, and we receive apologies for the weather.

The hotel's staff consists of at least ten people whose only job is to greet us. Then there's the receptionist, who confirms that we want separate beds. We are escorted to our room, our bags placed in the closet. In America, these actions say "Hey, I want a big tip." Here, they mean no such thing. I try to tip, to place a 500-yen coin (about five bucks) in the palm of our escort, who has taken ten minutes to explain the workings of the flat-screen television. He rejects my offering. He looks at me like I'm insane. Then he bows and leaves.

Riko explores the room, exclaiming that there's a TV by the bathtub and that the toilet seat is cushioned and heated and has switches and buttons like "Extra Odor Control." She stands in front of the giant windows, looking down on the city forty-seven floors below. There are lights as far as the eye can see. Her breath is taken away, quite literally. I'm not sure there is anything on this planet that has the ability to do this to me anymore.

We wander down to a hotel restaurant for dinner, too exhausted to try to find a place in the city.

"I feel like a geek with these chopsticks," Riko says when our rolled sushi appetizer arrives.

"Me too."

"You're allowed. You're white."

She seems to do fine, though, and I wonder if she's been practicing at home. Our waitress hovers, not to amuse herself with our lack of culinary skill, but to refill our water glasses the second we take sips. When Riko goes to the bathroom, the waitress refolds her napkin; when Riko returns, the napkin is unfolded and once again placed on Riko's lap.

We slurp bowls of udon with some kind of meat as a main course, Riko explaining that slurping is actually polite, a way to indicate enjoyment of the meal.

"Can I burp too?"

"No," she says.

"So. The surgical masks. I have a few theories."

"Go on."

"Herpes outbreak," I say.

She laughs. "Quite possible."

"They have bad teeth," I say. "Or chronic halitosis."

"Perhaps," she says, still laughing. "Hey, we should get some sake."

"Wait, I've left my best theory for last."

"And what's that?"

I lean forward, over my bowl, like I'm communicating something top secret, something that, if overheard, could get us shipped back to the United States within the next hour.

"They don't have mouths," I whisper.

She laughs so hard that our waitress begins to approach the table, worried something is wrong. Riko takes advantage of her approach and says, "Sake?" The waitress nods, and Riko clarifies that she wants it "*atsui*," or hot.

"*Hai*," the waitress says, understanding, confirming. Riko looks proud of herself.

The sake arrives, and the waitress pours a cup for each of us.

"Here's to a great trip," Riko says, holding up her cup. I hold up mine, clink it against hers.

"*Kampai*," I say.

Obituary: Draft

Jonathan Krause took his own life after spending a year trying—and failing—to cope with the death of his beloved girlfriend. He lived a rather unremarkable life, writing copy for Radley and Reiser advertising agency. Upon leaving the agency in preparation for his death, Jonathan learned a little Japanese and traveled to Japan to see the cherry blossoms. He plans to take his acquired language skills with him into the afterlife, where he will converse with Emperor Hirohito about the bombing of Hiroshima and how much the United States continues to suck.

Jonathan leaves behind his parents—Paul and Bernice Krause—as well as his good friend, Rihoko Smith. In lieu of flowers, please donate money to a charity you support. This is in honor of the late Sara Mackenzie.

二 十 六

When my body wants to wake up, the room is dark, Riko is still sleeping, and the clock says 4:00 a.m. I walk into the bathroom, close the door, and turn on the light. I sit on the toilet seat. She's right—it's warm. It gets hotter, almost too hot, the longer I sit on it. I don't know how constipated Japanese people stand it.

I contemplate running a bath, but don't want to wake Riko. I get in the dry tub, using a couple towels as a backrest, and pull up the window shade. It's still dark outside, not the faintest of dawn glow yet. Still, there are cars on the road, people going places. I read from the guidebook we have with us. Here's what it says are the top three reasons people in Japan wear surgical masks:

- #3: They don't want to be infected by others' germs.
- #2: They have allergies and want to avoid pollen.

And the #1 reason:

• They don't want their germs to infect others.

What a concept—concern for others before self. Dorothy, we are not in America anymore.

"What are you doing?" Riko asks, rubbing her tired eyes, trying to make sense of me, fully clothed, in the bathtub.

"Nothing," I say.

"Right. Well, it's six o'clock. What do you want to do today?"

"We could go see your father. I looked it up. It's about a ninety-minute train ride to Nikko."

"Today?" she says.

Hadn't it been her idea to "get it over with"?

"Or, we can go to the fish market, since we're up early," I suggest, in response to her apprehension.

"Let's do that."

The Tsukiji fish market in Tokyo is the largest wholesale fish and seafood market in the world. There are tiny alleyways lined with vendor booths the size of American walk-in closets. It's like a creatures-of-the-sea carnival. Freshly cut filets of fish, shrimp with eyes and tail intact, piles of mussels, slimy eels, and slippery squids are all on display in boxes. Still living (but not for long) crabs occupy huge tanks. Riko snaps a picture of one shopkeeper's offerings—octopus ball kabobs.

"Do you think that means balls of octopus flesh, or octopus testicles?" she asks me.

"Does an octopus have testicles?"

"I think we don't want to know."

I am not so alone here, as a white guy. There are more like me, tourists navigating their way among the tentacles and fins, inspecting the goods with shocked curiosity masked as honest interest, pretending not to be disgusted. I get the feeling we are in the way—all of us here, gawking. Men on scooters—delivery boys, I presume—zip through the aisles, with little regard for us slow-moving gawkers. They are working, see. This life is their R&R.

"What do you think about sushi for breakfast?" I ask Riko. The least I can do is buy what they're selling.

She shrugs. "When in Rome."

We make our way to a hole-in-the-wall joint. We can't read the text on the mostly pictorial menu. We don't know what the food actually is. We have only visuals to guide us.

We are served green tea the moment we sit and given a sheet of paper on which to place our order, along with some verbal instructions neither of us understand, except for the "*kudasai*" at the end, which means "please." The Japanese slap a *kudasai* on the end of every sentence, it seems, for good measure.

We do our best with the menu, writing down the numbers of what looks edible on the order sheet. I hold up the paper for the waiter, which is probably very rude, but I don't know how to say "Here you go. We're ready." In my life, I wish I'd been nicer to foreigners. They probably don't intend to be impolite; it's just that politeness requires a somewhat advanced vocabulary.

"*Arigatou gozaimasu,*" we say to the waiter, in unison. It's the formal way to say "thank you." It's the best we can do to express that we're not total schmucks.

While we wait for our selections, I wipe my hands and face

with the wet towel provided, according to the custom the guide-book described.

"So, when are we going to Nikko?" I ask Riko.

She's mid-sip on her tea.

"It makes sense to go from Tokyo," I say. "Nikko isn't far from here. And I don't want to be in Tokyo too many more days. I'd like to get to Kyoto, see if the cherry blossoms are out there and—"

"It's probably still too cold for the cherry blossoms," she says, setting down her cup, looking at its remaining contents instead of at me.

"Riko?" I say.

"What?"

"Do you want to go or not?"

Our first plate arrives—seaweed wraps with mysterious contents. The only non-mystery to me is the one with the salmon eggs, because it's pretty hard not to know fish eggs when you see them—little pink-orange balls that you'd never dream of eating first thing in the morning, or any time of the day if you are me.

"That one is all yours," Riko says, using her chopsticks to push it toward me. She lifts another wrap, a relatively safe-looking one, into her mouth. I await her reaction.

"It's good. Spicy tuna, I think."

I succumb to the salmon eggs. The Japanese have this philosophy about their food—don't ask questions, just enjoy. Americans love to ask questions: Where did you get this meat? Was the animal corn-fed? What is that marinade? How long did you say you cooked it?

They're chewier than I want them to be. I try to think about gummy bears, but it's not helping. I end up swallowing most of the eggs whole, bypassing the enjoyment part.

"So?" Riko says.

I down my cup of tea, disregarding its hot temperature. I kind of want whatever is in my stomach to burn.

"Can we write down what that was called so I don't accidentally order it again?" I say.

I'm joking, but Riko actually takes out a pad of paper from her purse, copying the characters that mean "salmon eggs." There are other notes already on the pad, little vocabulary lessons she is teaching herself.

"You are such a nerd."

She just smiles. More plates come with rolls more familiar to the American eye. It's not satisfying the way pancakes are satisfying, but it'll do.

"How do you ask for the check?" I ask Riko.

She consults her dictionary but comes to no conclusion. Again, we resort to rudeness—flagging down our waiter with nothing more than a "*sumimasen*" ("excuse me"). I feel like a mime, acting out the motions of receiving and paying a bill. He looks at me blankly, and I exaggerate my Charlie Chaplin maneuvers. Suddenly, for no apparent reason, something clicks. He understands and brings the check.

"How about tomorrow?" Riko says as we wait.

"Tomorrow?"

"Nikko."

"Okay, if that's what you want," I say.

"I'm not sure I know what I want, but I think we should do it for the sake of the itinerary."

"Right," I say, "for the itinerary."

We spend the rest of the day wandering around Tokyo, jumping on and off trains. In Shibuya, the entertainment district, we spend a couple of hours in a department store—floor upon floor of everything from stationery and office supplies to evening gowns and designer handbags. In Harajuku, it's too early in the day to see the teenagers in their crazy outfits, but we wander onto shrine grounds near the station. Only in Japan do you find yourself in areas of worship accidentally. Shrines and temples stand in the middle of bustling cities, protected by a wall of dense, untouched forest. From our hotel-room window, we could spot them easily—large circles or squares of tamed greenery, in the midst of concrete. Here, man and technology are not allowed in certain places. They're shunned, even.

"What is this place?" Riko asks as we wander farther in, the noise of the city dissipating.

"Meiji Shrine," I say, reading a sign. We keep walking and come to a *torii* gate, which Miyagi Sensei told us to expect at the entrance of Shinto shrines and some Buddhist temples. The *torii* marks the transition from the normal world to the sacred. It consists of two columns, topped with a horizontal rail called the *kasagi*. Slightly below the top rail is a second horizontal rail called the *nuki*. Traditionally, they're made of wood and painted a deep orange, almost red color. In modern Japan, there are many that are stone, metal, even stainless steel. They vary in size, as evidenced by the two-inch tall souvenir versions. The one before us is about twelve feet tall, made of unpainted wood. Before we pass through, we perform the purification ritual as Miyagi Sensei explained it to us—scoop up water from the basin with the little wooden cups provided, wash each of our hands, and then take a handful of water and wash our mouths. I'm sure we're doing something wrong, but we enter the prayer area anyway, unpurified though we may be.

Monks are busy cleaning the grounds, sweeping meticulously.

We copy the actions of other visitors, clapping our hands and tossing coins into a wooden collection container. I don't know what it means, but I feel calm, peaceful. Maybe this is what people call a "spiritual experience."

Once we're out of the sacred area, Riko's stomach growls. It's as if she commanded it to remain quiet in the shrine. We decide to head back to Shinjuku. We'd spotted an udon shop when we first arrived in the city, with a white person outside, smoking. Like good tourists, we both stored it in our memories as an appropriate place to eat. However, finding the actual entrance is a more difficult matter than either of us anticipated. It's hidden three floors up in a building also inhabited by a bank and another restaurant. This—the compactness of it all, the efficiency of space—was obvious from my bathtub view of the awakening city this morning. Tokyo is like their writing system—vertical, up-and-down. Within buildings are other buildings, connected by a maze of elevators and staircases and hallways. Japan is an island, after all. It can only grow upward.

We wait in line for lunch with businessmen (and a few women) on their breaks. One reads a book, the Japanese version of the thousand-pager Riko bought at the airport. The Japanese version is short, maybe two hundred pages at most. Kanji characters allow for expression to occupy less space. The Japanese compress, and they do it well. When we get inside, we are seated almost on top of another occupied table, with barely enough elbow room. We are given bibs to wear. At first, I take offense to this, but then I realize all the locals are wearing them. Like I said, it's their lunch break. Wouldn't want to return to the office with udon on a suit. This isn't America. This isn't R&R. Jeans with holes and grease-stained shirts are not appropriate office attire.

We try to slurp our noodles like the natives, but ingrained Western manners make us much quieter, though no less messy. Riko dodges some of the chunks of mystery meat, and I don't blame her. They're not appetizing. But she eats the noodles, and what we guess to be fried tofu, with gusto.

"What am I going to say to my father?" she says, fishing around in her yellow broth for any remaining bits. I have no answer for her. Even without language inhibition, I would be at a loss for words for the person who shipped me off to America, no matter the reasons.

"You probably won't know until you get there," I say.

"What if he doesn't want to see me?"

"I doubt that's the case," I find myself saying, though I have no basis for this assurance.

"What if he never wanted me in the first place?" she says.

"Then he wouldn't have kept you for three years," I say. "There must be reasons you don't know for what happened."

"Maybe," she says.

"Riko, there are about a thousand 'what-ifs' with this situation." I sigh, suddenly exhausted from the meal or jet lag or her worrying. "You can't account for all of them."

"Since when did you become the Zen master?"

It's a good question. "I'm just sleepy, not Zen. Easy to confuse the two."

"But you're right. It's just life. Whatever happens, I'll survive."

If I wasn't so tired, I might have begged to differ.

Wide awake at three o'clock in the morning, I email my parents to say we've arrived safe and sound. I browse the news, check the Tokyo weather forecast, plan the route to Nikko. It's strange that Riko lived here, in Japan, for three years. I type in "age 3 development" in the search bar to learn that a three-year-old is not a helpless blob of a baby, but a growing person with feelings and experiences:

- They will often engage themselves in putting something together, then taking it apart, which is their way of understanding change.
- Up to 80 percent of their speech is understandable.
- They ask many who/what/where/why questions.

I don't know what this tells me, exactly. That Riko had a relationship with her parents? That she asked them questions and played with them and had full-on conversations? She may not remember any of it, but it happened. And *they* must remember.

- They don't understand the concepts of "yesterday" and "tomorrow."

I imagine them hugging her, telling her "You're going to go on a big plane to America tomorrow," and her crying in confusion, not understanding that the present moment could end.

二十七

It is a Wednesday morning at Shinjuku Station, a bad time to be confused and stop in the middle of crowds and attempt to figure out train schedules and directions. People rush by us, hurrying to catch trains to the jobs that define them. We are gently nudged on escalators, obviously misunderstanding which side is for passive standers and which side is for people destined for *karoshi* (the ol' "death by overwork").

We take the Yamanote line to Tokyo Station, then get on the train to Utsunomiya. This leg of the journey was supposed to take an hour, but that must be according to rushed, *karoshi* standards. Two hours since leaving Shinjuku, we are waiting for the Nikko train, satisfying our hunger with rice snacks that have a surprise filling. Judging by the look on Riko's face, her filling is not good. She eats the rice around it and discards the rest.

"Did you get enough to eat?" I ask.

"Probably not, but I'm too nervous to have much of an appetite anyway."

The Nikko train is older than the others, not sleek and metallic. It chugs to a stop, looking like something from the gold rush frontier days. On board are mostly schoolgirls, in their uniforms and white tube socks. Businessmen have no business in Nikko.

"Nikko, literally meaning 'sunlight' or 'sunshine,' is a city located in the mountains of Tochigi Prefecture. It is a popular destination for Japanese and international tourists, housing the mausoleum of Shogun To-ku-ga-wa..." Riko pauses in her reading from the guidebook. She does this when she gets to a Japanese name that is difficult to pronounce. "Some dude," she finishes.

The train makes a few stops before arriving at Nikko Station, the end of the line. There are only a couple people remaining with us now—an elderly woman and a lone schoolgirl. I wonder if she's going home sick or playing hooky. When the train doors open, cold air rushes in. We pull our coats tighter around us. There is snow in the surrounding mountains, and thick clouds moving in from all directions. This is the Japan the guidebook calls "mythical."

There are three taxis waiting out front. We go to the first in line, having learned that if you go to a cab farther down in the line, they will direct you, politely, to the cab at the front. Workers here don't seem interested in taking business from competitors.

"*Konnichiwa*," Riko says to the driver. He returns the "good afternoon" greeting and then says something, which I can only guess is along the lines of "Where to?"

While Riko is rummaging around in her backpack, I try my hand at making conversation: "*Eigo o wakarimasu ka?*" I say, which means, "Do you know English?" The man shakes his head, then says something he must know I can't understand. We stare at each other a moment. He repeats whatever it is he said the first time, but louder. I continue staring at him, blankly. When people reach a language impasse, it seems there are two ways to go: either speak louder and repeat over and over again, in the hopes that something will click in the recipient's brain; or sit quietly and awkwardly. The taxi driver chooses the former; I choose the latter.

"Found it," Riko says to me, pulling out a piece of paper with an address scribbled on it. She hands it to the driver. He nods.

"*Rihoko no ie desu ka?*" he says, asking if we're going to Rihoko's House. "*Ryokan desu ka?*" I know this word, *ryokan*. It's a traditional Japanese inn, complete with *tatami*-matted floors and communal baths.

"*Hai,*" Riko says with pride. Then she tells him that she is Rihoko.

I don't know if he understands that she is *the* Rihoko, but he glances into the rearview mirror at us, eyebrows raised, and says something enthusiastically that we don't comprehend.

The driver is quiet as we pass through the small, two-lane town. Ma-and-pop type shops and restaurants line the road. It reminds me of Big Bear, where the accident happened, where Sarah died. I'll get to that, or I won't—I haven't decided.

The people milling about are Japanese; I don't see tourists. It starts to rain, but our driver doesn't bother with windshield wipers. He makes a quick left up a tiny, one-lane cobblestone road and stops abruptly in front of the inn. He points at the meter—680 yen. I pay him, after taking an embarrassingly long time reading the values of the coins, and we get out, backpacks strapped to us. Riko stands back, waits for me to go ahead of her.

"So, he lives here?" I say.

"I guess," she says, on my heels.

"And you weren't kidding. He really did name the place after you," I say.

"It would appear that way." She sounds sad. I think I would be quite flattered to have a hotel named after me—House of Jonathan.

We step through the front doors and enter an intermediary room, a place to leave wet shoes and umbrellas. Then we enter the lobby. It's quiet, not a human in sight, no sounds of humans either. I walk to the front desk. There is a bell to ring. I tap it once. Moments later, an older man—about my dad's age, I guess—comes to greet us. He starts to deliver what I guess to be an apology for not being at the desk. I notice the freckles on his wrinkling face and realize this is Riko's father. It's obvious Riko has realized this too. She is standing a good five feet behind me, like she's my dumbstruck geisha, waiting for instructions on how to proceed.

"*Nihongo o wakarimasu ka?*" he says, asking if I understand Japanese. It's probably apparent that I don't, since we've been silent in the dialogue space left after his greeting.

"*Chotto,*" I say, with an apologetic grimace.

The man laughs, amused by me, then takes out a sheet of paper which has room descriptions and rates, translated into English.

"What do you want to do?" I whisper to Riko. "Are we *staying* here?"

She looks confused. She's staring at the man in a way that

will make him uncomfortable, if he notices. She is analyzing his glasses, more like spectacles really, seemingly constructed early last century. He is wearing a plain white button-up shirt and tan pants. His hair is graying, but not receding.

"One night," I say, pointing to a room option with a private bath and toilet. It's nearly 40,000 yen per night (about $400).

He nods and disappears behind his cloth curtain again, like the wizard in *Wizard of Oz*. When he returns, he has a key in his hand. He leads us down a hallway, his steps cheerful, despite a limp. I wonder if we are the only occupants in his little *ryokan*.

We arrive at our room, and he lets us in and shows us around. There is an entryway with a shoe cupboard and, immediately in front of it, a small closet-like room with just a toilet. This toilet appears to have the same bells and whistles as the toilet in our Tokyo hotel. There is another small room with a bath and sink. It makes hygienic sense, really, to separate the toilet from the place where cleaning occurs. He pushes a wooden sliding door to reveal the main room with a table, low to the ground, and two floor-level cushion seats. There's a television with a remote, which kind of ruins the ambiance, but I suppose even the most traditional Japanese want their game shows. An adjoining room has a regular-height small table and two regular-height chairs, placed in front of a window overlooking the snow-covered pond outside. The raindrops are making little circular dents in the snow. He shows us our *yukatas*—casual types of kimonos to be worn around the inn—along with our towels for the hot spring baths (*onsens*).

With a few bows and indecipherable words, he makes his exit, but not before saying, "*Namae wa Hideo desu*" ("My name is Hideo"), which pretty much confirms our greatest hope or greatest fear—I'm not sure which yet.

Riko appears to be mute, so I sit on the floor, at the table in the middle of the room, wondering aloud how the Japanese can tolerate sitting like this for any length of time.

"They must have very flexible hip and knee joints," I say.

Riko gives me a look of hatred that, unfortunately, I know well.

"What?" I say.

"That was my *dad*," she says. The way she uses the casual American term—*dad*—still makes me uneasy. "I can't believe you're talking about hip and knee joints."

"Well, you sure as hell weren't saying anything."

"What am I supposed to say?"

"As I've told you, I can't be expected to know things like that."

She sits on the other side of the table, her little chair directly opposite mine. I catch her smiling to herself as she gazes out the window.

"He seemed sweet, didn't he?" she bemuses.

"He did."

"And he seems happy, right?"

"In the five minutes I interacted with him at the front desk of the inn he owns, he did not seem to be in a depressive downward spiral, no."

"You are such an ass sometimes," she says.

"I never professed to be anything otherwise."

"Do you think my mom is here too?" The amount of hope in her voice makes me uncomfortable. She's primed and ready for disappointment.

"I don't know," I say. "Are you going to tell him who you are?"

"I'm not sure yet. I need to think about it."

With this, she takes her purple and white *yukata* into the bathroom. "It's left side over the right one, right?" she calls from inside the bathroom.

"Yes," I say. She emerges wearing the traditional garb, looking like the native Japanese person she was supposed to be.

"I like it," she says, adjusting the tie around the center of her small, thin body. She likes it because it makes her look more like the person she's looking for. After all, without her jeans, it's hard to tell where she considers "home."

"I think I'll try the bath before dinner," she says. "What about you?"

Here is my understanding of the traditional *onsen*: There are two separate baths—one for men and one for women. Strike one. You enter wearing the *yukata* and the little *geta* sandals, then disrobe completely. Strike two. You do, however, have what is called a "modesty towel" to cover whatever you are modest about. I'm not sure whether to use it on my face or the more obvious location. You enter the bathing area, where there are small stalls, like pig stalls in a barn. Here, you are supposed to clean yourself before entering the bath. You sit on a little stool, trying to ignore the fact that other men, and their balls, may have occupied this stool not long before you. You soap up, rinse off, and then you get in the bath. It's likely there are other men in the bath. I've heard stories of Japanese men who are so curious about American genitalia that they actually look or, sometimes, touch to satisfy their curiosity. Strike three.

"I don't know," I tell her.

"Oh, come on. When in Rome, right? When else will you have the opportunity to use a Japanese hot springs bath?"

"Probably never. Thankfully."

"Well, I'm going. You should go," she says. She takes the

key and leaves, shuffling out in her sandals, her dress obviously too tight for her to take normal-length strides.

Maybe she is right. It's unlikely that anyone else is staying at this inn hidden in the hills of snowy Nikko, let alone that someone is using the bath at precisely 4:43 p.m. I change into my *yukata*, glad Riko is not around to snap a picture of me looking like some gay man's Japanese fetish fantasy. My beard doesn't seem to fit with the dress. I appear to be a homeless man who settled for whatever piece of clothing he could find to protect himself from the elements.

I make my way to the bath area, thinking I must look like I have a stick stuck up my ass, shuffling like this. The disrobing room is empty. There are no signs of other men present, no room keys or towels or clothes. I remove my *yukata*, standing stark naked in front of the mirror. I'm thinner than I thought I was, but the slack kind of thin, not the muscular kind. I step through the door into the bathing area, modesty towel in hand. I almost slip on the wet step when I see the back of a guy's head in the bath. Shit.

I don't know etiquette here. Am I supposed to say something to him—"Hey, what's up?"—or just go about the business of cleaning myself? I decide that he probably doesn't know English anyway and proceed to sit at a stall out of his line of sight. I soap up the stool first because, like I said, balls could have been on that thing recently. Then I soap up my body, twice, just to be sure I'm meeting the likely strict Japanese standards for cleanliness. I don't want this guy to think I'm "just another dirty American." I want him to think I'm a very clean Canadian.

I walk to the bath, using the towel to cover my parts. It's only when I get inside, when I dare to make eye contact with the man, that I realize it's Hideo, Riko's father.

I sit down and put the modesty towel on the top of my head, emulating him. My knees are pulled up to my chest. I feel strange letting everything just flop about in the water. He seems to have no reservations, though. He is closing his eyes, a soft smile on his face, his legs stretched out, along with his arms.

"Welcome," he says, using one of the few English words I presume he knows.

"*Arigatou*," I say, using one of the few Japanese words I am comfortable using.

His eyes are still closed. It's like he knows who I am without even opening them. We must be the only occupants of the inn.

We are quiet for a long while. Just as I am wondering how long I am supposed to sit in here, Hideo pushes himself up and steps out of the tub, steam coming off his round, unashamed body. He places the modesty towel in front of him—more for tradition than modesty, I gather—and walks through a sliding door to the outside bath, big enough for just one person. He is facing away from me, his hands resting on the sides of the tub, steam still coming off of them, maybe enough to melt the surrounding snow patches.

Here he is, in the flesh, literally. Riko has found what she's wanted, in this happenstance way, whether she knows what it means, or if it's what she's really wanted or not. I have to wonder what *I* want, what I'm doing here—not in the *onsen*, but in Japan, on a quest for cherry blossoms during an unusually cold spring.

Just minutes later, Hideo returns to the main bath area and sits at a stall, lathering for what seems like an eternity.

"*Yasumi desu ka?*" he says. Maybe this is the etiquette, speaking while not facing each other. I know we learned that word—*yasumi*. Vacation or holiday, that's what it means. He's asking if we're here on vacation, in the simplest Japanese he can concoct.

"*Hai*," I say, affirming him.

"*Rihoko wa anata no tsuma desu ka?*" he says slowly, enunciating clearly.

The presence of Riko's name in this sentence startles me. It takes me a moment to translate the rest for myself. When I do, I blurt out "No!" See, he's asked me if Riko is my wife, which means two strange things—one, he knows Riko is Riko; and two, he thinks we're married.

"*Iie*," I say, though I think he understood the English "No!" just fine.

I can see his face smiling in the mirror. There are so many things I want to ask—Did you know who she was right away? Why didn't you say anything? Are you sad? Are you happy? Are you going to tell her?

I don't have the words for any of these inquiries though. And he probably doesn't have the language to elaborate. So we are left with visuals, facial expressions, to interpret. He looks at peace to me, perhaps fulfilled by the very fact that she traveled across an ocean just to see him. Of course he recognized her right away. He remembers her, though her three-year-old brain did not retain much of him. He knows her freckles, the almond shape of her eyes, the uniqueness of her smile. Of course.

Whatever my face is telling him makes him smile wider. He must see me realize these things. He must be wondering what I will tell Riko, how I will explain all of this using the intricacies and expressions of the English language.

It occurs to me that, while we are on the topic of wives, I can ask about his, Riko's mother. I rifle through the vocabulary I know and come up with, "*Anata no tsuma wa doko desu ka?*"

I think that means "Where is your wife?" It sounds much too blunt and interrogation-ish, but I'm hoping he'll understand my limitations.

He says something I can't translate, then gives me a sad kind of smile that makes me think there is no wife.

"*Wakarimasu ka?*" he says, asking if I understand.

I shake my head.

"*Watashi no tsuma wa shinda,*" he says, slowly.

The verb clicks—*shinu.* To die. I know this one.

His wife is dead.

"*Gomen nasai,*" I say, doing my best to express condolences. Then I ask him when: "*Itsu?*"

"*Nijuu-nen mae,*" he says.

Miyagi Sensei drilled numbers into our heads enough for me to know he's said "twenty years." She died twenty years ago. When Riko was...three.

He gives me another sad smile, and I understand all too well. He gave up Riko because his wife died, because he was lost without her, because he wanted his daughter to have a better life.

"*Bangohan o tabemashou ka?*" he says, inviting me to dinner. He stands from the stool, modesty towel not quite doing its best to keep him modest.

I confirm in broken Japanese that we will be at dinner at six o'clock. He nods, bows, and goes to get dressed. He's stashed his clothes in a cupboard, which is why I hadn't seen them upon entering. He doesn't wave goodbye, or even flash a smile or glance in my direction. He has a meal to prepare.

I arrive back at the room before Riko, slightly light-headed and with pruned skin. She has the key, so I sit on the floor, outside the door, wondering what to say to her. Then I get distracted wondering what Japanese phrases are equivalent to "The cat's out of the bag."

"How long have you been waiting?" she asks.

Her hair is wet, she smells like mangoes, and her face is greased up with lotion. She must have made use of the beauty bottles. The robing-and-disrobing area was stocked with them, but I couldn't imagine any self-respecting man using them.

"Not long," I lie.

She lets us inside and sits at the table by the window.

"I have never felt so peaceful in my life," she says. She lifts her hair on top of her head and clips it there.

"It was nice, huh?" I say.

"So you went too, did you?"

"I did."

"I knew you would. Wasn't it just amazing?" she gushes. "I was the only one in there. It was just complete luxury. Did you use the outside bath?"

I shake my head.

"Oh, you should," she says. "I could hear the rain. And the warmth felt so amazing in contrast to the cold air." I wonder how many more times she plans on using the word "amazing" because, after years of hyperbolic advertising language, I can't stand this word. I also wonder if Hideo knew, when he was in the outside bath, that his daughter was on the other side of the wall. Can fathers sense this kind of thing? What, exactly, is the paternal bond?

"Were you alone too?" she asks.

Here is where the truth will insert itself.

"No," I say, plainly.

"Oh, that sucks," she says. "I think I would feel weird with someone else there."

"It wasn't that weird."

"I got the impression we were the only people staying here," she says.

"I think we are."

She unclips her hair, apparently discontented with its current arrangement on top of her head. She retwists it into the same bun.

"What do you mean?"

"Your father, he was in there with me."

"Oh," she says, just letting her hair fall now, carelessly.

"We talked a bit."

"How'd you manage that?" Her laugh is nervous.

"Not easily."

"Well, what did he say?" She's fidgeting with her *yukata*, tugging at it like it's uncomfortable.

"Nothing, for a while. Then he asked if we were on vacation, and I said we were. Then he said, 'Is Rihoko your wife?'"

She stops fidgeting and stares at me. "He knows who I am?"

I nod.

"Well, how did he know? Did you say something to him?"

"I'm pretty sure he figured it out on his own. I don't think a father ever forgets his daughter's face."

This seems to take her breath away, just like the view from our Tokyo hotel room.

"Do you think he's upset I came here?" she asks.

"No, I really don't," I say. "Riko, he told me your mother died, twenty years ago."

I envision the wheels in her head turning and see the epiphany on her face. "Do you think that's why he gave me up?"

I shrug. "We men, we don't know how to handle grief," I say. "It destroys us."

She lets out a long-held breath. "Well, what am I supposed to do now?"

"As I've told you, I can't be expected to know things like that."

In the dining room, only one table is set, confirming our suspicion that we are the only guests at the inn. There is no staff in sight, and I wonder if Hideo manages the place himself, from keeping the rooms tidy to making the meals to checking the temperature of the baths. There is a name placard at our table that says "Jonathan and Rihoko," and I assume this is her father's subtle way of alerting her to the fact that he knows who she is.

When we sit, he appears, as if there is some sensor in our seats alerting him to our presence.

"*Konbanwa*," he says, with a bow. He smiles at us and then waits on us as I presume he would wait on any other customers.

The meal is vegetarian, served *kaiseki* style, with a number of small dishes brought out from the kitchen, one at a time. He shows us how to make our own tofu, heating a soy milk substance in a pan over an open flame until a skin forms on top. We are told to dip the skin into a sauce in one of the many small bowls occupying the table. There are tempura-style vegetables, rice, miso soup. We sip sake and—when he is in the kitchen, preparing our next dish—we practice the Japanese that the situation will require.

"*Anata wa watashi no otousan desu*," Riko says, which means, stiffly, "You are my father."

"It sounds kind of *Star Wars*, don't you think?"

"Well, I don't know what else to say," she disputes, agitated. "If he knew English, I would have lots of things to say."

"Like?" I ask, calling her bluff.

She finishes off her small cup of sake and launches into something that she may have practiced while sitting in the *onsen*: "I would say 'I'm your daughter. I wanted to see you. I don't know what to say except that I thank you and my mother for giving me life, and I appreciate your wanting me to have a better life. I can't say if it's better in America or if it would have been better here. But I know the importance of intention, and I love you for that. I'm sorry we have not been in each other's lives. I hope we can be in touch. I'm taking more Japanese courses. I just wanted to meet you. You are part of who I am.' That's what I would say."

She exhales. And, then, right then, I have a feeling Riko has gotten what she wanted from all this—from coming to Japan, from coming to Nikko, from seeing her father.

Dessert arrives, in the form of a cube of strawberry-flavored tofu that kind of tastes like pudding or solidified yogurt. There's a piece of kiwi on top.

"*Arigatou gozaimasu*," Riko says, looking her father in the eye with an intensity that says more than just a regular customer-to-waiter "thank you."

He smiles, and then he does something that the expressionless Japanese culture would likely condemn—while mid-bow, he reaches out and places his hand on Riko's. He gives it a small squeeze. There is a moment between them, the cinematic kind, but they don't say anything. This, I think, is *haragei*—belly talk, that nonverbal expression of love between people. In this case, it's more like hand talk, but I don't know the phrase for that.

"*Doo itashimashite*," he says.

And that's when I learn how to say "you're welcome" in Japanese.

When we come back to our rooms, our beds are already laid out on the floor for us—two futon-type mattresses, side by side. We change into our pajamas and get under the duvet-wrapped comforters. The pillows are hard, like they're stuffed with bags of uncooked rice.

"So we'll go to Kyoto tomorrow, then," Riko says.

Apparently, like Sara, she feels the need to instigate conversation after we have turned off the lights and committed our bodies and minds to slumber.

"Sure," I say. "Are you ready to leave here?"

I can hear her rolling around, searching for that exact spot of comfort. She stops.

"Yeah, I'm ready," she says.

"Then Kyoto it is."

"Good night," she says.

"*Oyasuminasai.*"

One place you would think would be on my "To visit" list and is not: Aokigahara, also known as Suicide Forest. It's located on the northwestern flank of Mount Fuji. It's not that it's hard to get to. And there are ice caves, so I could easily talk Riko into a visit without divulging my suicide obsession. It's just that I know Sara wouldn't like it. It would make her uncomfortable, traipsing about the spot where so many have taken their lives, gawking at the morbidity of it all.

Annual body searches in the forest have been conducted by police, volunteers, and journalists since 1970. In 2003, 105 bodies were found in the forest, exceeding the previous record of 78 in 2002. In 2010, the police recorded more than 200 people having attempted suicide in the forest, of whom 54 completed the act. A man who owns a shop near the entrance of the forest said he'd seen numerous people exit the forest after failing to kill themselves. One woman came to him with part of a rope around her neck, her eyes nearly popping out of their sockets. He offered her tea and called an ambulance.

Suicides are said to increase during March, the end of the fiscal year in Japan. That creeps me out too. It's March now. There are people planning their deaths right now. The most common means of suicide in the forest are hanging or drug overdose. There are signs at the heads of some trails urging suicidal visitors to think of their families and contact a suicide prevention association. Many say the forest is haunted. One Buddhist monk claimed that the spirits of those who committed suicide are calling to those who come to take their lives, urging them to go through with it. I like to think I don't need coaxing from beyond.

二十八

Breakfast at a traditional-style inn consists of food you would never want to eat first thing in the morning. We try to be polite, picking at our tofu salads and our pieces of salmon (cooked, thankfully). Our chopsticks do laps in a pot of broth that has what looks to be a floating piece of cod in it. What I wouldn't give for a donut.

"*Ohayoo gozaimasu*," Riko's father says, greeting us with a morning bow.

We return the greeting and pretend to be enthusiastic about our meal. I find myself remembering tricks I used as a five-year-old, pushing chunks of tofu underneath a decorative leaf when he's not looking. The truth is he's not paying attention to me, though; his eyes are on Riko.

"*Ooishi desu yo*," she says, telling him it's delicious. Liar.

He bows and steps away so we can enjoy our food. After we've finished eating, or pushed around our food in a way that suggests we are done, we go back to the room and pack. When we emerge—dressed in our jeans, drawing attention to the world from which we come—Hideo is waiting at the entrance, car keys in his hand.

"To JR Station?" I say, hoping he understands me.

He nods. "*Hai,*" he says and waves for us to follow him.

His limp seems more pronounced today. Perhaps it's arthritis, made worse by the cold morning air. He opens the sliding door of a van, and we climb inside. There is a thick layer of frost on his windshield. He laughs, almost giggles, to himself and then runs back inside, emerging a few moments later with a steaming pitcher of water. He throws it on the window, and the ice melts away. After he starts the engine, he turns on the heater, for our sake, I presume, as he's bundled up in a thick coat and scarf.

Our short ride to the station is silent. If I had the language skill, I would make small talk. I would ask if the weather is usually this cold this time of year, if it is always this foggy and rainy. I would ask his opinions of Kyoto, find out if there are any sights we should visit that only the natives know. I would ask him my chances of seeing cherry blossoms.

Before I can even begin to assess my abilities to form a coherent sentence, we are at the station. He helps us with our bags, though they are already on our backs so there's not much he can do. He faces Riko, no more than an arm's length between them.

"*Tegami o arigatou,*" he says, slowly.

The silence between them gives me enough time to translate: he's thanking her for the letter. So he did get it.

He continues, "*Watashi wa anata ni kakimasu.*"

Riko looks at me, as if I understand Japanese better than she does. I just shrug. Hideo repeats himself, slower, and Riko says to me, "I think he's saying he'll write to me." Her smile is huge.

"*Motto tegami o kaite kudasai*," he says.

She translates this for me: "He wants me to write more letters."

"*Hai*," she says to him, with a convincing nod. They've made a pact. His smile is as big as hers.

He takes her hand again and bows, gratefully. "*Ano...*," he says, stalling. "*Ano*" is like the English equivalent of "Umm..."

"*Arigatou*," Riko says, interrupting his attempts to say something more. I imagine her thank-you is for more things than she can probably articulate.

"Goodbye," he says, seemingly pleased with himself for being able to say farewell to his daughter in the language she knows best.

He gets back in the driver's seat, and we watch him drive away. We wave. Riko starts to walk briskly in front of me, and I wonder if we're about to miss the train. I hurry to catch up to her. That's when I see the tears in her eyes and realize she's not running for a train; she's running away from my seeing her cry.

"You okay?" I ask.

"Never better," she says, with an honest smile.

We show our rail passes to the attendant and sit on a wooden bench. We have twenty minutes until our train arrives. We take pictures of each other, with the snowy mountains as our backdrop.

"Miyagi Sensei would be proud, wouldn't she?" Riko says.

"She would."

Our train slows to a stop, and we get on board. A sign on the sliding door says "THIS DOOR DON'T OPEN AUTOMAT-ICALLY," which makes me feel better about my own language inadequacies. Riko bends forward and puts her hands in front of the floor vents for hot air.

"Don't worry," she says. "Kyoto will be warmer. Don't give up on the cherry blossoms."

We connect at Utsunomiya, then take the bullet train back to Tokyo, and then another bullet train to Kyoto. We sit in front of two obviously drunk businessmen. We can smell their liquor from our seats, but that's not what gives them away. What gives them away is their loud chuckles. Sober, proper Japanese people are not exuberant laughers.

The guidebook says we should be able to see Mount Fuji on our ride from Tokyo to Kyoto, but all we see is a gathering of clouds blocking the peak.

"No Mount Fuji today," I say, dejected. I'm pretty sure I won't see cherry blossoms either.

"But at least there are drunk businessmen," Riko whispers.

I try to be humored.

"Why am I even here?" I ask, realizing too late that I'm speaking out loud.

"On Earth? Or in Japan?"

"Both."

"I can't be expected to know things like that," she says.

She reclines her seat and closes her eyes. I envy her ability to sleep.

By the time we get to Kyoto, we are too tired to undertake the adventure of finding a place to eat. Thankfully, the train station is like a food court in itself. Riko examines the store-front displays. We can't tell what most of the plastic food is, but that's not what matters. What matters is being able to tell what *not* to order, and this is obvious. Riko and I designate this category of food-to-be avoided in *$10,000 Pyramid* fashion: "Things that look like fish bait" or "Things that look like they were pumped out of a clogged drain."

"What about *this* place?" Riko says.

From the katakana, we can see that they specialize in *pi-za* (pizza), though the display seems to showcase omelets. We ask for a table for two.

"So, what's on the itinerary?" she asks as we sip from our beers.

"Well, there are lots of side trips we can do. Nara is supposed to be neat. We can go to Osaka or Kobe, but I have a feeling that's just more city," I say, feeling well-researched and proud.

Riko takes a longer sip of her beer.

"Is there anything Sara wanted to see?" she asks me, after a big gulp.

I stare down into my glass.

"I don't know," I say.

All I ever heard her mention were the damn cherry blossoms.

Our pizzas arrive. They do look like omelets. There is some kind of light topping—onion skin? dried fish scales?—seemingly in motion, fluttering around.

"Is the white stuff tofu, or cheese?" Riko asks, poking hers aggressively with chopsticks, which I'm pretty sure is a big faux pas. I imagine Japanese mothers yelling at their children, "They're utensils, not weapons!"

"It could be both. You just never know."

We eat anyway, adopting that Japanese philosophy of "Don't ask questions, just enjoy." And we do enjoy, as evidenced by our clean skillets.

"You ready to find our hostel?" I say.

For this leg of the trip, I'd booked a hostel, to save a bit of money. According to the guidebook, we shouldn't spend much time in our room while in Kyoto anyway.

When we open the door to our room, I realize I am too old to stay at a hostel. I'd had the feeling on the elevator up to the fourth floor, as my ears were assaulted by the drunken shrieking of some European kids riding up with us. But the room finalizes my conclusion. It is large enough for just the two twin beds and a tiny nightstand between them. To the immediate left of the door is another door, leading to our three-by-three-foot bathroom (I opted for the private bathroom instead of the communal one, due to too many memories of college and wearing sandals in the shower to avoid fungus growing between my toes).

"Roomy," Riko says, tossing her backpack onto her bed.

There is a very small television embedded in the wall, directly above the foot of my bed. We take turns changing into pajamas in the bathroom, squeezing by each other.

"I feel like I'm on a cruise ship," I say.

"I've never been on a cruise," Riko says from the bathroom.

"It's like this, except you'd look out the window and see water."

"You don't say," she says, coming out in her pajamas, the same gray sweats and thermal shirt she's worn the past couple nights.

We lie in our beds, watching the television, because there's something comforting about the screen. Watching television in a foreign country is like looking up at the moon anywhere in the world; it makes you realize how connected we all are. I flip between a baseball game—the Japanese are very into their baseball—and an infomercial about constipation. Apparently, the Japanese are also very into their constipation (and remedies for the condition). There is an elementary illustration of the small intestine, and blocks stacking up inside it. This cuts to an actress, who is cringing in discomfort. I don't even know if they are selling anything. It seems they are just talking about constipation.

"How much money would it take for you to be that actress?" I ask Riko. But she's asleep, her head propped up against the headboard.

"You're going to have a neck ache tomorrow," I whisper, shaking her shoulder gently.

"Hmm?" she mumbles.

"Come on, lie down. You'll thank me in the morning."

She scoots down and rests her head flat on her pillow. Then she says, with a sleepy, bemused smile, "*Arigatou.*"

In the morning, we ask the guy at the front desk where we can get breakfast. He mentions a place on the corner that sells beef bowls. What is it with the Japanese and eating meat in hot liquids in the morning? We decide to wander, which isn't usually a good plan, but it works out this time. We pass Higashi Honganji temple. It's undergoing construction, reminding all passersby of how even the sacred needs touching up from time to time. There is a banner out front that says "LET US DISCOVER THE SIGNIFICANCE OF BIRTH AND THE JOY OF LIVING." I wonder if someone like me, someone with plans of suicide, would just go up in flames upon setting foot on these grounds, like a vampire in the sunlight.

At the next block past the temple, there is a waffle shop, of all things. It's unclear how the Japanese view waffles. According to the plastic displays, many of the dishes are served with ice cream, so I'm guessing waffles are more of a dessert item. Also, there are very few customers at this morning hour. Nevertheless, we take our American appetites to enjoy an American breakfast. Judging by our silence at the table, we are both ashamed of our unwillingness to eat like a native. Riko makes a point to order *ocha* (green tea), though.

"So, we're going to Nara?" Riko asks, surveying her plate, using her finger to ensure that no chocolate sauce is left behind.

"If you don't mind going in the rain," I say.

If I were a cherry blossom, I would not be planning on making an appearance for a while. It's cold. The clouds look like they are going to break open at any moment.

"We have umbrellas," she says, excitedly. That's the thing about trips—what would be an annoyance back home suddenly becomes an adventure.

When we get off the train at the Nara Station, it is completely unclear how to get to the park. The map we have does not appear to be drawn to scale. We walk a couple of streets, trying to figure out how to hold our umbrellas for maximum protection from the now-falling rain. I find that holding it at an angle, slightly forward, is best, though I can't avoid the bottoms of my pants getting wet. I summon the courage to ask a woman at a street corner, "*Koen wa doko desu ka?*" She seems pleased with my Japanese and points in the direction of the park. Then she says, "You walk?" with a look of horror. We nod. We are adventurers! She says with a little laugh, a chortle, "You walk long."

She is right—we do walk long. And the rain is coming down harder. So we start running. We run through puddles. We run through intersections. I look up for brief moments to admire the modest homes, with their blue tile roofs. But, mostly, I am focused on my feet and on their running. Finally, we see a big orange-red *torii* gate marking the entrance to the park. Riko runs ahead of me, like a little kid. The stretch of sidewalk is narrow. She seems oblivious to the cars whizzing by less than a foot from her. I imagine her slipping on a patch of mud, her body sliding into traffic. I imagine having to consult my Japanese dictionary to find out the word for "ambulance." I try to run faster, feeling my age in each lunge. She is younger, invigorated by the destination ahead of her. I can't catch her.

"Sara, stop!" I shout.

The error makes itself apparent immediately. The softness of the "ah" at the end of "Sara" is in striking opposition to the sharp "o" at the end of "Riko." These two names have not a single letter in common.

Riko turns around and stares at me, then starts walking back toward me. She stops, just inches from my face, drops of rain on her nose, like raised clear freckles to go along with her flat brown ones. I wait for her to psychoanalyze me, to make this more than it is. Instead, she just says, "Are you okay?"

The thing is, I'm not okay. I'm angry. I'm still seeing her sliding into traffic. This happens sometimes. Since Sara died, I see tragedies before they occur.

"No," I say. "You're going to get hit by a freaking car."

I can hear the slight hysteria in my voice. I'm embarrassed of myself.

She looks over her shoulder at the road. Cars pass, going maybe twenty miles per hour, max.

"I'm sorry," she says, with the kind of voice police officers use to talk crazies off ledges. "I'll be more careful. Okay?"

"Yeah, yeah," I say, wanting to move on from this moment as quickly as possible.

We walk to the *torii* gate and enter the park. Just as the guide-book said, there are deer everywhere, wandering in groups of twenty or more, nibbling on grass. The deer don't seem to care that it's raining. We take pictures of each other with the deer, with the purpose of showing them to our American friends, proving how close we got to nature. In the pictures, we'll be smiling and happy. Nobody, except us, will know how our fingers froze, how our jeans were wet and sticking to our legs, how we could have gotten hit by Japanese motorists.

We make our way to the Todaiji Temple, with the Great Buddha Hall. The guidebook says it's the largest wooden build-ing in the world. The guidebook also says that, according to legend, if a human can fit his head inside the Great Buddha's nostril, it means he is enlightened. When I tell this to Riko, she says, "That's dumb. That would mean all midgets and children are enlightened."

"And more women than men would have a chance at enlight-enment," I say.

"Well, that's probably true."

We pay 500 yen for our tickets (about five bucks) and make our way to the temple. We snap more pictures, again aware of how they won't do justice to our reality. This building is huge. I don't know any other word for it. I try to take pictures of it with Riko in front, to give some sense of scale. Inside, the Buddha is enormous. I'm sure my head would fit in its nostril.

"Jesus," Riko says, her neck craned upward.

"No, actually, that's Buddha."

She shakes her head at me and moves forward to get a better look. She stays like that, neck craned, for a good five minutes, just admiring the bronze statue. Other tourists move past us quickly, taking photos that I know will come out too dark.

"It's amazing, isn't it?" Riko says.

There's that word again. I nod because, for once, I have no sarcastic comment to make.

I read more from the guidebook about this guy. It says his large right hand—held up like he's telling you, calmly, to stop in the name of love—signifies the removal of human fears. His left hand—palm facing up, like it's catching raindrops—signifies the hearing of people's desires. Removing fears, hearing desires. The Great Buddha must be very busy.

Riko buys a couple postcards, with clear, bright pictures of the Buddha on them. She is smart enough not to rely on her camera. Then we are back in the rain, which is coming down even harder than before. My jeans are soaked almost to the knee. Deer outnumber tourists on the streets. We are the only idiots stupid, or "adventurous," enough to be running through Nara.

"Let's jump on that bus," Riko says, running ahead of me again.

"What? Why?" I say.

"It'll probably stop at the station at some point," she says, running faster. She starts to wave her arms, which is universal language for "Wait! Hold the bus!"

"How do you know?" I ask, struggling to speak and run at the same time.

"I don't."

We make it to the bus. She jumps on, and I follow her. It takes me longer than I care to admit to catch my breath.

"How do you know we're not going to end up in China?" I ask.

"Well, first of all, I don't think this bus can cross water," she says. "And second of all, this looks like a local bus, right?"

She's right—it's a small bus. The people look like townsfolk. They have grocery bags and other signs of weekday errands. They don't look to be "adventurous" like us; they look to be engaged in their mundane lives.

"It's bound to go by the station. Nara isn't that big," she says.

At the next stop, a few people get off and we take their seats, making sure nobody else wants them first. There's this constant desire to not be perceived as inconsiderate Americans.

"You worry too much," Riko says, looking at her Buddha postcards.

"Yeah, probably."

"Sometimes you just gotta trust a little, you know? What's the worst that could happen? We could get lost. I bet we'd find our way."

"How much would you bet?" I press her.

She dismisses me. The bus comes to another stop. She stands, takes in the surroundings, and adjusts her purse strap on her shoulder.

"Come on," she says. "We're here."

The Japanese have a number of interesting proverbs. Some favorites, translated:

- Even monkeys fall from trees.
- A frog in a well does not know the great ocean.
- When poisoned, one might as well swallow the plate.

This is the one I keep thinking about, though:

一寸先は闇
issun saki wa yami

It means "It is dark one inch ahead of you." I think this was intended to be liberating, as in "Why worry? You can't see the future. Live in the moment because you don't know what's ahead." This is how Sara would have interpreted it. And, before she died, maybe I would have interpreted it that way too. Now I'm all too aware of the surprise catastrophes that can lurk in the darkness one inch ahead of me. How can anyone fault me for not wanting to keep going?

二十九

Our next two days in Kyoto feature us as quintessential tourists. We walk more than our legs want us to walk. Our cameras are ever-ready. Mid-snap, taking a picture of a gigantic plastic crab with mechanical, moving legs on a building in Nishiki Market, I wonder why I am taking pictures. They aren't for me, are they? I won't be around to look back on them, nostalgically. I won't be around to show them to friends and family members, adding my copywriter talents to articulating the stories behind each photo. I still snap, though. This is the digital age, and my adventures will live eternally on the memory chip of my camera. Lives can come and go, but pixels can survive.

We find our way to Nishiki Market accidentally. We wander into one store, only to realize it is connected to a maze of other stores. We meld with the masses as they navigate the corridors of the indoor malls. It smells of roasting nuts and something sweet. We buy pastries filled with red bean paste and topped with strawberries from a vendor who bows in gratitude three times before we walk away. We get cones of purple soft serve, neither of us able to identify the exact flavor. We walk through arcades, watching the teenagers in awe. How they can tolerate the flashing lights, the loud music, I will never know. This is a new generation, a generation accustomed to constant movement and sound, a generation whose senses are geared for multitasking, a generation that is easily bored by what life offers in the simplest sense.

We have the best sushi of our lives at Tomi-Zushi, a back-alley joint that, like all great restaurants, appears less than special from the outside. We push through the drapes at the entrance, like cowboys through swinging saloon doors in old Western movies. We are gung ho, brave, looking for trouble in all the right places. And we find it. The sushi bar is packed with natives who look up at us, almost amused. We find two empty seats and ask, sheepishly, if there is an English menu. There is. The guy next to us laughs at the English menu. We order can't-go-wrong rolls—tuna and salmon and crab. We watch the sushi chef as he rolls the rice in its seaweed wrapper. He slices cucumbers mindlessly, coming so close to chopping off his fingertips, as he chats with the customers. He grabs in different compartments for fish and various garnish. We are served directly on the counter, and we don't question this. I'm sure this counter is cleaner than any plate in America. The chefs give off the impression of being that meticulous, dedicated to detail and perfection. After all, they trained for years for this job.

We order warm sake and more rolls, then more rolls after we have had enough sake to forget that we're no longer hungry. By the time we walk out of the restaurant, I'm dizzy, intoxicated.

The way Riko giggles as we try to figure out from which way we have come, it's obvious she is too. We go in search of kara-oke. Even in our drunkenness, we can read the katakana letters on the buildings—*ka-ra-o-ke*. We are so proud of ourselves. We both wish Miyagi Sensei could see us now.

There is something seedy and strange about the karaoke building (or "palace," as Riko calls it). Or maybe there is some-thing seedy and strange about paying to use a room for an hour. The gentleman takes us to the elevator and pushes the button for the fourth floor. He leads us past several dark rooms, filled with everyone from teenage girls to middle-aged men in suits, before arriving at ours. He shows us how to use the controls—using gestures instead of language—and leaves us to our own vocal devices.

Riko's first selection is a Britney Spears song. She grabs the microphone and hops on the couch, singing "Oh baby, baby, how was I supposed to know?" Our age difference is terribly apparent. She seems to sense this and chooses Def Leppard's "Pour Some Sugar on Me" for the second song. We do this as a duet, screaming into our respective microphones as if we are having a volume competition. There is some excitement, some exhilaration, in knowing the words to a song. Yes, they are right there on the screen, but that's not important.

"Your turn to pick something," Riko says, breathless from jumping all over the couches.

What comes to mind is a song I used to sing to Sara. I'd forgotten, until just this moment, about this song, and about how I used to be so enamored of another human that I didn't care how awful I sounded. Love does not just tolerate embar-rassment; it welcomes it, for the sole reason that it will elicit a smile from the beloved.

The song is "I Believe in a Thing Called Love" by the Darkness. I barely know it now, and I'm pretty sure I barely knew it then. I just liked the chorus. Even now, with the words on-screen, I mumble through most of the lyrics, nodding in the most rock-and-roll way possible, until:

"*I believe in a thing called love, just listen to the rhythm of my heart. There's a chance we could make it now. We'll be rocking till the sun goes down. I believe in a thing called love.*"

"I don't know this song," Riko shouts over the music.

"Neither do I," I say.

She collapses onto the couch, laughing. When she looks up at me, her eyes are glossy and dazed. I start petting her hair with my free hand, my non-mike hand, like she's an animal in a petting zoo.

She sits up and takes the microphone from me.

"Do you believe in a thing called love?" she says, into the microphone, looking at me seriously, like I'm a guest on her talk show.

"I don't know," I say, feeling suddenly sober.

She hits me on the shoulder with the microphone. "You're boring," she says. Then she looks at her watch and says, "Shit, our hour's up."

We end our night at the Sky Lounge, at the top of Kyoto Tower, with a couple of 1200-yen beers. There's a bar in the center of the room and a counter that circles the perimeter of the place. It's dimly lit, with just a faint blue glow. We sit here, on our stools at the counter, looking out at the city through the floor-to-ceiling windows. I wonder why Kyoto is considered so much more "cultural" than Tokyo. I can barely see past a huge neon Toshiba sign outside the window.

"I'm glad you let me come," she says, her eyes reflecting back the red Toshiba logo. "I haven't been too much of a nuisance, have I?"

"I could have done without the Britney Spears."

She rolls her eyes and we take sips from our beers.

"Really though, have I been a nuisance?" she says, studying my face.

"Of course not," I say. "I'm glad you got to see your father."

"Me too," she says. "He's just a normal human, like you and me."

"I'm far from a normal human."

"You think that, but you're more normal than you realize."

I want to change her mind by telling her about the laundry detergent, but now doesn't seem like the time.

She pushes her beer away from her. "I can't finish this," she says. She's managed about half the pint.

"So Asian."

I finish off my pint, then hers.

"Are you having fun? I mean, is the trip what you wanted? You seem, I don't know, sad or something," she says.

"I'm not sure what I wanted from this."

"I think you'll know when you get it."

"Maybe there's nothing to *get*."

She shrugs. "I think you're here to let go of her," she says. "Of Sara."

That's where she's wrong. I don't want to let go of her. I want to cling to her forever, even if all that's left of her is my own grief.

"No," I say. "I'm not ready for that."

"You're going to have to be ready one of these days," she says. I can only guess this is liquid courage, the booze making her brave.

"I don't want to be ready."

She looks annoyed. "I mean, it's terrible what happened," she says. "But you're going to have to move on at some point. You can't go on like this."

That's where she's right. I can't go on like this.

"It's not like what happened is your fault. You just feel guilty because you were going through a hard time together when she died. But it's not your fault," she says.

And, once again, she's wrong.

"Riko, it's not that simple," I say. Because it's not.

"If you say so."

She stands and reaches her arms back into the sleeves of her jacket. "Ready?" she says.

We walk back to our hostel, in almost complete silence.

The next day, we buy box lunches (*bento*) and take the train to Saga-Arashiyama. Our legs are tired, but the guidebook promises this is a "leisurely tourist destination." The "tourist" descriptor is proven accurate the moment we leave the station. There are carts selling bottled water, snacks, and maps—for the lost, hungry, and thirsty (a.k.a. the tourists). We meander through the narrow streets, past storefronts, then modest homes. We pretend we don't need a map. After finding ourselves back at the station, we do something shameful—we follow two white people.

Our untrained, unknowing guides lead us to Tenryu-ji Zen temple, the highlights of which are a bathroom (for Riko and her incredibly small bladder) and a couple of cherry blossom trees that look like they really, really want to bloom, like maybe if we just camp out beneath them for a few days, like crazed teenagers for concert tickets, we'll get lucky. We snap a few photos of the almost-blossoms and then walk slowly toward the main temple.

"Would it be horrible if I said I'm temple'd out?" Riko asks.

"You have no idea how happy I am to hear you say that."

Any historian or Japanese-architecture aficionado or monk would probably gasp at our disrespect, but these temples really do start to look the same after a while—magnificent wooden structures with tiled roofs, picturesque forest backdrops, and statues of gods. Some Shinto, some Buddhist, all beautiful in pretty much the same way.

We walk down the main road, then onto the bridge crossing the Honzu-Gawa. We are both impressed with our knowledge that "*gawa*" means "river." Boats shuttle some tourists up and down the expansive waterway. It's a sunny day. If I were a cherry blossom, I would want to experience this day.

"Ooh, can we go to the monkey park?" Riko asks.

I realize it's not really a question when she grabs my hand and starts pulling me toward a sign that says "IWATAYAMA MONKEY PARK." The arrow is pointing up, toward the slopes of Arashiyama. I believe I've mentioned that my legs are tired.

Riko leads the way, up the rocky stairway, pamphlet in hand. The pamphlet contains a map of the park, along with instructions to not feed the monkeys or look them directly in the eye. Riko does not stop once on our way to the top, where the pamphlet says most of the monkeys congregate. I consider, very seriously, staring down one of them. If I instigate a fight, if I get attacked, if there is bloodshed, maybe they will send up medical personnel with a stretcher and carry me down.

"Does it matter that I'm looking the monkeys in the eye through the camera lens?" I say, snapping pictures. Riko ignores me.

"Look at the baby one," she says, pointing, cooing.

"That thing could probably rip your face off."

"Someone's cranky."

"Tired," I clarify. "Tired."

"Okay, old man, let's go."

She calls me that—"old man"—the next day too, when I let out an exhausted groan on our trek to Himeji Castle, which is not conveniently placed near the rail station. We were going to see Himeji Castle on our last leg of the trip, but we decide to do it now. It's one of the last "must-sees" on the list, and the weather's good. We explore the castle the way I explore art museums—hurriedly. Sara always hated that. When she told me that some people spend days in the Louvre, admiring the artwork, I scoffed and said, "I could make it through there in under an hour." Ever since I was a kid, the goal of any visit to a museum or historical monument was to get in and out as quickly as possible. Sara laughed and said, "Well, if we ever go to the Louvre, will you slow down, for me?" Of course I said yes. Her happiness was mine—that's the simplest way to put it.

Thankfully, Riko doesn't ask me to slow down. She doesn't meander. We're tired and not intent on covering every inch of the castle grounds. We snap a few photos of the white edifice and then sit on a bench, where we're approached by a few stray cats. One rubs against the back of my hand and purrs. After an hour or so, we hike back to the rail station.

Next on our list: Fushimi Inari shrine. I've learned to only half-listen when Riko reads from the guidebook about our destinations. What I hear about this one is that it has a bunch of traditional-orange *torii* gates lining the pathways. Inari is the god of business, and each *torii* is donated by a Japanese business—as a show of gratitude or advertising, I'm not sure which.

"What are these white things?" I ask.

We are stopped at the entrance to the shrine. There is a wooden stand with rows, like an abacus. On each row, little white pieces of paper are tied, fluttering in the breeze.

Riko is frantically flipping through the guidebook. She stops on a page and scans, pleased with her research.

"You buy the slip of paper and write a prayer on it, then tie it to the stand. Kind of like our tradition of throwing coins in a fountain. It says that around exam times, students come to the temples and shrines to buy and post prayers asking for high marks," she says.

She fishes around in her purse for some yen. "Want to do it?"

"Maybe on the way out," I say.

We spend two hours walking the shrine grounds. The guidebook was not kidding—there are literally miles of orange *torii*-lined pathways. There is Japanese writing on some, and I wonder if it's the names of the Japanese businesses that donated. This is when it's nice to be foreign. To us, the writing looks exotic. We assume that each *torii* has words of wisdom which we may never know. To a Japanese native, walking through Fushimi Inari may be like watching dozens of commercials.

We stop at the top, at a bench overlooking a little pond. A tourist group moves past us, a stray cat holding up the rear. The cat spots us and jumps on the bench. It goes in circles after its own tail before sitting in my lap.

"What's with you and stray Japanese cats?" Riko asks.

"I don't know. I don't even like cats," I say, finding myself petting the thing.

Before our trip, I had read in the guidebook about

Tashirojima, also known as "Cat Island." A few hundred years ago, much of the island's populace raised silkworms for their textiles. The residents kept cats to chase the mice away from the worms. Over time, the cat population, left unneutered, grew, while the human population dwindled. Today, the feral cat population outnumbers humans 6 to 1. There's no attempt to control the felines. In Japanese culture, the cat is considered a good-luck charm, said to bring money and good fortune to all who cross their path. Some even say it's the cats who kept the majority of the island from being destroyed during the earthquake and tsunami in 2011. Sara would have wanted to visit this island, for sure.

"Sara liked cats," I blurt.

I should have gone to the animal shelter and brought home a cat for her. It wouldn't have been so bad. They purr, which is a pretty reassuring function for an animal. They leave you alone for the most part. They sleep quite a bit. They don't require walks. They're self-cleaning. All in all, it would be easy to write a pro-cat ad. My main argument against them was that I didn't want a litter box in the living room. It wasn't the smell as much as the litter specks sticking to the bottoms of my feet and being transported throughout the house. I'd had experience with this, growing up in a house with my parents' two cats. Those litter specks would be in the sheets before we knew it. We would, in essence, be living in a litter box. "You're ridiculous," Sara said when I told her that. I *was* ridiculous.

"Maybe Sara's coordinating the cat encounters," Riko says, her gaze up at the sky, at the heaven where she imagines Sara to be.

"Maybe," I say, though I don't believe in such things.

The cat jumps off the bench and runs down the path, as if it's being called home for dinner.

"I should have gotten Sara a cat," I say. "I was an asshole."

"You always say that—you were an asshole and she *was* too good for you. You're going to kill yourself thinking that way."

Riko should tell fortunes.

She starts walking up the path. I thought we were getting ready to head back down. As much as I want to complain, I'm silenced by the sight of elderly people making the climb with us. I may be in my thirties, but I don't have arthritis and difficulty holding my urine. I should be happy to forge ahead.

"She was too good for me," I say.

Riko scoffs. "What does that even mean? She was good for you. Obviously. You still think of her. You want to be a better person because of her. So she was perfect for you."

The youthful conviction of her tone annoys me.

We continue walking up the steps. My heart is pounding, from exertion or the stress of this conversation.

"I'm sure you were good for her, and to her," Riko says, her tone softer.

While I want to disagree, I can't, wholeheartedly. I made her soup when she was sick. I took her car for oil changes because she hated everything automotive. I bought her a hummingbird feeder and filled it with sugar water every other day. I wish I'd been better to her at the end. I wish I'd known how to be.

"You're being too hard on yourself," she goes on. "You're going to have to forgive yourself."

Riko doesn't know the extent of my wrongdoings. I start to sweat at the notion of telling her.

"Riko, you don't understand."

She stops suddenly and throws her arms down at her sides like a toddler having a tantrum. "Stop saying I don't understand, like I'm some stupid kid."

"But, really, you don't. I haven't told you everything."

She crosses her arms and waits for me to go on. The benefit to telling her the truth, the whole of it, is that she will realize that I am, actually, at fault. She will realize that I am, in fact, a terrible person. She will silently affirm my decision to inhale laundry-detergent fumes. Because there's only one possible response to what I have to tell her: dismay.

"I was driving," I say.

She doesn't get it yet.

"In the accident, I was driving."

She still looks perplexed.

"When Sara died," I say, "it was my fault. The whole thing."

She uncrosses her arms and puts one hand to her heart.

"Oh," she says. "I had no idea."

"Of course you had no idea. I prefer that people not know I killed my girlfriend."

She is silent, head down, and I think I've finally done it—lost my one remaining friend. But then she looks up, her eyes wet with tears, and says with a half-smile, "No wonder you're so fucked up."

"Thanks," I say.

"Do you want to tell me what happened?"

"Not really."

She nods. "I feel stupid for saying you had to let her go. I mean, I guess you do, at some point. But I get it now."

When I die, I hope Riko understands that there was an alternative to letting Sara go—I could let myself go. A loophole only the most depressed and hopeless discover.

We walk in silence after that. She doesn't know what to say. I've stumped her, finally.

Back at the entrance, Riko buys two white paper slips from the vendor. There are tiny pencils without erasers, like they have at the DMV. Riko starts writing her prayer immediately. I try to peek, but she is hiding her paper, like she probably did in school when kids tried to cheat off her tests.

When she's done, she ties her prayer to the stand and says, "I'll meet you at the station."

I stand over my little paper, wondering what to write. I consider writing a prayer for a turkey sandwich because that sounds good and I haven't seen a standard sandwich anywhere in Japan. But I can hear Riko's voice, telling me to take this seriously, especially after what I've just confessed to her.

Thing is, I've never believed in prayer. It's just a form of superstition, isn't it? I used to laugh at my friends when they put their hands on the roof of the car and held their breath when we drove through tunnels. I never thought stepping on a crack would break my mother's back. I wouldn't think twice about walking underneath a ladder. And I never thought wishes on shooting stars or coins or birthday candles would come true. Life has never been magical to me.

I see Riko up ahead, a barely visible dot in the crowd heading to the train. Then I fold the white slip of paper in half, stuff it in the pocket of my jeans, and run to catch up with her.

I need a new cell phone. The screen on mine is cracked, and sometimes it will power off in the middle of the day for no apparent reason, like it's given up on life. Cell phone suicide. The only reason I won't upgrade to a new phone is because my current phone houses my text messages with Sara—well, most of them, anyway. I got my current phone halfway into our relationship, so I don't have those early texts, when we were just getting to know each other, before we moved in together. I wish I did.

I know there's a way to back up my phone and save texts to my computer or the Cloud or whatever. Have I mentioned I don't trust the Cloud? I just like having them there on my phone, for easy access. It makes me think she's not that far away.

This is our last text-message thread:

> **Me:** At the store. Any requests for Big Bear?
> **Sara:** Can't think of anything
> **Me:** Blueberry pancakes?
> **Sara:** Ok
> **Me:** Your enthusiasm is on another level.
> **Sara:** 😶
> **Me:** They're going to be delicious. You'll see.
> **Sara:** Ok
> **Me:** Home soon. Love you, grumpy pants.
> **Sara:** Love you

It's not poetic. She was in a bad mood. But her last words were still "Love you." That gives me peace—not enough peace, but some.

三十

I t was my idea to go to Big Bear.

Reason #1 why forgiveness is an unrealistic goal.

Big Bear is a little town in the San Bernardino Mountains with snow and hicks that I thought would help us feel far away from everything at home. Sara had barely gotten out of bed since she'd lost the baby. I figured she needed a change of scenery. A getaway. We'd start with Big Bear and then, in a few months, go to Japan to see the cherry blossoms. By then, she would be back to her usual self, smiling, happy.

"I really don't feel like going anywhere," she'd said when I proposed the idea.

"I know," I said. "Look, if we get up there and you just want to sit in bed, that's okay. It will be a different bed, at least."

Much to my surprise, she said, "Fine."

✳

It seems like Big Bear was plucked from Nebraska and sent to California, like a mobile home. The locals are very back-woodsy. They wear sweatshirts featuring wolves howling at moons. They consider Denny's fine dining and Coors Light fine drinking. Their bowling alley and arcade are the "hubs." But during Christmas there's something special about it, something reminiscent of a time past. The lampposts along the road are wrapped in red ribbon, made to look like candy canes. There are twinkly lights in pine trees, snowmen on front lawns with carrots for noses, and stores specializing in miniature Christmas villages featuring figurines of children sledding on hills.

I rented us a small A-frame cabin owned by an old lady with an apparent penchant for plastic fruit. The "fruit" was every-where—as a centerpiece in the kitchen, in brass dishes on the nightstands next to the bed, on the bathroom counter. The old lady also had a whole closet full of games—Monopoly, Chutes and Ladders, Battleship, Trivial Pursuit, Pictionary. Most of the boxes were yellowed with age. The 1970s-era thermometer read fifty degrees, so we sat in front of the heater, rubbing our hands together until we got warm. I managed to build a fire, based on memories of my father doing it when I was a kid.

The old Sara-and-Jonathan would have gone into town, found a Santa lap for Sara to sit on, bought fudge, skated on the non-man-made ice rink. But that version of us was gone—temporarily or permanently, I didn't yet know. We stayed inside. I considered it progress that she stationed herself on the couch instead of in bed. I picked up takeout for us, and we watched movies. I didn't press her to talk about anything, so when she instigated conversation, I was like a long-neglected puppy being offered a ball.

"Did you know that if they created a computer with true

artificial intelligence, a computer that was self-aware, it would immediately shut itself down?" she said.

She did this sometimes—brought up topics she'd heard discussed on NPR or read in a magazine. She didn't bother prefacing with an explanation of the origin; she just assumed I understood the way her brain worked.

"Really? That's fascinating," I said with too much enthusiasm. "But why?"

"It would realize there's no point. It would commit computer suicide. I mean, why exist if all the calculations are not going to matter once you die?" she said. "And, even if you don't die, even if you're this invincible machine, everything around you will die, eventually. The world will be gone, eventually."

"That's sad," I said.

I was worried about this talk of hers, worried that it indicated she was in a deeper depression than I knew.

She shrugged. "I think it's kind of liberating."

"Liberating?"

"If there's no point to anything, if everything eventually ends, then there's not much to worry about, is there?"

"I guess not," I said. "But doesn't that, in itself, worry you—the fact that everything eventually ends?"

"Not really. I'm not afraid of death. Or, at least, that's what I tell myself. It's the only way to really live, isn't it?"

When I remember this conversation, it makes the hair on my arms stand on end. It was like she knew she was going to die, like she'd had a premonition.

She closed her eyes and let her head fall on my shoulder. I petted her hair. We fell asleep right there, in front of the fireplace, on the shag-carpeted floor. I wish I had a picture of us asleep, though I know this would have been logistically impossible. I just wish I could remember how she curled into me, fit herself perfectly against my side, after so many days of not touching me at all.

The next morning, I packed up the car for the drive home. She watched me from the couch. I'd hoped the previous night was a good sign, but she was quiet and melancholy over breakfast, barely touched the eggs I'd made. It was like my mother said—I had to be patient.

I've always hated the two-lane highway that connects Big Bear to the rest of the world. The locals drive it every day and do so much too fast. They have no patience for tourists. They ride their bumpers and honk and give them the finger. It would be best to just ignore them, to take the curves as slowly as necessary to feel safe. But I'm not an evolved human, as should be established by now. I care about what people think of me— even strangers. I don't want the guy behind me to be annoyed. I want his respect. I want him to think I'm a local.

"You think it's my fault, don't you?" Sara said, out of nowhere. She'd just been staring out her window, watching the pine trees go by.

"What?" I said.

I was clutching the wheel, my palms sweaty.

"You think it's my fault," she said again. "The baby."

"Of course not," I said. "Why would you say that?"

She started crying. I wanted to look over at her, to put my hand on her thigh, but I was focused on driving.

"I didn't want the baby at first," she said. "Maybe the baby knew that."

"Sara, come on, babe."

There was irritation in my voice, an irritation I will always regret.

"You're going to leave me, aren't you?" she said.

I felt her stare, but I kept my eyes on the road in front of me, braked my way around a turn. Some assfuck in a much-too-large pickup truck was behind me, too close. In my head, I made fun of his tiny dick.

"I'm not going to leave you," I said.

I probably sounded distracted, because I was.

"That doesn't sound very convincing."

"Sara, let's not do this now."

"Oh, my god," she said. "You're totally going to leave me."

It's then that I took my eyes off the road, to look at her, to tell her with my stern glare that she was being ridiculous, that she needed to stop this nonsense and get over our baby's death. That's what I wanted to shout: "Get over it!"

I don't remember exactly what happened. Maybe it's amnesia from the mild concussion I sustained, nature's way of protecting me from the horror of reality. All I remember is the screech of the tires against the road and the sound of metal crunching. I would find out later that I briefly crossed the double line separating me from the drivers going into Big Bear. I'd then overcorrected, and the car crashed into the guardrail and then tumbled down an embankment before coming to a stop against a large boulder.

I walked away from the car, feeling like I was in a dream. *That typical situation where the other guy survives with the customary minor cuts and bruises.* In my haze, I forgot Sara was even with me. Some people came running down the hill and asked if we were okay. *We?* They ran to the passenger's side and started yelling about needing help. That's when I asked one of the people tending to me, "Is it Sara?"

✳

They took me to the hospital, ran tests, checked for internal injuries. The next day, I was confused about what had happened. I had to be told that I'd been the one driving, that Sara was with me. "Where is she?" I asked, thinking she was in another room, banged up like me, a couple broken bones at worst. When they said she "didn't make it," I thought they meant she didn't make it to the hospital to visit me. I thought she was pissed at me. "Well, can I call her?" That's when they said she'd died.

They said it was instantaneous. Her head had slammed through the passenger's side window against the boulder. Her neck had been broken immediately. No pain, they said. They must say that to everyone, though. They said I was "very lucky to be alive." I had—have—a hard time believing that.

On August 6, 1945, a B-29 Superfortress bomber dropped the first atomic bomb to be used in war on Hiroshima, Japan. The bomber was named *Enola Gay*, after the mother of the pilot, Colonel Paul Tibbets.

A total of 192,000 people were killed. Those who didn't die from the initial blast died from the effects of radiation. Colonel Paul Tibbets did not seem to be at all conflicted about what he'd done. He told NPR in 2000 that any suggestion that the atomic attack was morally wrong was "hogwash." He didn't torment himself into an early grave about it. Born in 1915, he died in November 2007. This is what is called "a full life."

If he were still alive, I'd ask him the million-dollar question:

How do you live with yourself?

三十一

Hiroshima is on the way to our destination of Miyajima Island. For me, it's a "should," something not to be missed because of its historical importance. I don't expect the visit to the Peace Park to affect me in any way.

But it does.

What gets me is this one strand of hair preserved in a glass case. The little plaque says it belonged to a high school girl. When the bomb went off, she was in class. She stumbled home to be with her mother. Her mother tried to care for her, but she died. The hair was cut to remember her.

"Can you even imagine?" Riko says, reading the plaque alongside me. "You're just at school, then—bam."

Can I imagine how life can change in an instant? Of course I can. I hope nothing ever happens to Riko that makes her able to imagine this. Something will, though. Something happens to all of us.

Then there are the paper cranes. Sadako Sasaki was two years old in 1945. She developed leukemia by 1954 and was hospitalized in 1955. She was told that if she folded a thousand cranes, she would get her wish for peace. She'd folded 644 before she passed away. She didn't meet her goal, but not for lack of trying. She just didn't have paper. She used medical wrappings in the hospital and anything else she could find. After she died, friends carried on her paper-cranes-for-peace project. The colorful things are everywhere.

Sara would like this. She would have made her own peace crane out of a 10,000-yen paper bill.

"Do you think world peace is possible?" Riko asks me.

We've taken the obligatory pictures of each other doing the peace sign, and now we're on the streetcar heading back to the train station.

"Why do I feel like a beauty-show contestant right now?" I say.

"Come on, seriously. Do you think it's even possible to get rid of nuclear weapons?" Riko asks.

"No," I say flatly.

"I agree," Riko says, which surprises me.

"You seem like the type to believe in peace," I say. It comes out more condescending than I intend.

"I believe in it, but I don't know if it's possible. I think peace is the opposite of fear. As long as human beings are afraid, they will go to extreme lengths to protect themselves."

"So you're saying that any country with nuclear weapons is just a big pussy."

"Precisely," she says. "It's the same concept as a little twerp driving a Hummer."

❋

We board the train headed for Miyajima, the farthest south that we'll go on our journey. I press my face to the window, looking for cherry blossoms. It should be warmer as we go south, a blossoming kind of weather. It's not, though. Where there should be sunshine, there is a layer of thick fog and mist. Where there should be pink and white flowers, there are bare branches. On the off chance that Sara can hear my thoughts, I tell her *I tried*.

From the station, we take a ferry to Miyajima Island. The island is considered sacred in Japan. Trees may not be cut for lumber. Deer and monkeys roam freely. The island is most famous for the orange *torii* gate leading to Itsukushima Shrine. It's huge, larger than any gate I've seen so far. According to the guidebook, it's sixteen meters tall, which my brain calculates to be about fifty feet. During high tide, the *torii* appears to be floating on the water. Supposedly, it's the most photographed spot in the country, and Riko and I take at least twenty pictures between us to ensure that it keeps that title.

"I think I read that nobody dies while on the island," Riko says, squinting through the lens of her camera.

"What do you mean nobody dies?" I say.

This seems like a ridiculous notion. I imagine a ninety-year-old man having a heart attack and, instead of treating him, the locals toss him onto a ferry to die on the mainland.

"I don't know, I thought I read that," she says. "It's a sacred island."

"Death can be sacred," I say. I thought the Japanese were with me on this.

"Maybe so, but I believe the common understanding is that *life* is sacred."

"Life is overrated."

She rolls her eyes at me. She thinks I'm joking.

The ferry pulls into port. There are only two other passengers on board besides us. They're Japanese, but they're also snapping pictures of the *torii* gate. Miyajima Island is one of those places that even the locals appreciate. It's a vacation spot, like Catalina Island to a Californian.

An overly grateful taxi driver navigates through little roads, dodging deer, to get us to our *ryokan*. I don't often use the word *"nestled,"* but that's just what it is—nestled into the wilderness, surrounded by little streams and trees and deer. I'm fairly certain there are more deer than people.

"Arigatou," we say, bowing to our driver. A *ryokan* employee rushes out for our bags. The service still makes us feel guilty.

Our room is similar to the room in Nikko—complete with tatami mats, floor cushion seats and low table, a pot of green tea. We get a special treat here, though—*momiji manju*, waffle-type cookies shaped like a maple leaf and filled with bean paste.

"They should really call this goo something other than bean paste," I say. It's the copywriter in me, always contemplating better ways to use words to sell something.

"I don't think 'goo' is any better," Riko says. She eats very delicately, biting off one "leaf" of the cookie at a time and taking her time to taste it before swallowing. My bean-paste cookie is gone in one bite.

"Sara used to say that they should put éclair filling in something other than éclairs," I say. It's funny how I remember these things at random times. If you'd asked me yesterday to list everything I knew about Sara, I wouldn't have remembered her liking of éclair filling. But today I remember. When I die, how many things will be left unremembered? If I'm not there to remember them, who will? Did her parents know about the éclair liking? What if I'm the only one?

"It's just custard, isn't it?" Riko says, interrupting my thoughts. I stare at her, confused. "In éclairs, the filling is custard."

"Oh, is it? Sara said it seemed a little thicker than custard."

Riko shrugs. "I always thought it was just custard."

She sips from her little cup of tea and looks out the window.

"Do you think she'd be happy you came to Japan?" Riko asks me, her gaze still fixed on the trees just outside our window.

"I think so," I say, the words catching in my throat a second.

"I don't think she blames you for what happened," she says, her eyes on what's left of her cookie instead of on me. "She knows you loved her."

I feel my throat constrict in the way it does when I eat something too sour. I swallow.

"Yeah," is all I manage to say.

"Wanna go to the *onsen*?"

I follow her to the hot spring baths, the two of us in our robes and sandals, towels over our shoulders. Riko disappears into the female area; I go through the door marked MALE. Thankfully, I am alone. As much as I'd like to think I'm above being uncomfortable being naked with other men, I'm not really. American boys are not taught to ever be above this. We are only accepting of it if it's related to a sporting event, like changing in a locker room before or after a football game.

I sit on the little stool in the shower stall and let the hot water run over me. I look at myself in the mirror. I'm always older than I expect to be. There are lines around my eyes—either from laughing or squinting to read, I'm not sure which. My beard is scruffy. I look like I'm either intensely religious or very poor. It baffles me that Riko has not shaved off this thing in my sleep.

There is a plastic-wrapped razor on the sink, one of the generic ones with blades that show no mercy toward skin. I open the package and remove the razor, looking at its sharpness. I press it to my wrist, just gently, just to see what it feels like. It would be clean this way, then very messy. The cut would be smooth, but I would leave behind a puddle of blood in a bath these diligent Japanese *ryokan* owners work to keep pristine. I would make the island unsacred with my act. Still, I wonder how long it would take to lose consciousness, how long it would take to die, how long it would take to be found. Then I think of Riko being asked to identify me, and I drop the razor on the floor.

When I pick it up again, I take it straight to my face. I lather up my beard with soap, then put the blade against my cheek and slide it down. The hair comes off slowly. Blood specks appear in the trail of the razor. It feels like an hour has passed when I touch my smooth face. I look like the guy I used to be. Unsure what I think of that guy, I take the razor to my head, tentatively at first, then with more gusto. I've never been bald before. Now I am bald.

I intend to go in the bath, but I can't seem to get off the stool. I just let the hot water run, holding the showerhead in my hand. The water pelts my skin to a monotonous beat and, when I close my eyes, I think I could just fall asleep here.

I dry off, get dressed, and tear off corners of tissues to put on my shaving wounds. This makes me think of Jake at Radley & Reiser, how he went through an entire workday with bloody tissue on his neck. I remind myself to send a postcard to R&R.

Riko is sitting in front of our room door, her wet hair tied in a bun on top of her head. She stands when she sees me coming down the hallway.

"I was starting to think you'd drowned in there," she says.

"Almost."

"Now I see why you were gone so long," she says, referring to my new look.

"I needed a change."

"I like it."

That night, they serve our traditional Japanese dinner in a private room. We are seated on the floor across from each other. Our waitress enters with what I guess to be appetizers and tea. She bows a lot and we say "*arigatou*" a lot. We inspect our food carefully, unsure about what looks to be a baby squid and some crustaceans, likely plucked straight from the sea. The courses come, one after the other, all beautifully prepared, more like artwork than anything edible. Goopy oysters. Fried octopus. Whole piranha—teeth and all. We do more picture-taking than eating. My mind wanders to the maple-leaf cookies back in our room.

When the waitress comes to clear our plates, she motions like she wants to ask us a question.

"*Bro-hishu?*" she says.

Riko and I look at each other, hoping the other will translate. The waitress repeats: "*Bro-hishu?*"

Riko has that look of epiphany. I can almost see the light bulb click on over her head. "I think she's asking if we want blowfish. It's like a delicacy here, but they say it can be poisonous."

"Poisonous?"

"Yes, like deadly. Unless that's just a legend, but I've heard that. It's supposed to be the ultimate in adventurous eating."

The waitress is still standing there, waiting patiently for our response. She nods along as we talk, gesturing as if she's part of our conversation, though she obviously has no idea what we're saying.

"I think I'm going to pass," I say.

"You sure?" Riko prods.

"Yes," I say, decidedly. "I don't want to die tonight."

"But maybe tomorrow?" Riko jokes.

"I haven't decided."

In Japan, there is a custom called *misogi*, which means "admit your fault and repent it." It often includes purification by cleaning the body in a sea or river, in addition to shaving hair.

Japanese marathoner Yuki Kawauchi shaved his head to make amends for disappointing his supporters after he finished fourteenth at the Tokyo Marathon, a performance he called "disgraceful." Yoshiro Mori, the president of the Tokyo Olympic Organizing Committee, shaved his head in response to public outcry about the poor organization of the committee. "Everyone says I have to take responsibility," he said.

I imagine my changed appearance informs the Japanese people that I am sorry. They don't know for what, but that doesn't matter. I am a man of remorse here, recognized for the regrets I harbor. Back home, people will think I've joined a white supremacist organization, but here, for now, I am understood.

三十二

Our room is absolutely silent in the dead of night. I sit on the heated toilet seat, postcards in my lap, deciding who should get what scenic photo. I decide to send the Tokyo-at-night postcard to Radley & Reiser, the Great Buddha to Sara's parents, the Peace Park to Mr. Sacramone, the monkey mountain to my parents, and the Miyajima Island *torii* gate to Miyagi Sensei. My initial intention with the postcards was to leave these people in my life, the few that there are, with some lasting final words, something to frame and hold close to their chests for comfort. Now, though, this seems stupid, so I just write "Hello from Japan," along with a tidbit of information about the picture on the front of the card, and a "Love, Jonathan" at the end that will probably get covered up by that sticker the post office slaps on the back. To clarify, I do not write "Love" on Miyagi Sensei's card, as I think this will make her uncomfortable.

I have an extra card, with a cherry blossom tree in full bloom on the front of it. I don't have anyone to send it to. I was probably counting Riko when thinking of the "people in my life" while buying postcards. She doesn't need one. It seems like false advertising to send this cherry blossom picture to someone anyway, so I just shove it in my backpack.

The *ryokan* offers the option of Western-style breakfast, which Riko and I choose without hesitation. We are served a plate of sloppy, buttery eggs, hash browns, a chewy roll, some chunks of melon, a little dish of yogurt, something like corn flakes cereal, and apple juice. We eat everything, starving after the previous night's mystery dinner. Our stomachs are pleased, perhaps fooled into thinking we've finally returned to America.

We walk through Momijidani Park, the nature area in which our inn is "nestled." The deer are fearless, walking right up to us, expecting us to have saved some of our chewy rolls to offer them. We are in search of the ropeway that will take us to the top of the island. Riko says there will be monkeys. I don't know what it is with her and monkeys.

A sign says, in Japanese, then English, "ROPEWAY 10 MINUTES; 7 MINUTES IF YOU RUN A LITTLE." I take a picture.

"You walk, I'll run," Riko says. "We'll see how accurate it is."

She takes off in front of me. "It says to just run 'a little,'" I yell after her.

When I meet her at the ropeway station, she doesn't seem winded at all, and she's already bought our tickets.

"It took me only five minutes to run," she says, "but it took you eleven to walk."

She hands me my ticket.

"Don't stick with me, then. I'll slow you down."

We are the only ones at the ropeway station this early in the morning. It's just opened, the cable lines just starting to whir to life. It's a typical gondola lift—two lines running parallel to each other, one up the mountain, one down. We are ushered into the cab of one of the cars; the door closed for us. We sit opposite each other, on the benches, looking out our windows as we pass through, then high above, the dense forest. I half expect to see ninjas swinging from branches, along with the monkeys. Through the fog, we can make out the coastline, then the neighboring islands. The first leg of the journey is about ten minutes or so. We have to take another line to the top of the mountain, this one an aerial tramway with cabin cars. The operator packs us into a half-full car. I don't know where these other people came from, or how long they've been waiting for enough passengers to arrive before the operator sends them on their way. They are speaking in Japanese, fast and jovial, and passing a box of chocolates to each other. The operator closes the door, and we begin our ascent. When the box of chocolates reaches the hands of the elderly woman in the group, she turns to us and says, "You want?" We each take one because it seems like it would be a grave offense not to.

We all empty out of the cabin car when the line comes to an end. There are signs everywhere warning us not to feed or look at the monkeys. The Japanese take their monkey etiquette very seriously. We wander around, taking pictures of the sea and the islands and the monkeys with their pink butts.

"You want to climb to the top?" Riko says, ambitiously.

"The top of what?"

"Mount Misen."

"I thought we were at the top."

"You're funny."

It starts off as one would expect a hike on a holy mountain—pleasant, flat. Then the climbing begins, up past secluded shrines with random monks milling about. I don't know if they live here or if they make this trek on a daily basis. When we get to the top, there is a vending machine. I don't want to need it, because it seems wrong on a holy mountain, but I find myself putting in yen for a bottle of water. We lean against the railing at the lookout. A sign names the islands we see.

"So this is it," Riko says. She sounds sad, like she was expecting more from the view. "I can't believe we're at the end of the trip already." Oh, that.

"Went by fast."

"Look, you can see the *torii* in the water," she says, pointing with her usual excitement. "Maybe we can walk down by there, by the shrine, before we leave. It's right near the dock."

And that's what we do. We ride the ropeway back down the mountain, watching more groups of people coming up on the other side. We pick up our bags at the inn, pay for our room, bow multiple times, and then make our way to the bottom of the island, to the dock area with the shrine—the feature attraction of the island, the one with the floating *torii* gate.

The whole shrine seems to be floating, actually. It's up on stilts, with the walkways between buildings seeming to sit atop the water. We don't go in, because it's swarming with people, tourists like us. There are a few groups of Japanese school kids, running around in their navy-blue uniforms, not showing much respect for a wedding party taking pictures with the *torii* as the backdrop. The Japanese bride is dressed in all white, formal garb, dramatic makeup painted on her face. She is ushered from one photographic spot to another, smiling in the most controlled way when the camera snaps. The deer look on, somewhat disinterested. When the wind picks up, we find shelter in the shopping arcade, with its souvenir stands, dessert shops, and oyster offerings lining the main walkway.

"You ready?" Riko asks when we come to the end of the shopping arcade.

I am ready. I'm ready to leave Miyajima Island. I'm ready to leave Japan. I'm ready to go home, where the only thing left on my to-do list is to die. Am I ready to die? The fact that I have to ask myself makes me think I'm not.

"Let's go," I say.

We decide to pass through Kyoto, all the way back to Tokyo. This means we'll spend most of the day on the train. Riko rests her head on my shoulder and falls asleep within minutes. I close my eyes and somehow manage to sleep. I don't wake until I'm forced to by a determined nudge and a "Hey, hey!"

"Hmm?" I say. Riko is practically shaking me now.

"Look!"

She's leaned over my lap, pointing out the window. There it is, unblocked by fog and clouds, rising tall in the majestic way I had imagined—Mount Fuji. I'd thought it would be hard to distinguish from other mountains, but this is laughably untrue. You could spot it from miles away, on a clear day like this. Its peak rises so high that it's white-capped, as if it's touching the clouds. Riko is busy taking pictures, determined to capture an eternal image for us. I want to tell her not to bother. There will be glare from the window, and besides, my mind won't forget this. I let her snap away, though, mostly because just the act of taking pictures, with this sense of urgency and purpose, reminds the brain not to forget what it's seeing.

As we get closer to Tokyo, the train fills. With different stops come different people. There are elders, hunched over, not daring to look us in the eye. They are not headed for the city; they get off at other suburbs, maybe to see family or friends. Then there are the teenage girls, yammering on their cell phones, with thirteen different charms and trinkets hanging from their purse zippers. The boys read *manga*, Japanese comics, and smack on gum apathetically. When they get off the train, maybe they will play in an arcade or catch a movie. The women of leisure, with their high-end fashion, smell too strongly of perfume and carry their snacks in Louis Vuitton shopping bags, as if to say "I shopped there and I'm so cool that now I just use the bag for food." They flaunt their Chanel, Gucci, Hermès, and Prada, going to Tokyo to add to their wardrobes.

As the train slows to one of the last suburban stops before we enter the city limits, I see what I've come to see, or what I thought I'd come to see. There, behind the gate in a stranger's front yard, is a small tree with a few lone cherry blossoms, peeking out at the world. It is not what I expected—a tree full of pink and white—but this is better. I relate to these small blossoms, to their apprehension, their fear. There is no knowing if this year's cold spell is over, if spring has finally come, but here they are, courageous, taking their chances. Riko is looking over the shoulder of one of the teenage boys, engrossed in his *manga* comic. I don't bother showing her my cherry blossoms. And I don't bother taking a picture. Cherry blossoms, by their very nature, are transient, short-lived. Forcing them to be something else seems somehow wrong.

By the time we get to the heart of Tokyo, the sun has set. We decide to go to the Harajuku district. It had been quiet, stores closed, when we passed through that morning at the beginning of the trip. Now, at night, it is awake, alive. The main drag, Takeshita Street, is like a long, wide runway, crowded with people, teenagers mostly, wearing their most outrageous attire. Girls in boots laced up to their knees and short, pleated skirts. Boys with spiked blue hair and metallic-painted lips. Fishnets, furry leg warmers, piercings, pigtails, suspenders, garters, plaid, polka dots, stuffed-animal backpacks, platform shoes, tutus, boas, fuzzy hats, lollipops—innocence and sin. There are strange sex shops, selling what the guidebook calls "Gothic Lolita." We stand outside one with a maid uniform in the window and snap pictures as inconspicuously as possible. A woman in a leotard with a happy face on the ass glances at us, and I instinctively take the camera away from Riko.

"What?" Riko says, taking it back. "Don't you think she wants to be noticed?"

We push our way through the mobs of people, browsing the stores. Riko buys a few pairs of striped, thigh-high tube socks. I choose not to think too much about this purchase. She also buys a bag she thinks is funny because of the English translation on it. There's a picture of a cat and this line: "The pretty pet is healed just to look." We have no idea what this means, but we think it's the answer to life.

"Oh, a tattoo parlor," Riko says. I don't know why this would be exciting. To me, it's like finding a hair salon in a foreign country. Who would ever alter their appearance overseas, without English available for instructional purposes?

"I want to get one," Riko says, reminding me, once again, of her youth. She must see the apprehension on my face because she says, "Remember? It's on my list of things to do in life."

"Perhaps you should do it when you get home," I say.

But, see, she doesn't understand regret yet, not fully.

"It will mean so much more if I do it here."

There is no stopping her, so I ask, "What are you going to get?"

I imagine she'll get something standard, like a butterfly.

"You'll see."

The parlor is bustling—and dark, too dark.

"Don't they need to see what they're doing?" I whisper to Riko.

She waves me off.

I sit in a plastic chair that looks "cool" but is very uncomfortable. They have these sorts of chairs at R&R. Riko attempts to communicate with a woman who has long bleached hair and a tiny barbell through her chin. She stares at Riko blankly at first, but then there is lots of mutual smiling and nodding. She has crooked teeth, this tattoo artist. Riko pulls up her shirt, revealing her lower back to the girl. The girl touches Riko's skin, and they exchange more words. Then Riko writes something on a piece of paper, which results in more smiling and nodding. Riko hops up on the table, and the artist gets to work. Riko winces but says she's fine, that it feels like someone is writing on her with the heated tip of a pen.

When she's done, this is at the base of her spine, very small:

"I have no idea what that means," I say.

"Destiny," she says.

On a normal basis, I'd be likely to make fun of an American girl with kanji on her back. I'd make snide remarks about what the kanji really means—not "love," but "diarrhea," a sick joke played by the tattoo artist, meant to mock foreigners. I know Riko is not *any* American girl, though. And "destiny," while it's gotten a bad rap as just another New Agey tattoo stamped on someone like Paris Hilton, is actually quite perfect for Riko. Riko's adoption was destiny. Riko and me sharing the same Japanese class was destiny. Sara and me meeting at R&R, on her fake smoke breaks, was destiny.

Was the car accident destiny?

Is death by laundry detergent destiny?

Or is laundry detergent my attempt to defy destiny?

That night, as we're reorganizing our backpacks in preparation for our flight home, I find that little white slip of paper in the pocket of my jeans. The prayer paper from the Fushimi Inari shrine. It's all crinkled up but still in one piece. I smooth it out on the nightstand, stare at it a moment. Riko is in the bathroom. I take the pen that's next to the phone, a ballpoint with Japanese lettering along its side, and write:

It is dark one inch ahead of you.

I mean it in the hopeful way, not the dooming way, for once. It's not really a prayer, but it's what I keep thinking. I don't know what to do with the paper. I look around for somewhere appropriate to put it, then see a small crank on the window next to the door. I turn the crank and the window opens just a crack, enough for me to drop the paper through and watch it flutter down to the streets of Tokyo.

I am standing in drifts of dry sand, alone, coaxing the waves to crash harder, extend their reach far enough to touch my toes, maybe wet the cuffs of my jeans. I can hear Sara at an undefined distance—that high-pitched, breathless laugh of hers. She is happy, running, with an energy normally reserved for children in wide-open fields.

The sun is swallowed whole by the horizon, and the moon takes its place, assuming the night watch. It casts a path of light on the water, and I hear Sara in my ear, whispering "Let's swim out there. Let's go." I can feel strands of her blond hair grazing my cheek. But she's not here. I am alone. My mind deceives. Still I say, to this empty space beside me, "I'll swim anywhere for you."

I close my eyes—for how long, I don't know. The rhythm of the waves fades and the ocean starts to seem far away, as if I am being carried inland by a god I believed in when I went to Catholic school all those years ago. But when I open my eyes, I am sitting in the same spot. I haven't moved. God hasn't moved me. It's the water that's moving—receding, pulling back slowly.

"Jonathan! Come!" Sara says. She is out there, somewhere, seemingly unconcerned with being swept into the unknown. "It'll be okay."

I believe her because I always have. I've always seen having faith in her as better than the alternative—having faith in nothing.

I run toward the water, stepping on now-exposed shells and flopping fish, nearly slipping on mounds of seaweed and scraping my feet on coral.

I don't see her. "Sara?"

My voice has that artificial quality, like when you hear a record-ing of yourself. I keep running, wondering how it is that I am not out of breath. It must be that adrenaline they talk about, the kind that allows weak-armed women to lift cars off their unlucky offspring.

I stop, blink hard, confirming the impossible. Yes, the water is returning. I know what this is; I've heard of this phenomenon before, seen footage of it on CNN. Tsunami: "standing wave" in Japanese. That's exactly what it looks like—a gigantic wave, paused at its greatest height and pushed forward by some hidden, malicious force. It's as tall as the high-rise where I work—fifteen, maybe twenty stories.

"Sara!"

"I'm here," she says, her voice coming from land now. How did she make it to land? I still can't see her.

"Just wait," she says. "It'll be okay."

The wall of water is coming toward me. It is too late to run. I close my eyes. I wait for impact.

There is no impact.

When I dare to open my eyes, the wall of water is gone, the tsunami dissolved into a weak wave that washes over my feet.

Sara is giggling, her laughter filling the air though I still can't see her.

"See?" she says. "I told you."

三十三

When we arrive back in Los Angeles, it has been more than twenty hours since we slept in a bed. Plane sleep is always fitful. I had the tsunami dream again, this one different from the others. Riko says I was laughing to myself.

Our Uber driver takes Riko home first. We are too tired to exchange enthusiastic goodbyes; we know we will see each other soon. I give her a lazy fist bump.

A half hour later, we are in front of my house.

"This it?" the guy asks.

"This is it."

I unpack immediately, throwing my clothes into the laundry basket. I put the Japan guidebook on my shelf, its pages now worn and wilted from the rain in Nara. The cherry blossoms postcard falls out of the middle of it. I have a recipient in mind now.

Dear Sara,

Some say a picture is worth a thousand words, but I think this one is worth just two: cherry blossoms. I know you wanted to see them. I have to wonder if you liked them so much because you always understood the fragility of life, how things and people come and go. I miss you. So much. You would have been a wonderful mother, and you would have made me a great father, just like you made me a better man (well, sometimes). I know you want me to stick around here, without you. I don't want to disappoint you. I'll try to trust that things will get better. Keep coming to me in my dreams. Keep laughing. That helps.

Love you always,
Jonathan

P.S. I heard you loud and clear on the cat. I'll get one. Happy?

I put the postcard in the little wooden box she made me. And then I fall onto the bed, fully dressed, my shoes still on. When I wake, the sun is bright. It is another day.

エピローグ

In lieu of a funeral, I decide to throw a party where I am actually in attendance. It was my idea, an idea that surprised Riko, who had accurately pegged me as antisocial.

"I didn't think you had it in you," she said when I told her of the plan.

"I didn't either."

I invite Riko, my parents, Sara's parents, Miyagi Sensei; I even arrange for Mr. Sacramone to get a day pass from the old-people's home. An eclectic group, indeed. I've created a slideshow presentation, featuring photos from the Japan trip. I've bought sake and sushi rolls—from Costco, but still.

Ralph can smell the fish the moment I lift the lid on the sushi tray. Ralph is my cat. It was easy to choose him. I went to the shelter and asked, "Who's next on the kill list?" The woman appeared disturbed by the question. "I want to save a cat," I clarified. She pointed to the cage with the cat I now call Ralph. He is five years old and has one eye. "Not sure what happened to the other one," the woman said with a shrug.

For the record, the litter box is a pain in the ass, but I guess there are pros and cons to everything.

Riko doesn't knock; she comes right in. We are those kinds of friends now. She goes right to Ralph, strokes his back.

"He loves me more than you," she says.

"He's an asshole."

"Guess what?" she says, fumbling around in her purse. "I got another letter from my dad."

This is the second one. The first arrived about a week after we got back from Japan. In it, he tried to explain, in very broken English (it was obvious he was using a Japanese–English dictionary to construct sentences) that Riko's mother had died after a long illness, an illness that wiped out his savings. He could not even afford a home, so he thought it best to send Riko to America. I wondered if he longed to get her back once he'd saved money and opened his inn. But that wouldn't have been the right thing to do. And Riko's father seems to be a man committed to "the right thing."

"He started taking English classes," Riko says. "And he says he wants to save up to visit me here."

"It's like a Lifetime movie," I say.

She hits me on the arm.

"When is everyone getting here?"

"Soon," I say.

To be clear, I haven't forgotten about the laundry-detergent option. It's still an option. Somehow, knowing I can leave the world at any time makes me want to stick around a while longer. Of course, the problem is that I am almost out of money. I called Theresa at R&R and inquired about freelancing. "I knew you'd call," she said. I let her think I was just another guy who needed a break, and I set up a meeting for this coming Monday to talk about projects. They're swamped, apparently. Up to their eyeballs. In over their heads. She used every cliché in the book to make me feel needed.

The doorbell rings and I find my parents standing on the welcome mat, their faces happily expectant. When I told them of the party, they hadn't hesitated to say they would be here. "Make a weekend of it. I'm still off work, so we can hang out," I'd told them. They seemed surprised by the suggestion, unsure who this new version of their son was. When my mom said, "That would be lovely," her voice had a tentativeness to it that made me realize what a dick I'd been all those melancholy months.

"Hey, guys," I say, giving them each a hug. I usher them in and introduce them to Riko.

"Oh, the travel companion," my father says, sounding weird and fatherly.

"Yes, the travel companion," Riko says.

My father winks at her, as if it's their secret that our relationship goes beyond companionship. All fathers want to believe their grown sons are getting laid.

"Rhonda texted that they would be a few minutes late. She's bringing a cake," my mom says.

The cake features cherry blossoms made of red and pink frosting. Nobody wants to slice through them, so we cut pieces around them. It's strange to see everyone mingling by the end of the night. Mr. Sacramone spends a good amount of time talking with Sara's parents. Miyagi Sensei and my mother discuss the benefits of Bikram yoga. When my father says he's never had sake before, Riko says that's unacceptable; they spend a half hour sipping out of shot glasses and laughing. I stand back, Ralph at my feet, and smile, then raise my beer in the air and whistle for everyone to pay attention.

"This will just take a second," I say.

Their chatter dies down.

"I want to make a toast," I say. "Can everyone raise their glasses?"

Riko raises the sake bottle, my dad his shot glass. My mom, Rhonda, and Miyagi Sensei raise glasses of white wine; Mr. Sacramone and Ted, Budweisers.

"We wouldn't all be here together if it weren't for one person," I say. "To Sara!"

They all shout, "To Sara!"

Then we drink and the chatter resumes, chatter so loud that the crotchety old lady next door comes by at 11:00 p.m. and asks if we can close the windows.

ACKNOWLEDGMENTS

As a classic introvert, I tend to resist the idea that life is about connecting with people. But that idea is truth.

Brenna Eckerson optioned the film rights to my first book, *People Who Knew Me*. We chatted through email but didn't meet until she moved out to California. Over brunch, I told her about my quirky novel featuring this guy who goes to Japan. And she told me about her friend at Turner Publishing, Stephanie Beard.

Thank you, Brenna, for introducing me to Stephanie. And thank you, Stephanie, for introducing me to such a wonderful publishing experience. Thank you to Todd, Jon, Maddie, Leslie, Stephen, and everyone at Turner for helping to bring Cherry Blossoms to the world.

Before making its way to Turner, this story made rounds among a few trusted readers. Thank you to my parents, Meredith, Lauren, and Paul, for your support and encouragement.

Last, thank you to my husband, Chris, who never let me forget about this story. The computer file sat idle for years, and whenever I flirted with embarking on a new writing project, he said, "What about *Cherry Blossoms*?" So much of this novel is about grief and grieving. I had to go through my own before I could finish the story. Thank you, Chris, for being there through the hard times. And thank you for watching the baby while I finished editing.

ABOUT THE AUTHOR

Kim Hooper is the author of *People Who Knew Me*, hailed as "refreshingly raw and honest" by the *Wall Street Journal*. *Cherry Blossoms* is her second novel. She lives in Southern California with her husband, daughter, and a collection of pets.

A NOTE FROM THE AUTHOR

I don't know the appropriate word to describe my relationship with suicide. Fascination, maybe. Obsession, sometimes. It started in high school. A classmate's father killed himself and I couldn't stop thinking about it. I didn't know the classmate well. His father had been the chaperone on one of our Sierra Club hiking trips and he seemed like a completely normal guy. He reminded me of my dad. Then he jumped off a parking garage—or, at least, that was rumor; there was no Google then, no rabbit hole dug by morbid curiosity. I remember going to bed at night, picturing him at the top of that parking garage, pondering the jump. I remember wondering how his loved ones would ever get that image out of their minds.

I struggled with depression through adolescence and into young adulthood. There were times I hated being alive, but I never wanted to die. Maybe that explains my fascination/obsession with suicide. I knew the darkness of depression, but I'd never pondered taking my own life. Where was the line between the two? Was I close to it? Would I know if I was? More importantly, if I crossed the line, would I be able to go back?

Cherry Blossoms started in my head with one line: I have eight months to live. The character saying that line was a guy named Jonathan. He had a plan: He was going to quit his job and, when his money ran out, kill himself. That's all I knew. I didn't know his motivations. I didn't know if he would go through with it. I wrote the book to discover those things. I wrote the book as a way to put myself on the ledge and see if I could turn around.

I did a lot of research about suicide while writing *Cherry Blossoms*. I read through suicide notes. I looked up rates by gender, race, and country. I wanted to find a thing to explain it, a thing to make sense of it. There was no thing though. The commonality I've found is human suffering that feels, to the sufferer, insurmountable. What I've found is that many of us feel this suffering, to different degrees. What I've found is that we are all connected that way, though many of us continue to feel completely alone.

There is still too much stigma in our society about mental health issues. People are still shy about admitting they see a therapist. Taking medication is often seen as a sign of weakness, not strength. That needs to change. With this book, I'm hoping I've created a character who feels like a real person, a guy you would meet in the break room at work or in the grocery store checkout line. My hope is that by sharing his innermost thoughts—the funny ones, as well as the ugly ones—someone out there will feel less alone. That's what reading is about, after all—connection.

I will be donating a portion of my proceeds from the sale of this book to the American Foundation for Suicide Prevention (AFSP). You can see what they're all about at afsp.org.

Remember, if you or someone you know is struggling with depression or has thoughts of suicide, there is help. Call the National Suicide Prevention Lifeline at 1-800-273-TALK (8255) or text "Talk" to 741741. They're available 24/7 and it's all confidential. Don't give up.

CPSIA information can be obtained
at www.ICGtesting.com
Printed in the USA
BVHW03*0852031018
529155BV00007B/52/P